Number
Eleven

Number Eleven

A Love Story in 1960's Bombay

Zia McNeal

ARCHWAY
PUBLISHING

Archway Publishing books may be ordered
through booksellers or by contacting:

Archway Publishing
1663 Liberty Drive
Bloomington, IN 47403
www.archwaypublishing.com
1 (888) 242-5904

ISBN: 978-1-4808-1507-0 (sc)
ISBN: 978-1-4808-1505-6 (hc)
ISBN: 978-1-4808-1506-3 (e)

Library of Congress Control Number: 2015902306

Print information available on the last page.

Archway Publishing rev. date: 3/10/2015

AMIR VIRANI'S FAMILY TREE

Parents:

Karim (father, deceased) and Shakila (mother)

Siblings:

Farid (older brother) married Rehana
Rabia (girl) and Rafiq (boy)

Bandra (older sister) married Salim
Daania (girl)

Nilofer (older sister) married Nadir
Zarin (boy) and Yasmeen (girl)

Nadia (younger sister) married Kassim
Tarik (boy)

CHAPTER 1

Sunday, August 7

"SO FAR, SO GOOD"

The jet lag had not yet hit him, and hopefully it never would. He simply didn't have time to be tired. This was the first prospective bride meeting. There were going to be nine others - nine additional formal dinners, lunches or afternoon teas. Maybe this girl would be good enough, and they could start planning the wedding. They would need all of the three weeks he had. But, first, he had to meet her, and if not her, the next one on the list. Oh, these dinner parties were going to be torture!

Running on adrenaline, Amir reviewed the notes his sister-in-law had scribbled on a piece of paper. "Nargis, twenty-five years old, third year of medical school, two brothers, father is a doctor." *Well, she seems fine on paper*, he thought happily. *In fact, she seems better than fine, she seems great!*

Amir smiled widely as he checked his necktie in the hall mirror for the third time in ten minutes. He was wearing the navy blue suit he had custom made in Hong Kong only days earlier. Adding that quick stop before this trip to Bombay was his travel agent's idea. He considered it an odd suggestion at first, but the more he thought about it, the more it made perfect sense. The forty-eight hours in Hong Kong were his last chance to see a part of the world before he got married. His future wife might not like to travel. She might not like to see new places. She might not like to do anything he liked to do.

1

The doorbell rang and Babu, his brother's servant, stomped with heavy feet toward the front door. His footsteps on the freshly waxed hardwood floors echoed like thunder bolts on a stormy night. Babu was a large man with a broad chest and large muscles. He walked with hunched shoulders and eyes downcast from years of servitude. Stepping onto the Oriental carpet, his footsteps were briefly muffled before the thunder bolts returned as he resumed his steps on the wood flooring.

Turning from the hallway mirror, Amir faced the front door. Babu reached the entry, turned around to face the assembling group, and placed his hands behind his back awaiting permission to open the door. He stood with his legs slightly apart and filled the entire door frame, reminding Amir of a defensive lineman on his favorite football team, the Green Bay Packers.

His older brother, Farid, and his wife, Rehana, hurriedly entered the hallway from the living room. Farid looked very prim in his light blue suit and his usual brown tie. He stood rigid, exuding an air of being the master of the castle. Once the three of them were in place, and Rehana had whisked away a stray piece of hair, Farid gave Babu a single nod. The trio watched as the door slowly opened to allow Nargis and her parents to enter the three bedroom flat.

The flat, as the British and hence Indians call it, or condo as the Americans call it, belonged to Farid and Rehana. Amir fondly recalled he had lived here, along with their mother, before he left for America eight years ago. However, when Rehana was about to have their second child, Farid moved Mummy into a ground floor flat. Amir was staying in the guest room in her flat during his visit.

An elbow to his ribs brought Amir back to the present. Farid wanted to know Amir's initial reaction to seeing the first girl on the list. He glanced at Nargis. She was very pretty. If all the girls were this pretty, finding "the one" would be difficult. His family knew his brief criteria for a bride. But he had failed to mention his preference with regard to looks: long hair and little make-up. Amir smiled to himself as he noticed Nargis met both of these unspoken criteria.

Nargis glided into the hallway with her head held high. She was shapely and attractive and seemed to know it. Her pink sari had small silver beads along the hem that sparkled with the overhead light of the hallway chandelier. Her black tresses were carefully draped over her right shoulder exposing her left shoulder and armpit around her sleeveless sari blouse. Was that intentional? Maybe that was how women wore their saris nowadays. Very unlike Rehana and his mother who covered all of their bare skin. However, neither had long hair like Nargis.

She seemed tall, or was she wearing high-heel shoes? Amir immediately glanced at her feet to see her footwear. Nargis was wearing open-toe sandals or *chappals*. Looking up at her face, he concluded she was a couple inches shorter than him. *So far, so good*, he thought. His sister-in-law had selected a good woman to be the first one for him to meet. Maybe this evening would be successful. They would like each other and then that would be that. Three weeks to plan a wedding. It was possible. Yes, it was possible.

Amir wet his lips and was working up the courage to move his right foot forward when Farid and Rehana both stepped forward and approached the guests. In turn, each of them gave welcoming hugs and kisses - one kiss on each cheek. They appeared to know the three guests very well. Yes, of course, they knew them from the Jamat Khanna (JK) where they attended religious services almost every Friday night. The JK was where Ismailis pray to His Highness the Aga Khan, high priest, as well as Allah, God. In fact, all of the women on the list were from the JK, at least that was what Amir had been told.

One by one, the potential groom was introduced to the guests. He flashed a brilliant smile at Nargis. At least he hoped it was a brilliant smile. He wanted to impress this woman. She might be his future wife.

He gestured with an open hand for her to follow his brother into the living room. They stepped onto the very large burgundy and navy blue Oriental carpet in the center. Farid had written him last winter that Rehana's brother had given her the rug as a birthday gift. Rehana adored the rug and upon hearing of Amir's visit, began updating the entire room to match the carpet.

As they walked into the living room, Amir glanced around the room for the first time in eight years. The furniture now had a burgundy hue, a nice update from the previous olive green. The furniture arrangement was more or less the same as he remembered. The sofa was on the far wall, under an Indian landscape painting. The matching love seat was perpendicular to the sofa separating the living room from the dining room. There was a comfortable looking navy blue English style high-back chair opposite the love seat. Behind the chair were two wooden steps leading to the veranda door. The cream colored curtains were pulled to the side allowing the last glimmers of sunlight to enter the room.

Chuckling, Amir recalled his brother's complaints about Rehana's efforts to find the English style high-back chair. She had scouted at least a dozen furniture stores before she found "the perfect one". Amir was anxious to sit in the chair he had heard so much about. Plus, it would give him an ideal view of everyone.

The group followed Farid's cues and took their seats in the living room. The potential bride and her parents sat on the sofa, her father placing a navy blue cushion behind his back. Nargis was in the middle with her mother on the side closest to the love seat. Amir headed toward the high-back chair but immediately frowned when he noticed his mother already sitting in it. *Darn!* She didn't move that fast! Maybe she'd been sitting there the whole time. Yeah, that made sense since he couldn't recall seeing her in the entryway.

With his lower lip pouting slightly, Amir headed to the only available seats. The six dining room chairs were lined up on the far wall and still offered a decent vantage point for watching Nargis. The wooden chairs were a bit out of place in the newly updated room, but even Rehana admitted they provided the much needed seating these meetings required.

Aiming for his chosen spot next to the small wood bookshelf, Amir quickly searched the shelves for the carved elephant he gave Farid a few years ago. To his dismay, he only found small plastic toys and well-read children's books.

Farid stood behind the high-back chair and introduced his mother to the young lady and her parents. Mummy recognized the ladies from JK, and with a large smile, she slowly stood up and greeted each guest with the customary welcoming hugs and kisses.

All of a sudden, Amir's chair made a slight rubbing sound as he shifted his weight slightly. He guessed the sound was from his new trouser fabric rubbing against the stiff plastic seat covering. The conversation abruptly stopped. Amir felt all eyes turn and stare at him, his mother's eyes penetrating into his soul.

Smiling weakly, he waved his right hand and simply uttered, "Hello." He slowly exhaled. *Just calm down*, he told himself. *Breathe. Breathe. Don't screw this up before she even speaks!* Rehana, stifling a laugh, excused herself to check on dinner preparations.

After the initial embarrassment, Farid saved the day by asking Nargis' parents about their trip to the flat. Her father straightened his back and began the uninteresting story of their journey. The story ended when he said his wife's heel had got stuck in a sidewalk crack in the front courtyard. They contemplated leaving the shoe behind, as they didn't want to be tardy for this meeting. The group laughed at the thought of Nargis' mother with only one shoe. Noticing Nargis was laughing, Amir faked a chuckle.

When the laughter had sufficiently subsided, Farid steered the conversation to Amir and his recent arrival from America. Amir spoke briefly about his multiple airplane rides, his layover in London, and concluded with his arrival earlier that day from Hong Kong. He noticed Nargis gave a wry smile when he mentioned Hong Kong. Maybe she was intrigued by the city? He wanted to impress her if he could. After all, she was going to be the mother of his children, right?

He continued to speak about Hong Kong, focusing on how he had a tailor make two suits for him. The tailor measured him from all sorts of angles, just like they did in India. Although tempted to purchase a half dozen suits, he could only afford two. Consequently, he picked the two most popular fabrics - navy blue and charcoal gray. He purposely mentioned he was wearing the navy blue suit that evening for their visit. Nargis and her parents nodded their heads. Amir smiled to himself thinking they must be sufficiently impressed.

Farid glanced in the direction of the dining room, probably hoping to see his wife waiting to tell them dinner was ready. She was not to be seen, which meant he needed to keep the conversation going. Reaching into his right trouser pocket, he retrieved a piece of sky blue paper that looked like some sort of list. Glancing at the paper, he turned toward the bride prospect, "Nargis, Rehana and I know you and your parents very well. However, as you now know, my brother has newly returned from America. Could you please tell him a bit about you and your family?"

Nargis blushed, and Amir noticed she looked startled by the question. She glanced at her father and then directly at Farid. Speaking a bit too quickly, "I'm the oldest of three children. I have a brother in University studying Engineering and another beginning University this Fall to study Accounting." Feeling she had said quite enough, she leaned back on the sofa with a huge sigh.

"We are very proud of our children. Very proud." Nargis' father said with his chest puffed out like a rooster, "We insist all our children be college educated."

"*Aacha.* Good. That is what I insist as well," Mummy said with a slight head bobble. She leaned forward with her hands on her lap and declared proudly, "All of my children are college educated. In fact, my youngest daughter is in medical school." She was referring to Amir's younger sister, Nadia. She had attended medical school at Seth G.S. Medical College in Bombay for two years. She met her husband through a group of friends. Both families were pleased and they married one month after his graduation. Nadia had intended to continue her studies the following semester, but she got pregnant on their honeymoon. That was four years ago and now she is pregnant with their second child.

"Nadia hopes to continue her studies next term," his mother added. Amir knew his sister would not be continuing her medical training. At least, not until their children were older. But, he didn't want to add that bit of information to the conversation. Not yet.

Thankfully, Rehana entered the room and all eyes shifted from his mother to her. Nodding to the group, she informed them, "Dinner is served." The group noisily stood up and followed her to the dining room.

CHAPTER 2

"SAFE TOPICS"

Everyone gathered around the table crowded with delicious looking plates. Rehana proudly explained each dish, waving a hand toward each one as she described it. "Here we have the typical hot steamed *basmati* rice. Next to it is *Rojan Gosh*, made using my mother's recipe for the lamb curry. Next to Amir is the *Khoja-style Daal* which has three different lentils and also lamb meat. Next to Farid is *Masala Chana*. The chickpea curry is usually very spicy, but I had Babu make it bland as I wasn't sure if Amir was used to spicy food living in America." Nargis giggled. Amir wondered, *Does she have a good sense of humor?*

"In front of Nargis," Rehana continued, "is *Palak Paneer*. I had Babu lightly fry the *paneer* cheese to give it a nice contrasting texture to the creamed spinach. Next to the *paneer* dish is *Dahi* Curry. Unlike other yogurt curries, I added *besan* cubes as Farid likes a bit of texture. The cubes are like un-fried *bhajiyas* or onion fritters." As the guests eyed the various dishes, Babu brought out a plate of hot bread shaped like pitas. "Ah, here comes the *naan*." Turning to her servant, she added, "Place it next to the *raita*." He complied and placed it next to the bowl of plain yogurt with cucumbers and onions.

These were a few of Amir's favorite Indian dishes. Rehana must have made this meal especially for him. *How thoughtful!* Farid was right in suggesting they have the dinner parties at their flat, rather than trying to cram this group into their mother's smaller flat. Also, Rehana loved all the details and parties. Their mother did not.

Slowly, the guests and then Virani family, picked up one of Rehana's precious gold-rimmed china dinner plates and began circling the table. Amir, suddenly realizing he was very hungry, took three spoonfuls of *Rojan Gosh* and two spoonfuls each of the *Khoja-style Daal* and *Masala Chana*.

Once everyone had returned to their seats in the living room, they began eagerly eating the flavorful meal. A few of them mixed their food with the rice and ate with their fingers or a fork. Others tore pieces of *naan* and scooped the food with their fingers. After glancing around to make sure everyone else was eating, Amir picked up his fork and started devouring a piece of lamb. Delicious. Hopefully his wife will be able to cook this well. *Can Nargis even cook?*

"Amir, could you tell us a bit about your life in America?" Farid suggested.

Glancing around the room, Amir's eyes grew wide. As he slowly chewed on a tender piece of lamb, he lifted his forefinger to indicate he would need a moment. He would actually need a few moments. What was the right thing to say? Should he tell them about his job? The city? His Indian friends? His American friends? His American ex-girlfriend? No, definitely not the ex-girlfriend. This was not the right time, maybe it never would be. *I'll start with my job and maybe talk about the city. Safe topics.*

"Well," Amir finally said gulping down the piece of lamb, "I work for a large company called Allen Bradley in Milwaukee, Wisconsin. They make electrical controls and switches. I'm a member of the plant engineering group."

"What's a plant engineer?" Nargis asked meekly. Amir noticed she rarely looked at him. Did she find him repulsive or was she just trying to act demure in the traditional Indian way? She seemed to play with the hem of her sari often. Was it beginning to unravel?

Amir leaned forward in an attempt to make eye contact with Nargis, but she kept her eyes on her sari hem. "A plant engineer is an engineer that works in a plant. In other words, I help to make sure my company's factory floors are producing products efficiently and safely."

Nargis nodded and returned to her meal. Amir watched as she expertly tore a piece of *naan*, scooped up the lentils of the *daal* and placed it in her mouth. She pushed back her hair with the back of her hand and repeated the tear-scoop-eat process.

It was her father's turn next. After swallowing a finger-full of *paneer*, he asked with raised eyebrows, "Are you the head of the plant engineering group?"

"No," Amir responded. Sensing the father was disappointed with that answer he added, "Not yet."

The conversation bantered for a few more minutes, discussing Amir's career and life in America. When he thought he had sufficiently updated the group on his life, he paused and quickly took another bite of lamb.

After a few more mouthfuls, Farid reached into his pocket and glanced down at his notes. Much to Amir's relief, he swayed the conversation back to the prospective bride, "Nargis, what year of medical school are you in?"

Nervously glancing at her father, Nargis responded, "I'm about to start my third year of medical school." She tilted her head to Mummy, "Aunty, you said your daughter attends Seth G.S. Medical School." She waited for Mummy to nod acknowledgment, then added, "That's where I attend classes."

"That is a good school. A very good school," Mummy announced proudly with a slight head bobble and a flip of her hand.

"What is your field of study?" Rehana asked as Babu began to collect the dinner plates from each guest.

"Well, Aunty, I want to be a surgeon." Nargis replied glancing again at her father. She bit her lower lip and added, "It's a seven year program and... and... I want to finish my training here... in India."

Amir's mind raced. *What?! Did she just say she wanted to finish her seven year program here in India? That would be what, four more years?! Four years they would be apart? That she, his wife, would not be in America with him? What about children? He wanted them soon, and that would be impossible if she was here. No, this would not do. Why hadn't Farid and Rehana found this out before we spent the whole evening with these people? Really nice people.*

"Wh...What?" was all Amir could muster to say.

"I love my college and my professors. I want to finish my medical degree here in India."

"As a result, if you two did marry," Farid clarified, "you wouldn't be going to America for another four years?"

"Yes, Uncle, that's correct." Nargis responded with growing confidence.

A hush fell over the group. Babu brought small finger bowls for everyone to cleanse their fingers, using the small piece of lemon in the bowl to help remove the curry stains from their skin.

The silent awkwardness continued as Babu brought out small crystal bowls filled with a creamy rice pudding called *kheer*. He had them on a sterling silver serving tray and offered each person a bowl and little spoon. When everyone was served, Farid finally broke the silence, "Well, Amir. What do you think?"

Amir took a bite of *kheer* to stall a moment longer. As he crunched on the slivered almond garnish, he watched Nargis gulp the rice pudding. No wonder she had seemed so nervous. She wanted a marriage on her own terms. She was pretty enough. In fact, she had beautiful hair and a lovely body. But there was no way he was going to wait four years. He was already thirty years old and he couldn't wait, didn't want to wait, to have a wife and children. He closed his eyes and placed his head in his hands.

He glanced around the room. His family seemed dumbfounded at Nargis' bombshell of four more years of schooling in India. They all assumed she would continue her medical school training in America, as many others do. Amir glanced at Farid and shook his head. Farid cleared his throat and said, "Sorry, Nargis, this match will not work. Good luck in your medical studies."

"I understand," she replied. She didn't seem surprised by his response, "Let me know if you're still looking for a bride in four years." The group laughed, breaking the tension in the room. *She does have a good sense of humor*, Amir thought to himself. *She could have been a good wife.*

They allowed Babu to collect the crystal dessert bowls. Given the futility of further discussions, Nargis and her parents stood and said good night. Rehana offered to make them tea, but they politely declined. They thanked Farid and Rehana for being lovely hosts and complimented Rehana on a very tasty dinner. Before they left, Farid pulled her parents aside and assured them that although a match did not occur, they are still friends and they would welcome each other at JK.

As Babu shut the front door, Rehana exhaled a huge sigh. She tried to cover up her disappointment by faking a smile. Cocking her head to the left, she announced "Well, that one didn't work. We just move down the list. We meet another woman tomorrow."

"Another doctor?" Amir asked for clarification.

"No," she replied proudly, "Tomorrow's prospective bride is a *nawabzadi*."

"An Indian heiress?" Amir grinned, "This could be interesting. Very interesting."

CHAPTER 3

Monday, August 8

"A REALLY BAD IDEA"

The next morning, Amir awoke feeling refreshed. He had slept soundly with not a hint of jet lag. The guest bed in his mother's flat was very soft and comfortable. Much more comfortable than his bed in Milwaukee. Stretching his arms wide, he tilted his head from side-to-side, ridding himself of any left-over cobwebs.

Amir smiled to himself as he continued his stretches. A *nawabzadi*! Wow! When did Farid and Rehana meet wealthy land-owners? What did Rehana say the name of the province was? As he touched his toes, Amir's mind began to wander. *How prosperous was the province? Would the heiress be okay leaving her luxurious life in India to live in America?*

He consoled himself that he did have a good job, but realized his salary was not enough to keep an heiress in the lap of luxury. He had no servants. His car was used. He had a two-bedroom apartment. His lifestyle was not affluent. His wife would have to do the laundry, the cooking, the cleaning and ideally work outside of the home. Not a lifestyle for a *nawabzadi*. Maybe meeting her was a bad idea. Yes, a really bad idea.

Slightly panicked, Amir rushed from the guest room directly to the hall telephone. He quickly dialed his brother's telephone number, and impatiently tapped his foot as he listened to the phone ring. Suddenly, Babu picked up the receiver, and told him no one was home. Frustrated, Amir left a message asking one of them to call back immediately. It was very important.

Drudging back to the guest room, he changed into a short-sleeve shirt and khaki pants. As he was buckling his belt, he remembered he had brought gifts for everyone. He had been too rushed with the bridal viewing yesterday to sort through his suitcases. Ramu, Mummy's servant, had offered to unpack the bags for him, but Amir refused. Living in America, he was used to doing things on his own.

Shopping was not his forte. Therefore, he had sought the help of the various department store sales clerks and just hoped for the best. Knowing that 1966 Bombay was still a bit formal, he brought silk neckties for the gents and knit shawls for the ladies. Someone at work told him all kids like chocolate, so he packed two dozen Cadbury chocolate bars. He also indulgently purchased a dozen Toblerones at the Heathrow airport. Toblerones are his favorite chocolate and nearly impossible to find in Milwaukee. He decided to distribute these last, so he could eat any triangular Swiss milk chocolate bars remaining.

He picked up the egg-shell colored shawl he had purchased with his mother in mind, and quickly walked into the dining room. She was sitting at the head of the table enjoying her morning tea and lightly buttered toast with orange marmalade. They greeted each other warmly, and he presented the shawl to her as he sat down.

"Oh, Amir, *khubsoorat!* Beautiful!" she said. She immediately put the shawl around her shoulders, bobbing her head in approval, "*Shukriya.* Thank you."

The doorbell rang, and Ramu crossed the room to open the front door. Amir noticed the servant had a spring in his step. Very different from the thunder bolts of Farid's servant. Ramu looked very different too. He was a tall, lean man and looked like a scientist with curly hair and black eyeglasses.

His mother's flat was much smaller than Farid and Rehana's place, but it was still comfortable. Amir had heard all about her move to this flat a few years ago during one of their evening chats last summer. She had said she liked the flat and was thankful to only climb four steps from the front courtyard to the ground floor. No other stairs and no need to wait for the building's slow lift. She did complain about the iron bars on the windows, but after a bit of pushing from Amir, she admitted it was a common security feature in ground-floor flats.

The move was hard for Mummy at first. She said the flat was too quiet. But, she knew Farid needed the room for his growing family. With tears in his eyes, he had told her he felt guilty moving her to a flat all alone. As the eldest son, it was his responsibility to take care of her. Even though the move and the change was difficult for her, Mummy told Farid she still felt protected by him since she was in the same building. After a few months, Mummy actually began to enjoy the quiet of her new flat. Especially after an evening with the noisy grandchildren.

Ramu opened the door, and Nadia waddled into the room. "Hello, Mummy. Hello, Amir." Plopping down on the living room divan, she added, "Tell me about the woman last night. She's a doctor, no?" Mummy had mentioned his younger sister, Nadia, came to visit her two to three times a week. She often brought three-year old Tarik to visit with *Nanima*. His maternal grandmother. Was this one of those days, or was she here to gossip?

Amir was not really in a talking mood. He didn't like to gossip and he didn't was to rehash the disaster of last evening. Plus, he really needed to talk to Rehana about the *nawabzadi*. When was she going to call him back?

Grudgingly, Amir retreated to the guest room to retrieve a shawl, necktie and Cadbury chocolate. Returning to the living room, he lovingly pushed her long legs to the side of the divan, and presented her with the gifts. She immediately put the shawl around her shoulders and turned from side to side, "Looks good, no?" Their mother laughed and did the same. Amir just shook his head. Women.

"Thank you for the gifts. Tarik loves chocolate." She removed the shawl from her shoulders. Sitting up and propping a pillow behind her back, she leaned forward placing a hand on his arm, "I'm listening. The woman was good, no?"

Not wanting to relive the evening, he summarized the conclusion. Nadia gasped and said, "But, that would mean you would be apart for the first few years of your marriage." She repeated the obvious. "What did you say?"

"Farid told her it wouldn't work, and then she left." He replied very matter-of-factly.

"There are more, no? Who does Rehana have next on the list?"

"A *nawabzadi* from a small province," Amir replied standing up. He was tired of this conversation already. "That's all I know. Rehana doesn't want me getting stressed before each meeting. She gives me a few details just before the woman arrives."

"She's coming to dinner, no?" Nadia asked with a bit of enthusiasm in her voice, "Shall I come?"

"Yes, she's coming to dinner, but no, you cannot come." Amir said as he waved his hands at her, "It's hard enough with Mummy, Farid and Rehana there."

"But, I want to help," she pleaded like a little girl.

"How?" Amir replied throwing up his hands, "You'll ask silly questions. Farid came prepared with a list of good questions."

"Well, maybe I would ask silly questions, but I'd like to meet the girl anyways." Nadia paused and pouted her lower lip. She blinked her eyes repeatedly like she did when they were younger. "I want to make sure she'll take care of you."

She and Amir had always been close. They were only two years apart in age and had been playmates in their younger years and confidantes during their teenage years. Nadia was the only one of his siblings Amir trusted to be level-headed enough to think of him first. She would indeed look out for him. "If any of the women make it to the second round, then you can meet her."

"Fine," she agreed. Placing her hands on her hips, she added, "So, what questions do you want Farid to ask?" It wasn't proper for the groom to ask questions directly to the prospective bride. He had family members do that, in this case, Farid or his mother. On the prospective bride's side, it was not proper for her to be alone with the groom. She had to have an escort, usually her parents or siblings. Consequently, a simple conversation between two people turned into a large family meeting.

"Hmm," Amir paused. He had started compiling a list when he boarded the airplane in Hong Kong. He had scribbled about a dozen questions on the cocktail napkin he received with his complimentary soda. Unfortunately, he didn't guard the napkin and the stewardess removed it when she cleared his empty cup. Looking up at the ceiling, he tried to recall some of his notes, "I'd like to know if she can cook."

"Great question. Especially in America since you can't come to Mummy's for dinner. What else?"

"Um, I'd like to know if she likes to travel." Amir really hoped she did.

"That may be a hard question to ask at the first meeting. Don't you have any general questions? About her age, her schooling or what her father does?"

"Farid has some of those questions on his list. Plus, we know a bit about each woman because Farid and Rehana know the families from JK."

"*Aacha.* Sounds like the first encounter is covered." Nadia said reassuringly. She stood up and patted Amir on the top of the head like a small child. "You'll find the perfect wife in no time!" Blowing him a kiss, she disappeared down the hallway in search of their mother.

Shrugging his shoulders, he looked down at his feet and mumbled, "I hope so." *Finding a wife is going to be harder than I thought. Isn't there a woman who wants a bit of adventure?*

Looking up from his feet, Amir glared at his reflection in the window. His hair was jet black and parted on the left with a bit of hair oil to keep his cowlick from springing up. *This is the modern look, right? The nawabzadi should be impressed by that. But, what if she is looking for someone less modern?*

He walked quickly to the hallway mirror, and looked closely at his cheeks and chin. The slight beard stubble could be fixed with another quick shave before she arrived. *My eyes look fine,* he convinced himself, *much better without the bags under them.* Smiling at his own reflection, he admonished himself for the silly grin. Trying three or four different smiles, Amir finally found one he liked. *What about the rest of me?*

Leaning closer to look at his shirt, he concluded the hall mirror was too small. Anxiously, he retreated to the guest bedroom, hearing the murmur of Mummy and Nadia's voices. Their voices were hushed, so he couldn't make out what they were saying, but he knew they were talking about him.

The two large cherry-wood armoires sat side by side along the main wall. The one on the left was filled with Mummy's extra saris. The one on the right contained his sparse belongings. He opened the armoire doors, and stepped back to examine himself in the full-length mirror drilled into the door. The shirt was fine. But, what about the suit for tonight? He looked at the gray suit and noticed it was slightly crumpled. The blue one from yesterday had creases from sitting! Yikes! That would not do to meet a *nawabzadi* or really anyone. Grabbing the suits he called, "Ramu!"

Amir could her the quick footsteps of the servant rushing toward his door. Ramu knocked reluctantly, "Sah'b, you called?" Ramu said quietly in Hindi.

"Ramu. No wrinkles." Amir said slowly in English, hoping the servant could understand his American accent. Handing him the two suits, he added, "Back quickly."

It had been about a year since his mother had visited him in America, and Amir found it more and more difficult to converse in Hindi. Growing up, he had attended English speaking convent schools as his parents believed they offered the best education. After he went to America, he rarely spoke Hindi, even when he got together with his few Indian friends. Some of them spoke their local Indian languages such as Telugu or Gujarati. More often than not, the conversations were mixtures of English and other languages. He found it hard to follow them, so he just spoke English.

Ramu nodded and said, "*Aacha*." He took the suits and scurried off.

"Okay," Amir said to himself. *Everything will be fine.* His mother used a variety of vendors nearby to do specific chores such as washing, ironing and tailoring. He was confident Ramu would take his precious suits to the ironing guy. It would cost only a few *rupees* and he would look sharp for tonight's meeting. That was, if Ramu understood what he said and the guy didn't destroy the suits. He was half-tempted to run after Ramu, and tell him to forget it. But, it was too late.

Nadia left the flat soon after Ramu, but not without stopping by to remind Amir of his promise to allow her to meet any women that passes the first meeting. Once she left, the house was immediately quiet. Amir glanced into his mother's room. She was laying on the bed quietly snoring. Nadia must have exhausted her.

Returning to his room, Amir picked up the book that lay casually on the bedside. It was a book of love poems. *Mummy is relentless.* He flipped a few pages, and decided he needed to do something else. Throwing the book onto the bed, he strode into the living room. Ramu had returned from his errand, and was in the kitchen boiling water for them to drink. Amir nodded to him, and left the flat.

CHAPTER 4

"NEVER BE AFRAID"

The five-story Ivanhoe Building was squeezed between two other condo buildings in central Bombay. It was built in the art-deco style, perfectly located between Marine Drive and the Bombay Harbour. Rehana and Farid had been living in their fourth-floor flat ever since her parents had bought it as part of her wedding dowry. Recently, her parents also updated the kitchen so Rehana could enjoy cooking more efficiently.

Amir hummed as he skipped down the four steps into the front courtyard. The pleasant fragrance of the jasmine flowers wafted through the air, and he inhaled deeply. Smiling, he continued through the iron gate to the surprisingly quiet sidewalk. Recalling from memory his route, he turned right and headed down Prakash Pethe Marg to the very busy intersection at Madame Cama Road. A legless beggar on the corner caught his eye, and he tossed him a few *rupees* before crossing the intersection to head east.

The toxic smell of the vehicle combustion filled his nostrils. Amir coughed. He had forgotten the assault on one's senses. The smoke of pollution, the honk of horns and the explosion of people. This is why he left Bombay. He passed a small group of beggars with one holding a hungry-looking toddler on her hip. *Such poverty in this city*, he sadly thought to himself. He gave them a handful of *rupees* hoping they would use the money to buy food for the baby.

Continuing his mission, Amir passed the Prince of Wales Museum. During his teen years, he had enjoyed visiting the different rooms with the variety of paintings and artifacts. His favorite exhibits were the Indian miniatures, especially the ones painted on palm leaves. *I should visit it again*, he told himself, *but not today.*

He continued east toward the Bombay Harbour and the Gateway of India. He quickly glanced to his right. Normally he would admire the glamorous Taj Mahal Palace Hotel (Taj Hotel), but today he kept his eyes on the sidewalk searching the crowd. Not finding the person he was seeking, he moved toward the large plaza in front of the Gateway of India. The plaza was full of camera-toting tourists. As with any tourist attraction, there were a handful of various vendors trying to sell them various things from balloons to lamb kebabs.

Finally, Amir spied the man he was looking for. Rushing to the vendor's side, he ordered a coconut by lifting his forefinger and mumbling, "*Ache*. One." Amir had forgotten the Hindi word for "please", but he did remember the word for "thank you " and he muttered it as he watched with delight as the coconut-*walla* used his dull machete to skillfully chop the top off the young coconut. He quickly paid and cheerfully took hold of the prized fruit. *Aaah, fresh coconut water.*

There was an empty bit of sidewalk with a view of the Harbour. Amir took a straw from the coconut-*walla* and rushed to the vacant spot. He sat with his feet dangling over the brick ledge, and inhaled a long sip of *nariyal pani*. The trickle of the coconut water on his throat brought back memories of family vacations in Matheran, a nearby town.

After the long railway journey to the resort town, his parents would stop and refresh the family with fresh coconut water. He closed his eyes, and travelled back in time to those simpler days when his father was alive. He had died a decade earlier from a sudden heart attack, and Mummy missed him immensely. Amir was convinced that was a biggest reason she was pushing him to get married - she was most happy when she was married.

He laughed as he recalled his mother's determined visit to Milwaukee last summer. Since he was the only one of her five children not married, she had packed up the traditional Indian matrimonial garb, and flew from Bombay to New York. Not knowing much English had not stopped her; but to ease his own mind, Farid had arranged for stewardesses on Air India to escort her to the correct planes in London and New York. After she passed through U.S. customs, Amir was there to drive her to his home in Milwaukee. The fourteen-hour car drive in his forest green Ford Falcon was cramped but pleasant.

Amir had enjoyed Mummy's visit to his home. She pampered him by cooking his favorite Indian dishes, and introducing him to a few new ones. After dinner, they sat for hours at his small kitchen table sipping tea. Mummy spoke almost exclusively in Hindi, and Amir had worked hard to understand and converse with her. Their conversations were filled with updates on the family, but most of the discussions, during the drive and for the two months of her visit, were about his marriage. He had no current prospects, so when she left, she made him promise to either find an "Ameer-ic-kan" girl to marry or return to India to find a bride. They agreed on a one year deadline. Amir knew he would need that year to save enough vacation time to make a trip to India worthwhile.

A few months after Mummy left, Amir met a wonderful American girl named Diane. She had long brown hair and a great sense of humor. He enjoyed spending time with her as she was also self-confident and full of life.

After three months of dating, Amir thought Diane might be "the one". She was the perfect height, she could cook, and she even enjoyed Indian food. Unfortunately, when he started talking about marriage, Diane abruptly broke things off with him, saying he was "moving too fast". Those were the words she used when she left him sitting alone at the restaurant. He remained at their table until the candle in the center extinguished.

Sipping cup after cup of coffee, Amir resolved he didn't want to marry an American girl. Instead, he wanted an Indian girl who was ready for marriage. But, he enjoyed Diane's self-confidence. He wanted his Indian wife to not only survive here; but also thrive, in what Julia Child termed "the servant-less America".

Remembering the promise to his mother, and now a bit more excited at the prospect of an Indian bride, he called Farid and told him he was coming in August. He gave basic criteria: college educated, fluent in English and self-confident. Working with that criteria,

Rehana, Farid and his mother had created "Amir's top ten list". They are meeting the second name on the list tonight.

His blissful thoughts were cut short by the blaring sound of a boat horn. HONK! It repeated. He watched as a tourist boat returning from nearby Elephanta Island almost hit a commercial fishing boat. The two captains were frantically waving their arms, while the tourists watched helplessly. It reminded him that he was now basically a tourist too. His body didn't have the same immunity it did when he left Bombay. *Am I going to get sick from the nariyal pani?*

The tourist boat backed up, and awkwardly swerved around the fishing boat. Ignoring the chaos, Amir resumed eating his delicious coconut. The tasty water was now gone, but the best part was yet to come. Scrape. Scrape. Scrape. With his mouth open wide, he swallowed a long slippery sliver of the coconut flesh.

Fresh coconuts had always been a treat for him. In fact, he insisted his going-away party end early, so he could indulge in this delicacy. Nadia brought an autograph book to the Harbour, and the members of the group wrote their parting wisdom as they sipped *nariyal pani*. The one memorable entry was his Mummy's. She had written, as an excerpt from his father's diary:

> "Instructions to my children:
> Anything can happen.
> Every difficulty can be overcome.
> Above all things, never be afraid."

The last line struck him. Never be afraid. Good advice for someone leaving their homeland to settle in a foreign land.

The next day, Amir dragged his heavy metal steamer trunk and his mother's beat-up leather suitcase, and boarded the impressive cruise ship, the *S.S. Chusan*. The fairly new boat was built for the Peninsular and Oriental Steam Navigation Company, or as the stewards called it, "P&O". The passengers had renamed it the "B&O", as they had found out very quickly the vessel didn't have air conditioning. The rooms were very stuffy, and the passengers very stinky.

Amir ate another bite of coconut flesh. *Darn, Ravi!* He was recalling the misadventure with his shipmate, Ravi. They had become fast friends during the long, boring hours on board. When they arrived at the first stop in the Port of Aden, Ravi invited Amir to join him at his Aunty's for lunch. Since he needed to replace his suitcase in town, he gladly accepted the lunch invitation.

Ravi's family had sent a car and driver to pick him up. Before going to lunch, they briefly stopped at a shopping area where Amir was able to find a decent replacement suitcase. They both thought the two hours remaining would be enough time for lunch. They were wrong.

Since they had not seen Ravi since he was a small child, his extended family was eager to chat. Amir was introduced to the group, and the two of them were the center of the conversation for almost an hour.

The clock was ticking, and Amir was relieved when Aunty finally ordered the cook to start heating the food. She wanted to serve the guests a hot meal the traditional Hindu way - *thali* style. Each of them was given a steel tray with small steel bowls placed around the edge. The middle section was empty for mixing the food prior to eating. Amir had not had a *thali* meal in years, but he did remember it took a long time to prepare the full meal as each dish was warmed individually.

Part of the enjoyment of the *thali* meal was the variety of dishes. Amir sighed as the cook slowly filled one of his bowls with spicy mango pickle and another with cooled *basmati* rice. The clock ticking seemed to grow louder as the cook waited for the *tawa* to heat so he could make hot *chapattis*. The *bhendi* and *aaloo* curry had been prepared earlier and was leisurely being warmed on the *chulla*. When the cook was satisfied, he spooned the warm food from the pot on the *chulla* into the steel bowls on their trays.

Aunty's okra and potato curry was indeed delicious, but the clock was ticking. Tick. Tick. Tick. Only thirty minutes before the boat departed, and the boat dock was about twenty minutes away, if Amir had timed it correctly. Mummy's warning echoed in his mind, "Don't miss the boat!"

The cook now began making the *chapattis* directly on the *tawa*. Amir's heart was beating fast, and he worked up the courage to say they had to leave. In retrospect, he wished he had been more adamant, but he was a guest in their home and didn't want to offend them. The Aunty waved her hands dismissively, and said, "Don't worry, don't worry. Our driver will take you there fast, fast."

Ravi seemed oblivious, and continued to eagerly eat the curry with the freshly made *chapattis*. As the cook started heating an eggplant dish, Amir stood up, and insisted they return to the boat. This time, Ravi relented. Much to Amir's frustration, good-bye hugs and kisses took another ten minutes. The driver did his best weaving through the streets, nearly hitting two cars along the way, but they arrived at the dock too late.

"Damn!" Amir swore as he looked at the boat floating away. Ravi suggested they go back to Aunty's to finish their lunch, and Amir shot him a frustrated look. Maybe Ravi didn't comprehend the magnitude of what just happened. He might be able to take a different ship to London, but Amir was not so lucky. He had to get back on that ship. Not only to get to London to catch his scheduled boat to New York; but also, because all his precious belongings were on board in that steel trunk.

They had two choices - fly to Gibraltar, the next port, or hire a tug boat to take them to the *S.S. Chusan*. Neither option was good, because it would use most of his money. After much discussion, they decided on the least expensive option, and split the cost of the tug boat.

Churn! Churn! The tug boat churned slowly through the water, and it took over an hour to catch up to the ocean liner. The crew from the *S.S. Chusan* saw the little craft speeding toward them. When it was close, they lowered the Jacob's ladder. Amir tied his now costly suitcase to the ladder first, and watched as it was hauled onto the deck, bashing into the side of the ship a few times as it ascended.

The crew lowered the rope ladder again, and the two men grabbed hold of it. Climbing was difficult as the ladder flailed against the ship, and the salty water made the rope slippery. When they finally reached the main deck, the gathered crowd broke into a round of applause. The weary and embarrassed travelers were wrapped in blankets and escorted to their cabin. His mother's warning still haunting him, he swore he would never tell her. He still hadn't.

Missing the boat seemed like a lifetime ago, and an unfortunate start to his American adventure. He felt guilt over hiding the boat fiasco from Mummy, especially since she had been so supportive of his decision to stay in America.

Amir missed her and India. Unfortunately, his opportunities to remain tied to the Indian culture were limited. There were only a few Indians in the Milwaukee area. Last spring, soon after his break-up with Diane, his work friend Kabir Mehta suggested they drive two hours to "Little India" in Chicago. Miraculously, Kabir's rusty Volkswagen Beetle didn't overheat, and they made it to Devon Street.

Kabir and Amir gorged themselves on a lunch buffet, and then wandered in and out of various Indian themed stores buying decorations for their apartments and snacks for their sweet tooth. Just before they returned home, they stuffed themselves on a dinner buffet and ordered *samosas* to take home. The outing made Amir realize how much an Indian wife would mean to him. She could enjoy "Little India" as much as he did. Diane would not have appreciated it. Not at all.

Amir scraped the interior of the coconut, and realized it was spent. Oh well. He glanced again at the boats in the Harbour, and stood up to stretch his legs. As he retraced his steps to home, he deposited the coconut in a garbage pile. Sadly, he thought, *the little food left might be a meal for someone later today.*

He walked past the majestic Taj Hotel. Everyone in town knew it was considered a five-star hotel, which meant it was as impressive inside as it was outside. He strained his neck to glance into the lobby. Several uniformed bellman were helping people with their luggage. Each wore a clean white jacket with a Nehru collar and black vest. Some of them wore turbans with obnoxious ostrich plumes. Maybe one day he would have enough money to stay at this hotel.

"Is The Sea Lounge just up the Grand Staircase?" a woman asked Amir. Startled by the question, he turned to notice the person standing next to him. She was an elegant older lady wearing a burgundy sari, and a matching ruby and gold necklace and earrings.

"Um, I believe so." Amir answered. The woman thanked him and proceeded into the Taj Hotel. She must have asked the same question to one of the bellmen as he pointed his white-gloved hand to the Grand Staircase and then motioned to the right. *She must be eating dinner there*, he thought. A quick glance at his watch and he realized he would be late for his own dinner with the *nawabzadi*. Hopefully Ramu had returned with his suits pressed and ready.

CHAPTER 5

"I LIVE IN A TOWN CALLED MILWAUKEE"

Hurrying back to the flat, Amir found his mother impatiently waiting. She was elegantly dressed in a vibrant green sari, tapping her foot repeatedly. Amir smiled weakly at her, and dashed into the guest room to change. Thankfully, Ramu had both of his suits hanging on the armoire door. He wiped himself with a wet cloth, trying to clean the car exhaust smell from his body, and slipped into the charcoal gray suit. *Oh, this feels great!* The recent pressing had softened the stiff fabric a bit, and made the lapels lay perfectly. He looked great. Actually better than he expected.

Knotting his tie, Amir looked at himself in the mirror. The slight beard stubble was now a light beard. *Too late for a shave,* he told himself, *Mummy was waiting.* There was a clump of hair standing a bit too high on the back of his head. He added a dab of hair oil, and combed it through. *Darn cowlick.* He combed it again, and gave up. Hopefully no one would notice. Especially the heiress.

Mummy led them to the lift, and they entered silently. *She must be upset because we're late.* Amir pulled the outer and inner scissor doors shut while his mother repeatedly hit the button for "4". The lift jerked, and began its slow ascent. Amir noticed the box was big enough for four, maybe five, medium size people. Tight fit. After what seemed like minutes, the lift reached its destination. Amir pulled the scissor doors open and his anxious mother strode down the hall. He followed close behind her, nervously patting down his hair, and cursing his cowlick.

Just like the entrance to Ali Baba's cave, the door silently opened as they approached. Farid rushed up to Mummy, kissing her on both cheeks. Rehana came out of the kitchen to also welcome them. She was wearing an attractive blue sari. Both of the ladies were dressed up to meet this Indian *nawabzadi*. Amir nervously patted his hair down again. Suddenly, he remembered he had left their gifts downstairs, again. The guests were due any minute. There wasn't enough time to get the gifts. *Shoot. This evening isn't starting out very well.*

The aroma of the food wafted into Amir's nostrils, and his stomach growled loudly reminding him that he had only had a coconut for lunch. Rehana handed Amir a piece of paper with her notes, "Shalimar, eighteen, oldest daughter of the *Nawab* of Jaipura, two sisters."

Only eighteen. Wow, a twelve year age difference. A ten or twelve year age difference wasn't uncommon in Indian marriages, but it was uncommon in America.

Amir looked up from the notes, to notice his brother sitting very uncomfortably. "What's wrong, Farid?" Amir asked as he sat down next to his brother on the love seat.

"*Kuch nahih.* Nothing," Farid replied as he shook his head and waved his hands, "You just concentrate on the *nawabzadi* tonight. Don't worry about me."

Before he could respond, the doorbell rang. Babu walked heavily to the door, and waited for permission to open it. The family scampered to form a welcoming party in the hallway. When everyone was in place, Farid nodded to Babu. The servant opened the door to reveal a small group standing in the doorway.

First two large men, probably the guards, entered the flat. They both wore red baggy pants, a large hat with a purple ostrich plume, and small swords sheath on their right side. The second guard carried a large intricately-carved mahogany chest. As they entered the flat, they appeared to scan the room for danger. Satisfied, they stood at attention in front of the wooden bookcase.

Next floated in Shalimar's younger sisters. They giggled at the Virani group standing in the entryway, and held hands as they found seats on the sofa. There was a pause in the procession, and then the lift bell rang again.

The *nawabzadi* was dressed in a bright yellow sari. An unusual geometric pattern ran throughout it, stitched with silver thread. Much to Amir's disappointment, she wore her sari *pallu* draped over her head. The extra sari fabric surrounded her head and made her face difficult to see. *Is she being discreet or is she hiding something?*

Shalimar's father was a loud man. His voice boomed throughout the flat with every word. He marched into the room like a movie star, shooing the sisters from the sofa. The teenage girls giggled again, and moved to the loveseat. Mummy sat in the high-back chair, and the remaining hosts found seats on the dining room chairs.

They exchanged pleasantries, but the first few minutes were tense. Amir glanced often at Shalimar, but still could not see her face. She was practiced at keeping her face covered, and her eyes cast down. Indian women were supposed to be discreet, and mysterious, but this was borderline ridiculous. He wanted to see his bride before their wedding day. This wasn't an arranged marriage!

"How was your journey?" Farid asked the *Nawab*, Mirza.

"Very nice," Mirza replied, "We enjoyed the rail journey very much. Our first class cabin was most comfortable. My daughters and I are staying not far from here at the Taj Hotel. We go back home to Jaipura tomorrow," he paused for effect, "Unless a match occurs."

Amir's mind began to race. *First class cabin. The Taj Hotel? They must have wealth. What can I possibly offer her? This is a mistake. Did Babu even give them the message I called?*

"Very nice hotel," Mummy replied calmly, "Where exactly is Jaipura?"

"Humph!" Mirza snuffed, sounding displeased, "You are not familiar with our lovely province? Jaipura is close to Ahmadabad. Do you know where *that* is?" He waited for Mummy to nod, and then continued, "We have talented textile makers, who specialize in the geometric patterns my daughters are wearing. Our saris are prized all over Northern India."

"Lovely saris," Mummy said as she scanned the intricate patterns on the three young ladies, "Beautiful patterns."

Suddenly, the *Nawab* snapped his fingers. The bulky guard holding the chest stepped forward, and placed the box on the coffee table almost knocking over the bowl of Bombay Mix snacks. The chest landed with a heavy thud, causing the water in the nearby flower bowl to slosh back and forth for several seconds.

With exaggerated bravado, the *Nawab* lifted the antique brass latch on the chest, and threw open the lid exposing the colorful contents. He waved his forefinger once. The two young girls obediently rose from the loveseat to gracefully hand a sari to each of the host women. Mummy admired her pink sari with a swirling pattern, while Rehana gazed at her purple sari with a geometric branch pattern.

Amir was impressed at the generosity of the *Nawab*. Throughout this exchange, he noticed the eldest daughter did not move or say a word. She kept the top of her sari covering her forehead. Her eyes only snuck glances occasionally. He wondered, *What does her voice sound like? Is she so quiet, because her father is so flamboyant?*

The current *Nawab* proudly explained Jaipura was originally settled by Sultan Ahmed Shah in 1421, a decade after he settled Ahmadabad. Mirza's family was also interested in the land, consequently they fought and beat Ahmed Shah's army. They renamed the province Jaipura as a tribute to one of the first *Nawab's* wives.

The conversation they were having was in broken English. The *Nawab* and his three daughters had learned English, but preferred to converse in their local language of Gujarati. The *Nawab* slipped between the two languages as he spoke. Amir had a hard time following the conversation, and he hoped the heiress spoke fluent English because he knew very little Gujarati.

Babu entered the living room to announce dinner was ready. The procession slowly followed Babu into the dining room. The two young ladies were first, followed by Shalimar and Mirza, Farid and Amir, and finally Mummy and Rehana. The guards followed Babu into the kitchen for their meal. It was not proper for the hired staff to eat with their bosses.

The food was arranged on an off-white linen table cloth, with a crystal vase full of yellow carnations in the middle. Similar to the night before, Rehana explained each dish to the group. As Amir's stomach growled again, he picked up a plate and followed his brother around the table. These were Farid's favorites, and probably dishes Rehana made often: Shrimp Curry with Onions, Chicken Curry with Coconut Cream, *Dudhi Daal* and *Matar Paneer*. A bowl of hot *basmati* rice and plate of *chapattis* sat next to the *raita*.

Amir noticed the heiresses took very little food on their plates. Were they vegetarian? He shrugged his shoulders, and ladled the *Dudhi Daal* into one of the bowls sitting next to the serving platter. He planned to eat the squash and lentil dish like soup just as he did when he was a child.

He continued sneaking peeks in Shalimar's direction, as he spooned the shrimp curry onto his already full plate. His glances paid off, when he noticed her reach for a *chapatti*. The sari *pallu* slipped onto her shoulders before she hastily snapped it back over her head. The quick glance was enough to notice she was comely, with a pointed nose and soft cheekbones. That was all he could see in that millisecond. He now watched her nonstop, hoping for another slip of the sari *pallu*. She did not let it happen again.

The assembly seemed to enjoy the food. Eagerly, Amir sipped the *daal* savoring the thick consistency of the broth. The lentils were so tender and had been mashed carefully leaving only a few of the lentils whole. No wonder this is Farid's favorite *daal* dish! As Amir finished the last bite of *dudhi*, he licked his lips. He was tempted to lick the bowl as he did when he was a child, but he thought better of it.

Suddenly, the conversation changed from Jaipura to America. This was Amir's chance to impress the guests with his life and adventures abroad. He cleared his throat and speaking slowly, so they could understand his American English, he explained, "I live in a town called Milwaukee. It's in the state of Wisconsin about sixty miles north of Chicago." *Everyone knows where Chicago is, don't they?* He had hoped that mentioning Chicago would impress the *Nawab*. He seemed to be the one to please.

"Is that near New York or Los Angeles?" The *Nawab* roared.

I guess not everyone knows where Chicago is. Amir explained, using his hands for a visual aid, "Well, New York is on the east coast. Los Angeles is on the west coast, and Chicago is in the middle."

"*Aacha*, in the middle," Mirza replied with a scowl. He turned to direct his words to Farid. "I thought this young man," he said indicating to Amir with a dismissive hand, "was from New York. A town of culture and near members of my family. This town of Meala-wok-kay, I have never heard of it."

Farid remained silent, touching his forehead with his fingertips. Amir ate the last few bits of shrimp on his plate, while attempting to think of a comeback. After a loud gulp, he clarified, "Well, Milwaukee is not as famous as New York or Los Angeles, but it does have culture. From Germany. The town is known for its sausages and beer." *That should impress him, right? Maybe it's not Indian culture, but it's still another ethnic background. He could expand his and Shalimar's horizons by learning about another culture!*

"Sausages and beer?" Mirza exclaimed with wide eyes, "Have you tasted them?"

Amir hesitated. He had not tried the sausages, but he had sampled a couple pints of beer during his college days. He was suddenly nervous because Muslims don't drink alcohol or eat pork. "I did try a beer a few years ago."

The *Nawab* slightly rose from his chair in indignation. He caught himself, and sat back down. "Humph! And you call yourself a good Ismaili?"

"Ismailis are a more forgiving sect of the Muslim religion," Farid defended, "As you know, they are a blend of Muslim and Hindu traditions. Amir *is* a good Ismaili."

The father shook his head in disagreement. Putting his hand up to his temples, he closed his eyes and his nostrils began to flare. Amir immediately regretted his comments. *Shoot. Why didn't I just say, "No". But, then I'd be lying. Better to tell the truth, and face the consequences. Anyways, she doesn't look interested in me or the conversation. At least Nargis had asked a question or two.*

Amir watched as Mirza looked away from them. As if contemplating his reply, he scooped a handful of *Matar Paneer* curry and placed it into his mouth. Using his forefinger and thumb, he swiped the plate clean capturing the last two peas and one large cube of *paneer* cheese with the last bit of *chapatti*. Once he finished chewing, he wiped the corners of his mouth with his cloth napkin, folded it haphazardly, and placed the soiled napkin back onto his plate.

He whispered in staggered breaths, "Farid. I sought *you* out at the Jamat Khanna. I wanted to find a *suitable* Ismaili husband for my eldest daughter. A New York penthouse would have been fine. But, now. Now, I find out your brother lives in a beer and pork-filled city... in the middle of nowhere!"

Farid and Amir exchanged glances.

The *Nawab* continued, "I cannot consent to this match." He glared at Amir, "Good luck finding a wife." Turning to Rehana, "Thank you for dinner."

With a snap of his fingers, the entourage filed out of the living room. The guards put down their half-eaten dinner plates to rush from the kitchen and into position in the entryway. With a slight nod of the *Nawab's* head, the group silently departed.

"Well, that was no fun," Amir said as he leaned back in the high-back chair. He finally got to sit in the prized spot since his mother had not yet returned to the living room. He closed his eyes and dropped his head back on the seat cushion, "Cross number two off the list". *What kind of screening did Farid and Rehana do before my arrival? This is the second woman to eliminate herself from the list? At this rate, I'll go home without a wife. How am I supposed to find "the one" if no one makes it to the second round?*

CHAPTER 6

Tuesday, August 9

"WHERE'S THE SPARK?"

The evening with the *Nawab* and his daughters had been exhausting. As a result, both Farid and Rehana realized they needed to review "Amir's top ten list" to ensure there weren't any remaining bombs. Over breakfast, they discussed the remaining names and concluded Afsan, the fifth name on the list, should be moved to the end, as she was more modern looking than the other women. They didn't want to cross her name off the list just in case "modern" was what Amir wanted.

"The remaining names are fine," Farid said with a heavy sigh. "Let's just call them all, and be done with it."

"Come now, Farid. You know it would be in bad taste to have all those ladies parade around here like show ponies." Rehana said shaking her head. "Besides, Amir agrees with me. He wants to meet them so he can get to know them and make a good decision about the girl he wants to marry." She glanced down at the list and drank the last sip of her now cold tea, "This revised list is good, but, I think we need to find one or two more women willing to move to America. Amir only has two and a half weeks left in India. We need to help him find a wife!"

Farid slumped back in his chair with a slight groan. Rehana placed the back of her hand on his forehead and said, "Why don't you go back to bed and rest a bit? I'll make a few phone calls. Don't worry." Farid nodded, and returned to the bedroom without another word.

Giggling like a young schoolgirl, Rehana phoned a few of her friends for advice. One proposed returning to the JK to seek out additional eligible women. Another suggested attending the Ambassador's Meet and Greet events. A third friend recommended they go visit to the nearby University to find women willing to go to America.

Rehana thanked her friends, but concluded only the second idea made sense given their short timetable. She knew the Ambassador by reputation as a decent matchmaker, and she and Farid had even attended one of his Meet and Greet events a few months ago. He hosted them every Tuesday night as a way to give back to his community, and of course, to collect a match-making fee. Since today was Tuesday, it was worth a try. Rehana was determined to be the one that found the girl for Amir to marry. She didn't want her sister-in-law, Bandra, to have that honor!

The third bridal meeting was to be during afternoon tea, a nice change of pace from the formal dinner parties. Amir whistled as he tied the knot on his tie. He was hopeful this meeting would go well, especially after Rehana explained they had moved the one potential bomb to the end of the list.

He re-read the notes she had dropped off for this meeting, "Chandni, twenty-six years old, stewardess, one older brother, father owns a travel agency." A stewardess. She must like to travel and her father owns a travel agency, so he could arrange it. *This could be perfect,* Amir thought. *In fact, this is perfect! Maybe she wants to see the pyramids in Egypt or the Great Wall in China as much as I do!*

Chandni arrived without pageantry with her mother and brother. Her father, her mother explained, was working with a client moving to Perth, Australia and so unfortunately, he was unable to attend the meeting. After the welcoming hugs and kisses, Farid excused himself to lay down in his bedroom. Rehana was concerned about her husband but still had to play hostess. She led the group into the living room and placed Amir and Chandni next to each other on the sofa. Chandni's mother sat softly on the loveseat and Rehana sat next to her. Mummy took her usual spot in the high-back chair. Chandni's older brother stood next to the high-back chair for a moment, then settled into one of the dining room chairs, occupying himself by biting at a torn fingernail.

Amir was pleasantly surprised that Chandni wore a pink *salwar kameez*. The color of the two-piece outfit looked lovely against her skin. The long tunic hung loosely about her torso and she wore the matching scarf *dupatta* loosely around her neck so he was able to see her face clearly.

She was definitely shorter than him, maybe a foot shorter. She had an oval face with chubby cheeks, and wore her hair in a single braid that reached her tailbone. He watched her for a few minutes. She seemed very pleasant, making eye contact with whomever she was talking. With her stewardess training, she must be used to meeting new people.

Babu brought the silver serving tray with the usual afternoon tea essentials – steeping Darjeeling black tea in a teapot covered with a tea cozy, a small bowl of sugar cubes, a small pitcher of fresh cow's milk, and of course, a variety of bite-size desserts. Rehana had Babu make a special trip to Lookmanji's sweet shop to get *malai khajas* and an assortment of *barfis*, Indian fudge. The *malai khajas* were one of Amir's favorite desserts and a special treat for this afternoon tea. The pastries were made of several layers of flaky crust with sweet cream in the center. They looked similar to baklava but without the honey or nuts. Rehana had cut the large squares into four pieces, so they were easier to share but just as messy to eat.

The ladies received their tea first. Amir watched as Chandni waited politely for the other ladies to add their sugar and milk. When it was finally her turn, she scooted closer to the tray, picked up the silver tongs, and slowly dropped four lumps of sugar into her tea. Adding a large dash of milk, she stirred the contents with a little spoon. Her first sip looked as if it burnt her lip, and he laughed to himself as she made a distorted face. She leaned back in her seat, and continued to stir the tea.

Preferring coffee over tea, when it was his turn, Amir mimicked Chandni's mixture. He smiled at her as he sat back on the sofa to stir his tea. Their eyes met, and she smiled back. *What a nice friendly smile.* He waited for his insides to warm from the smile, but they didn't. *Shouldn't I be feeling something?*

"Chandni, as a stewardess, you must travel all over the world. What routes have you travelled?" Rehana asked sipping her brew.

"Well, I've been flying with Air India for almost four years now." She took another sip of the tea. "Lately, I've been mostly working the Bombay to Calcutta route. But hopefully I'll be promoted to international flights soon."

Calcutta. The city name made Amir think of his job interview with Tata Steel. The interview had gone very well, but the city was too overwhelming for him. The sights, smell, and sounds of Calcutta had sickened him. It was on the long trip back to Bombay that he decided he could not live there, no matter how much he might enjoy his job. Amir asked, "Isn't the train ride between the two cities really long? How does it compare to the airplane ride?"

"*Ji, huh*, Amir, the train journey is almost two days." Chandni took another sip of tea. "The airplane flight is only three hours. It's a very popular option and the flights are often full."

"Have you only travelled to Calcutta?" Rehana wondered.

"Oh, no, Aunty. I've also been to Delhi for training."

"But your father owns a travel agency. Don't you travel?"

"Not yet, Aunty." Chandni said putting her empty cup of tea on the table, "My father wanted me to marry first. He said I should see the world with my husband." At her response, the group smiled and nodded.

Amir was actually impressed with her answer. She was pretty, straight forward, and wanted to travel. She's perfect! Finally! But, wait, there's something missing. He watched her talk, but didn't feel any tingling in his fingers. *Why am I not physically attracted to her? What's wrong with me? Where's the spark?*

Chandni nervously poured herself another cup of tea. Her hands were trembling as she added the lumps of sugar and milk. Maybe he just needed to get to know her better. He sat forward, and asked, "Chandni, why don't you try a piece of the *malai khaja?* Lookmanji's makes the best in town."

She turned to face him, and their eyes met again. Beautiful eyes, but still nothing. Marriages have occurred when there was no physical attraction. The love grew over time, they said. *Sure, I guess it could happen. But, if I'm going to take her all the way back to America with me, I would prefer to be attracted to my bride. Is that too much to ask?*

"Thank you, Amir. I would like to try one." She leaned forward, selected a piece of the flaky dessert, and placed it on her palm. She took a dainty bite and the flaky pastry crumbled in her fingers. She quickly took another bite to finish the *khaja* piece, and rubbed her messy fingers with a napkin. Amir smiled at her awkward moment. *She seems like such a nice woman. I could enjoy getting to know her.* "They're messy, but good." He picked up a piece and had the same experience. They shared a laugh at the impossibility of eating the *khajas* without incident. Still no spark.

The group departed shortly thereafter. As soon as the door closed, Rehana asked Amir what he thought. "I like the more casual setting," he started, "the tea was good."

"But what did you think of Chandni? She seemed to like you. You two exchanged smiles a lot. Is she the one?"

"She seems like a nice lady, and I like that she wants to travel," he responded picking up another piece of *malai khaja*. "But, honestly, Rehana, I felt nothing. No spark. We did exchange smiles a few times, but each time I felt as if I was smiling at you rather than my future wife. I want to marry someone where I feel some …" He couldn't say the word passion but that is what he wanted to say, instead he said, "… well, something."

"*Aacha*," Mummy announced. "Then we keep looking. There are other girls." She reached over, and patted her son on the knee. "I want my son to be happy." She turned to Rehana, "When do we meet the next girl?"

Rehana retrieved the list, and glanced down at the names, "We meet Parveen for dinner tomorrow."

"No one tonight?" Mummy retorted impatiently.

"I thought Amir might want a night off. I wasn't sure if he would still be jet lagged. We have been meeting girls every day."

"I'm over the jet lag," Amir responded. Jumping up, "I would like the night off, though. I want to visit Nilofer and Nadir. I haven't seen my older sister since I arrived."

"Good idea," Rehana quickly responded, "They've been wanting to come visit you, but I told them you were too busy."

"Great," Amir said with enthusiasm, "I'll visit them, and you three can have the night off to rest. How's Farid?"

As he said this, Farid hobbled into the room, "I'm feeling much better."

"You look much better," Rehana said as she stood on her tip toes, and gave him a kiss. Amir heard her whisper into his ear, "I'm glad you're rested. We have a party to go to tonight."

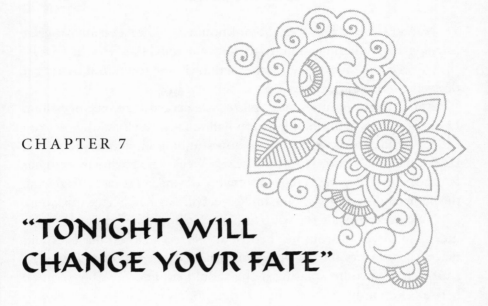

CHAPTER 7

"TONIGHT WILL CHANGE YOUR FATE"

"*Beta*, why are you staring out of the window?" Ammi asked Nazeera, as she walked into her bedroom.

Nazeera was staring at the whisper of clouds, trying to conjure up an excuse. "Ammi," Nazeera whined, "I really don't want to go to this party. There won't be any good men there. As usual."

"I know you don't want to go, but we have to. You have refused so many suitors, you may never get married. You want a husband before you lose your looks, no?" Ammi leaned forward, gave her daughter a kiss on the side of her head, and began adjusting a bobby pin.

"Yes, but, all the guys you've introduced me to have had big ears or yellow teeth." Nazeera said sarcastically. She sat still as her mother fiddled with the bobby pin. Nazeera preferred to wear her hair long, parted on the right side, and draped over her shoulder. When she did so, her hair reached the middle of her chest. Tonight, her mother had insisted she wear it in a bun with a few ringlets framing her round face. It had taken Florence, their hairdresser, almost an hour to make it look perfect. "What makes you think tonight will be any different?"

"Aaah, *Beta*," Ammi replied stepping back to look at her fix, "My *jyotishi* said the planets are aligned in your favor tonight. In fact, he said, tonight will change your fate."

Nazeera rolled her eyes, "You know I don't believe any of your astrologer's predictions. But, to make you happy, I'll go to the party."

"*Theek hai.* Good. Your father will be home soon. You better get dressed. *Juldi, juldi.* Hurry up!"

About thirty minutes later, Nazeera emerged from her bedroom. Looking at herself in the full-length hall mirror, she fixed the bolts on her 22K gold earrings and admired how stunning she actually looked in the turquoise silk sari. No wonder Eve's Weekly magazine wanted her to model again. She had enjoyed showing off the latest fashions during the photo shoots, but standing on her feet all day had been exhausting.

"We need to wait for your father. He should be home any minute." Ammi yelled from her bedroom. Nazeera closed her eyes and placed her fingers on the bridge of her nose. *Great, now I have to wait.* She was contemplating if she should sit, and possibly wrinkle her sari, when the door opened with a flourish.

"Daddy," she said with delight, "you're home."

Her father, Rahim, was an impressive man - six feet tall and muscular build. Nazeera loved his trimmed mustache, as she thought it made him look distinguished. He had been the district collector for most of Nazeera's childhood. Being a high government official, similar to the mayor in many American cities, had its perks including a nice home, servants, and usually a car and driver. They had moved back to Bombay, only six months earlier, when he had been given a different position. But, he and his family still enjoyed the same privileges.

"Nazeera, you look lovely," her father said. He was standing just inside the doorway, next to her favorite pencil sketch hanging above the settee in the living room. It was a sketch he had done a few years earlier of a long haired woman playing the sitar. The woman resembled her, and she liked to think she was the woman in the sketch though she had no idea how to play the sitar.

The three of them lived in a two-bedroom flat in the Yashodham building in central Bombay with other government officials. It was a five minute walk to the Arabian Sea, and a twenty minute walk to the Gateway of India. The building had five floors, and they lived on the second floor.

Their main room was a long rectangular room that her mother had arranged into two sitting areas on either side of the veranda doors. The area closest to the dining room had a large sofa and three padded chairs. The area closest to the front door had a long settee and two wooden chairs. Two photographs sat on the coffee table in the main sitting section. One of the family standing with Prime Minister Jawaharlal Nehru and another of Nazeera and her two older brothers at her oldest brother's University graduation.

He repeated his words to bring her attention back to him, "Shall I have the driver pull the car around?"

She blinked her eyes to return to the moment, and replied, "We'll wait until you're ready. No need to rush to get there." In fact, she'd be happy if Daddy said to forget the party. But, she knew Ammi would be disappointed, and the stars were aligned tonight, right?

Her father quickly changed his clothes, and they were off. The Ambassador's "Friends Circle" Meet and Greet event was a couple miles away. They could have walked to the building, but it was more impressive to emerge from a car. Plus, with her and her mother all dressed up, the walk in a sari and fancy *chappals* was not a pleasant experience.

Nazeera entered the building, stepping over the well-worn threshold into the lobby. The lobby was an airy room with a skylight in the center ceiling. The heavily waxed floors reflected the last glimmers of daylight, and made the room sparkle as they approached the staircase. There was an easel at the base of the staircase where someone had written with a thick black marker, "Meet and Greet - 2nd floor Ballroom".

The trio climbed the winding staircase to the second floor, and were met with a murmur of voices. Nazeera's heart began to pound from sheer nervousness. *Maybe this is a bad idea.* She was just getting comfortable with her life after University. Sure, all her friends were starting to get married, but not all of them were yet. Plus, she had two older brothers that were not yet married. *Why aren't they here?*

Sensing Nazeera's hesitation, Daddy took her hand, "*Chalo.* Let's go." They stepped through the double doors, and into the main ballroom with Ammi a few steps behind them. Nazeera was immediately impressed by the scene. The rectangular ballroom was half-filled with people. Tables with bowls of punch were on the left, and rows of chairs were on the right. The long vertical windows lined with heavy maroon velvet curtains were tied back to allow the assembly to see the Bombay skyline. These were mainly Muslim events where soft drinks and lemonade were usually the only drinks served. Sometimes they also served light snacks or desserts. Apparently today, they did not.

Nazeera dropped her father's hand, and confidently strode forward maneuvering around the guests hovering in the entry way. She scanned the room looking for her friends, and inspecting who all was there. The party seemed just like all the others - guys on one side, gals on the other. Parents were sitting in chairs or standing near the punch bowls watching the young ones; but also, giving them freedom to wander the room.

"There's Nusrat Aunty and your cousins," Ammi said joining her and pointing toward the punch bowls. Nazeera barely heard what she said as she continued to scan the crowd for her friends and of course, good looking guys. Nusrat was married to Ammi's older brother, Jhoma, and they had three children - Pinky, Dolly and Khazim. No one remembered how or when the girls received the nicknames, but everyone used them, including their parents. Pinky and Dolly were slightly younger than Nazeera, and this was their second Meet and Greet event.

Waving to her cousins, Nazeera continued to scan the room. She was not in the mood to hang out with her younger cousins. Pondering aloud she said, "I wonder if Farah and Aaliya are even here yet?" She enjoyed their company at these parties, as the three of them would hang out in one corner and find fault with each boy that walked by.

Her mother didn't appreciate them giggling at each boy, and so when Nazeera got on her tip toes to look for them, her mother sighed deeply. "Aha, there they are!" Nazeera noticed both of her friends, and started heading toward them.

Farah and Aaliya greeted Nazeera warmly with air kisses so no one would spoil their make-up. They immediately got into party-mode and began glancing around the room, one-by-one noticing each guy. "He has a hook nose," Farah started, "Oh, the one next to him has white hair. He must be old!" Aaliya added, "What about that one? His tie is all twisted!"

They continued to scan the crowd, finding some sort of fault with each guy. After ten minutes, a man with salt-and-pepper colored hair approached their small group. He was clearly nervous. Shifting his weight from his left foot to the right, he mumbled, "Hello. My name is Asif. Would you like some lemonade?"

Surprising herself, Nazeera didn't immediately dismiss this guy. His complexion was fair and his eyes were soft. She agreed to the lemonade, and Asif turned and headed toward the refreshments table. As she watched him go she thought he seemed nice enough. *His ears aren't too big, and his teeth aren't yellow. But, he did have some white hair. Maybe he was old. 30? 40? Is he the one that's going to change my fate?*

As Nazeera contemplated his age, Asif returned with two glasses of lemonade. He smiled as he handed her one. *Nice smile.* She thanked him, took a sip, and waited for him to say something. He opened his mouth, and she leaned forward to hear what he was going to say. Amazingly, he excused himself, and scurried to his friend in the corner. She watched him whisper to his friend and wipe his brow. *Why has he left me so abruptly? Maybe he'll return. Maybe not. Fine, onto the next guy.* She sipped her lemonade, and glanced at her mother who was smiling approvingly.

Nazeera continued to sip the lemonade. Several men walked by and smiled at the group. The ladies smiled back and then exchanged whispered comments on the guy. A good-looking guy in a dark brown suit approached Farah. He whispered something to her, then scampered off to get her a lemonade. Farah giggled and said she didn't want to hear their comments on him. Moments later, he hurried back with the filled glasses, and they again began whispering to each other. Nazeera noticed Farah was smiling, and batting her eyelashes more than usual. *Maybe this will be a good night - for her.*

When Nazeera turned her head back to where Asif had retreated, she noticed he was no longer there. She scanned the crowd for him, but he was gone. *So much for him changing my destiny.* A bit disappointed, she shrugged her shoulders, and leaned toward Aaliya for an update on the rest of the crowd.

Out of the corner of her eye, Nazeera noticed a woman in a sea green sari approaching her small group. She was older than her, and wore jewelry indicating she was already married. *Why is she approaching us? She looks too old to be here for herself, and too young to be the mother of someone here. Maybe she knows something about Asif or Farah's brown suit guy?*

"Hello," the woman said, "My name is Rehana Virani. I noticed you from across the room. I was wondering if you're still in University."

Nazeera was skeptical of this woman, but responded to her question, "Uh, my name is Nazeera Khan. I graduated from University a few months ago." This exchange was very peculiar. Never had a woman approached her at these type of events. *Why is she even here?*

She must have noticed Nazeera was thinking this was strange, as she clarified, "I'm here looking for a bride for my brother-in-law."

That makes more sense, and explains why she's here. Nazeera's interest was piqued, "Your brother-in-law?"

"Yes," Rehana responded, "he's from America, and only has a short time to find a bride and get married. So, my husband and I are looking for potential wives."

This was becoming more interesting. She had heard of sisters and sisters-in-law making lists of potential brides, but this was the first time she had heard of one for an American, "Your husband?"

The older lady nodded in the direction of a man leaning against a pillar. She retreated and escorted Farid back to Nazeera's side. After he introduced them, Farid asked, "Are you here with your parents?" Nazeera explained she was, and indicated where they were standing. The guy didn't make eye contact with her or even look at her parents. He was staring at the ground, and was either disinterested or ill. After a few more questions, the two of them abruptly left.

Thinking the exchange was over, Nazeera was stunned when the couple returned with an older woman. "Hello," she said, "my name is Shakila Virani. We are looking for a bride for my son."

Nazeera introduced herself a third time. This was getting crazy. *When am I going to meet the guy? Is he next? Maybe there's something wrong with him. Maybe he's crazy or ugly.*

"Are you college educated?" the mother asked interrupting her thoughts.

"Yes, Aunty, I recently graduated from the University in Poona." Then she volunteered, "I'm currently living with my parents, and taking an Interior Decorating class at the local University." She looked in the direction of her parents again.

Shakila exchanged eye contact with both of her parents, and they nodded to each other. Speaking to no one in particular she concluded, "*Aacha*, she will do. Add her to the list. Number eleven."

CHAPTER 8

Wednesday, August 10

"HER PARENTS KNEW BEST"

Nazeera tried reading her book on the veranda. The fresh sea breeze, and incessant horn honking made reading difficult. She allowed her thoughts to drift from the words on the page to her various suitors - Armaan, Kassim and Habib. *Would any of them make a good husband?* Probably not, each of them had a fault. Why did she need a husband anyways? She was smart and pretty. She could support herself! She could find work. But, what career could she have with an English degree? Maybe she could work in a boutique. And there was also the modeling.

But, her parents wanted her to marry. Oh, but whom to marry? There had been many suitors over the years and even a few proposals - but none of them seemed right. Not good husband material. Handsome and respectful. *Is it really that hard to find? Maybe in India it is.*

There was Armaan. He seemed respectful but his bad teeth were distracting. Oh, and that smelly breath. Maybe, Kassim. He was wealthy but was neither handsome nor respectful. Definitely not. Lastly, there was Habib. He was handsome, as for respectful, well, she wasn't sure. Ammi thought he might be sending a proposal. She would have to figure out how she felt about him soon.

And then there was William. He was a friend. A good friend. *Would he ever think of her in a romantic way or would they always be just friends?* They met during her college days in Poona. He was charming, and his mother was a sweetheart. They would sip afternoon tea and discuss Art, books and her fledgling modeling career. In fact, it was his mother who had encouraged her to try modeling. But, alas, William had big plans for his life. Plans that involved the Army and India, not her and marriage.

Forget about William, she scolded herself. *What about the guys from last night? What happened to Asif? Why had he disappeared so suddenly? And who was this mysterious brother-in-law Rehana spoke about? Why wasn't he there? Was he still in America? What was his name?*

"*Beta?*" her father asked stepping onto the veranda. His voice brought Nazeera back to reality. He held two tall glasses of *falooda*, "Can we chat?" She was immediately suspicious. Daddy knew *falooda* was her favorite summertime drink.

"Thanks Daddy," Nazeera replied taking her glass. She swirled the long spoon to stir up the sabja seeds, boiled vermicelli, rose syrup and milk. *He must want to chat about something important. He even had Akbar add a scoop of malai kulfi on top.* The added iced cream was just the way she liked it. "Did you want to chat about something?"

"Well, yes. I know you're meeting Jaya for lunch today. She's been married now for over three months." He took a sip. "I want you to be happy for her."

"How can I be happy for her if she's not happy? I'm not going to pretend." Nazeera replied, her heart beating faster. "That's why I want to meet her. To see for myself if my best friend is really happy."

"I know, *Beta*," her father was trying to empathize with her, "I know Jaya was not enthused about her arranged marriage, but her parents thought she was ready. They carefully selected the guy. He comes from a good family. A very good family. And has good prospects. Her parents knew best."

Nazeera took a long sip of the *falooda* drink contemplating her response. The sabja seeds swirled around the glass like a tornado. "That's what Uncle said when I pleaded with him."

"You what?"

"Oh." She took another sip. *Whoops.* "I visited Jaya's father before the formal engagement. I told him she was just not ready to be married. She wanted more time. She was scared to talk to her father. So I did."

"What did he say?" Daddy asked with his eyebrows bunched together.

Shrugging her shoulders, Nazeera added, "Well, he basically told me it was none of my business. He knew best for his daughter."

"*Aacha,*" Daddy said as he nodded his head. "That's what she will tell you today. She will tell you she is happy, and that will be that."

"I hope so, Daddy. I just don't want her to end up like Aeesha *phupi.*"

Her father almost choked on the sabja seeds. Clearing his throat, he said, "My younger sister was so beautiful inside and out. She had an infectious laugh that lit up a room. She had just turned fifteen when our parents arranged her marriage. As you know, I was already married to your mother, and we were living in Surat. I should have gone home to help them find a decent husband for her...." His words trailed off as he sipped his *falooda.*

After a minute of silence, he added, "Her marriage was not a good one. I admit that. Not all arranged marriages work and hers was one that did not." He paused again and sipped his drink. With a tear in his eye, he added, "After we learned of the physical abuse, your mother and I helped your *phupi* get out safe."

"Yes, but she had been beaten for years before you intervened. She was terrified to leave him for fear he would track her down and kill her." Nazeera could tell her father was remembering how they helped his sister and her two children escape to London. It took her another year to work up the courage to file for divorce.

Nazeera drank the last sips of *falooda,* and was relieved when her father said somewhat cheerfully, "But it all worked out. She's happy now. You have to believe that Jaya will be happy."

"I want to believe it." *Thank goodness he's letting me chose my own husband! Maybe, I have Aeesha phupi to thank for that.* She rubbed her hand along her father's arm to let him know she would think about his words.

"*Bas,* enough. Let's chat about something else," he suggested, "What book are you reading?"

Fumbling with the book that had fallen to the floor during their discussion, she picked it up and handed it to her father. "The book is called *Rebecca,* written by Daphne De Murier, one of my favorite authors." Putting her glass onto the side table, she leaned forward and continued, "The story is about a woman who marries a man she hardly knows and goes off to a far away land."

"Sounds like a fairy tale."

"Not quite." Nazeera admitted, "It doesn't have a happy ending. The man is accused of a crime, and there is some drama. But in the end, the couple ends up together."

"So, it does have a happy ending." Her father said handing her back the book.

Reflecting for a moment, "Well, I guess it does. The couple overcomes the obstacles together, and their marriage is stronger. So, yes, it has a happy ending."

"I'm sure Jaya's story will also have a happy ending."

"I hope so, Daddy. I hope so."

CHAPTER 9

"AREN'T THEY ALL MARRYING A STRANGER TO GO TO AMERICA?"

The flat was quiet when Amir woke. The visit with his older sister, Nilofer, and her husband, Nadir, had been very pleasant. The three of them spent a large part of the evening discussing life in America. It was enjoyable discussing familiar topics without being judged or questioned. Nadir had received an engineering degree from an American University, and was one of the inspirations for Amir applying to University abroad.

Amir's original plan was to learn about air conditioning, return to India, and utilize his unique degree. He and his family speculated that since India got very hot and humid in the summer months, a degree in air conditioning would be in high demand. However, once he completed his two-year Associates Degree, Amir determined a four-year Engineering degree was needed to best utilize the distinct knowledge. Since he was already in Wisconsin for the Associates degree, he enrolled at the University of Wisconsin - Madison. After graduation, he was thrilled to find a job at the Allen Bradley Company. The company sponsored his work visa and he was allowed to stay in America.

Nilofer and her family lived in an affluent part of town on Peddar Road. Her teenage kids, Zarin and Yasmeen, were well-mannered during dinner and cheered when Nilofer declared they were having *kulfi* from Parsi Dairy for dessert. Nadir and Zarin had the mango flavor, Yasmeen and Amir had the *malai* flavor, and Nilofer had the *pista* flavor. The kids updated Amir *mamu* on their various activities, and when their *aaya* came to get them ready for bed, they moaned as all kids do when they're having a good time. They each kissed their *mamu* on the cheek, and retreated. Once the kids were out of the room, Amir asked guiltily if he could try the two other flavors. Always indulging her younger brother, Nilofer had the cook bring out a dish each of mango and *pista kulfis* for Amir.

When Amir had finished his sweet indulgence, the three of them moved to the living room, and continued to chat about life in America. None of them realized how long they had chatted until Nilofer yawned and declared she couldn't keep her eyes open any longer. After saying his good-byes, Amir was pleased to see the driver had waited for him to return. The drive back to his Mummy's flat was not a long one, but it was long enough for him to fall asleep.

The next morning, Amir discovered his mother already at the dining room table, sipping her tea. Instead of her usual buttered toast with orange marmalade, she was eating something resembling scrambled eggs - an Indian version with green chilies and cilantro. She greeted him in English, "Good morning. How your evening?"

"Wonderful," Amir replied pleased his mother was attempting English. "I had a great evening with Nilofer, Nadir and their two kids. Zarin and Yasmeen are interesting teenagers. Did you know Zarin loves football and Yasmeen adores horses?"

"Yes, I does." Mummy replied, struggling with the verb tense.

Learning Amir preferred coffee, Ramu proudly strode into the dining room holding a pot of instant coffee. Eager to try the brew, Amir watched as Ramu nervously poured a cupful. Blowing on the steam, Amir continued, "Nilofer served *kulfi* from Parsi Dairy for dessert. It was delicious! After the kids went to bed, the three of us talked until well after midnight. Did I wake you when I came home?" Amir asked as he sipped the freshly poured coffee. It was actually good. *Better than the tea.* He nodded to Ramu to bring him some Indian scrambled eggs, too.

"No, you do not. We be nice evening at Ambassador event." Mummy paused a moment, then added, "We meet one more girl."

"So the list is getting longer not shorter?"

"Just *ache* more."

"So, the original ten plus one. That is eleven. You added number eleven." Amir scowled at his mother, and sat back slightly as Ramu laid a plate of eggs in front of him.

"Amir," Mummy pleaded flipping her hands as Indian mother's sometimes do. Speaking now in Hindi, she added, "We are trying to help you find the right girl."

"I know Mummy," Amir said patting her hand lightly. "This whole process is just taking more time than I thought. Can't I just meet them all at once and pick one?"

"That would not be fair to you or the girls. You know that. A bride parade is not the right way to meet a decent young lady." She took the last bite of her scrambled eggs, and sighed, "Maybe Rehana can bring over some photos. We can discuss the next few girls and..."

"That's a great idea." Amir said interrupting her. He excitedly took another sip of coffee. The coffee was decent, but the eggs were too spicy with all the green chilies. He pushed the plate aside, "I'll go up and see them right now."

"*Aacha*, have them bring everything here. I am tired."

Amir frowned, and looked at his mother carefully. She was indeed looking more tired today. The event last night must have taxed her. Amir hummed as he slipped on his shoes, and headed to the hallway to call the lift. It was a very slow machine and more than once he considered just taking the stairs.

The slow climb to the fourth floor was almost as tedious and frustrating as it was waiting for the lift. *How can they live on the fourth floor?! This is crazy!* He walked down the hallway losing all the excitement he had felt just minutes earlier. He was dreading this visit now. He should've just called them. *After all this, they better be home!*

Babu opened the door, and thankfully both of them were home. After a warm greeting, Amir pleaded, "This bride finding business is taking too long. Can't we look at some photos and narrow the choices? Especially before one of them embarrasses me again!"

Farid laughed, "Rehana and I were just discussing the same thing. I called Mummy. We'll go downstairs as soon as I finish my tea."

"Fine," Amir said shaking his head, his heart still pounding wildly. His brother had used the telephone. What was that commercial - let your fingers do the walking? He slumped onto the sofa, and began playing with the wilted flower floating in the bowl on the coffee table. His finger snagged on a petal, and he had just broken it free of its entanglement when Rehana entered the room with some papers.

"*Chalo,*" she declared. "Let's go."

They decided to use the stairs, and descend carefully so as to not lose any of the precious papers. When they arrived at the ground floor flat, Mummy was already in the living room resting on the divan.

"I've brought information on the next three women." Rehana said clearing a space on the small coffee table. She made a pile for each potential bride. A photo of each woman was paper clipped to the top of the manila folder. Amir leaned closer trying to sneak a peek at them. "I only know one of them personally."

"Okay, Rehana, walk us through them," Amir said waving his hands in a circular motion to hurry her up. This process was so tedious. But, then again, he was excited to have such choices. What an effort all three of them had put into this bride-finding business. *Did I ever give Rehana her shawl?* He frowned, because he didn't think so. Maybe he should get her something more too. He made a mental note to go shopping somehow, and buy her something special.

Rehana picked up the papers from the first pile and handed Amir the photo. "This is Parveen. We have dinner scheduled with her tonight. She graduated with a degree in Philosophy. She is twenty-three and the youngest of five girls. Their father owns a tire business. All her sisters are married, so the family has accepted she may live abroad. She has a great personality, though a bit shy."

"Hmm," Amir said as he looked carefully at her photo, and considered what Rehana had said. "Look at her eyes. There's a sadness in them. I don't think she would be okay leaving her family. And you said she was shy? She would definitely have a hard time moving all the way to America. I don't think so."

"I see what you mean about her eyes. Hmm...." Rehana conceded as she flipped Parveen's photo face-down on the first pile. She picked up the photo from the second pile, and handed it to Amir, "This is Amara. She's twenty-six years old, and has a degree in education. She's been working with rural children in the poverty-stricken areas of India for the past three years. She's hoping to make some American connections so she can send money back to India. She wants to open a school."

Picking up the photo, Amir studied it carefully. She had an enchanting smile, and small dimples in her cheeks. She looked young and hopeful. "She has a very pleasant face. Her eyes are not sad. What do we know about her family?"

"She's an only child. Her parents live in Kenya. Her father is in the United Nations, and speaks several languages, I believe."

Amir glanced at the photo again. "How do you know her?"

"I know her uncle from JK," Farid interrupted, "We don't know much about her family, but her uncle tells me that she is eager to meet you."

"Has she seen a photo of me? Why is she so eager?"

"As Rehana said, she wants to go to America to make connections."

"So, she is willing to marry a stranger to go to America?" Amir questioned, "I don't know about this one. A bit too eager."

"Aren't they all marrying a stranger to go to America?" Farid responded.

Amir stared at his brother a moment. He was right. The perfect woman had to be a bit adventuresome to consider moving away from her home. He stared at Amara's photo again. Maybe this one would be okay. She wanted to help the poor children in India. *A worthy cause.*

"I will arrange for her to come to lunch today. Her uncle said they were available for either lunch or dinner. If you like Kulsum, I'll see if she can come for dinner tonight. Here's her photo."

Taking the photo of the third girl, Amir immediately shook his head. She had auburn hair, black hair dyed reddish brown using henna. She wore a lot of makeup on her oval face, and modern Western clothes. Her two nose rings were distracting. He wanted a modern Indian girl, but this was a bit too extreme.

"This is Kulsum. She's...."

"No." Amir interrupted Rehana, "No. Too modern for me."

"She's very self-confident, and we knew you wanted that. Her parents were anxious to add her to our list. They've been searching for a groom for awhile. Are you sure?"

Amir nodded. Rehana added, "*Theek hai*, I'll call the family, and let them know. That leaves Amara for lunch. I'll call and make the necessary arrangements. Here's her photo and info." She placed the photo on the table in front of Amir.

He nodded again as he stared at Amara's photo. A teacher, a lovely face, and those cute dimples. She had potential. "Thank you, Rehana." She just smiled at him, and scurried after Farid.

Mummy had been quiet this whole time, but now spoke, "I think you will like this girl. She likes children." *Is that a subliminal message? Yes, she likes children and hopefully that meant that she... no, we would have them soon. Being a father would be a good thing. A very good thing.*

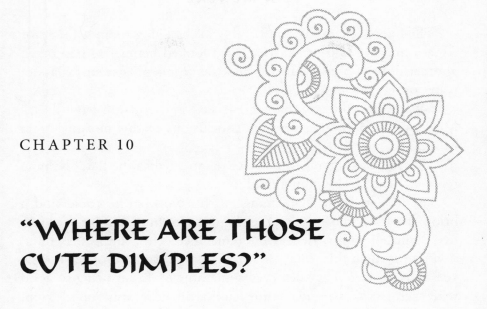

CHAPTER 10

"WHERE ARE THOSE CUTE DIMPLES?"

This was the first lunch meeting Rehana had arranged. She told Amir later that she had struggled with the menu, but decided to serve the leftover shrimp and onion curry as it was barely touched the previous night. She justified it by saying the spice flavors would have developed even more overnight. With her approval, Babu whipped up vegetable *korma* because the vegetables from the vegetable-*walla* looked fresh and ripe. She also had Babu make chicken *jalfrezi,* using a recipe she received from a friend, so there would be another non-veg dish to offer their guests. As usual, hot *basmati* rice, *raita* and warm *naan* were to be on the buffet table.

To help with the meal, Nadia brought over her brother's favorite dessert, *gulab jamuns.* She boasted how she and Tarik had personally made the *jamuns* or fried dough balls. Lingering in the living room, she said she specifically made them last night so they would have enough time to absorb the rose-water simple syrup before they were served. She insisted the more *gulab* or rose infused syrup the *jamuns* absorbed, the softer and tastier they became. Dropping several not so subtle hints that she wanted to stay for lunch, Amir shooed her away. She made him promise her again she would meet any woman that made it to round two.

The four of them sat comfortably in the living room waiting for Amara and her uncle to arrive. Farid looked better. He had taken another dose of pain medicine, and was sipping his second glass of water of the morning.

"Were you able to contact Parveen and Kulsum's families?" Mummy asked making sure the conclusions of this morning were executed.

"Yes, I called them as soon as we returned to the flat," Rehana replied as she sat down in a thud.

She looked exhausted, doing all this work so he could find a bride. It would make his mother happy. No, finding a bride would make himself happy. At least he remembered to bring a shawl and necktie for them this time! He threw a few extra chocolates for the kids into the bag. They deserved something extra for being so good with their *aaya*, Jasminda. Amir had hardly heard any sounds from them during the dinner parties.

"Rehana, I appreciate all you've done for me - all this planning and cooking. How about for the next meeting, we go to a restaurant. You don't need to keep playing hostess."

"I really enjoy cooking, but it would be a nice change to go out," Rehana replied with a smile. "Thank you, Amir." She slipped the pale blue shawl over her shoulders, and waved her head back and forth trying to see how it looked on her. She slipped it off, and smiled as she laid it on the arm of the sofa.

The doorbell rang. As was now routine, Babu thunder bolted to the door and waited for Farid to give the nod. Receiving it, the servant opened the door to Amara and her uncle. Her uncle was a large balding man. He wore a bright green *kurta pyjama*, with a vibrant almost joking voice.

Amara appeared to be the opposite of her uncle. She was very thin, almost frail, and talked in a timid manner. She wore a brown *salwar kameez* with a *dupatta* that matched the embroidered threading on the hem. The *dupatta* was draped around her neck like a long necklace. *At least I can see her face!* She wore her hair in a long braid that reached to her mid-back. Amir thought she looked rather plain. Similar to a homely mother bird, trying to camouflage herself so the predators would not find her or her young. *What has changed? Why does she look so different from her photo? Where are those cute dimples? Where's her self-confidence?*

Amir noticed right away the latest bride prospect acted reserved. He tried to make eye contact with her a few times, but was not successful. Amara kept her hands in her lap and focused her eyes on them the whole time. *Is she nervous or just shy? Is she acting like a good Indian girl by keeping her head down? Is she intently listening to my American accent?* He wished she would look up so he could see her face again. He wanted to see those cute dimples. *She's going to be the mother of my children, right?*

The conversation seemed to bounce between Farid and Amara's uncle. Discussions were had about their journey, the weather and even American baseball. Amara sat quietly during the half-hour discussion, almost as if she wanted to be invisible.

However, she lit up the room when Rehana asked her about her work with the rural poor. Amara's eyes glistened, changing from dull brown to fiery bronze. Her face was ablaze with movement and passion. Using exaggerated hand movements, she looked each person directly in the eye, and spoke of the injustices of the poor. She talked at length of parents abandoning their children because they could no longer afford to feed them; how girls were killed at birth because the fathers only wanted sons to work in the fields; and, how only sons were sent to school because educating girls was considered a waste of time and money. It was wonderful to see her so alive and passionate. Amir smiled to himself. *There's her spirit. There's the self-confidence!*

When the conversation changed to the more light-hearted topic of the international cricket match between the West Indies and England, the prospect's face faded. The passion in her eyes turned to dust, and she retreated into her cave. She did not look up again.

"Lunch is served," Babu announced. Rehana led Amara and her uncle to the buffet table to describe the various dishes. Amir watched as Amara filled her plate with small spoonfuls of rice and vegetable *korma*. The braised vegetables did look vibrant in the yogurt and cream sauce. The potential bride ignored the two non-veg dishes. Is she vegetarian? Her uncle was the opposite, filling his plate with several spoonfuls of each dish. In fact, he took four spoonfuls of the chicken *jalfrezi*.

Amir wasn't sure what to think of this girl. Amara had passion for the children and her social work, that was obvious. *Could she spare some of that passion for me? Would she be a good mother to our children? Does she even want her own children or is she too concerned about other people's children?*

The meal proceeded uneventfully, and while they were eating the *gulab jamuns,* her uncle asked Amir, "Could you tell us a bit more about your life in Amir-ika."

Amir swallowed his bite of the sweet *jamun* and said, "Sure, Uncle." Did he just pronounce America with his name in it? Amir-ika? No, he must have heard it wrong.

Shaking his head to clear the thought from his mind, Amir went on to describe Milwaukee and his job at the Allen Bradley Company. It was the same basic description he had given to Shalimar's family. This time he was hoping to avoid the beer and sausage conversation that had gone wrong. So horribly wrong.

As they sipped their hot Darjeeling tea, they returned to the conversation of the weather. This time, they discussed the weather differences between Milwaukee and Bombay. Since it was August now, autumn would be approaching soon which meant cooler weather in both cities. "And during the winter, we get snow," Amir admitted. "At first, I didn't like it, but now I find it very pretty. It's still a challenge to drive in."

"What kind of car do you drive?" her uncle asked. He then took a long sip of tea, dripping some onto his chin.

"I drive a green Ford Falcon." Amir replied trying not to laugh at the fiasco around the Uncle's mouth. "It's a small car, but it was something I could afford after college. Once we have children, we can get a bigger car. Maybe a large sedan or even a station wagon."

Amir happily noticed Amara was listening to this exchange. But, she didn't seem interested in it or in him. She hadn't spoken since before they ate lunch. Maybe a direct question was needed, "Amara, is there anything you would like to know about me or America?"

The mother bird looked up from her hands, and directly into Amir's eyes. Her eyes were comforting, but there was no hint of a smile. *Where did her dimples go?* She looked away from Amir and glanced around the flat. After a few seconds, she simply said, "No". She had made up her mind. She was clearly not interested.

As if waiting for a cue, Amara stood up, giving her uncle a slight nod. He stood up with a surprised grunt, dripping some tea onto the Oriental rug. He thanked Farid and Rehana for the meal and complimented Rehana on the perfect amount of green chilies in the chicken *jalfrezi*, "It had the perfect amount of heat, the added cream balanced the spices wonderfully. Delicious! Simply delicious!" Amara simply nodded to them as her good-bye. She didn't say another word. *Why is she so anxious to vacate the flat? What's her hurry?*

After Babu shut the door, Amir turned to Farid and asked, "What the heck happened? I thought she was anxious to meet me. It seemed she couldn't get out of here fast enough!"

Farid shrugged his shoulders. "I was watching her listen to you describe your life in Milwaukee. She shook her head as you talked about your engineering job. I think she was expecting a social advocate like herself. Someone to save the world and its children. Not an engineer wanting his own."

"Humph, didn't you give them a good description of me?" Amir said thrusting his hands into the air in defeat. "What other girls have the wrong impression?" Seriously! Another rejection. Was this bride-finding business that difficult? It was obvious Farid and Rehana had no idea how to find a bride for him. Maybe he should just allow his mother to arrange the marriage. Then they would meet on their wedding day, and she wouldn't have time to reject him. That would be easier on his nerves...and his heart.

"Amara's parents live in Kenya. We weren't able to speak to them directly. We did speak with the uncle. I know him from JK." Farid said defensively. "All the other girls have a good description of you. Trust us."

Amir shook his head and trotted back to the dining room. *Trust them. Trust them to more of this heart-ache?* He picked up a fresh crystal bowl, and scooped two *gulab jamuns* into it. He poured a generous amount of syrup over the golden fried donuts, and plunked down on a dining room chair. Cutting the sweet balls in half, he ate each half slowly savoring each bite. They were perfectly sweetened as his sister had suggested.

What do I say to them? He had to make them feel okay, though he was extremely frustrated. Sighing Amir said, "I do trust you, but this is getting ridiculous. I feel like we're just wasting time with these women. Are there any on the list that have real potential?" Turning to Farid, "Can you help me find a wife or should we just forget this whole thing?"

"There is Chandni." Mummy suggested with a glimmer of hope, "She is pretty, and you two got along."

My mother the optimist, Amir thought. Yes, there was Chandni. She was the only one so far to not rejected him outright. She was pleasant enough, and easy to talk to. They could be good friends. But friendship wasn't what he was looking for. He wanted a wife. Someone to share his life and his bed. Was he expecting too much? Maybe being married to a friend was the best he was going to get. Maybe the love would blossom. Maybe the passion would develop. Maybe it wouldn't. Maybe passion was for other people. Not for him.

CHAPTER 11

Thursday, August 11

"WELCOME, YAAR!"

Just before lunch, Jamila's father called the flat and asked to speak with Farid. Jamila was the bride prospect the four of them were supposed to meet for dinner that evening. The father had called, with apologies, requesting they postpone the dinner meeting as he was currently dealing with a work emergency. He wanted to attend the meeting, but wasn't sure he would be able to leave work until very late. Wanting to accommodate a potential bride and consulting with Rehena, Farid rescheduled Jamila for dinner the following day. Suddenly, they had an evening free.

The two of them decided this was a perfect time to call the match-making Ambassador to set up a meeting with Nazeera. She was appealing. She had the energy they thought Amir wanted, and hopefully she would not reject him right away. Even though she was not a member of the JK, she was still a Muslim and good enough to be added to "The List". It also gave Rehana one more chance to find the right bride for Amir. Bandra's choice was coming up soon.

The Ambassador returned their phone call several minutes later. He said he had set up the meeting with the "ladies' side" as they had requested. Given his schedule, he could not meet for dinner, but he was able to set up afternoon tea at his office. Since he was going out of town for a week, the meeting had to be today or it would have to wait a week. Farid quickly updated Amir and Mummy.

This meeting needs to be perfect, Amir thought as he chose the blue-green tie with his blue suit, rather than the red one. Maybe a change in ties would change his luck. He patted his hair as they walked to the Ambassador's office. *Darn cowlick.* Their destination was a government building just behind the Prince of Wales Museum. He hadn't noticed it before when he walked this direction a few days ago. But then again, he was not looking for it either. He glanced at his shoes as they walked up the front three steps to the main entry. They were a bit scuffed. He wiped them quickly with his handkerchief as they entered the lobby. Okay, now he was ready.

The skylight over their heads allowed streams of light to show onto the heavily waxed floor. There was a dark wooden desk off-center with a lone man sitting and reading *The Times of India* newspaper.

"Excuse me," Farid asked after clearing his throat, "Can you tell me where to find the Ambassador's office?"

The man looked up grudgingly from his newspaper. Amir noticed he was probably in his mid-forties, but since he had shaved his head, he looked older than his age. The bald man looked at each of them, and grunted, "Third floor. You can take the lift over there." He thrust the crispy newspaper in front of their faces and resumed reading. So much for customer service.

They looked around the lobby, and finally found the lift. The ride to the third floor was quick, much faster than the lift in the Ivanhoe building! Wandering back and forth down the red carpeted corridor, they scanned the dull brass plaques on the doors until they found the one they were seeking at the far end of the hallway.

Pushing open the heavy wooden double doors, the foursome hesitated in the entryway. The Ambassador's secretary looked up from her desk, "Come in, Come in." With a grand smile and a wave of her hands, she ushered them into the outer office.

The room had two other visitors, and Amir scanned the room for four chairs near each other for them to sit in. To his surprise, the secretary marched her new guests past the open chairs, and directly into the main office. "The Ambassador is expecting you."

H.H. Ismail looked up from his desk. He forced a smile, and motioned for them to sit in the wooden chairs on his right. "Welcome, *yaar*. Welcome, friends." The group sat in the chairs well worn from previous suitors. H.H. came and shook each person's hand several times repeating, "Welcome, *yaar*, welcome."

When the Ambassador was done making their wrists sore with the repeated handshakes, he stepped into the outer office to chat with his secretary. The Viranis waited.

Enjoying the cool breeze from the Arabian Sea, Nazeera and her mother were chatting and chortling about her lunch with Jaya. The lunch had exceeded Nazeera's expectations and she was in a lively mood.

Her father stepped onto the veranda, "Sorry, *Beta*, the phone just rang." Nazeera was surprised her father was delivering the message personally. *Where's Akbar? Why is Daddy home so early? Is something wrong?* He continued, "It is the Ambassador. He has invited us to afternoon tea with an interested suitor."

"They gave a name, no?" Ammi asked with a glimmer of hope in her voice.

"*Ji, huh.* Yes. Amir Virani. The Ambassador says Nazeera met his brother and sister-in-law at the Meet and Greet event on Tuesday." Turning to his daughter, he asked, "Do you remember meeting them?"

Nazeera smirked. "Yes, I remember meeting them. I thought the whole scene was odd. First this woman comes up to me and asks me questions. Then, she leaves and returns with her husband and then he asks me questions. Then, finally, they both leave and return with his mother. She asked me to point the two of you out to her. Do you remember that?" Daddy shrugged his shoulders. "I guess now they want me to meet the guy. He's from America."

"*Kya?* What? This guy is from Ameer-ic-ka?" her father asked raising his voice an octave. "You're not leaving here and moving to Ameer-ic-ka. Forget it. We're not going to this tea."

"We *have* to go to this tea," Ammi insisted, "It's excellent exposure for our daughter. It shows she is still on the market and desirable." Ammi leaned toward her husband, "Plus, Nazeera has turned down so many suitors, we're in jeopardy of being removed from party lists. We want to continue to get invitations from the Ambassador, no? He throws the best parties, and has very good connections. Very good."

Daddy frowned. "I do not like it." He stepped toward his daughter, and patted her on the head like a small child, "Ameer-ic-ka is very far away."

Nazeera looked up at her father, and blinked her long eyelashes playfully, "I know it's far away, Daddy, but they have me curious. I want to meet this mystery guy. You know I love mysteries."

Ammi whispered loudly, "She'll probably say "no" to him anyways. Why not meet the boy, and maintain our social invitations?"

Her father looked at his wife and then his little girl. Frowning, he relented, "*Theek hai*. Fine. We will meet the boy." He turned and marched back into the living room. Nazeera could hear him reluctantly accepting the Ambassador's invitation. *Poor Daddy*, she thought.

Ammi grabbed Nazeera's arms and the ladies looked at each other with *mushti* in their eyes. Mischief! They would need to continue the conversation about Jaya later. There was a suitor waiting!

With the help of their servant, Shanti, Nazeera dressed in a deep magenta sari with small silver flowers randomly stamped throughout the fabric. She knew the rich color of the fabric and the glisten of the silver stamping would compliment her complexion and accent her facial features. Expertly pulling her hair into a soft bun, Shanti pinned a dozen black bobby pins to hold it in place. The two of them were discussing jewelry options when Ammi entered the room.

Her mother had changed from her every day lily-white sari to a stunning mango floral sari. As usual, she had put too much white powder on her face. *She wants to look fair and beautiful, but she ends up looking like a pale ghost instead*, Nazeera thought and just rolled her eyes.

The pair watched as Shanti placed two different necklaces around Nazeera's neck. The three of them looked at her reflection in the mirror, and Nazeera tilted her head left and right until her mother declared the second one was best. Nazeera agreed. The filigree of the silver flowers on the string necklace matched the stamping in the sari almost exactly.

As she twisted the bolts on the matching earrings, Nazeera reminded herself, *I deserve someone that will treat me and my family with respect. Someone that will love me and only me.* Maybe then she could be happy in marriage, at least happier than her parents.

They had to walk to the Ambassador's building this time, as her father had sent the car and driver home for the evening. The walk was amazingly pleasant, as the evening was still warm but the breeze from the Arabian Sea had removed the heaviness in the air. Her parents were walking slowly two paces ahead of Nazeera. She wanted to hurry them, but was suddenly struck with nervousness. *Who is this guy? Why wasn't he there at the party? What are they hiding? Is he ugly? Rude? An American snob?*

Just as Nazeera's mind began to race in millions of directions, they arrived at their destination. Stepping over the entry threshold they had crossed two days earlier, Ammi declared they were taking the lift to the third floor. She added her right leg was beginning to swell from walking in the fancy *chappals*. Daddy helped Ammi walk across the lobby and over the threshold of the lift. He offered his arm again as they walked down the red carpeted hallway toward the Ambassador's office. Nazeera was touched by the tenderness they shared. *Hopefully, one day a man will take care of me.*

After a deep exhale, Nazeera pushed the heavy wooden doors to enter the Ambassador's outer office. The chamber was empty save for the secretary who hurriedly came from around her desk. She greeted them, smiling widely, and said the Ambassador was expecting them. The other family was already waiting inside. Nazeera's heart started pounding in her chest. *They're already here. Oh my. How long have they been waiting? What does the mystery guy look like? Is it too late to turn around and go home?*

The secretary opened the door to the inner office, and gestured for them to enter. Nazeera choked on the yellow haze hanging in the room. The office was crammed with stacks of papers, binders, and books everywhere. Maneuvering left and then right toward the row of unoccupied chairs, Nazeera hit a small stack of books with her right foot. The top book fell to the floor with a thud. The Ambassador looked up from his desk, and smiled when he recognized her father. Shaking their hands repeatedly he said, "Welcome, *yaar*. Welcome."

The meeting seemed to start awkwardly. Nazeera recognized three of the four people sitting across from her. Farid, Rehana, mystery guy and the mother. *The mystery guy must be Amir,* she thought. *He's a good looking man. Not too much hair oil, but enough to keep his hair in place. Nice blue suit, and, oh, his peacock blue tie is fabulous. How did he know I adore that color? He gets a point for that!*

Nazeera watched Amir for several seconds. He sat confidently in his chair, leaning forward slightly. He glanced about the room, probably inspecting the members of her family. When his glimpse drifted toward her, their eyes met. She quickly turned her gaze away. She didn't want him to think she was a flirt or too forward. But, her curiosity was too much for her, and she discreetly glanced back to him. He was still staring at her.

The Ambassador played his part by introducing each member of the two groups to the other. He then leaned back in his chair, and continued editing a thick document with his squeaky marker.

After a moment of silence, Rehana finally said, "Nazeera, it's so nice to see you again. You're looking lovely this afternoon." Nazeera sat up and involuntarily smiled, quickly moving her eyes from Amir to Rehana.

"Nice to see you again, Aunty. Thank you." She bowed her head demurely like a good Indian girl. *No more stolen glances.*

Thankfully for Nazeera, the secretary brought a wooden tray of Darjeeling tea and English digestive biscuits. She served each guest a cup of tea, and silently retreated. The distraction made the conversation pick up pace. Soon the whole group was conversing, even laughing, openly. Nazeera decided she would be an active participant in the conversation. *Heck with being a good demure Indian woman. If Amir didn't like it, tough.*

Amir described his life in America to her father. Nazeera was half-listening to his words. He had a strange accent that was hard to understand at times, so she decided to watch him talk instead. She noticed he made eye contact with whomever he was speaking. When he noticed she was listening, he made eye contact with her as well. *Impressive. Two points.*

Suddenly, there was a knock on the door. Poking her head into the room, the secretary apologized for the interruption. She explained the Ambassador had an appointment on the other side of town. The Ambassador glanced at his watch, and winced. With a turn of his head to both sides of the room, he said, "Sorry, *yaar*, I've got to keep this appointment. We can meet again when I return next week."

"*Ji, nahih.* No," Farid declared, shaking his head stubbornly. Then leaning forward toward her father, he asked, "The conversation is going well, right? Let's continue talking at the CCI. It's just a short walk from here."

Daddy glared at his daughter with a hard stare indicating he wanted to go home. But, Nazeera was enjoying this meeting and she didn't want it to end. Not yet. This guy seemed different from all the others. He was a bit mysterious. And, of course, he was wearing a peacock blue tie. Yes, he was definitely worth a few more minutes of their time.

Nazeera returned her father's glare with a light-hearted smile. Knowing she could melt her father's heart with her smile, she was not surprised when he accepted Farid's invitation.

CHAPTER 12

"I HOPE HE CAN DANCE!"

The CCI. A easy-to-pronounce abbreviation for The Cricket Club of India. During the British Raj time, it was an exclusive club for the British elite. After partition, some twenty years ago, the CCI opened its membership to Indians. Well, Indians that could afford the membership dues. It was a prestigious place to relax and socialize.

Farid explained to the group during their fifteen-minute walk from the Ambassador's office to the CCI, that he had purchased the membership a few years ago to entertain current and potential clients for his stock exchange business. Over the years, he allowed his family to use the membership and found his children loved splashing in the large swimming pool during the hot summer months. He admitted he preferred watching cricket matches over swimming in the pool. Rehana added she preferred when there were no cricket matches, so they could have tea and snacks on the lawn. It was a rare opportunity to walk on grass.

Nazeera and her family knew the CCI and its facilities well. It was literally across the street from their Yashodham building and she could see the swimming pool from the second floor veranda. Her father was also a member of the exclusive Club. He had received a discount on the membership dues due to his high position in the government. Laughing at Farid's comment about the cricket matches, her father admitted he's also watched dozens of cricket matches. Nazeera was about to admit she too had attended several games - but to check out the guys, not to watch the cricket. She changed her mind though and held her tongue. *It was too soon to be sarcastic.* Ammi eagerly added she enjoyed her weekly bridge games. She continued prattling on to anyone who would listen about her various partners and her latest card match.

Since several cricket players were on the lawn practicing their bowling or catching, much to Rehana's disappointment, the group settled on eating snacks in the Club restaurant. The sound of the rock and roll music surrounded them even before they stepped into the building. *It must be Thursday. It's the only night the CCI has a live band.*

Clearly distressed, Farid shook his head and pounded his fist twice on the reception stand. Finding no one there to seat them, he snaked his way to a few empty tables in the back corner, as far away from the band as possible. The group slowly followed with Ammi arriving at the table last. Her feet were still swollen and hurting. She was most pleased to be able to sit down.

Waiting for everyone to be seated at the two pushed together tables, Farid ordered hot tea and three orders of finger sandwiches from the white gloved waiter. It seemed just a moment later, the waiter returned with the items on a silver tray. Without a word, he placed a steeping teapot on each end of the long table and the three tiered trays of bite-size sandwiches evenly between the guests.

As host, Farid offered the ladies the sandwiches first. He commented the egg and cress sandwiches were his favorite. Nazeera politely declined a sandwich and simply sipped her tea. After a few very hot sips, she noticed Amir was sitting opposite her and next to her mother. She had a unique and wonderful view of him. Farid was sitting next to him and trying his best to encourage his guests to eat.

Nazeera used her cup as a protective shield to hide behind. Peeking over the top of it, she spied Amir scan the tiny treats, and pick up an English cucumber sandwich. The triangular wonders were common for afternoon tea as the thin slices of English cucumbers on the lightly toasted crust-less white bread were refreshing. It was traditionally made with butter, but Nazeera preferred when it was made with cream cheese. *How did the CCI make it?* She tried to see what spread was on the bread, but she couldn't. It wasn't until Amir bit into one corner, and wiped a bit of butter from the side of his mouth that she knew.

Her suitor finished the sandwich in three bites, then turned to her mother sitting on his left. He had not spoken to her all evening. Maybe he thought this was his chance to make a good impression, *"Aap kyaa huh?"* What yes?

Stifling a laugh, her mother responded to his attempt at a conversation. Encouraged, Amir continued, *"Mujhey theek, shukriya."* So much fine, thanks.

Ammi was trying to respond the best she could, but it was clearly difficult for both of them to converse. Nazeera giggled under her breath as this silly American man was not speaking well at all. He was trying hard to impress her and her mother, but he was actually doing the opposite. Obviously, he was out of practice with speaking Hindi. He had forgotten words, syntax and basic grammar. *Incredible! And he wants to marry an Indian woman?*

After a few minutes, she saw him turn to her and with a slight plea asked in English, "Would you like to dance?"

"Sure," Nazeera replied. *Anything would be better than watching him hack the Hindi language. Did he notice me laughing? Since he can't speak properly, I hope he can dance!*

Amir stood up and came around the table to where she was sitting. He offered his hand in a gallant way but Nazeera ignored it. Instead, she stood up on her own and strode to the dance floor. *That will show him I'm independent. If he doesn't like it, tough. Oh, he must be fine with it, he's following me.*

The band was playing Chubby Checker's, "The Twist". Dancing to that modern song in this sari would be a challenge. Nazeera quickly glanced around the dance floor at the four other couples, as they stepped onto the parquet floor that had been laid over the bright orange and green carpeting. The ladies were twisting their torsos to the beat of the music. *Simple. I can do that.* Trying to replicate what they were doing, she leaned forward onto the balls of her feet and started twisting her torso, her bent knees and arms swinging back and forth in opposite directions. *Left-right-left, this isn't too hard to do.* Once she had perfected her dance steps, she turned her eyes to her dance partner. Amir looked lost. He was standing there just shifting his weight from side to side. *What is he doing? Why isn't he twisting like everyone else?* "Don't you know how to do The Twist?"

"No, not really. I prefer the waltz or the fox trot."

Sensing she was watching him, Amir added a slight arm movement to this weight shifting. He looked as uncomfortable dancing as he did speaking Hindi. *What is he doing with his arms? Is he trying to impress me with his dance moves? It isn't working!*

Nazeera just had to ask, "Are you sure you're from America? Aren't you supposed to know all these fancy dances?"

"I guess I should," Amir admitted, "I don't go dancing much."

That was obvious. They danced silently for a moment. The band started playing "The Mashed Potato". This one she knew. Nazeera squatted slightly and started raising and lowering her arms. After a few mashes, she noticed Amir was still shifting his weight from side to side. *What a pathetic dancer. Well, at least he's trying. He probably just wanted to get away from talking to Ammi.* She laughed to herself, "I saw you chatting with Ammi."

"Yes, Aunty seems very nice," Amir replied adding a clap to his weight shifting.

"It's funny." she said ignoring the clap, "People go abroad and forget how to speak Hindi. How long have you been in America?"

"I've been in America for eight years. I really like it there. It's much cleaner than Bombay and there are far less people," he said. Looking down at his own dancing feet, he admitted, "And honestly, my Hindi wasn't too good to start with. I went to Catholic convent schools that taught in English. I much prefer to converse in English."

"Obviously," she teased. *This guy can't dance and can't speak Hindi. No wonder he needs help finding a wife. But, at least he's honest about it. That's something he had going for him. He's different from the other guys. A bit odd, but definitely different.*

The music changed to "Blueberry Hill" and they both agreed it was time to rejoin the table. He offered his right hand, and Nazeera was tempted to take it. Instead, she politely refused and strode back to the table with him close at her heels. All sets of eyes were on them. She noticed her mother had a huge smile on her face, and her father wore a scowl.

CHAPTER 13

Friday, August 12

"WOULD SHE REJECT ME NOW OR LATER?"

Propped on his left hand, Amir lay on his bed staring at the book of love poems on the nightstand. Wow, the girl from last night had some spunk. She's beautiful and witty, though a bit sarcastic. *She's everything I'm looking for in a wife. Well, I could do with a little less sarcasm.* Finally, Rehana had introduced him to someone that he liked. Nazeera could be more than a friend - she could be a wife. Someone to not only share his life; but also, enrich his life.

What did he really know about her? His sister-in-law had not given the usual slip of paper with notes. He didn't know how old she is, how many brothers or sisters she has, or what her father does. *Hmm... Does she know how to cook? Does she like to travel?*

Just having spunk may not be enough. But it was a good start. Nazeera would be okay in America. In fact, she would be more than okay. She could thrive there. She was definitely the best choice so far. *And, she's beautiful! Her eyes are mesmerizing, her hair was pulled up but it looks long and thick. Her face is very pleasing and her body, oh, her body is perfect. But, how does she feel about me? Would she reject me now or later? I have to make sure the next meeting goes well.*

He began to hum, surprising himself that he was humming, as he stood up from the bed and began to change from his night clothes. He decided to skip wearing a tie today as he was going to be a bit more casual. A bit more relaxed. *Maybe that would help. It sure couldn't hurt*, he thought.

Still humming, he joined his mother at the dining room table for breakfast. Ramu saw him enter and obediently went to make his instant coffee. "I see you are in a good mood this morning," Mummy commented in Hindi to her son, "That's good."

"*Ji, huh*, good mood." Amir replied in Hindi, keeping his words and grammar simple. "Nice girl last night." He made more effort to speak in Hindi this morning. He needed to improve a bit before he conversed with Nazeera's mother again. And her father!

"You two seemed to get along. Maybe you need to meet more girls on the dance floor."

"She said I not dance well." He replied in simple Hindi, "She wonder if I from America because I dance bad."

Mummy frowned, "Humph, she sounds a bit forward to me. Not respectful. Too independent."

Amir reflected for a moment and then replied in English, Hindi was just too hard, "I don't think she's too forward." Amir sipped his coffee and took a bite of the Indian scrambled eggs that Ramu had just placed in front of him. "She's just someone with a lot of..." he searched his memory banks for the correct Hindi word to help his mother understand, "*utsaah*... spirit...spunk."

Mother and son continued eating their breakfast in silence with Mummy shaking her head every once in awhile. Amir ignored her and smiled to himself as he thought about Nazeera and their dances. The telephone rang, and Ramu walked spryly to answer it. Amir could hear him talking but couldn't make out the words.

"Ma'am Sah'b," Ramu announced as he entered the dining room and addressed his mistress, "Rehana-*Ji* is on the telephone. She wants to speak to Amir." *Why couldn't he tell me directly? Well, I guess Ramu works for my mother, not for me.* Amir gave Ramu a look, and headed toward the telephone.

Hmm, Rehana is calling. That will be for information on the next meeting. He wiped the corners of his mouth with his fingers before picking up the telephone receiver on the hallway table. He answered with his American greeting, "Yallo."

"Good morning! I hope you were able to sleep well," Rehana replied without allowing him to answer, "I was able to move Jamila to an early lunch today. Then we meet Dilshad for afternoon tea. I know it's a busy day, but Farid and I want to go to JK tonight to see if we can meet any other women for you. It's Friday you know, and everyone should be there."

Amir frowned. This was going to be a busy day with two meetings. But, she was right to keep this process moving and present as many women as she could. He had only so much time, and he was only halfway done with "The List". Nazeera had been met out of order because the Ambassador was leaving town. Maybe he was more than halfway done meeting the women. Hopefully he was. Anyways, he had a lot more women to see. "Okay, let's do it. Did you pick a restaurant so you don't have to cook?"

She had, and gave him the details. Rehana had selected the restaurant at the Oberoi Hotel. It was a bit expensive, especially for his limited budget, but it would make a good impression on, what was her name? He glanced at the name he had scribbled on a scrap of paper, Jamila. Hopefully this Jamila will like it and he would have another option. If not, then at least they had a nice meal and Rehana had a break from cooking and hosting.

Glancing at his watch, he concluded he had some time before they needed to leave for lunch. He thanked Rehana for arranging this and returned to the dining room to inform his mother and finish his breakfast. She smiled at the name of the restaurant and patted his hand as he sat down at the table.

"Lunch be good, Amir," she said confidently and with a motherly head bobble, "This Jamila will be nice, nice girl." She used the double adjective as they often do in Hindi grammar. Well, at least she said her words in English so he could understand. That was progress.

Amir's appetite was gone. He hoped his mother was right and this Jamila was a nice, nice girl. But, Nazeera was a nice girl. In fact, she was more than nice. He would compare Jamila and any other girl he meets to her. She was the new, what was the term? Show horse? No, lead horse? No. Well, it didn't matter, she was the one he would compare any other girls to. So far, he had two girls in the running, Chandni and Nazeera. Hopefully the girls today would be worth his time and not reject him quickly. More rejection would be hard to take.

To make sure they got a table large enough for the whole group, the four Viranis arrived at the Oberoi Hotel a few minutes earlier than the arranged time. The maitre d' at the Ziya restaurant wore a long-sleeved black cotton shirt and black cotton trousers, both freshly pressed. His ivory vest was buttoned and he had a small red handkerchief poking from the small chest pocket. Amir thought the man looked very formal in his western clothes. *Do I look formal too?*

As the group approached the mahogany table stand, the maitre d' looked up from the reservation book and smiled. He nodded slightly as Farid gave the name and time of the reservation, and then bowed his head and scanned the lines of the reservation book. His fingers traced the various lines and names and then he found the reservation. It was the first one on the list. With another smile, he gallantly gestured with sweeping arms toward the empty dining room allowing his gold nametag, bearing the name "Kumar", to sparkle in the small amount of light that shone from the nearby window. Since they were eating an early lunch, the Viranis were the first ones to arrive when the restaurant opened. They really didn't need a reservation, but it didn't hurt and the maitre d' seemed to expect it.

The foursome followed his gesture and stepped into the dining room. Since the room was empty, Mummy suggested they be seated facing the front entry so they could see their guests arrive. Kumar nodded and they followed him to a group of tables along the far wall. He minutely nodded to the waiters standing at the ready and they silently rearranged the tables for the party of eight. Once the tables were arranged, two waiters held out a chair for Mummy and Rehana and allowed them to sit comfortably before disappearing into the shadows.

Amir glanced around the restaurant. It was very formal but unexpectedly comfortable. White linen tablecloths lined each table with small crystal vases of red roses in the center. The golden chairs with ebony black lacquer trim were slightly pulled out to make sitting in them easier. Each table setting had a golden charger plate framed by sterling silver utensils. The crystal wine glasses on the upper right hand side of each charger added a bit of shine and sparkle. Impressed by the table setting, they took their seats at the table. Farid and Rehana sat on one end with Amir and Mummy in the middle.

The complimentary *papadams* were brought by "Rupali" their server. She wore a similar outfit to Kumar but instead of trousers, she wore a long black skirt. Her hair was pulled back into a tight bun and it glistened from the glare of the overhead lights. She smiled as she laid the snacks on the table. Farid was the only one to take a *papadam* and everyone at the table turned to watch him eat the fried cracker. The crackers are notoriously messy and this one was no exception. Rehana rushed to place a plate under her husband's chin as the *papadam* fell apart with his first bite. Unfortunately, she was too late and most of the flaky pieces landed on the table in front of him. Farid stoically gobbled the rest of the cracker as the rest of the group shook their heads. So much for first impressions and in such a formal restaurant.

Although tempted, Amir decided against the delicious *papadams*. He didn't want to make the same mess as his brother had just done.

Jamila and her family strode toward them as Farid picked up another cracker. Amir immediately noticed she had some spirit. She walked very confidently in the front door and followed closely behind Kumar as he led her group to their table. She had chubby cheeks and was a bit overweight, but she carried it well. She wore a blue sari with white circles running throughout the fabric. Her hair was long and she wore it draped over her right shoulder, just as Nargis had done.

The two men stood as the group approached. Jamila placed her hands together and said to each of them the customary Ismaili greeting, "*Ya Ali Madad*". May the Exalted Ali help you.

They each replied with the correct Ismaili response, "*Mawla Ali Madad*". May the Exalted Ali help you, too. The small group all sat down at the same time with Jamila across from Amir and Jamila's mother across from Mummy. Both her brother and father sat on the opposite side of Farid and Rehana.

Speaking first as she placed the cloth napkin on her lap, Jamila said, "So, Amir, I hear you're from America." Amir suddenly realized he had not studied the notes Rehana had given him. He wasn't sure of her background, in fact, he didn't know anything about her, other than her name. A wave of panic overwhelmed him. He breathed heavily and then concluded, heck, maybe it was for the best. He would get to know her the American way, by just talking to her like he did with Nazeera.

"Yes, I'm from America." He gave her a short summary of his work and life there. She listened intently to every word and asked clarifying questions. When he concluded his summary, he took a long sip from the straw. They had ordered a round of Coca-Cola drinks while he had been telling about his life in Milwaukee.

The conversation paused for a moment, and Amir glanced at Farid. This is when his brother would asked a question from his blue piece of paper. Much to Amir's dismay, Farid was mindlessly crunching on a *papadam* and didn't see his brother's cue. So much for that. *Okay, I can think of a question on my own. What do I want to know?*

Before he could formulate a question, Jamila's mother, Meena, asked him one. "What are your thoughts on The Partition?"

Really? This was not the time and place to discuss a politically charged question. The Partition was the nickname for the nightmare that occurred two decades earlier when the British left the Indian subcontinent and partitioned it into three countries – East Pakistan, India and West Pakistan (later Bangladesh). The reason for the partition was to accommodate religious differences between Pakistan, which has a majority Muslim population, and India, which is primarily Hindu. It was thought to have been a good idea since then both religions could practice as they preferred, but it ended up creating hostility between the regions that continues to this day.

The boundary lines drawn by Lord Mountbatten were debated almost immediately. In fact, they are still fighting over the area of Kashmir which had been composed of princely states at the time of independence, and thus had not been assigned to either country.

Immediately after the new countries were created, millions of people moved, some forcibly, from their homes and their land. Muslims moved from India to Pakistan and Hindus moved in reverse. Such a large double exodus, with limited government guidance, allowed for exploitation. The strong overpowered the weak in the form of beatings, rape and murder.

"Well," Amir started. He didn't want to get into a political debate, so he kept his reply personal, "Although we are Muslim, my family decided not to move to Pakistan. My father had started the first Ismaili bank here in Bombay, and he wanted to stay and make it a success. So, he and my mother took a chance and stayed. However, Mummy's younger brother moved to Pakistan. He set up a household in case things got tough here and we needed to move quickly."

"*Aacha*," Meena replied. Turning to Mummy, she asked, "Is your brother still in Pakistan?"

"*Ji, huh*, he lives in Karachi. Do you have family there?"

Meena smiled, "Yes, we do. All of my family, including my parents and siblings and their families, moved soon after Independence. I stayed here with my husband, as his parents were elderly and could not travel. They have now passed on, so we have no ties left in Bombay other than our two children. We will go wherever Jamila goes."

"So, you would move to America?" Amir clarified.

"Yes, we would move to America with Jamila. We could help set up household and watch over the children."

Amir was a bit overwhelmed. He wasn't planning on getting a set of parents with his bride. He would need to buy a bigger place, maybe a house, and that would cost a lot. But, then again, he would get Indian cooking every day. That was worth something. It didn't matter if Jamila couldn't cook, as he was pretty sure her mother cooked very well. And, they would help with the children! That would be good as he had no desire to change dirty diapers. *Yes, this might work out just fine.*

The lunch arrived, and Rupali supervised as the wait staff circled the table with the steaming hot dishes to serve each guest. Each person was able to say yes or no to each dish presented. When the plates were sufficiently full, the hot *naan* was laid on the table. As the wait staff retreated, Rehana asked, "Jamila, who is the woman that sits with you and your mother at JK."

Wiping the corners of her mouth with her napkin, she answered, "That's Arzoo, my brother's wife. They have four boys. The boys all sit with Hasan on the men's side during the prayer services. She sits with us."

Amir used the sway in the conversation to consult his notes. He reach into his pocket and panicked for a second as they were not in his right trouser pocket where he usually kept them. He patted himself to locate the slip of paper. They were actually in his shirt pocket. With a sigh of relief, he unfolded the paper and read: "Jamila, twenty-seven, Art degree, one brother, parents run a hotel."

The group looked at Hasan who just nodded and lifted his right hand at the mention of his name. He resumed eating, so Rehana turned her eyes toward Meena and asked, "So, you would be fine leaving your son and grandchildren to move with Jamila to America?" Most Indian parents live with their son since the daughter moves into her husband's home.

Meena looked at her son and then sheepishly replied, "Hasan is well settled and his wife takes great care of him and their children. She is very... organized. Jamila needs my help."

The wait staff came again to offer the food dishes to each guest. Hasan and Farid each enjoyed another serving of chicken *tikka*, while Amir chewed for the first time on the *papadams*. They were cold and not as tasty as they would've been fresh, but he didn't care, he was stalling while he formulated the next question. This girl seemed nice enough but the parents would be there too. *What will they do all day?*

"Masud, do you and Meena still run the hotel?" Farid asked as if reading Amir's mind.

"We sold the hotel six months ago." Jamila's father quickly replied. He was a soft spoken man of medium build and a high forehead. He had a small pot belly that overflowed his belt buckle and his temples were showing hints of gray. He still looked young for his age, but Amir could tell that he didn't speak much. Meena did most of the talking.

As if on cue, Meena interrupted, "Yes, we sold the hotel for a good profit, and now we are, what they call, retired." She straightened her back, lifted her chin in the air, and added, "Masud and I spend our days at The Willingdon Club."

Impressive. The Willingdon Club was the short name for the

Royal Willingdon Sports Club of Bombay. It was the first such Club to allow indigenous Indians membership and has been a prestigious club for decades. It is best known for its eighteen-hole golf course. Amir asked, "Do you play golf there?"

"Well," Masud shriveled up his face and said, "Well, I try." The group burst into laughter, with Meena laughing the loudest.

The wait staff began to clear the table and dessert menus were handed to each guest. Lunch was going very well and Amir was enjoying the conversation. Farid glanced at his watch and then nodded to Amir. They had time for dessert. After the dessert orders had been placed, Jamila looked at Amir and whispered with a bit of conspiracy in her voice, "What types of Art do you like?"

The question took Amir by surprise. He hesitated and then answered, "Well, I don't really like Art. I mean…. it's a bit pointless, isn't it?"

Jamila sat back in her chair. She stared at him as tears began to well in her eyes. "I'm sorry, Amir, did you just say you don't like Art?"

What did I say? Why is she reacting this way? What's the big deal? Then it dawned on him. She was an Art major. She likes Art. "Well, Jamila," Amir whispered, "I guess I do like Art. But, I don't really know how to appreciate it."

Wiping a tear from her right eye, she allowed the one dripping from her left eye to fall down her cheek, "Art. It's…it's something that moves you. It touches your soul. By you saying you don't know how to appreciate Art, it's like saying you don't know how to appreciate your own soul."

Amir shook his head in disbelief. *What is she saying? What does she mean by Art and soul? Seriously.* "I understand Science. I don't always understand Art." He stared at her a moment, "I guess what touches my soul is different from what touches yours."

She sniffled and replied, "Yes, Amir, I guess it is."

The desserts were distributed, eaten and cleared before Jamila said another word. Amir asked her a few more questions but she didn't respond. She was no longer interested. He had lost her. The table grew quiet as they had all witnessed the exchange between the two prospective spouses. When the wait staff offered tea, Farid looked at his watch and shook his head. No, there was no time for tea. Thank goodness.

He had to fix this before the door was shut to Jamila forever. Art wasn't so bad. Granted, he thought it was pointless, but he could learn to appreciate it. Amir leaned forward and touched the table near Jamila's hand. "Jamila, I'm sorry if what I said offended you. I know I could learn to appreciate Art." He smiled, "I just need a good teacher. Someone like you."

Jamila looked up. Her cheeks were still moist from the tear drops but she was no longer crying. "No, Amir, I'm sorry for falling apart. I really do like you, and maybe things could have worked out between us. But, your love of Science and my love of Art makes us incompatible. I'm sure you can learn to appreciate Art, if you really try, but it will never affect your core being, as it does mine. I do hope you find a good teacher, but, that person will not be me."

Farid paid the bill, and the group got up to say their good-byes. Hugs and kisses were exchanged and Jamila even managed a smile. She and her parents thanked them for a nice lunch and left the restaurant without an indication of interest in another meeting. As she walked away, Amir thought, this time it wasn't the timing or the city he lived in that caused the rejection, it was him. He and Jamila were just not right for each other. And to think he was that close to having Indian food every night.

CHAPTER 14

"DON'T YOU LIKE TEA?"

The foursome returned to Farid and Rehena's flat after lunch. The next guest was to arrive in half an hour, so the group prepared for her arrival in their own ways. Rehana was in the kitchen supervising preparations for the afternoon tea. Farid was in the bedroom taking a quick nap. Amir and Mummy were on the veranda enjoying the fresh air and trying to stay out of Rehana's way. After a brief conversation between mother and son, Mummy leaned back on one of the plastic chairs and began to doze from the large lunch they had just consumed. Amir stood up and leaned on the veranda railing, letting his eyes wander to the people passing by and in turn, his mind wander to Jamila.

The girl from lunch was definitely self confident. She was interesting and pretty, but her passion for Art, and his love of Science, did not make them a good match. *Darn.* She had not rejected him, so the door may still be open. Amir mentally put her in the "maybe" pile, took a deep breath, and exhaled to clear his mind. *Okay, onto the next girl.*

He unfolded the paper in his hand, and glanced at the notes Rehana had given him. The handwriting was different. It wasn't hers, but it did look familiar. Was it his mother's? *Hmm...* The note read, "Dilshad, twenty-eight years old, widow, school teacher, father is a shopkeeper. Friend of Bandra and Salim." Ah, yes, that's whose handwriting it was – Bandra's. Now that he thought about it, Rehana had mentioned something about this. Bandra was his eldest sister, just two years younger than Farid, and two years older than Nilofer. Her real name is Badra, but since they had spent so much of their childhood in the nearby Bombay suburb of Bandra, her name evolved. No one remembers who gave her the nickname, but it stuck.

The doorbell rang, and Amir could hear the heavy footsteps of Babu pounding from the kitchen to the front door. A moment later, the entryway was filled with the sound of Bandra and Rehana's voices. Deciding he better go in and say hi, Amir stepped down the two wooden steps from the veranda and joined the two ladies in the living room. Bandra rushed to him and kissed him multiple times on each cheek. She made some excuse about the business being so busy, and Salim was sorry he was not able to attend this meeting. That was fine with Amir. Less people, less formal.

His older sister was dressed in a gray sari with dark blue flowers. She wore eyeglasses with thick black frames that made her look much older than she was. Her hair was cut short like their mother's, and her temples were beginning to gray the color of her sari. She carried a canvas tote that must have been heavy because the strings of the bag made a slight indent in her right arm. After greeting Mummy who had just joined the group, she sat down on the sofa with an exhausted thump. She paused for a moment, and then leaned forward to open the mysterious bag. She pulled out something rectangular and handed the wrapped parcel to Amir, "Welcome to India".

Grinning like a child receiving a gift he eagerly reached for the bundle. This was the first gift he had received in India. *Shoot, if I knew she was coming, I'd have brought her a shawl. Maybe there's still time to get it?*

"Open it," Mummy urged as she eyed Babu bringing in a box of sweets. Babu had again been asked to get sweets from Lookmanji's. They were sold out of the *malai khajas,* so he selected an assortment of Indian sweets including *khaju kathri.* The diamond shape cashew treats were special because they had edible silver foil on top. The sweets were a favorite of Mummy's, and she watched with a smile as Babu moved the pieces from the box to a cut crystal platter.

Amir unlaced the twine from around the parcel, and carefully unwrapped the brown paper wrapping. Then there was a layer of bubble wrap. Someone had wrapped this very well - as if they were wrapping it to go overseas. Oh, that's probably exactly why they wrapped it like this. He could then re-wrap it and take it home. Smart sister. He unwrapped the bubble wrap and held up an earthy brown soapstone box. It was very heavy indeed. Amir turned it from side to side to get a better look at the carvings. The sides had a carved lace pattern and there was the typical red, blue and green gemstones tulip on top. It was a very nice gift and must have cost her a bit of money. She was definitely trying to butter him up for this meeting.

"*Shukriya-ji*. Thank you." He said looking at Bandra. Even if she was buttering him up, it was a thoughtful gesture just the same. "I brought you and Salim gifts from America, but they're in Mummy's flat. I'll get them after tea."

"That's fine, Amir. Don't worry about it." She was clearly being nice. Nicer to him than she had been in a long time. *She clearly wants me to chose Dilshad as my bride.*

Suddenly Bandra began to laugh at something Mummy said, and Amir was transported back to a time when she had laughed similarly. He was about eight years old, so she would have been in her early teens. The two of them were sitting cross-legged on the veranda of their childhood home eating peanut *chikkis*. The *chikki* was a peanut, sugar and jaggery brittle candy they only got to eat occasionally. A pair of black-faced monkeys leapt onto the veranda railing startling both of them. Bandra stood up, and with hands akimbo shooed them away. Or so she thought. One of the monkeys climbed to a nearby tree, and leapt onto the railing closer to Amir. He was dumbfounded, and just sat there in shock as the monkey approached him, slapped him in the face, and scampered away with his *chikki*. Instead of yelling at the monkey or consoling her brother, Bandra had simply laughed. Just as she did now. That was over two decades ago, but the memory of that incident was as fresh in Amir's mind as if it happened yesterday.

The group took turns admiring the soapstone box, and Rehana commented on how "heavy it was". The words brought him back to the current moment and Amir began thinking about the weight of it too. *How am I going to take this back to America? Is there a weight limit on each suitcase? Is this another game by Bandra? What is she up to?*

The doorbell rang, and everyone anxiously looked toward the front door. They were here. Amir swore under his breath that he should have put a tie on for this meeting. Maybe he could still borrow one from Farid? No, all his ties were shades of brown. *Darn.*

Babu stomped from the living room, and walked quickly to the front door. He received the nod from Farid, and opened the door to the small group. Dilshad's father was the first to enter. He was followed by his wife and daughter as well as two sons. Big group; so much for a small intimate meeting.

The five guests were greeted by the five hosts with a warm welcome. Bandra kissed them all on both cheeks, then lovingly grabbed Dilshad by the arm and introduced her personally to each member of her family. The other guests just laughed at Bandra, and introduced themselves. Amir's first impression was that they all seemed like nice people with a good sense of humor. Dilshad wore a green sari with gold embroidery along the edge. She also wore a heavy gold necklace and earrings that chimed softly each time she moved her head. Her hair was loose and fell slightly below her shoulders. She wore black eyeliner like most Indian women did, on her upper eye lids and on the inside of her lower lid. It made her lotus shaped brown eyes mesmerizing. She looked enchanting, and he instantly understood why Bandra had added her to the list.

Wetting his lips and raising his eyebrows, he followed the group into the living room. Bandra still had Dilshad by the arm, and led her to the loveseat. She moved onto the sofa leaving the seat next to Dilshad vacant. Amir wondered if she had done that on purpose for him. Of course she did, as she was glaring at him to sit on the loveseat. He understood her cue, and sat down next to the bride prospect.

The chatter in the room grew in volume. Even though she was only inches from him, it was hard for Amir to hear what Dilshad was saying. He turned to get a better look at her, and noticed her eyes were indeed lovely. She was listening intently to Bandra explain something, so he just watched her for a moment. She sat quietly with her hands clasped loosely on her lap. She did not act demure or shy. In fact, she glanced at him occasionally as though she was also sizing him up. She was a widow, so she had been through this whole marriage process before. *What happened to her first husband? Can we ask that question? Maybe I'll ask Bandra later. She would know.*

Holding the silver tray of steeping tea and crystal platter of sweets, Babu carefully placed it on the coffee table moving the bowl of flowers to one side. After pouring each of the ladies a cup of tea, Rehana asked Babu to offer the platter of sweets. When it was her turn, Mummy pounced on the *khaju kathri,* taking three pieces. She gobbled the first one as if she had not eaten in days. Then ignoring her indiscretion, she mindlessly nibbled on the remaining two pieces, appearing to savor each bite.

"Would you like to try the *khaju kathri?*" Amir asked Dilshad after watching his mother. *If she does wants a piece, she better grab it before Mummy eats it all.*

Dilshad blinked her eyes, and coyly replied, "*Nahih, shukriya-ji.* No, thank you." She took a sip of her tea, then shook her head violently. She quickly sat forward, adding three more cubes of sugar and a large amount of milk to her brew. With a half-smile, she stirred her mixture as she sat back. "Don't you like tea?"

Amir returned her half-smile. She must have noticed he had not taken any sips of his tea. "No, not really."

"Add several lumps of sugar. That'll help."

"Maybe. I actually prefer coffee. In fact, Americans don't drink tea very often. I think it has to do with the Boston Tea Party or something. I'm not sure," he admitted. "Anyways, everyone drinks coffee. So, I guess I got used to drinking coffee, too. They have coffee breaks over there like Indians have tea breaks."

"Do you have your own coffee-*walla?*"

He laughed. She laughed nervously along with him. "No, I don't. Nobody does. In fact, I have to get my own coffee. At work, we have a machine in the break room. You put your money in one slot and then push a few buttons and voila, hot coffee."

"Really!?" she said in disbelief, "That's certainly different from here."

"Yes, but you..." Amir started.

"Dilshad," Bandra interrupted, "Tell them about your classroom."

She turned her face away from Amir, and blinked a few times. Her long eyelashes bounced gently up and down on her cheeks. They were enticing and her profile with those long eyelashes was striking. He sighed. Now that he was looking at her eyelashes from this angle, they looked oddly familiar. As if he had seen them somewhere before.

Dilshad began to describe her classroom. "I have only eight children in my class, mostly boys, ages nine and ten. My favorite student is Nirmil. Now, I know we're not supposed to have favorites, but he is so funny. The other day he ...."

Amir's thoughts began to wander. He was simply captivated by those eyelashes. *Why am I so obsessed with them? Where have I seen those eyelashes before? Maybe in a photo Bandra sent me? No, there is no photo. Maybe I've seen her on the street? When I got the nariyal pani?*

Then, as if hit by a bolt of lightning, he remembered where he had seen those eyelashes. It was on Nazeera. Those were her eyelashes, too. Dilshad and Nazeera both had long lovely eyelashes and lotus shaped eyes. *Somehow the eyes and eyelashes are even more lovely on Nazeera. And her face, her skin...it's smooth and luminous. And her mouth...her lips...full and pouty. Oh, and her slender body and...*

The group laughed, and Amir snapped back to the present moment. He laughed though he didn't know why. "And the principal is very fair," the woman sitting next to him continued, "He always makes sure the girls are treated with respect."

"How long have you been teaching?" Rehana asked her.

"This is my third year. After my husband died in a car accident, I went to work at the English convent school. I really enjoy teaching there, but I think it's time for a change."

"Is that why you're interested in going to America?" Farid summarized, wincing a little as he spoke.

"Yes, I love children," she answered, "but, there aren't enough students in the school and there is talk about combining classrooms.

The other teachers have seniority, so I may be dismissed. I like teaching in English and would like to try and teach in America."

Babu poured a second cup of tea for Farid who seemed to be holding the tea cup tighter than usual. *Is he in pain again?* The servant circled the group offering a second or in some cases, third cup of tea and then retreated to the kitchen to make a fresh pot. The *khaju kathri* was gone and the other sweets were close to being gone. The meeting had been a huge success from the length of the conversation. But a failure as Amir had not heard most of it.

"We must be leaving shortly," Farid announced, "We are meeting some friends at the Jamat."

"Oh," Dilshad's father responded sounding a bit disappointed the meeting was ending, "Who are you meeting?"

"My friend Noorudin and his older brother Noorudin."

"They have the same name?" Dilshad's mother, Husna, asked in disbelief.

"Yes, their parents named the older son and His Highness the Aga Khan named the younger one."

"He can do that?" Husna responded with a bewildered look on her face. She explained they were not Ismailis and had never heard of this tradition. Farid responded that His Highness the Aga Khan was not aware of the older son's name when he named the younger one after one of the prophets of the Ismaili faith.

"I was named by the Aga Khan too." Amir piped in finally entering the conversation. Dilshad shot him a shocked look, "Really?" Amir hoped she had not noticed that he had not heard much of what she had said.

"Yes, Prince Aly Khan came to visit our home soon after I was born. He was a friend of my father's from a personal favor he had done for him. Anyways, as leader of the Ismaili religion, he was asked to give a blessing to the latest birth, which was me."

"He named you Amir?" Husna questioned.

"Actually, he was named Jooma," Mummy inserted, "But Karim and I preferred the name Amir, so we made Jooma his second name." Dilshad's parents simply nodded.

Dilshad turned to look into Amir's eyes. Whispering, she asked, "Do you go to the Jamat very often in America?"

Amir broke her gaze and looked down at his feet kicking an imaginary stone, "No, not really. I'm not very religious. I haven't been to JK in quite awhile." Surprisingly, she sighed with relief.

Her mother must have been intrigued by the naming of babies, as she continued the conversation best avoided on a first encounter – religion. Amir now wished he had kept his mouth shut about being named by the Aga Khan. Dilshad's family were not Ismailis but they were Shias, so they shared many views of religion. He and Farid tried to focus on the similarities of the two Muslim sects and steered the conversation away from the differences. They were successful for the most part.

"*Bas,* enough. We really need to go." Farid said looking again at his watch and standing up. It had been almost thirty minutes since he had first mentioned they needed to go. They were going to be late. "It was great meeting you all."

The visitors finally got the hint and stood up to leave. It took a long ten minutes of good-byes before they left. Apparently, they were in no hurry to leave and even Dilshad lingered awhile longer in her good-bye hug to Bandra. Farid and Rehana changed quickly and Babu wrapped a plate of fruit as their offering. Neither Mummy nor Amir wanted to go to the JK that night, but they both did.

CHAPTER 15

"MAYBE WE CAN MEET FOR TEA?"

Nazeera returned from her Interior Design class, mentally exhausted. She had taken the class believing it would help her decorate a home one day. What she didn't realize was the class was more about flower arranging than about home decorating. She loved flowers, but after seeing dozens of cut flowers needing to be arranged as instructed, she didn't love them as much. Slumping into the sofa, she was shocked how the aqua blue upholstery of the furniture contrasted so sharply with the hot pink sari she was wearing.

The telephone rang, and Nazeera hoped it was for her. She desperately needed a distraction. Maybe it was her cousins Pinky or Dolly with the latest gossip. She now regretted not chatting with them when she saw them last Tuesday at the Ambassador's Meet and Greet. But, she was distracted with finding her friends and when she went to look for them later, they were already gone. They weren't allowed to stay out late, that was clear.

It was made very apparent earlier that summer. The three of them had gone to a movie, and Nusrat Aunty had told them to be back by 9:00 pm. Rather than leave the movie early to make curfew, and miss the exciting ending, Nazeera had insisted they stay until the movie was over. When they returned home at 9:45 pm, Aunty shook her forefinger and clucked, "Good girls do not stay out past curfew".

Nazeera had calmly explained the curfew was not fair as the movie ended at 9:30 pm and it took fifteen minutes for them to return home. Aunty did not understand her logic, nor appreciate her disobedience. She grounded her cousins for two weeks and complained to Ammi about Nazeera's reckless behavior. Thankfully, Ammi took it in stride and just warned her to be more careful.

"*Beta*," Ammi called, "telephone."

With a huge smile, Nazeera jumped up and almost skipped to the telephone. "Pinky?" she started, "Is that you?"

"No," a deep voice replied, "It's me, William."

William. A flood of memories rushed into Nazeera's mind, like a flashback in a Bollywood movie. He was a handsome man of six foot. He played cricket for his college team, and looked very dashing in his uniform. His mother had hoped they would marry and he had even jokingly proposed twice in the three years she had known him. But, she knew he was not ready to settle down. His proposals were for his mother's sake, not out of love for her. So, she had politely declined each one, not even mentioning his proposals to her own mother. They were still good friends, and she enjoyed talking with him.

They met when their families both lived in Poona in the government housing. Their backyards were kitty corner to each other. Nazeera's father was the collector, a high civilian official. William's father, as well as Jaya's father, were two-star generals in the Indian Army.

One day just after lunch, she and Jaya were chatting about the movies playing in the local cinema and deciding if they should see a show that evening. William's mother was in the yard watering her plants, so Nazeera waved to say hello. At that moment, William walked out of the house.

He was wearing his white cricket uniform, and the sunlight made his silver buckles sparkle. He looked like a Bollywood movie star stepping onto a movie set. Full of confidence and utterly gorgeous. His mother returned her wave to Nazeera and said something to her son. He shrugged his shoulders and proceeded to walk diagonally across the yard to the fence she was leaning against.

Smelling slightly of sweat, she assumed he had just returned from a cricket match. His musky aroma filled Nazeera's nostrils and made her swoon. Her lips parted, and she smiled slightly in spite of herself. When she looked up from her demure pose, she saw him staring at her. He briefly greeted Jaya and then returned his attention to her, explaining he had heard a lot about her from his mother.

The three of them spent the afternoon together on her veranda chatting about a variety of topics. Jaya left about tea time, so William and Nazeera continued their conversation alone enjoying lukewarm tea and finger sandwiches. He told her about his University life, his dream of joining the army and his goal of becoming a general like his father. When it was her turn to speak, he listened intently as she spoke of her goal of running a boutique and meeting new people. She remembered thinking he was the most handsome man she had ever met.

"Nazee, are you there?" Nazee was his cute nickname for her.

She blinked her eyes, "Yes, William, I'm here."

"I'm home for a few days. I was hoping I could come to town to see you."

"Yes, I'd like that."

"Great. Next Tuesday, Mummy has to get a necklace fixed and cleaned for an upcoming wedding. She wants me to bring her to TBZ. Isn't that close to where you live now?" TBZ was short for the Tribhovandas Bhimji Zaveri Jewelry store. It specialized in gold sets for weddings and other high-end jewelry.

"*Ji, huh.* Yes. TBZ is just a couple blocks from here. I'm sure Ammi would enjoy having you and your mother come to our flat for tea," she replied. Nazeera was actually excited to see both of them again. *Maybe he's going to tell me he has quit the army and is ready to settle down. If he did, would I consider him?* Moving every three years, as the government and army require, was a hard way to grow up. *I don't want to do that again as an adult!*

"Let me just check with Ammi," She put down the telephone receiver and rushed to check with her mother. Her mother was clearly excited but cautioned Nazeera not to get her hopes up for "that boy". Ammi didn't quite understand how the two of them could be friends without wanting marriage. She thought it was unnatural. Cradling the receiver, she huffed, "That will work just fine, William."

"I'll see you then, Nazee." She hung up the telephone receiver and smiled from ear to ear. He was coming here! She could get his thoughts on Jaya's marriage as well as their opinions on her suitors. He could give her a guy's opinion. That was, unless, he wanted to be a suitor too! *No, probably not. He's just being friendly.*

Nazeera missed the long chats she used to have with William. Chats she used to have with her brother, Aziz, when they were growing up. He had been sent to supposedly better schools in Bombay for most of his childhood and had not moved around as she had. He had a stable home with Nusrat Aunty and Jhoma Uncle for almost a decade. Nazeera often wondered if he thought of Pinky and Dolly as sisters more than her.

She had hoped they would become close again once she and their parents moved to Bombay. But he kept his distance. He rarely came by the house and blamed Ammi for the trouble with Hamid. It wasn't her fault his wedding had been a disaster. Well, not totally.

Maybe William could help her bring Aziz back into the family. It was worth asking him. She missed her older brother.

CHAPTER 16

Sunday, August 14

"I'M NOT GOOD AT BARTERING"

Amir had met the ninth lady on the list last night for dinner. Koyal was beautiful with long brown-black hair and high cheek bones. Her self-confidence was evident as she lit up the room when she entered it. She had an electric smile, and Amir was hopeful for a pleasant evening. His hopes were smashed as she walked closer to him and opened her mouth. Using a baseball analogy, she had struck out.

Koyal was naturally tall, probably two or three inches taller than him. He could have dealt with her height, after all his own sisters were as tall or taller than him. However, she insisted on wearing her sparkling high heel shoes all evening, refusing to remove her footwear as most people did when they enter a home. He noticed how very tall she was, when he tried to gaze into her eyes, and only saw her chin. It was a lovely chin, but he couldn't imagine being married to a woman that liked being taller than him. Strike one.

Both Farid and Koyal's father were elders or senior leaders at the JK. Since this was the first time the guests were invited into their home, Rehana wanted to impress them with a few of her favorite recipes. As she proudly explained each dish with a wave of her hand as she usually did, Amir noticed Koyal turned her head away from the table as if the sight of the food made her sick. Holding her breath, she took a small spoonful of the *Daal Saak* and a *naan*, and swiftly retreated to the living room.

During the dinner conversation, she boastfully proclaimed she only took a little of the lentil and potato dish as it was the only vegetarian dish offered. She was amazed Rehana had served mainly non-vegetarian food, insisting all meat eaters were sinful. She further explained she only cooks and eats vegetarian meals. Amir did not think of himself as a meat eater, but he did like to eat meat almost every day. He could get used to eating vegetarian meals, but he could not get used to marrying a woman that so blatantly insulted his family. Strike two.

The final strike against Koyal was her pampered lifestyle. She had worn a very expensive looking sari and 22k gold jewelry. That was not unusual attire for special occasions and maybe she considered this meeting to be special. Nonetheless, during the course of the evening, she dropped several hints about her family's wealth and their many servants. At first, Amir thought she was just nervous and saying these things to convey her family was not poor; but when her father added he had just bought her a Mercedes Benz for her birthday, he knew her expectations of lifestyle were more lavish than his. He was still in the early part of his career and at this point, didn't want a wife that would spend all his money. In fact, he was hoping she would work to contribute more to their monthly income. Strike three.

Amir opened the veranda door of his brother's flat, and climbed the wooden steps. *Some fresh air will do me good.* As he stepped over the threshold and onto the cool tiles he heard the deafening sound of horns honking. He walked forward two long strides, and leaned forward against the flimsy railing to watch people as he sipped Babu's version of coffee. There was a man selling fresh vegetables and another man selling marigolds strung on a string. How simple their life was. They would just accept whatever arranged marriage their families organized. This semi-arranged marriage business was difficult. Selecting Miss Right after just a meeting or two was difficult, nearly impossible. *How am I supposed to get to know someone in just a few days? How am I supposed to make a life decision without all the facts? More Art and less Science? Maybe Jamila is right. I need to get in touch with my soul.*

The last girl was coming for afternoon tea. Amir let his mind wander to his short list of potential brides. Nazeera and Dilshad. But, then there was Chandni. He liked her too, but more like a friend than a wife. *How do Nazeera and Dilshad feel about me? Neither have rejected me, so that's a good sign. No second dates until all the girls have been seen. Is that Rehana's rule or Mummy's? It didn't matter. It's a silly rule. I'm running out of time! I leave in two weeks, and I'm still in the first round!*

Frustrated, Amir stomped back into the living room and announced, "I'm going out." He noticed only his brother and mother were still at the dining room table, "I think I'll visit the Prince of Wales Museum."

"Great choice," Farid replied with a soft voice, clearly struggling to speak, "They have a...great exhibit of...weapons.... My favorites... are the daggers...and the...Oh!"

Amir looked at his brother who was clearly in pain, "Farid, you don't look well. Are you sure you're okay?"

His brother tried to smile, but did so in vain. He grabbed his right side with his hand and closed his eyes. "No... not so well." He whispered, "I had...blood...in my urine."

"Goodness, Farid! You need to go to a doctor right away!"

"Rehana is calling Dr. Bumbadelli now."

"*Beta*, go lay down!" his mother ordered. Farid looked to his mother and just as he did when he was a child, he pouted his lower lip and nodded, "Yes, Mummy."

Farid slowly got up from the table, and leaning with his left hand on one of the chairs for support, walked himself slowly from the dining room to the bedroom. His feet moved in a shuffle, his pace much slower than he normally walked. He was clearly in pain. Amir laughed to himself. Farid was almost 40 years old, but still a child in his mother's eyes. And, he still obeyed his mother. As a matter of fact, so did he. Isn't that why he's here now?

"I hope you feel better soon," Amir called to Farid as his brother shut the bedroom door. Turning to his mother, he said in a softer voice, "I'll be back in a few hours."

He followed the same route he had days earlier when he walked to the Bombay Harbour for the *nariyal pani*. Tossing a few *rupees* to the beggars, he admitted the walk itself was delightfully pleasant. It was only mid-morning and most of the stores were still closed. He passed an occasional shopkeeper on his way to his shop or an excited tourist wandering around with a guidebook. He watched a pair of lovers walk hand in hand, and then kiss.

As he approached the Regal Circle area, the noise level increased and the foot traffic tripled. Amir contemplated skipping the Museum in favor of walking down the Colaba Causeway. He wanted to get a few souvenirs for his co-workers, and Colaba was a good place for shopping. He continued on Madame Cama Road and then had to decide which way to go. *Left to the Museum or right to Colaba?*

Amir glanced at his watch. He needed a distraction right now more than he needed trinkets. Besides, most of the shops were not set up yet. Turning left, he crossed the road and entered the Museum. He felt a weight lift from his shoulders as he accepted this semi-decision. He started to whistle as he walked slowly through the Indian miniatures. They were his favorites, and the palm leaf paintings were amazing. He crossed to the other side of the foyer and climbed a flight of stairs. *Where is the weapons display? Aha, there it is.* He carefully studied the various swords and daggers, marveling at the various ways man devised to hurt one another. *What is that saying, make love not war?*

Emperor Akbar's shield hung off to one side behind a thick wall of glass. He studied it closely, and recalled something he had read in his history books. Akbar had three wives, a Hindu, a Muslim and a Christian. He loved the Hindu wife the most as she bore him a son, but still, he had two other wives. *What would it be like to have three wives? He could marry Nazeera, Dilshad and Chandni. Would that be a fantasy or hell?*

Wandering around the Museum for another thirty minutes, Amir decided he had seen enough. He glanced at his watch as he exited the Museum, and concluded the stalls should be open by now. Surprisingly, he felt a surge of excitement. It had been a long time since he had been on Colaba. *This will be fun.*

Colaba was usually filled with tourists, but hopefully it was still too early and they weren't there in droves. He was fairly confident he would find some handicrafts or incense holders, but he was really hoping to find some brass trinkets. *Yes, this will be fun.* He picked up his pace a bit and started to see the stalls ahead.

He crossed the road carefully checking for traffic the whole way. There was no such thing as a crossing guard and red stop lights were merely suggestions to the speeding cars. Successfully crossing the street, he smiled to himself. *Yeah! I made it.*

Amir started walking down the Causeway. It was packed with locals and tourists, just as he feared. An elegantly dressed woman, already loaded down with shopping bags, was holding a beaded purse and offering a number to the shopkeeper. The man stood up from his stool, bobbled his head and barked a number back to her. She waved her hand and laughed, offering a slightly higher number. *Yikes! That's right, they may want to haggle. No, they will want to haggle. I'm not good at bartering, haggling, whatever it's called. Negotiating. Never was. Shoot! Maybe this won't be fun after all. Oh, heck, I'll just do my best. As soon as I open my mouth and they hear my American accent, they'll probably double or triple the price anyways.* These vendors knew foreigners were bad at bartering, and would often happily pay more just to get the trinket.

Continuing past the bartering pair, Amir walked past stalls of handmade bags, leather *chappals*, shiny rocks, and plastic toys. *What the heck. Even if I pay double what the locals pay, it will still cost a fraction of what it would cost in America. So what if they took advantage of me? I'll still get a good deal, and they will get a bit more money in their pocket. I'll be helping them survive another day.* He smiled to himself feeling like a noble hero.

He approached a stall with wooden bangles he imagined his female co-workers would like. Asking the price, he was surprised by how little they cost. He attempted to negotiate but did so only half-heartedly. He just handed over the money and since he didn't want to go through that uncomfortable experience again, he bought a few more sets in a variety of colors. *Pitiful haggling, but at least I got a few souvenirs.*

Hurrying along the sidewalk, Amir stopped at another stall selling a variety of carved wooden animals. He picked up an elephant and a lion. They seemed to be very crudely carved. Amir was about to say something to the shopkeeper when he noticed the man was lame, and leaning on a well-worn crutch. The vendor had white hair, his clothes were torn and slightly soiled. He greeted Amir when he picked up the carvings, showing he had several missing teeth. Although Amir knew he could find better quality carvings elsewhere, he decided to buy half a dozen from this guy. He feebly haggled, basically giving the old man his very high asking price. This time when he walked away with his treasures, he wasn't mad at himself.

With a light heart, he continued walking down the sidewalk and crossed another intersection. As he skipped onto the new sidewalk he noticed the sign for "Rajsi's". *Oh, that name is familiar.* He had seen several bags from this store in his brother's flat, so Rehana must liked this store. *This would be the perfect place to get her something special.*

Stepping into the store, he heard a chorus of small bells ring. The store interior was extremely quiet compared to the hustle and bustle on the street. He glanced around quickly, and noticed an older lady looking at a cotton *salwar kameez.*

Spotting a mannequin with a long patterned blouse and cotton trousers, he quickly decided he would try and replicate that look for Rehena. He could buy her a *kameez* and she could match it with her choice of trousers. *That's fashionable, right?* He passed the older lady and continued walking to the back of the store, glancing around as he walked.

Not finding what he wanted, he approached the glass counter hoping for assistance. The woman behind the counter bowed her head slightly, raised both her hands in front of her face, pressed her palms together, fingers pointing upwards and thumbs closest to her chest and welcomed him, *"Namaste".* This was typically a Hindu greeting, but was becoming commonplace in India since Hinduism is the prominent religion.

He replied in English, and then immediately regretted it. *Shoot! There go the prices.* He tried to converse in Hindi, but it was too difficult, so he just sighed in defeat and asked for a *"kameez* only" in English. He accepted he would just pay extra.

"What color?" the shop lady asked with a heavy accent in

simple English. She had pulled out several dozen different shirts each wrapped in a plastic bag. She pointed to one near Amir's hand, "You want see?"

"Sure," he replied not really know what else to say. He had no idea which one to get, and even less clue as to what size his sister-in-law is. The shop lady pulled the shirt from the plastic bag, and with a quick flick of her wrist, the shirt was thrust into the air and gently floated down to the table. It was a ruddy red with a black geometric pattern running horizontally across the chest. As he looked at it, he recalled Rehana had something similar to this. Maybe she would like it.

"*Theek hai*," Amir replied and nodded, "Okay."

The shop lady smiled, skillfully folded the shirt back into thirds, and slipped it back into the plastic bag. She touched another plastic bag, "You want see?" He simply nodded and the flick, float and fold continued for a few minutes. He had agreed to four different shirts. He now glanced at them a bit more closely and decided to purchase the two that were the biggest sizes. *Better to be too big than too small, right?*

Taking a deep breath, he asked the price. The shopkeeper had already begun to put the rejects back on the shelf, so she had to turn around to give him the price. He knew from his limited experience today, this was his cue to start haggling. He wished they just had set prices like they do back home.

"*Ji, nahih, ji, nahih.*" she said impatiently. She added in English, "Fixed price. Fixed price."

Amir's heart felt like it was leaping out of his chest. *Fixed prices just like home! Awesome. I don't have to haggle after all.* He would need to remember this store and come back here if he needed more shirts. His smile must have been apparent as the lady turned back to him and said, "Look more?"

He simply shook his head, and asked her to write up the bill. Obeying, she handed him the receipt. He reached for the shirts, but she shook her head and pointed to the cashier near the front of the store.

First stop, the cashier. The lady he had seen earlier in the shop was now standing in front of him in the queue. He watched her slowly count her *rupees* one-by-one. As he patiently waited, he wondered how this country functioned. The shopkeepers outside had low over-head, but the price of their goods fluctuated based on the customer's negotiating skills. The formal shops like this one had a higher over-head, but had fixed prices for their goods? *Which method makes more money?*

After the cashier, he stood in another line at parcel pickup. Amir handed his stamped paid receipt to the young lady. She mindlessly took it, and handed him a brown paper bag with the Rajsi's name and logo stamped on the side. He glanced inside the bag to confirm the two *kameez* he had just bought were inside. They were. He stepped through the exit door, but not before he had to pass one more check-point. A burly man compared the receipt to the bag of goods. With a grunt, he allowed Amir to pass.

The sidewalk was busier and noisier than he remembered when he entered the shop. More sidewalk stalls were open and there was a multitude of new customers. He glanced at his watch again, deciding he had done enough souvenir shopping for now, and it was a good time to head back to the flat. Maneuvering past a man with two small kids, he retraced his steps past the lame carver, past the bangle-man to Madame Cama Road.

Finally at the Regal Circle intersection, he noticed a *pani puri-walla* on the corner near the YWCA. The aroma of the round puffed pastry filled with a mixture of flavored water or *pani*, tamarind chutney, chilies, potatoes, onions and chickpeas made his stomach growl. This was the quintessential Bombay *chaat* or street food. The best part of this *chaat* was the *pani* that dribbled down the throat as you eat the little filled *puris*.

Crossing the road, he stood in line for a snack. He watched the man for a moment. *Was this safe?* He never had to worry about that before, but now that he lived in America he heard about all the warnings about the water. Don't drink the water. Don't eat the ice cubes. Don't eat food cooked in water unless it has boiled. *Boo. That makes the trip less fun. I'm going to do it. He looks like a decent clean guy. He looks like he would boil the water all the way. Sure his clothes smell a bit and his hair is unkempt, but he still seems relatively decent.*

Decidedly, Amir stepped forward and ordered a dish. He watched as the vendor selected a Styrofoam bowl from his lop-sized stack and spoon two heaping scoops of *puri* mix into it from his large container. Then, using a large stainless steel ladle, he drizzled the tasty *pani* sauce over the *puri* mix. Amir's mouth was already starting to salivate. Finally, he added a scoop of extra spices and thrust a white plastic spoon into the mixture.

"100 *rupees*," he announced as he handed the bowl to Amir. Smiling with anticipation, he gladly handed the man a 100 *rupees* note, not even worrying about how many US dollars that translated to.

Amir took a quick bite, then began walking precariously with the Rajsi's bag tucked under one arm, and the plastic bags with the souvenirs dangling by their handles from his wrist. After a few more steps toward the flat, he stopped for a second bite. *This tastes incredible! Yum!* The spicy *pani* was sweet but still tangy. The potatoes and onions were diced into one inch cubes which allowed him to spoon a few of them with each bite of *puri*. The round chickpeas were a bit hard to keep on his spoon, but he preferred to eat them separately anyways. *Oohh. This is so good. Definitely a good choice.*

He was about halfway to cloud nine when he decided to just stop for a moment to totally savor the experience. There were a lot of people and animals on the sidewalk, and if kept walking and eating, he would probably bump into someone or something. Leaning against a lamp pole, he dropped his bags into a heap and took another bite. He was in heaven. Hopefully he would not regret it later, and be in hell.

When Amir was about halfway done, he paused to do some people watching. It was definitely busier now. Taxis swerved here and there. Fiats and Ambassador cars whizzed by. An oxen and cart were hauling firewood through this chaos. Only in Bombay.

Resuming his snack, he noticed a few drops of the spicy *pani* had dribbled from his chin to his shirt, and he swore at himself for not grabbing a few napkins. Amir covertly glanced around, like a child checking to see if anyone noticed him stealing a cookie from the cookie jar. Thankfully, it appeared no one had. He wiped the excess moisture with the back of his sleeve, hoping either Babu or Ramu could find someone to get the stains out.

Now losing a bit of his appetite, he glanced around the intersection. To his right, there was a bit of a commotion. Two familiar looking ladies were trying to cross the road carrying several shopping bags. *Why do they look familiar? Did I see one of them on a movie billboard? At the museum?* As the older lady began to cross the road, the flimsy straw handle on one of the shopping bags broke, and the contents fell into the street. The younger lady scooped the shirts into her arms and they hurriedly continued weaving between cars while balancing their bags. They glanced in his direction, and Amir immediately recognized them. It was Chandni and her mother! *I should call out to see if they need my help.*

"Hey, Chandni!" he called. The ladies must have been too far away as they did not react to his calling. Amir was about to call out again, when he decided to stay silent due to the stain on his shirt.

He watched them finish crossing the road adeptly dodging the moving cars. Chandni lifted her hand and after a few seconds, a taxi veered toward them and stopped. She leaned into the front passenger window, probably to give the driver their destination. He nodded, and motioned for them to enter the taxi. They awkwardly climbed into the back seat with all their precious belongings. They were so crammed in the back seat that Amir saw Chandni move a few bags to the empty seat next to the driver. Before they were totally settled, the taxi pulled away and they were gone.

Chandni. She's pleasant and had a good personality. *Why am I not attracted to her? Am I shallow in wanting to marry a woman I'm attracted to both mentally and physically? No, I'm a man. Just a man. A man with just one more name on the list. What time are we meeting today? Is it for tea or dinner? Hmm.... yes, it's for tea! What time is it now? Yikes! It's nearly tea time! I better get home before Mummy has a fit!*

Amir gobbled the rest of the *pani puri* and headed quickly back to the flat. He entered the lobby and decided the lift was too slow. He rushed up the stairs two at a time to the fourth floor. He hesitated only a moment to catch his breath, and then pounded on the door. He heard Babu's familiar footsteps approach the door and then ask who was there.

"This is Amir. Is my brother back from the doctor?"

It was silent for a moment, then Rehana came to the door. "Farid is laying down for a bit. The doctor says he has stomach issues. He gave him some medicine, and told him to stay in bed the rest of the day."

Trudging into the flat, Amir gave the Rajsi's bag to Rehana without comment. She accepted it with a puzzled look on her face, and then cautiously opened the bag. As she retrieved the two *kameez* she exclaimed, "Amir, they're splendid. Thank you!" She laid the ruddy red one and an aqua blue one on the table. Glancing at each of them, she put the ruddy red one back into the bag.

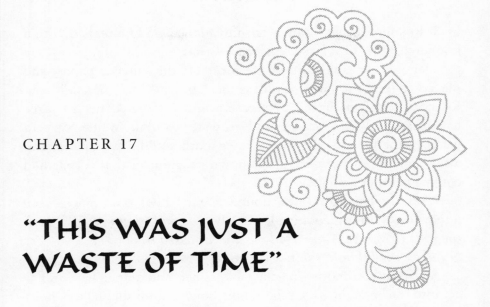

CHAPTER 17

"THIS WAS JUST A WASTE OF TIME"

Nazeera walked into the kitchen wearing her headphones. They were camouflaged under her long hair, so she thought her mother wouldn't see them. She didn't think she need to learn to cook. She was convinced she was going to marry a man who could afford a servant and a cook... a driver and a car were, of course, a plus. If her modeling career wasn't successful, she would run a boutique shop selling the latest fashions. Then if she got restless or bored with that, she could do charity work. There would be no need for her to know how to cook. This was just a waste of time.

In spite of Nazeera's protests, Ammi insisted she learn the basics - how to boil water to make sure it was safe to drink, how to cook an egg at least three ways and how to make a few Indian curries. Today, her mother was going to teach her how to make her father's favorite dish, *Kofta* Curry. Meatball Curry.

Akbar leaned on the doorsill between the small room which served as his living quarters and the kitchen. He had recently returned from the butcher shop with the freshly ground lamb required for the recipe. *Is he hovering there to encourage Ammi not to make the huge mess she usually does in the kitchen?*

Nazeera was glad he was lingering in the corner. She might need his help later. She shot him a friendly glance, and he replied with a knowing smile. *Can he see my headphones?*

Her mother gently lifted the meat off the butcher paper, and placed it into the large stainless steel bowl Akbar had laid out for her. She then turned to Nazeera and instructed her to place two pieces of bread into some clean water to soak. While Nazeera watched the bread soak, she saw her mother add a few spices, and a few pinches of *kothmir*, also known as cilantro, that Akbar had chopped earlier.

"You ain't nothin' but a hound dog...." Elvis is so much more interesting than this cooking lesson. *When can I be done? Why soak the bread? Maybe Ammi told me and I missed it. Should I ask her? No, then she'll know I'm not listening.*

Suddenly, her mother reached across her, and dipped her forefinger into the bread bowl. Grabbing the bowl, Ammi slipped the moist bread from the bowl into her spicy meat mixture. She was mouthing something and making hand motions that looked like she was grabbing something small. *What is she saying? Combine? Sure.* Nazeera began to combine the bread and meat with her hands. *This is actually fun. The mixture is cool and the squishiness of the mixture is like playing with wet sand on the beach.*

Her mother bobbled her head, and leaned forward to glance in the bowl. "*Theek hai.*" So far, so good. She glanced down at the recipe and ordered, loud enough that Nazeera could hear it through her headphones, "Akbar! *Tel garam karo.*" Heat the oil.

Nazeera watched her mother take a small handful of the meat mixture and roll it between her palms to make a small meatball. She proceeded to make three more before she pushed the large bowl with her elbow toward Nazeera, and lifted her chin to indicate her daughter should continue.

This was simple. Nazeera had made these several times over the years helping her mother in the kitchen. She grabbed a small handful of the mixture and performing almost as well as her mother, made the rest of the *koftas*. When she was done, she looked up to see her mother staring at her looking very impressed. *Maybe I can cook after all!*

They moved closer to the hot skillet and after checking the oil was hot enough, Ammi slowly dropped three *koftas* into the hot oil. After a few moments, she took her favorite ladle off the hook on the wall, and moved the koftas around in the pan. When they were browned, she deftly removed the *koftas* from the hot oil, and placed them onto a plate covered with a cloth. She handed the ladle to Nazeera and said something.

"....Heart..break..hotel, I'm so looonelee, babee...." *What is she saying? She is actually letting me use the ladle? The ladle her mother gave her? Wow, this is the first time I've been allowed to even touch this ladle!* Nervously, Nazeera took the ladle from her mother and mimicked exactly what her mother had done.

Suddenly, Akbar stepped on her foot. Nazeera turned to him with a stern look, and was about to chastise him, when she noticed her mother was washing her hands and jabbering. *Oh, maybe he's trying to get my attention.*

Nazeera moved the headphones off one ear, so she could hear her mother's babbling. Akbar moved closer to Ammi, and proceeded to check the water temperature turning the hot and cold faucets to the left and right to make the water warmer than colder. Frustrated with his interferance, Ammi shut off the faucets and repeated the question. This time, Nazeera heard it, "What do we do now?"

Shrugging her shoulders, Nazeera replied, "I'm not sure, Ammi."

Her mother shook her head, *"Baap-re!* Yikes!" Thankfully, Ammi answered her own question and began explaining how to make the curry. Nazeera leaned behind her mother so she could not see and mouthed *"Shukriya"* to Akbar. *He has saved me once again.*

Ammi explained the various steps to make the curry or sauce for the meatballs, and proceeded to make it with very little input from her daughter. When the curry was done, she placed the *koftas* in the curry and sprinkled two pinches of freshly cut *kothmir* on top of the dish as garnish. Holding it in front of Nazeera, "See how pretty the dish looks. Always put the fresh *kothmir* on top to add some color and flavor."

Nodding, *"Shukriya-ji,* it looks very good, Ammi. Daddy will like it." She turned and began to walk away.

"Beta," she said as she bobbled her head, and grabbed Nazeera's arm, *"Beta,* it's your turn."

Nazeera's eyes grew, and she looked to Akbar in panic. "My turn? I just helped you make *Kofta* Curry."

"Exactly. Now, you know the basics. You need to make a different dish. I'll write the directions to two dishes and you can select the one you want to prepare for dinner tomorrow." She glanced at the wall clock and added, "It's time for cards. Are you coming to the Club?" She gave her daughter a hug with her right arm and vacated the kitchen before Nazeera could protest.

She looked after her mother and pouted. Akbar laughed, "Baby Sah'b". Sahib, or the abbreviated Sah'b, were polite names to address the master or mistress of the home. Since he had started working for them, Akbar had called her "Baby Sah'b" to indicate she was the young lady of the household. It was his special nickname for her and she cherished it. "Baby Sah'b," Akbar repeated, "I help you."

"*Shukriya*," Nazeera replied, "Thank you, Akbar." She desperately needed his help. Akbar had helped her with some simple cooking steps in the past. It was their secret. Really, if she had paid attention to what her mother was showing her, she would be a good cook. But, now, it was just easier to continue the game.

She found sanctuary in her bedroom. She laid on the bed for a long moment and resolved to get dressed to go to the Club. The cricket matches were always fun to watch. Well, really, the boys were fun to watch. Maybe Farah or Aaliya would be there too.

Nazeera stood in front of her armoire looking at the various choices. *Hmm…. Something eye catching but not too bold. Something that'll make me look pretty, but not look like I'm trying.* She selected a bubble gum pink sari, and called for Shanti to help her change. Shanti came running from the living room where she had been sweeping the floor for the third time that day.

When she was dressed, Nazeera sashayed into the kitchen. Akbar had the bowls and dishes all cleaned and put away. The room was spotless. *How very efficient!* He was sitting on the stool in the corner reading a small paperback book written in Hindi. He looked up as she stepped into the kitchen.

"Baby Sah'b," he said in Hindi, "Which recipe do you want to make?" Nazeera glanced at the two recipes her mother had left for her: *Bhendi Ki Subji* or *Bombil*. Both were important dishes, but for very different reasons. *Bhendi Ki Subji*, or stir fried okra, was one of her mother's specialties. *Bombil*, also known as Bombay duck, was fried fish. The fish was commonly found in the waters around Bombay, and her personal favorite fish dish.

Nazeera knew she should really learn to make these dishes, but she convinced herself, she had time to learn. She pointed to the *Bombil* recipe and thanked Akbar again for the work he was going to do on her behalf. He smiled a wide smile, which she returned, before she disappeared around the corner.

CHAPTER 18

Monday, August 15

"HALL-LOW"

The afternoon tea yesterday was a bust. Even Rehana admitted Afsan was not a good match for Amir. The bride prospect had been moved to the end of the list for the same reason Amir rejected her - she was just too modern. She wore bell-bottom pants with a flowing flower print shirt. Her hair was cut shoulder-length with a slight flip at the bottom. She spoke very good English, but inserted "far out," "outta sight", or "groovy" into every sentence. Amir thought she looked like the flower-power women in the Sears and Roebuck catalog.

Soon after the tea was finished, the guests were thanked for coming and basically shooed out. Rehana, Mummy and Amir had another cup of tea as they discussed the next step. An exhausted Farid retired to the bedroom, once again.

Amir concluded he would like to see Nazeera and Dilshad again. He wanted to get to know both of these ladies better. And quick. After much discussion of the other women, they resolved to add Chandni on the second round list. Rehana suggested that meeting her again might spark something. Amir shrugged his shoulders, another one on the list wouldn't hurt. *She did seem nice.*

Setting up meetings was the logical next step and Rehana was volunteered to call the ladies the next morning. Time was of the essence. Amir insisted they meet the ladies at the CCI or a restaurant, so he could see how each of them interacted with others. He also mentioned Nadia had to be at these meetings. He had promised her she could meet any girl that made it to round two. *A promise is a promise.*

The rain was still gently falling on the veranda, when Nazeera strolled into the dining room for breakfast. Daddy had left for the office at least an hour ago. The light drizzle of the rain was comforting and made it hard for her to wake up. She had quickly changed from her overnight clothes into a festive maroon *salwar kameez*, placing her long flowing black hair into a ponytail. She was still a bit sleepy as she slouched into a dining room chair. Yawn!

Her parents would be eating the meal she supposedly cooks for dinner tonight. Hopefully she and Akbar can pull the ruse on Ammi again. She would need to check on Akbar's progress before her mother woke up. Hearing Akbar clanking pans in the kitchen, she told herself, *I'll ask him after I finish my tea. I need to wake up first.* Yawn! Nazeera poured a cup of hot tea from the steeping teapot on the sideboard. She added two cubes of sugar and a dash of milk. *This will help.*

As she cradled the hot mug of tea, she closed her eyes to let them rest. Yawn! It was going to be harder to wake up today than she thought. *Wearing Khushboo's favorite color is a good start. I can't wait to meet her at Sumrat!* She and Khushboo had only known each other for a few months before her friend had returned home. Khushboo sprained her ankle when her left *chappal* got caught in the wood planking on the stairs outside University Union Hall. Her family concluded if she was such a klutz after being away from home only six months, she couldn't handle living away from home for four years of college. Sad to see her go, the two of them swore to keep in touch, and they had - writing letters often and telephoning each other several times each year. After Nazeera moved to Bombay, Khushboo came to visit her every month via a two-hour train journey from her hometown of Thane. Since Khushboo is vegetarian, their restaurant of choice was Sumrat. It was convenient to the train station and just as importantly, the food was great. After lunch, they would continue catching up by listening to the latest records at Rhythm House. Nazeera was hoping Elvis or Pat Boone had a new album released so they could listen to it today.

"Baby Sah'b," Akbar said holding a food platter out for her inspection. He had made the *Bombil* following her mother's recipe. She raised her eyebrows at him in nervousness, and he smiled his toothy smile in reassurance. All was set. Nazeera approached him and using her pinky finger dipped the tip into the curry and in one motion touched it to the tip of her tongue. *It tastes wonderful.* She licked the remaining curry off her pinky and nodded, *"Bahut maze daar huaa.* That was very delicious."

She began to hum just as her mother did yesterday, and resumed her seat at the dining room table. The ruse would work!

The telephone rang. Akbar placed the platter down on the corner of the table, and quickly moved toward the land line. "Hall-low." His best version of English with his Hindi accent. Akbar listened to the caller's words and slowly looked in her direction. "Baby Sah'b," he simply said.

Nazeera smiled and skipped to the telephone, half expecting it to be Khushboo confirming their lunch plans. She was still smiling when she took the receiver from Akbar and said in a sing song voice, "Hel-loo."

The voice on the other end was not Khushboo. "Good morning, Nazeera. This is Rehana. Amir would like to see you again. Are you available for dinner tonight?"

"Good morning, Aunty," Nazeera replied quickly shifting her thoughts from Khushboo to the caller. Rehana... Amir... oh, yes, the guy that makes eye contact. *He wants to see me again? Really? What should I say? Daddy will not be pleased. But, he's an interesting guy. Different from all the others.* "Sorry, Aunty. We have dinner plans for tonight, her *Bombil,* but I think we are free tomorrow night. Let me check with Ammi."

Placing the receiver down on the side table, Nazeera quietly knocked on her parents' bedroom door, "Ammi, are you awake?" She leaned forward and put her ear on the door to try and hear any sound she could from the interior. She heard nothing, so she returned to the telephone, "Aunty, sorry, my mother is not available at the moment. I'll phone you later this morning."

"That's fine. Please try and call back before lunch as I am going out this afternoon."

"I'll try." She put the receiver back into place and skipped into the kitchen to check with Akbar. He was cutting up fresh *kothmir* for the lunch meal. He looked up when she entered the room, and tilted his head toward the platter now sitting on the sideboard. She sprinkled some of the freshly cut *kothmir* on top. *Always add a kothmir garnish, her mother had said. Well, at least I did that. All is set. Ammi will never know.*

❋ ❋ ❋ ❋ ❋

Amir paced impatiently in his mother's living room. "Has Rehana called with an update yet?"

"No, *Beta*," Mummy replied. With a nudge of her chin she added, "Why don't you go up and see if she has any news."

"Good idea!" Amir abruptly left the flat, heading directly to the lift. He pushed the call button and waited only a second before pushing it again. He pushed it a third time, and looked up at the floor indicator. The arrow was pointing to the third floor. *Forget it.* He turned and headed down the carpeted hallway toward the stairway. Without hesitation, he began to climb the steps.

I hope one of them can meet tonight, he said to himself as he climbed the stairs. He repeated the wish again and again, until he reached the fourth floor. Wheezing slightly, he hurried down the hall and knocked loudly on the door to his brother's flat. He waited only a moment before he knocked again. *What's taking so long?*

He heard the quick step of heavy footsteps, and stepped back from the door. As expected, Babu opened it and stepped aside to let him enter the room. Amir rushed in, calling, "Rehana, Farid."

Babu started to tell him they were in the bedroom, but as he did so, Rehana entered the hallway. "Amir, what's the matter?" she replied shutting the bedroom door quietly behind her.

"What's the update? Did any of them accept my dinner invitation?"

"Well," Rehana started, gesturing with her hands for him to

calm down. "I did phone all three of them. First, I phoned Nazeera, but she has plans for tonight and is checking with her mother about tomorrow night. I then phoned Dilshad. But, she was not at home, so I left a message for her to ring me back. I then went ahead and phoned Chandni. She is free tonight, so I made dinner plans with her."

"Okay, good work." Amir said with a slight smile. "Dinner with Chandni will be good. When are Nazeera and Dilshad going to call back?"

Rehana laughed, "Wow, I have never seen you like this." Whispering, she added, "*Chalo*. Let's go talk on the veranda. Farid is laying down."

"Is he still not feeling well?"

"He's better. The pain medicine from the doctor is helping."

They walked side by side through the living room, and he allowed her to proceed up the steps first onto the veranda. Following close behind her, he sat down in the chair nearest the door. He wanted to know the moment the phone rang. The chair he now sat in was the one usually avoided. It has one leg shorter than the others and thus wobbled a bit. Amir began to rock back and forth, impatiently.

The odd pair sat silent for a few long minutes, both of them lost in their own thoughts. Amir finally broke the trance, "Why are they not calling back?"

Rehana laughed again. "Be patient. I've asked both of them to phone before lunch if possible."

The silence resumed. Amir was amazed at how slow the clock ticked while he waited for a simple phone call. *Why am I so nervous? Or am I excited? What if they rejected me now. Maybe that's why they're not calling! Oh, enough of this!*

Troubled, Amir leapt from the wobbly chair, and leaned on his familiar spot on the veranda railing. *Maybe people watching will take my mind off this waiting!* A taxi drove by. Then a pair of motorcycles, one with three people on it. Another car. The distraction was starting to work and Amir's heart beat was beginning to slow. An old man with a cane walked slowly down the sidewalk. He walked a few paces, stopped to catch his breath, and then continued for a few more paces before resting again. His pace was slow, but he made it to the end of the block and then shuffled out of view.

Rehana stepped back into the house and brought out a deck of cards. She began to shuffle the pack. "I think we both need a distraction. Me from Farid's illness and you from the telephone. Let's play a game of Rummy."

Amir mumbled under his breath and returned to his wobbly chair, "Okay."

She proceeded to shuffle the cards one more time and then dealt the cards. Picking up his thirteen cards, Amir scanned them for runs or pairs. *Yeah!* He already had a run of Clubs. *Great.*

The flipped top card was one he quickly determined he didn't need. So, he picked up the top card of the deck and added the Queen of Hearts to his hand. He already had the King of Hearts. "Hmm…" he said aloud, partially in thought and partially to throw off his opponent. If he got the Jack of Hearts, he'd have another run of three cards. *Okay, I'll keep the Queen.* He dropped the two of Spades.

Rehana yipped and picked up the two of Spades. She rearranged a few cards in her hand and then dropped the nine of Diamonds in the discard pile. Well, he had two other nines, might as well pick up a third for three of a kind. He did so, dropping the Ace of Diamonds.

She let that one go. She picked up the top card from the deck and dropped the Jack of Hearts. *Yeah!* Amir quickly picked up the discarded card and added it to the Queen and King. *Nice little family. One more run to win.* He scanned his cards and discarded the only one that did not have a possibility, the three of Hearts.

They continued playing Rummy for another four turns, and then Amir placed the seven of Diamonds face down to end the play. He had won that round. *Yeah. Now, if only one of them would call.*

Two more hands of Rummy distracted them both from their worries. Rehana was shuffling the deck to deal the fourth hand when they both heard the telephone ring. Amir held his breath. He didn't hear any footsteps but after a moment, Babu stepped onto the veranda, "Ma'am Sah'b, telephone call for you."

Rehana stepped lightly back into the living room and walked quickly to the telephone, "Hello." Amir's heart resumed beating faster. *Who is she talking to?* Was it Dilshad or Nazeera returning her call? Was it Chandni cancelling dinner for tonight? Had she seen him standing there with a *pani puri* stain on his shirt and changed her mind?

After what seemed like a very long phone conversation, she returned to the veranda wearing a huge smile. Amir was relieved, she came bearing good news. "Nazeera is all set. We are meeting them for dinner tomorrow night at the CCI."

"The CCI again?" Amir asked, "Why didn't you suggest somewhere else? The Oberoi or the Willingdon Club? Isn't your dad a member there?"

"Yes, but, we're meeting Chandni at the Willingdon Club tonight and I didn't want to go there two nights in a row. Besides, the CCI is across the street from Yashodham, so Nazeera and her parents could walk there."

"Fine." Amir sighed, "What time do we meet Chandni tonight?"

Nazeera laid down the receiver after her call with Rehana, and immediately called for Shanti. She had to finish getting ready for her lunch with Khushboo but more importantly, she had tea with William and dinner with Amir tomorrow. She needed to go through her wardrobe.

Shanti came to her side and listened to her mistress' detail description of the upcoming events. Nazeera briefly explained what she wanted to wear, the color and how much jewelry. She knew Shanti would be able to assemble the perfect outfits for her to review and approve.

Soon after Shanti began working with the Khan household, she had been given the task of ensuring Nazeera's outfits were laid out as specified each day. To aid in this task, she and Nazeera had spent endless hours flipping through fashion magazines looking for different ways for Nazeera to wear her hair, her sari *pallu* and even her jewelry.

The servant must have taken the task to heart, as Nazeera often found her in the kitchen corner carefully studying the magazines pages. To feed her interest, Nazeera made sure she gave Shanti the latest fashion magazines whenever she was done reviewing them. Over time, Shanti had developed a keen eye for color and quickly became an expert at matching the solid-colored sari blouses with the multi-colored sari patterns.

"*Mujhe pani, chahiye*! I want water!" Her mother yelled from the bedroom. Nazeera heard her mother's words and rolled her eyes. She glanced at the wall clock, concluding her mother would not be well enough to do anything today. When she got into these fits, she liked to stay in bed all day. Hopefully she would be well enough for the events tomorrow. *It's a good thing we aren't meeting Amir for dinner tonight.*

Knowing Shanti was scurrying around in her bedroom, she stepped to the hallway. Akbar was just entering her parent's bedroom holding a glass of cold water on a tray. He smiled his toothy smile as he passed by her. Nazeera waited a moment, then entered the bedroom just as Akbar was exiting.

Her mother looked tired but otherwise fine. She was more pale than usual, and closed her eyes at the touch of her daughter's hand. Nazeera sat down by her mother's side, stroking her fingers over the back of her mother's cool hand. It was best for her to rest now so she could recover by tomorrow. If she didn't, Nazeera would call the doctor to make sure it was nothing serious. He was used to making house calls for Ammi.

What can be wrong with her? She seemed fine yesterday. Maybe she just had too much rich food at the Club last night. Nazeera patted her mother's hand again and stood up to leave. "You rest now," she said softly just above a whisper. She left her mother's side and went to her bedroom to inspect Shanti's progress. She was pleased with the outfits and jewelry that had been laid out. As expected, they were perfect.

117

CHAPTER 19

Tuesday, August 16

"WHAT AN ENCHANTING EVENING"

The toe tapping was getting louder and louder. Nazeera couldn't wait for William to arrive for afternoon tea. But, he was late. *What could be keeping him? Is Aunty's appointment running long, or are they stuck in traffic? It is today, right?*

As the various scenarios played out in her head, Akbar came to check on her twice. When he returned the second time, he brought her a glass of chilled mango *lassi* to keep her occupied. The tall glass filled with the marigold colored yogurt drink already had beads of sweat dripping down the sides. *It's going to be another hot day.* The air in the living room was already stifling. The ceiling fan was on high, but it only moved the hot air from one end of the room to the other. Nazeera carried the drink onto the veranda hoping to catch a slight breeze from the Arabian Sea. Any breeze would do.

She sipped the *lassi* slowly. With the last sip, she stood up and strode back into the living room. Picking up the telephone receiver, she listened for a dial tone. *Theek hai, it works. Something must have happened.*

They were very late. Much later than was fashionable or even acceptable. A sudden thought struck her and she rushed quickly back to the veranda and peered over the railing edge to make sure he wasn't sprawled out on the pavement. There was no one in the courtyard except for a passing beggar. His face and arms were covered in skin sores and his fingers were knotted, indicating he suffered from leprosy. What a nasty disease.

She heard footsteps rush across the living room. Then she heard the faint sound of the telephone ringing. *It's William calling!!* She closed her eyes and waited for Akbar to come to the veranda. After a moment, he joined her and said, "Baby Sah'b, William-*Ji* calling."

Finally! She smiled, and rushed past him to the telephone. "Hello," she said as calmly as she could.

"Hello, Nazee?" the familiar voice answered. "It's William. Unfortunately, we won't be able to make it to tea today. Mummy's appointment has run very long and we must return to Poona tonight."

She was very disappointed but did her best to keep her voice steady, "*Theek hai,* I see. When will you be coming back to Bombay?"

"I'm not sure. I head back to the Army barracks next week. I'll try and come up to see you before I go."

"That would be nice," she said with some hope. "Give my regards to your Mummy."

"I will. Give your Mummy the same. Good-bye, Nazee."

Slamming the receiver back on the telephone, Nazeera slumped into a chair. *Darn.* She wanted to talk to him about Jaya. Her friend had shown a brave face when they had lunch last week. But, was she really happy? Could she be happy married to a stranger? Arranged marriages had been around for hundreds of years and the divorce rate was very low. So, it must work. Parents selecting the spouses for their children seemed like such an odd concept in 1966, but it still worked. Her own semi-arranged marriage was more like a dating game or a series of blind dates. At least she was able to say no. Jaya couldn't.

A quick glance at the wall clock confirmed the lateness of the hour. She had waited for William and his mother for most of the afternoon! They only had an hour before dinner with Amir and his family. *He's never kept me waiting. Well, we've only met once, but that one time, he didn't keep me waiting.*

To spite William, she was determined to have a good time tonight. *That will show him!* She flipped through the records she bought at The Rhythm House yesterday with Khushboo, and found Elvis'

Paradise, Hawaiian Style. As she removed the record from the cardboard jacket, she wondered if the movie portrayed what life was really like in Hawaii. *Probably not, just as his movie "Harum Scarum" is not at all like the Middle East.*

Placing the vinyl disk onto the record player, Nazeera carefully placed the needle at the edge. It created the well-known crackle, and then the room filled with the booming voice of the American singer. Shaking her hips, she danced her way into the bedroom to get dressed for dinner.

Nazeera followed closely behind her parents as they walked into the CCI. She was wearing a vibrant cinnamon red silk sari with delicate gold stamping. She wore a gold choker necklace and chandelier earrings with specks of rubies. Her earrings chimed with every step she took. Ammi wore a rich brown-tea colored sari with dazzling copper swirls. She was feeling much better after the days rest, and had even complimented Nazeera on her *Bombil* dish. *Had she figured out Akbar really made it?*

Daddy arrived home soon after Elvis started singing. He was tired and not happy to be visiting with the Ameer-ic-kan boy again. After some prodding by Ammi, he changed from his work clothes into a very smart looking navy blue Nehru jacket. Nazeera noticed he was working later and later at this new government posting. When he was a collector in Poona, he seldom worked past six. Now, he seemed to work until seven or even eight, and sometimes didn't make it home for dinner. He mentioned a few times he felt he needed to work twice as hard as everyone else since he was one of the few Muslims in the primarily Hindu government.

They stopped at the entry desk, and Daddy signed the Members' Book. They had been members for a few months now, well, since her parents had moved to Bombay. It was a nice haven for all of them to visit during the hot summer. Tonight, the evening was delightful, the sky was as dark as the kohl on her eyes and the stars were beginning to sparkle like diamonds in the sky.

The CCI had lights strung from the various trees and they lit their path and gave the evening a festive air. A great night to sit on the lawn and eat dinner.

They followed the curvy red brick path into the heart of the Club. The activity at the swimming pool had lessened as the sun set. The four swimming lanes of clear blue water now contained only two serious lap swimmers. The snack bar next to the pool was overcrowded with guests. Waiters carrying platters of steaming hot *samosas* and tea were hurriedly weaving from table to table.

The attendant taking the trio to the Virani clan, pointed his hand down to the puddle of water near the flowers as a warning. *Probably left by one of the gardeners watering these aromatic flowers.* Nazeera carefully lifted the hem of her sari, and delicately stepped over the puddle with her jewel studded *chappels.* Her mother did the same. Her father walked defiantly through it.

They continued following their guide until they reached the fork. Normally, her parents would walk to the left to one of the many meeting rooms where they played cards. But, tonight, they turned right and walked toward the outfield entrance of the cricket field. The main action was on the other side of the field, but Nazeera preferred this side because it gave her more opportunity to check out the players and spectators. She had been here on Sunday with Farah and Aaliya, doing just that.

The young employee led them onto the cricket field and pointed to a group seated in the center. Nazeera noticed there were tables and high back cane chairs scattered in small groups on the outfield. This was really special - to sit on the lawn. She had never done this before!

Her father glanced around, and saw Farid frantically waving his arms. He grunted and the trio started walking toward him. *Great. Three against one, two... eleven, twelve. Three against twelve. Really?*

Nazeera noticed there were only two pairs of open seats. Her parents quickly grabbed two and like musical chairs, she sat in one of the remaining open seats. The seat next to her was not open for very long as Rehana came and sat next to her. "Good evening, Nazeera. You're looking very lovely tonight."

"Thank you, Aunty. You look lovely too." Nazeera had spoken the truth, Rehana was looking lovely. She wore a pale yellow sari with a sparkling flower filigree along the edge. She seemed especially cheerful today.

"So, you had told me you had completed University. Where did you attend school and what degree did you receive?"

"I have a degree in English Literature from the University of Poona."

"*Aacha*. But I thought I overheard at tea that you're still taking classes."

"Yes, Aunty, I'm taking a class in Interior Decorating."

"Oh, are you getting a second degree?"

"No. I just thought it would be a good class to take since I hope to run a household one day. I thought I should know how to decorate the ... interior. Unfortunately, it turns out, this class is mostly about flower arranging." They shared a laugh, and Rehana returned to her seat next to Farid. Nazeera noticed he was looking pale and sipping something reluctantly through a long straw.

The seat next to Nazeera did not remain empty for long. As she watched Farid greet Rehana, a tall pregnant woman approached her. The woman introduced herself as Nadia, Amir's younger sister. She collapsed into the cane chair. After some pleasantries, she asked Nazeera if she was a good cook.

"Um," Nazeera said as she recalled her latest cooking episode with Ammi and Akbar, "I am taking lessons. I just recently learned how to make *Kofta* Curry."

"*Aacha*. Good." Nadia replied with a relieved smile, "That's a wonderful dish. What else can you cook?"

Nazeera tried to recall her other cooking lessons but all that came to mind was her mother teaching her how to make eggs. She straightened her back and proudly said, "I can cook eggs three different ways." They discussed the three different ways for a few minutes.

"Excellent, my dear. Have a pleasant evening." Nadia awkwardly stood up and returned to her seat. Nazeera blinked her eyes a few times to shake the interrogation feeling from her bones, and motioned to the waiter for a soft drink. He brought her a Coca-Cola, but she was only able to take two sips before the adjacent seat was occupied again.

"Nazeera?" the lady asked. She stood with her hands folded in front of her. "My name is Bandra, Amir's eldest sister. My husband

Salim is over there." She pointed to a lone gentlemen sipping a brown drink with ice cubes. He noticed Bandra pointing at him and he held his glass aloft in a sort of greeting response. "Have you ever left home?"

"No, Aunty, I have not. I have never left my parent's home. My elder brothers both were sent to boarding schools, but I remained at home with my parents."

"Humph! Have you ever taken care of household?"

"No, Aunty, I just finished my University degree."

"I see... but you know how to sew, right?"

"Just a little, Aunty. I know how to make petticoats."

"*Bas.* Enough." Bandra exclaimed as she threw her hands into the air. She abruptly turned, stormed across the lawn, and resumed her seat next to her husband. She took a long sip from her glass and started conversing covertly with him.

Sipping her soda, Nazeera glanced around the cricket grounds, absorbing the scene from this angle. The monsoon rains last month had encouraged the bougainvilleas to bloom. The pink and white flowers were climbing everything, including the trellis near the stairway leading to the upper observation area.

The waft of the jasmine in the nearby flowerpots was intoxicating. She closed her eyes, and inhaled the perfume. Her lips parted, and she inhaled again. *What an enchanting evening!* Blinking her eyes open, she become aware of Amir's mother slowly walking across the horseshoe sitting area to her side.

"Hello, Aunty, nice to see you again," Nazeera said in perfect Hindi. She initially seemed pleased by Nazeera's greeting, but, then frowned. *Why? Maybe I should've let Aunty speak first. All this formality!*

"How are you this evening?" Shakila asked, dropping into the cane chair next to her.

"I was just enjoying the fragrance of the jasmine. I find them so enchanting."

"So, you like flowers?"

"Yes, Aunty, very much. I would love to have a garden one day. I like jasmine, but the bougainvilleas are my favorite."

Shakila leaned back in her seat and seemed to need a moment of rest before she started her questions. Nazeera took this opportunity to take another sip of soda. "What does your father do?"

She was a bit taken back by this question. The Ambassador should have already told Amir's family about her family. He was the matchmaker after all. "Well, my father," she started looking in his direction, "works in the government office. He was the collector in Poona until just recently."

"*Aacha*," She nodded knowingly, as if confirming something she already knew. "Do you know how to cook?"

"*Ji, huh*," Nazeera responded proudly. She was going to respond she knew how to cook an egg three ways but upon further thought, she suddenly recalled two more ways. She added, "*Ji, huh*, Aunty, I can cook an egg five different ways." *That should impress her, right? Maybe, I should have paid more attention to my mother's instructions!*

"Have you travelled much?" Shakila asked with a slight head bobble.

"Well, Aunty, as I just said, my father works for the government. So, as required, we have moved every three to four years. I have travelled through most of Northern India."

Shakila leaned back again in her chair as if the correspondence was too much for her. After a moment, they both watched the slight commotion on the other side of the horseshoe. Nazeera's brother, Aziz, walked across the lawn and stood next to their parents as one of the waiters moved a cane chair from a nearby group to their area. "I see your brother has joined us. What's his name?"

"His name is Aziz. He is three years my senior." Nazeera replied. They both continued glancing in his direction. He finally noticed they were watching him, and waved to them. Nazeera was very surprised to see him. He had been extended invitations to these courtship meetings for months, but this was the first one he had attended in almost four weeks. She wanted to ask him what made him show up tonight, but that would have to wait.

"What does he do for a living?"

"He's an engineer. He works for a British company that makes engines."

The older lady reached forward and patted Nazeera's hand. "*Theek hai*," she said with a head bobble. Groaning as she stood up, she said good-bye, and slowly walked back to her seat next to her youngest son.

Amir looked from his mother to Nazeera and smiled. *What a pleasant smile*, she thought. She smiled back at him. Suddenly her heart began to beat a little faster. He was watching her. *What is he thinking?*

She took another sip of her soda, and another woman approached. "Hello, I'm Nilofer, Amir's older sister. It's nice to meet you. I have just a few questions. You have graduated college, no?"

"Yes, I graduated a few months ago...."

"And, you have two brothers?" She seemed so excited about asking her questions she had cut off Nazeera's answers. Was she verifying information they already knew or did the Ambassador not tell them everything?

"Correct. My brother Aziz is over there," she pointed in his direction, "and my eldest brother Hamid is in Delhi." She didn't want to offer any additional explanation about Hamid. There was no need to get into that now. It would come out if Amir was serious about marrying her. *How much do they already know?*

"*Aacha*," she responded as if the answer didn't matter. She paused for a moment and then asked, "Do you know how to sew?"

Embarrassed to admit she only knew how to make petticoats, she shyly said, "No, Aunty, I don't know how to sew." Nazeera was waiting for the cooking question next. She was going to say she knows how to make *Bombil*. *Well, she has a good recipe.*

"I can tell you speak good Hindi. Do you also speak good English?"

"Yes, Aunty, I'm fluent in English."

Nilofer hurriedly stood up and scurried off with her answers. Nazeera was alone for only a moment when the waiter came to her side and offered her a *samosa*. She was famished with all these questions, so she took a *samosa* and a spoonful of tamarind chutney. The group must have been watching her eat because as soon as she took the last bite of the *samosa* Rehana sat down next to her.

"Nice evening, isn't it?" she started.

Nazeera swallowed the last bite of pastry and potato and responded, "Yes, Aunty, enchanting evening."

"I was just wondering if you know how to cook?"

The answer to this question was apparently very important. She didn't want to be deceitful, as she only knew a few dishes, so she responded, "Well, Aunty, I only know a few things."

"And you speak fluent English."

"Yes, Aunty, I was taught in English convent schools. My parents thought they were better than the local schools. So, I learned to speak fluent English."

Rehana was about to ask another questions when she saw Farid double over in pain and nearly fall out of his chair. "Oh, my! Farid!!" Rushing to his side, she clutched his hand. A passing waiter laid his tray down to helped Farid rise to his feet. The waiter, Amir, and surprisingly Aziz helped the couple to their car.

When the commotion was done, Amir came and sat down next to Nazeera. "Good evening, Nazeera."

"Good evening, Amir," she blushed and kept her eyes downcast. *A good Indian girl is demure.* She kept repeating this over and over in her head. She had that message drilled into her head by both the convent schools and her own mother.

"Please, look at me," Amir said as he softly touched her chin with his fingertip, and tilted her face toward him. Their eyes met, and she blushed, "You're looking lovely tonight." He dropped his hand, "Rehana took Farid to the hospital. He hasn't been feeling well for a few days now."

"Oh, my! I hope he'll be alright," she genuinely said.

"He's a great brother. Very patient."

She smiled coyly and flirted her long eyelashes. His eyes twinkled, and he opened his mouth as if he was about to say something. He closed it, and just kept smiling, reaching for her hand instead. Winding his fingers around hers, they noticed Salim approach and stand by Amir's side. *Go away,* Nazeera thought, *I want to talk to Amir alone.* Reluctantly, he released her fingers and said good-bye. Salim sat down and cleared his throat, "I have been asked to find out if you speak English fluently."

Nazeera cast her eyes down, and replied in perfect English, "Yes, Uncle, I do."

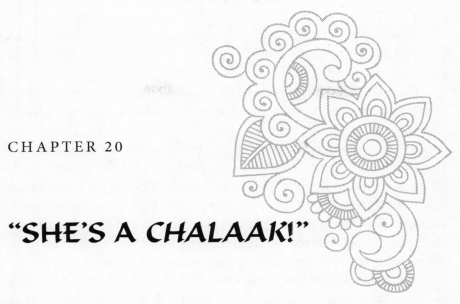

CHAPTER 20

"SHE'S A CHALAAK!"

Farid and Rehana returned from the hospital to a flat full of anxious family. The dinner party had dispersed soon after they left, with Bandra insisting to the Khan's that the family was too concerned about Farid to think about socializing.

Amir agreed they had mostly asked their questions, but he wanted to spend more time with Nazeera. He apologized to her parents for the abrupt ending to the evening, and asked if he could walk with them back to their flat. Thankfully, Nazeera agreed. It was a short walk, but it gave him ten more minutes with her. Ten precious minutes. They talked about the flowers and the weather. The conversation was not important. He just wanted to be near her.

During the three hour wait for Farid to return, the women nervously chattered as they drank Babu's bitter tea. Salim and Nadir both returned home giving different reasons. The noise level in the living room rose as the ladies tried to talk above each other. Covering his ears, Amir sought solace on the veranda. There he was free to recall the short walk with the Khan's, how Nazeera smelled and the shape of her face. He was worried about his brother too, but he knew there was nothing he could do at that moment to help.

Suddenly, the front door opened and a pale man leaning against his wife hobbled into the hallway.

"What's wrong, Farid?"

"Did they run tests?"

"What did the doctor say?"

"Is it an ulcer?"

The barrage of questions nearly knocked the couple over as they barely stepped into the flat. Rehana put up her hand, and simply said, "*Ache* minute."

Following the pair into the living room, like paparazzi following a Bollywood movie star, they allowed Farid to ease into the high-back chair, recently vacated by Mummy. Amir had heard the commotion and joined the frantic group. He watched as Rehana scurried to the bedroom and brought out a blanket placing it over her husband's legs and torso. Farid seemed to relax a bit and closed his eyes. She ordered Babu to bring Farid a glass of water and herself a fresh cup of tea.

Once Farid had taken a few sips of water, and Rehana had added the milk and sugar cubes to her tea, she sat down on the arm rest of the chair and announced the doctors believe he has kidney stones.

The questions as to what to do bombarded them again and Rehana sighed. Amir thought he could read her expression, "*Too much family*".

She waited for the questions to cease, then added there was nothing they could do other than to give him pain medicine and water, and wait for the stones to pass. This could take several days and the pain would get worse before it got better.

The family was amazed something so small could cause so much pain. Bandra insisted her doctor could give better care. What kind of doctor allows his patient to suffer so? Nadia suggested Farid drink hot water to dissolve the stones. Even Mummy gave her advice. She insisted Rehana rub Tiger Balm on his torso. The family favorite ointment always worked.

The suggestions bantered about the group for several minutes before Farid put up his hand, and weakly announced, "*Bas*. Enough. Let's talk about something else. What happened with the girl?"

The conversation quickly changed to that evening. The room was filled with their observations:

"She's a great cook – she can cook eggs five different ways."

"She told me *three* different ways."

"She told me she can't cook!"

"She can't sew!"

"She sews her own petticoats."

"She's travelled all over India."

"She has never left her parents home."

In a huff, Bandra said, "It seems her stories are very inconsistent." Folding her arms in front of her, "She just told each of you what you wanted to her. No one knows the truth. Amir, she's got you bewitched. She's nothing but a *chalaak*! Scam artist! My Dilshad is a lovely woman. Much better choice."

"We must have made her nervous," Nadia defended. "There were all of us and only her."

"No, she's a *chalaak*!" Bandra repeated with a dismissive wave of her hand, "She's cunning, this one! Like a snake! You cannot trust her!"

"*Bas! Bas!*" They all looked toward Amir who had yelled at them in Hindi - something they all knew he rarely does. He stood next to Farid's chair with frustrated eyes staring at them and his fingers on his temples. "I think she figured out what you all were trying to do, and outsmarted you all! She purposely told you different answers to confuse you." He laughed to himself, "She's got spirit!"

Mummy shook her head, "Are you sure she wasn't tricking us?"

"*Ji, huh*, Mummy," Amir repeated. "She is exactly what I'm looking for. None of the other girls have her spirit." He turned to Bandra, "Not even Dilshad."

Bandra groaned and started to protest, but Amir put up his hand to stop her. She ignored him and complained, "But, you haven't even given Dilshad a real chance. When are you meeting her again?"

"We're meeting Dilshad for dinner tomorrow at the CCI. We can do the same questioning with her and then Amir can decide," Rehana defended. "As for Nazeera, I think Amir is right. She outsmarted us. I've chatted with her a few times. She's no snake."

"Um, I'm confused," Nilofer piped in. "We've only been talking about Nazeera and Dilshad. Wasn't there a third girl? What's her name? Cha... something?"

Rehana leaned toward Nilofer, whispering, "Let's not talk about that now. I'll tell you about her later."

"No," Amir declared, "Let's just talk about it now. Everyone wants to know everything and give their two bits. So let's update the group on the events of last night." Amir slumped onto the sofa and sighed. "Well, the four of us met Chandni and her parents at The Willingdon Club for dinner last night. As usual, we arrived a few minutes early so we could ensure we got a good table."

"… They were already there," Rehana interrupted. "We all sat down for dinner and it started out just fine. The servers brought the food and walked around the table offering the different plates. You know, like they normally do." Rehana paused to make sure all the ladies were following her set-up. "One of the waiters was standing between Amir and Chandni. Amir was telling a story about something and he gestured with his hands." She demonstrated his wild hand movements nearly knocking Nadia in the face.

"Oh, my! What happened?" Nadia asked with concern.

"I accidentally smacked the server and the chicken curry poured all over Chandni," Amir admitted.

"She started crying," Rehana continued the story. "I think she over-reacted because she was scared to tell us she had just received a job offer for the Bombay-London route. She wanted to take the promotion but that would mean she wouldn't be able to marry Amir. She was nervous to tell us."

"This one is the stewardess, no?" Nilofer asked trying to keep up with the list of girls. Amir nodded.

"Fine. So Chandni is out. That makes it simpler." Bandra summarized, "You meet Dilshad tomorrow night at the CCI. We question her as we did the girl tonight, and then you can decide which one you want to marry. The school teacher or the scam artist."

CHAPTER 21

Wednesday, August 17

"WE ALWAYS
TRAVEL FIRST CLASS"

Ammi rushed into her daughter's room dragging the telephone and its long extension cord along with her. They had meant to call Amir's family that morning to check on Farid, but the telephone call they received changed all that.

Nazeera was telling Shanti what she wanted to wear today. The fresh air and discussions from the night before had made them all sleep a bit more soundly and well into mid-morning. It was now close to eleven and Nazeera was just now getting ready for the day.

"*Beta*," her mother blurted, "The Abdullah family just phoned. They are in Bombay! They travelled all the way from Hyderabad, and want to speak with your father." Ammi started giggling, "I think they're coming to present a proposal!"

The Abdullah family. Habib. She had met him twice before. He was a handsome man - tall enough, slim enough and wealthy enough. He had recently returned from a University in Canada, either Montreal or Vancouver, she couldn't remember which. They had been able to converse, under chaperone, a few times and he seemed fine, though a bit arrogant. There was something else that bothered her about him, but she couldn't put her finger on it.

"*Juldi, juldi*! Hurry up and get dressed!" Ammi insisted, "Wear your bright green sari and the earrings we gave you for your birthday last year. You know, the ones with the little emeralds."

Nazeera's heart began to flutter. Maybe she's right and this is a proposal. After all, the family had come here from Hyderabad. That was a good sign. Hyderabad wasn't too far away, maybe a day's journey by train. Or, maybe they came by airplane. That was faster, but much more expensive. If she remembered correctly, flying would be more consistent with what she knew of them.

Hastily, she changed plans of what she was going to wear that day, throwing the sky blue sari onto the bed. With Shanti's help, she wrapped the bright green silk sari around her waist and deftly flipped the sari *pallu* over her shoulder. After searching through her various pairs of footwear, Shanti found the perfect *chappels* for her to wear. She was hurriedly screwing the tiny bolt on her birthday earrings in her left ear when her mother returned.

"Are you ready yet?" her mother said out of breath as she entered the room. She had also quickly changed clothes, without Shanti's help. She was now wearing an indigo sari with stamped steel-gray accents. She had said she would wear this sari only to receive Nazeera's proposal. She had been saving it for the past three years... waiting.

Her mother had bought it at a little shop in Mangaldas Market. It was a very expensive sari due to the new fashion of stamping patterns on the edge of the sari. Well, new, three years ago. Daddy had thought it was too extravagant, but Ammi insisted she wanted something special to remember the occasion. It was an important occasion after all!

"Ammi," Nazeera said as she stood up to get a full body look at her mother, "You look divine! That color is wonderful on you. Do you really think this will be a proposal? He may just want to meet again."

Her mother smiled a grand smile, creasing the layers of powder on her face. Bobbling her head, "Yes, *Beta*, I'm positive he will bring a proposal."

The ladies floated into the living room where her father and brother were waiting. They wore suits and fashionable narrow neckties. Nazeera was surprised to see them both in the middle of the day, but her mother said she phoned them and insisted they be present for the proposal.

"You look lovely, *Beta*," her father admired as he flipped down the newspaper. "Those earrings look perfect. Are they the ones we gave you for your birthday?"

"Yes, Daddy, they are," Nazeera gleamed. The earrings did match the sari perfectly. *Is it worth sitting down and getting wrinkled?*

She spotted Aziz on the settee sipping a lemonade. Taking small steps to avoid her sari coming undone, she crossed the room and stood by his side, "Can't stay away from me?"

Aziz looked up into her eyes and simply said, "Yup." He told her later that since it was a slow day at work, he decided to take the afternoon off to meet Habib. Especially since his mother thought he was presenting a proposal of marriage to his little sister.

Jabbar, Habib's father and head of the Abdullah family, had said they would arrive at noon. It was now a quarter past noon. They were late. Ammi sat down on the sofa, patting the seat next to her. Nazeera took the hint and complied keeping a small distance from her mother.

They waited for twenty minutes. It seemed like a lot longer because of the loud ticking of the mantle clock. Tick. Tick. Tick. Any conversation that was started was short lived.

In the first ten minutes of their wait, Ammi yelled from her spot on the sofa for soft drinks. Shanti came into the living room carrying a wooden tray with empty glasses and bottles of Duke's Mangola and Duke's Lemonade. She seemed unusually anxious. *Is she nervous or excited?*

In the second ten minutes, Ammi shouted again from her throne on the sofa. Akbar came running from the kitchen at her beckoning. She insisted he check again to make sure the Nehru tea set was ready.

They had two tea sets consisting of a tea pot, creamer, sugar bowl and matching cups and saucers. The tea set they used for everyday use, and casual entertaining, was cream colored with small royal blue flowers. The other tea set was used only for special occasions. It consisted of a tall white tea pot with gold trim along the handle, spout and base. A solid gold band encircled the lid and the top of the pot just where the handle met the tea pot. The bottom half of the vessel was solid white, while the area between the solid gold band

and the imaginary center line was filled with a band of silver filigree and a band of gold filigree on a yellow background. The matching creamer and sugar bowl were equally stunning. Rather than use the matching serving platter, Ammi insisted Akbar polish the silver tray so the cups and saucers could be carried out with the tea pot.

The latter tea set had been nicknamed the "Nehru tea set", because it had been used when they entertained Prime Minister Jawaharlal Nehru on his visit to their home in Ahmednagar a few years ago. As the then collector of the town, her father had played host to both the prime minister and the governor at the opening of a local school. When they needed a place to have their afternoon tea, Daddy had invited the elite group into his own home.

A photograph had been taken for the local paper of her parents sitting next to Mr. Nehru with the three kids standing behind them. Ammi wanted to remember that moment forever, so she had the photograph framed and placed on the living room coffee table for all to see.

As ordered, Akbar returned with the Nehru tea set on the freshly polished silver tray. The tea set was cleaned to the point of sparkling and looked very much ready for the guests. Ammi simply nodded her satisfaction.

Everything was set. Tick. Tick. Tick. The sound of the mesmerizing clock ticking was finally broken by the ringing of the doorbell. Akbar spryly walked to the door and looked to her father for approval to open it. He received the nod and the group stood up and straightened out their clothes. Nazeera took a few breaths and exhaled slowly to try to calm her nerves. This was it!

The door opened and the procession started. First was Habib's father, followed by two men that looked like they were Habib's brothers, and then finally Habib. Introductions were made to Aziz as the group had not met him before today. Nazeera sat in her previous spot next to her mother on the sofa. She thought it would be the perfect spot to hear the whole conversation. She didn't want to miss a word.

"How was your journey?" Daddy started.

With a bobble of the head, Habib's father, Jabbar, replied, "Long journey. Very long. Over six hours on the train. But we travelled first class, so it was not too uncomfortable."

"*Ji, huh*. Yes. We always travel first class," blurted Habib. Nazeera was sufficiently impressed. That was, until he added, "Why sit next to a dirty peasant when you can pay to have someone serve you hot tea, right?" He laughed awkwardly hoping others would join him in the laugh. No one did.

Aziz change the subject. "So, Habib, since I missed the first few meetings, why don't you tell me a bit about you and your family?"

"*Theek hai*," Habib said with a dismissive wave of his hand. He cleared his throat and turning to face Aziz began, "I'm the only son of Jabbar. My mother is from the Nizam family, very well known in Hyderabad. Very well known. She had been married to my father's brother for many years. But after he died, she married my father. I have two half-brothers. This is Shazad," he turned to indicate the older brother with gray temples. Turning to the other brother, "and my brother Adham. Between them they have six children with one more coming soon."

Habib continued, glancing in Nazeera's direction, "I'm just now returning from studying Business at the University in Vancouver. I'm ready to marry and set up household."

"Would you be setting up household in Hyderabad?" Aziz questioned.

"*Ji, nahih*. No. I'm planning to live here in Bombay. My father and I are opening a shop here." Nazeera began to get excited. If she married him, she would stay in Bombay. *Yeah!*

The conversation continued about Habib's schooling and life in Vancouver. Abruptly, Jabbar turned to her father and asked, "Where do we pray?" Strict Muslims pray five times a day. It is one of the pillars of Islam. The faithful face Mecca, sit in a prone position and bow to pray with their forehead touching the ground in respect to Allah. Men and women pray in separate areas, rarely together. So, Jabbar probably expected a quiet room away from Nazeera and Ammi.

"Come this way," her father motioned as he lead them to her parent's bedroom. Her father also prayed and had prayer rugs already on the floor facing Mecca. He did not pray five times a day as these faithful did, but today he joined them in the prayers. So did Aziz.

The ladies glanced at each other. They said their prayers occasionally, but did not get down on the ground each time. Today, they turned and faced Mecca and said their prayers enunciating each word carefully. They were good Muslims but did not follow this pillar strictly. In fact, Nazeera considered herself a practical Muslim.

When the prayer time was over, the men rejoined the women in the living room. They seemed solemn but refreshed. As they settled back into their seats, the older brother, Shazad, asked Ammi, "I noticed neither of you wear *burkhas*. You know, the full length outfit that covers all but the face of a woman."

Ammi opened her mouth to respond, but at that moment, Akbar entered the room carrying the polished silver tray with the Nehru tea set. He had four tea cups filled with steeped tea and began circling the group offering each guest a cup of tea, the milk and the sugar.

A moment later, Shanti entered the living room carrying a wooden tray. She silently followed Akbar, offering each guest a piece of *barfi* to accompany their tea. When they had completed the circuit - Akbar had to return to the kitchen for the second set of four tea cups - they placed their trays on the table in front of the sofa and returned to their at-ready positions just outside the kitchen opening. Akbar paused only a moment before vacating it and retreating into the kitchen.

Observing Habib, Nazeera noticed his expression changed when Shanti entered the room. Both he and Adham seem to watch Shanti's movements with interest. Habib pursed his lips as he took a piece of a coconut treat from her tray. Adham wet his lips seductively as she laid the tray on the table. She ignored them both. They continued to gawk at her as she crossed the room to stand near the kitchen opening. *What are they thinking?*

Rolling her eyes, Nazeera said philosophically, "I believe one's actions speak louder than one's words." She was not a fan of hypocrites, not since the visit from the Omar family a few years ago.

Mr. Omar was a professor at her University in Poona and a friend of her father's from the mosque. He and his family needed a place to stay for a few weeks, so her father generously offered space in their Poona house. The Omar family of eight slept in the two bedrooms while the Khan family slept in the living room. Rather than be grateful, Mr. Omar constantly criticized Daddy for his liberal views - allowing Nazeera and her mother to wear saris rather than *burkhas*, allowing his daughter to attend University, and even allowing her to drive a scooter!

Nazeera was beginning to feel guilty until she witnessed Mr. Strict-Muslim, fondling a woman at the University. A woman that was not his wife! In fact, she was a student of his! What a hypocrite! What a dog!

Since the day she saw Mr. Omar kissing a student, she discounted every word he had said. His poor wife and children! There was no way she was going to marry a man that said one thing and did another. No way!

Ammi shot her daughter a look as if to say, "Please be quiet". Realizing she had blurted her thoughts aloud, Nazeera bit her lower lip but continued to watch both of the brothers. *Are they eyeing Shanti or is it my imagination?*

Habib changed his focus to the tray of sweets, but Adham intensified his glare at her servant. She watched as Shanti began frantically glancing around the room. She looked to the sofa, then the mantle clock, then the front door. She saw her peek to see if Adham was still staring at her. When the two of them made eye contact, Shanti quickly glanced away from him toward her father to see if he had noticed any of this exchange. He had not. She glanced away again to the wall and finally rested her eyes on her own feet.

"So, you do not wear the *burkha*?" Jabbar summarized with a slight head bobble.

"Shanti, could you please pour another cup of tea for everyone," her father ordered, possibly trying to change the subject. He added, "Please everyone, try the sweets. I especially like the coconut *barfi*. It has just the right amount of *ghee* and sugar."

Nervously approaching the group, Shanti walked behind the chairs and entered the semi-circle between her father and Adham. As she poured the tea, Nazeera stared as Adham was following her with interest. She refilled Jabbar's cup and then Habib's. As she moved toward Shazad, her sari *pallu* slipped from her shoulder allowing a brief glimpse at her neckline. The two younger brothers exchanged wry smiles and nodded knowingly.

Panicked, Shanti quickly flipped the sari fabric back over her shoulder and poured the cupful for the eldest brother. Her hands seemed to shake as she continued the tea service. When she had refilled everyone's tea cup, she swiftly retreated into the kitchen nearly tripping on her own sari as she scurried. *Is that a tear in her eye?*

They sipped their hot tea in silence. Tick. Tick. Tick.

After finishing his tea, Jabbar sat forward in his seat, placing his tea cup and saucer next to the tray of sweets. "This is not just a social visit, Rahim. We have some business to discuss." Nazeera's heart started to beat faster. *This is it!*

"This is not unexpected," her father replied, "please proceed." He said these words very calmly, but Nazeera noticed his voice was quivering. *Is he nervous?*

Jabbar declared turning to indicate Ammi and Nazeera, "Business should not be conducted with ladies present."

All eyes turned to the sofa and the conversation paused as the group waited for the ladies to leave the flat. She had never been excused from a room like that. "Humph!" Ammi said as she frustratingly pushed the button to call the lift. "I guess we will have to wait to hear the details!" They trudged down the block to the CCI being careful not to get their precious outfits soiled. After they found seats at the snack bar, they each ordered a mango *lassi* to calm their nerves. They slowly sipped their drinks as they watched the youngsters dive into the swimming pool.

A small group of cricket players approached the snack bar and ordered some drinks and snacks. They were noisily discussing the West Indies cricket team's tour of England. The two teams had just finished their fourth match yesterday and the two men were debating if England's Ollie Milburn's elbow injury would force him to retire from the sport altogether. The ladies shook their heads at each other and smiled. They would need to wait.

After a long two hours of sipping mango *lassis* and nibbling on Bombay snack mix, Daddy and Aziz joined the ladies at the CCI. Her father seemed solemn and stood behind Nazeera's chair. He began to stroke her hair, "Well, they did propose marriage."

Ammi's cheeks turned rosy red with excitement, "Very good. And you like him, no? You like him very much." Nazeera did like him.

He seemed like a nice enough guy. Well, except for the gawking he did at Shanti. *What was that about?*

Aziz waved to the waiter to bring them a round of Coca-Cola and then he sat down next to Nazeera, "He seems very interested."

"*Aacha, w*hat else did they say?" Ammi looked like she was going to burst with excitement.

Sighing, her father sat down in the empty chair between his two ladies. "Let me tell you the whole proposal. Habib does like Nazeera very much and wants to marry her. They are fine with her running a boutique or performing some sort of charity work as long as it does not interfere with her running the household." *So far so good. I could run the boutique as I always wanted. Maybe selling fashionable saris or something more modern like the flower prints they're wearing in London and America.*

Daddy cleared his throat. That was usually a sign he was nervous about saying something. *What is he nervous about?* Taking Nazeera's hand in his, he continued, "They will not require you to wear a *burkha* in Bombay, but all the women in the Hyderabad household wear it. Consequently, you will need to wear one whenever you visit there." *An odd request, but one I can live with.*

After a pause, he added, "And as Habib's father said, you would be living here in Bombay." He paused again. Nazeera nodded, yes, she knew that. *Why is Daddy stalling?* "On Malabar Hill."

"Ooh! That's a very nice part of town. Very nice." Ammi encouraged with a head bobble, "You'll have great views of the Arabian Sea. And you'll be far away from the filth. Very good! Very good!"

Daddy looked annoyed by his wife's interruptions. He squeezed Nazeera's hand and looked into her eyes, "And as part of the dowry, we would supply the furnished flat."

"As part of the dowry?" Nazeera repeated returning his strong gaze. "What do you mean? What else is in the dowry?"

He hesitated, then added, "A car and driver."

Nazeera's head spun. A furnished flat on Malabar Hill would cost a lot of money, a few *lackhs* for sure. She knew her father had not saved a few hundred thousand *rupees* for her dowry. Government employees had perks, but they didn't make a lot of money. And a car with a driver! That would mean an annual payment for the rest of her life. This dowry demand was outrageous!

There was no way she was going to let her darling father go into substantial debt for the rest of his life just to get her married. If Habib's family was so wealthy, why couldn't they just buy the flat. And a car! Oh, this was too much!

Daughters are expensive in India. Parents are often forced to pay a dowry to get one married. So, if the parents don't have much money, the daughters are often married into poor families or families that treat them poorly. In an effort to try and combat this abuse, the government recently outlawed the concept of dowry. It was hoped it would reduce the number of women beaten or even killed because a dowry demand was not fully paid or paid on time. It has helped some women, but in most cases it has just been renamed "wedding gift".

But, what Habib's family was asking for wasn't an extravagant wedding gift like jewelry or clothes. They were asking for a lifestyle dowry. An expensive demand for him to marry her. "First class" he and his father had kept repeating.

"As you know, *Beta*, I don't have that kind of money saved," her father shared with his head down. He looked up at Nazeera with a half-smile, "but I will make a loan if this is the marriage you want."

Nazeera shook her head, "*Ji, nahih*, No! There is no way I want you to go into debt to marry me to someone." She leaned forward and gave her father a strong hug. "I see this dowry demand as extortion. You shouldn't have to bribe someone to marry me. I know I'm a beautiful woman and if Habib, or anyone else, wants to marry me, they're not getting a dowry! Not a single *rupee*!"

Aziz just smiled. He stood up and excused himself, saying he needed to use the restroom. She watched him leave their little group and realized a few people were staring at them. She needed to calm down. *Breathe in and out, in and out, in and out.*

A bit more calmly, she added, "I would have enjoyed running a boutique, but not at this high cost. I will not marry him."

Her parents both stared at her. *Did they really expect me to say "yes"? Are they glad I said "no"?* Ammi must have been surprised by her defiance, "Are you sure, *Beta*? He seems like a nice boy."

She added a head bobble, "Very, very handsome. And this marriage would give you a good life, *Beta*. A very good life."

She had to admit, Habib was a handsome man. Good body and movie star good looks. Ammi obviously liked him. But how could she marry a man forcing her father into the poor house? And to support his own lavish lifestyle. No way!

"Ammi, I will not allow you or Daddy to suffer for me. If Habib wants to marry me, he can lower his dowry demand."

Aziz returned and propped his feet up on an empty chair. "If they lowered the dowry demand, would you really reconsider the proposal?"

Nazeera reflected for a moment. *What does he mean by that? Did he also seen Habib gawking at Shanti? Was he really gawking? Maybe he was just noticing her hairdo or a spot on her clothing. Did it mean he had a wandering eye and he would cheat on her?* For now, she would give him the benefit of the doubt, "Yes, I would consider it."

"*Theek hai*," her father said a bit relieved and picking up a cold *samosa*. He motioned to the waiter to bring some fresh hot ones. "I will phone Jabbar when we return to the flat. In the meantime, let's enjoy this time as a family. It is nice to have Aziz here."

"Yes, *Beta*," Ammi said placing her hand on her son's knee, "We don't see enough of you."

CHAPTER 22

Thursday, August 18

"SHE CAN'T SAY NO"

The dinner with Dilshad had gone very well. Amir listened to every word she had said, and discovered she was a very interesting woman. She would make a wonderful wife to someone. Just not to him.

He admitted she was everything he was looking for in a wife - beautiful, self-confident, educated. But, something just didn't feel right. She seemed to be trying too hard to please him. She had said nothing to offend him or anger him. In fact, she had laughed at all his jokes, said all the right things, and even smiled at all the right times. But, it all seemed fake, forced.

When they were alone for a moment, he stared into Dilshad's dazzling brown eyes, hoping to find a hint of affection. Instead, he found a desperate woman. He could grow to love her, but it was hard to build a marriage without love or hope.

These feeling were hard for Amir to put into words, and Bandra had a very hard time accepting them. She pleaded with him to meet Dilshad one more time. But, Amir knew the clock was ticking. He was supposed to leave in ten days and he still had to propose and marry someone!

After meeting with Dilshad, he was determined to marry Nazeera. She had spirit and was gorgeous. He could imagine a life with her. Only her. If she said "no", well... no, she can't say no. He would convince her himself. He would propose himself.

"Farid," Amir started his conversation slowly as to not disturb his ailing brother, "What are some good restaurants around here? I want to ask Nazeera to dinner."

Amir's older brother smiled. He had not seen Amir this excited in a long time, "Well, there are several around here. Um... there are the restaurants in the hotels, like Ziya we visited a few days back. There is Talk of the Town near Marine Drive. That's a very popular place. Oh, there's The Bayview Restaurant, The Ritz Hotel Restaurant. Hmm, there's Sumrat, but that's vegetarian."

"No vegetarian. Isn't Talk of the Town very crowded? I want something a bit quieter."

"Quieter? I've been out of the loop for the last few days. What is the status of the love search?"

"Well, brother, I've met all eleven women and have selected Nazeera. I'm planning to propose to her tonight! That's why the restaurant must be quiet and special."

"*Kya*? What? You are going to propose? Amir, that's not how it's done. You need to send a formal proposal to her father. He will consider it and once you receive their acceptance, *then* you can talk to her about it."

Amir shook his head, "I know that's the Indian way. But, I want to ask her myself... the American way."

"Highly unusual," Farid replied. After a moment he added, "If you insist on proposing yourself, you should go to the restaurant at The Ritz Hotel. It's fairly close and I think there is music tonight. You two looked great dancing together at the CCI. You could have a moment alone with her on the dance floor."

"That's a great idea!" Amir exclaimed. He could propose to her on the dance floor like the American's do. But, he would not get down on one knee. Well, maybe he would.

Amir called The Ritz Hotel and confirmed they did have dancing that evening. He made dinner reservations for seven assuming Nazeera's parents would come along to chaperone. He informed Rehana and his mother of his intentions and though his mother agreed with Farid that this was "highly unusual", they went along with Amir's plan. She did however, declare she was too tired to attend the dinner tonight. The late evenings over the last week had made her weak and she needed to retire to bed early. He called The Ritz Hotel again, changing the reservation to six. *Okay, now, to get Nazeera to accept the dinner invitation.*

Nervously, he dialed the number Rehana had given him. He heard the phone ring once… twice… then he hung up. Boy, this was going to be harder than he thought. He dragged the phone onto the veranda and shut the door. Maybe a bit of privacy would help. He picked up the receiver and dialed the numbers again. The phone on the other end began to ring again…once… twice…."Hall-low" a voice said.

"Um, Hello. This is Amir," he gulped, "Is Nazeera at home?" He was half hoping she was not at home. His heart was beating so fast he thought he might faint.

"*Ache* minute," the male voice answered. He must be one of the servants. If it was her father or her brother they would have responded differently. He waited for what seemed like several minutes before the voice came back on the line, "*Ache* minute."

Amir waited patiently as the telephone was handed to Nazeera. He could hear her footsteps and her picking up the receiver, "Hello?"

"Um. Hello, Nazeera. This is Amir" He paused, waiting for her to respond that she remembered him. "I…I would like to invite you and your parents to dinner tonight."

Nazeera paused for several seconds and then responded, "What? Dinner? Oh, that would be fine. When?"

Amir laughed, "Tonight, 8 o'clock." *So far so good*, he thought.

"I'm not sure about tonight. My parents may be busy and I'll need to find a chaperone."

How was a couple supposed to get to know each other with others always eavesdropping. Trying to be helpful, he offered, "My brother and his wife will be coming. They can be the chaperones."

"*Ji, nahih*, No, that will not do." He heard her fingers strumming on a table, "Hmm… I'll see if my brother is available. Otherwise, we'll have to do it another night."

"Okay. I'll plan for you to be there. Call Rehana if you're not able to make it. Good-bye, Naz." Amir added softly, "I hope to see you tonight." He hung up the phone before she could reply. Whew! He was anxious just talking to her on the phone. What if he was too jumpy to say the words tonight. He closed his eyes and exhaled. Well, at least she hasn't said "no" yet.

Smiling, Nazeera replaced the telephone receiver. Amir was still interested in her. Even after all those questions from the other night. And had he just called me "Naz"? A nickname already? Well, he seemed nice enough. One more meeting wouldn't hurt. Then she would decide if she liked him or not. Maybe he could get her mind off of Habib and his demands.

Picking up the telephone receiver, she phoned her brother. He had met Amir once, so hopefully he would be willing to escort her tonight. He had to help her. She really didn't want to ask her parents. They had a huge fight this morning after her father reviewed the latest invoice from her mother's shopping spree. He had left the flat in a huff and didn't return as he normally did for lunch. Nazeera knew when her parents have these fights, they could last for several awkward days.

Aziz was supposed to be at work at this time of the day. But, his secretary said he was at a customer, due to return in a few hours. After two frustrating hours of waiting, Nazeera phoned him again. This time, his secretary politely responded her brother had returned but immediately rushed into an important meeting. Disappointed, she left another message.

Reluctantly knocking on her parent's bedroom door, Nazeera entered the room and informed her mother of the dinner invitation. Ammi was clearly in a bad mood and flipped the back of her hand to shoo Nazeera out the door. There was no way they would escort her tonight.

Promptly one hour later, Nazeera phoned her brother again. The lady on the other end must have guessed it was her, as she said the meeting was almost over before Nazeera even introduced herself. Frantic, she left a third message now stating it was urgent for him to phone her back. It was nearly five o'clock and she still was not sure if she would be able to meet Amir for dinner at eight.

Throwing down the receiver, she stormed from the living room to her bedroom. The room was hot and stuffy. She pulled the cord for the ceiling fan and took out her frustration on the window sill as she lifted it. A slight breeze blew in rustling her hair. She leaned out the window and allow the wind to play with her hair. *Why isn't he calling?*

Nazeera turned from the window and opened her cupboards. The four new saris her mother had purchased, the ones that caused her parent's quarrel this morning, were neatly hanging in her cupboard. *Well, let's see if these saris are worth it*, she said to herself. She lifted each one off the hanger to admire them. A chocolate sari with gold stamping, lovely; a hot pink sari with silver beading, interesting; a *mehndi* green one with some sort of swirls, probably for the wedding ceremonies; and an apricot chiffon sari with yellow and white circles. *This one is obviously for my mother. I would never wear something like that!*

"Hall-low," Akbar's familiar voice said. *I didn't even hear the phone ring. Is it Aziz? Oh, I hope so.* A moment later, Akbar knocked on her bedroom door and announced her brother was indeed on the telephone. Would she like to take the call? Excitedly Nazeera dumped the saris on the bed and yelled, "Yes! I'll take the call!"

Leaping toward the telephone. "Aziz!" she said a little out of breath. "It's about time!"

"Sorry, Ra-Ra." He hadn't called her by that nickname in years. Pinky gave her that nickname so the three cousins could each have silly nicknames. For some reason, her brother used it now. Maybe he was missing her. Yes, he must be missing her as much as she missed him. Could they go back to the way it was before Johara and Hamid changed it all? "I have three messages and my secretary said it was urgent. Are you ill?"

"Aziz, I need a favor," Nazeera spilled, "I need you to be my escort tonight at dinner. Amir will be there. So will Farid and Rehana."

"What about Ammi and Daddy?" he asked.

"They're fighting again. Ammi bought some expensive saris and...and, she's been spending money on those astrologers again."

"What are the *jyotishis* saying now?" he laughed. "Are the stars in alignment for you?"

"The one that came two days ago said I'd be married before I turn twenty-one."

"That's in four months, Ra-Ra. But, really, that's not too hard to imagine. You were offered a proposal yesterday. Ammi needs to stop consulting with these *chalaaks*."

"That's what Daddy said too." Nazeera sighed, "Are you coming to dinner or what? I need to get out of this house!"

"Anything for you," Aziz responded. "Just tell me what time I should be at the flat."

The driver slowed the car at the entrance to The Ritz Hotel. The emerald green and snow white covered canopy was inviting and the pair were impressed by the uniformed bell hop who stood at attention at the top of the stairs. As the car stopped, he descended the steps and opened the car door. Nazeera slid out of the car, using the bell hop's offered hand for leverage. Aziz hustled around the car and took his sister's arm as he led her up the cherry red carpet to the glass doors.

Stopping at the maitre' d desk, Aziz asked for Amir's table. The tall lean gentlemen in a white *salwar kameez* type outfit nodded and asked them to follow him. Nazeera lifted her mother's newly purchased hot pink silk sari as Shanti pleated it a bit too long in front. She followed her brother through the weave of white linen topped tables to one near the dance floor. *Great, more dancing.*

The other three guests were already seated and sipping mango *lassi* drinks. Rehana jumped up first and gave both of them welcoming hugs and cheek kisses. She seemed more happy than usual.

Nazeera grinned at her greeting and sat down next to her suitor, with her brother on her right. After the initial introductions, Aziz leaned toward Farid and asked him about his current health. Farid smiled weakly and replied he had just taken some pain medication and was fine for now. Rehana, maybe trying to change the subject, asked where their parents were. The siblings exchanged glances and Aziz just simply said they were busy tonight.

Two more mango *lassi* drinks were ordered as well as a variety of starters. When they were served, Aziz helped himself to the spicy chicken *tikka* while both Farid and Amir began with the fried potato and onion *pakoras*. The gentlemen nibbled on the bite-size servings, licking their lips to savor all the flavors.

The ladies both passed on the starters and sipped their *lassis* instead. Nazeera noticed the *lassi* had a wonderful rich mango flavor just like Akbar's. *They must use fresh mangos. Yum!* She eagerly sipped the drink and was tempted to ask for a second glass. The wait staff must have read her mind as a few seconds after she finished the last sip of *lassi*, a fresh one appeared in front of her. *Impressive!*

The main course dishes were served with the flourish only good restaurants can achieve. The wait staff encircled the table, offered each guest the platter of food, served a generous portion and then silently withdrew. The conversation between the five of them was lively with topics ranging from the weather, to the food, to the latest cricket match. Nazeera observed how well they all got along and began to imagine having other conversations with this group. She was most impressed with Amir. He seemed a bit nervous and didn't speak much, but he paid attention to every word she said and never let his eye stray from their small group. *No wandering eye with him!*

As the dinner plates were being cleared, Amir leaned forward and whispered in Nazeera's ear. She was surprised he was being so forward. No man had ever whispered in her ear before. "Would you like to dance?" There it was. He wanted to dance again. It was a slow song, so maybe he could do his waltz. She glanced quickly at Aziz who gave her a smile and a nod for encouragement.

She followed her suitor silently to the dance floor. Amir took her right hand in his and placed his other hand gently on the small of her back and began to float her about the room. *He actually does know how to waltz! At least he can dance the slow dances. That's something.*

They waltzed in a large circle for several minutes before either of them spoke. His hands felt strong on her waist and he made her feel safe, protected. She was floating on a cloud!

His words brought her crashing back to Earth, "If we marry, I would like for you to work. The cost of living is higher in America."

What did he say? Work? Is he serious? She burst out laughing. "Moi?" she teased in French, "Work?" She turned to face him and he looked very serious. Hmm...maybe he was serious.

"And..." he continued ignoring her previous comment, "I have to return to America soon, so we would need to have the wedding next week."

Nazeera giggled, "It would take at least two weeks to put together my trousseau." She glanced at the table and noticed Aziz and Farid were in a deep discussion about something. Rehana was chatting with a waiter, probably ordering tea and dessert for everyone.

He twirled her around the dance floor for another minute. This was an enchanting dance. An enchanted evening. *Isn't that a song?* He slipped his hand to her lower back and pulled her closer. She tightened her grip around his neck. He smelled like gardenia flowers and hair oil.

But, wait, wasn't he the American? Didn't Mallika marry an American. She backed away suddenly breaking his hold on her, "Do you have any …. emotional attachments?"

"What? You mean, girlfriends?" He asked with a grimace on his face. Nazeera nodded. "No…I dated a few American women but I have no girlfriend."

"No live-in girlfriend? No wife in America?"

"No," he said making eye contact with her. Then he added his quirky smile and said gently, "You would be my one and only wife."

They danced silently for another minute before returning to the table. The trio at the table welcomed them back and they enjoyed their tea and bowls of *pista kulfi*. Nazeera wasn't sure what to think of their conversation. *What is he trying to tell me?* She glanced over to him. Amir looked relieved and eager to end the evening. *Did I say something wrong? What is he expecting?*

They walked toward the front door together. Aziz and Farid had called the drivers and so both cars were waiting to escort them home. They wished each other well and said good-bye. On the way home, Nazeera relayed the conversation she and Amir had on the dance floor. Aziz listened and then summarized, "I think that was his version of a marriage proposal."

Nazeera laughed, "Really? I don't think so. I think he was just trying to make conversation." She looked out the window at the buildings whizzing by, "Did Farid say something to you?"

Turning to his sister, Aziz replied, "Ra-Ra, Farid said Amir really likes you. He likes your spirit and he has chosen you above all the others. You have gone from number eleven to number one. He wants to marry you."

She stared at him for a long moment. *That was a proposal? Really?* She knew the wedding would have to be quick because he was only visiting, but next week? And work? Is that what he was saying? "What do you think?"

"It's not up to me," Aziz responded, "But given what I've seen of him so far, he seems to be good husband material. What does your heart tell you?"

The prospective bride stared out of the window. He was good husband material. He made eye contact with her, treated her with respect, never looked at other women and most importantly, he was not afraid of her wit and self-confidence. In fact, he liked it. She smiled to herself.

They arrived at the Yashodham building. As Aziz exited the car, he called back to Nazeera, "*Chalo*, let's tell Ammi and Daddy."

CHAPTER 23

Friday, August 19

"WAS IT A PROPOSAL?"

Thankfully their parents were asleep when Nazeera and Aziz returned home from the dinner last night. Not wanting to stay, Aziz hugged her good night and returned to his flat a few blocks away. She wished he would have stayed longer as she really wanted to discuss the dinner events with him.

She wasn't sure how to tell her parents of this proposal. Was it a proposal? Aziz said it was, but she so wasn't sure. Amir had not said the word "marry". Well, maybe he would be sending the formal proposal today. In any case, she must tell her parents something this morning.

Changing into a casual blue paisley *salwar kameez*, she haphazardly braided her hair, and took a deep breath. As she entered the dining room she noticed her mother sorting through some envelopes. She seemed to be in a better mood than yesterday. *Let's hope she stays this way. Here we go.*

"Good morning, Ammi," Nazeera said as cheerfully as she could, "*Aape kasee hai*? How are you?"

"Good morning, *Beta*," Ammi responded with a smile. She reached out and touched her daughter's forearm as she sat down next to her, "*Theek hai*. Fine. How was last night?"

"Last night was good." Akbar brought her usual cup of tea and she took a long sip, "Aziz and I had a nice dinner with Amir, Farid and Rehana. Amir and I danced again."

Her mother looked up from the letters and frowned, "You danced again? Did he dance better this time or did he do his silly dances again?"

"Ammi!" Nazeera laughed nervously, taking another long sip of tea. "We slow danced and he danced wonderfully. He knows how to waltz. I was floating and twirling... It was a nice dance...." she let her words trail off.

"*Aacha,*" Ammi responded with a head bobble and a twist of her hand that Indian mothers' have perfected, "A nice dance. All this boy does is dancing! What are his intentions?!"

"Yes, Ammi, we danced again," Nazeera hesitated and then blurted, "He wants to marry me. He sort of proposed to me last night." Nazeera let her words sink into her mother's brain. She waited for a reaction... any reaction.

"*Kya*? What? Did I hear you correctly?" her mother put the letters down and looked directly at Nazeera. Talking with expressive hand movements, "You said, *he* proposed? That is highly unlikely. The proper way to deliver a marriage proposal is through *us* not through *you*. You must have misunderstood."

Nazeera reflected a moment, "Maybe...he was telling me things. He didn't actually say "marriage" or 'marry me". In fact, I didn't even know it was a proposal until Aziz told me Farid told him it was. It wasn't at all like the American movies. He didn't even get down on one knee."

"See," her mother answered standing up and giving her daughter a reassuring hug, "You and he simply had the conversation before the proposal. I'll have your father phone them and see what is really going on."

Ammi picked up the telephone, dragging it and the long extension cord into the bedroom. Nazeera wished she had made the call from the living room. *Why does she need privacy? This is my proposal!*

She took another sip of tea to finish it. Sulking, she drudged to the veranda. Leaning forward she glared at the world below. There's a man carrying a wicker basket full of mangoes. Across the street is a woman and two small boys on their way to the CCI swimming pool. Here comes a man pulling a wooden cart. It's loaded with odd shaped pieces of wood. *He has his life figured out. He doesn't have to figure out if the proposal was a proposal.*

Looking toward the sky, she watched the birds flying around darting in and out of imaginary circles. Nazeera's mind wandered to her dilemma. *Was it a proposal? If it was, what's my answer? Amir seems like a nice guy. But America? Is it at all like the movies with big cars and big homes? Lots of wide open spaces? But, he said I'd have to work! What does that really mean?*

And what about my life here? My family? My friends? Jaya? Maybe I should marry Habib. Then I can stay in Bombay, and my life wouldn't change too much. Are there any other suitors to consider? William? But Ammi's jyotishi said I would marry before I was twenty-one. Would I receive any other proposals soon? Maybe these would be the only two proposals I'd ever get? No, there have been others, but I've rejected each of them. Should I say yes to one of these? Which one?

Nazeera sighed. She needed help. Jaya would help her decide. Yes! She was wise and had gone through this already. Granted, she had an arranged marriage, so it was different, but still, she was the closest thing she had to a confidante. She rushed back into the living room with the intention of calling her friend but found her mother still had the phone in the bedroom.

She glanced at her watch and shrugged her shoulders. *Darn! I'll have to call her after class.* Grabbing a banana and her purse, she left the flat with a simple nod to Akbar. The fresh air would do her good. A walk to class will help clear her mind and the exercise would be good. The walk quickly turned into a skip, well, rather a spry step. This was the last Interior Decorating class of the summer semester and she was more than happy it was ending. It had been tedious learning how to arrange flowers in crystal vases and matching fabric swatches to paint colors. But, today, the class would be a nice distraction from her reality.

Later that afternoon, the front door slammed shut, and Nazeera heard a thunderous roar. She had recently returned home from her class and was enjoying the cool afternoon breeze on the veranda. She looked up from the pages in her book and watched her father stomp around the flat. Was he looking for her?

"Nazeera?! Nazeera?! Lailaa?!" he called. Apparently he was looking for her. She waved her hand and he must have seen it from the corner of his eye as he turned his head and stomped onto the veranda. He eyed her suspiciously as he loudly plopped down on the chair next to her. The plastic seat cushion gave a little squeak as he sat down. He leaned forward to talk to his daughter, his nostrils flaring. Nazeera speculated this was about the latest proposal and she needed to calm him down a bit. She met his gaze and blinked her eyes innocently, "Did you want to talk to me, Daddy?"

Her father's deep frown softened a bit. It was working. She was calming him down. "*Beta*, I talked to Farid." He paused for a moment and Nazeera could see he was breathing deeply, "Amir did propose last night."

Nazeera froze. So, it was a proposal. How odd! Why had he not done it the traditional way? No wonder her father was upset.

"I'm not sure... about this... boy," he started, visibly trying to calm himself down so he could talk more smoothly. "Maybe this is how they do it in Ameer-ic-ka, but here in India, he needs to present a proposal to me first. Just as Habib did."

Great, here we go. Nazeera knew her parents would be upset about her moving out of Bombay and this would be even worse, as she would be leaving India. Life here was all she knew and she secretly wanted to see more of the world. An adventure! Just as Lady De Winter from her book had married a stranger and moved to a new land, so would she. Or so her romantic thoughts had convinced her.

"Daddy," she began, placing a bookmark on the page she was reading and shutting the book, "you know I love you and Ammi." She waited for him to nod before she continued, "I'm ready for marriage and I think Amir is good husband material."

"Yes, but Ameer-ic-ka? Also, what do you really know about his family and his life in Ameer-ic-ka?"

Nazeera reflected for a moment, casting her eyes downward, "Not much." Then she looked up at her father and confidently said, "He told me he has no girlfriend. No wife in America. I believe him."

"*Aacha...chaa...chaa...*" her father said with a slight head bobble, "What if he lied... like Khurram lied to Mallika?"

"He's not like Khurram. He did not lie to me." Nazeera said with a raised voice. She had not often raised her voice to her parents. It surprised her a little.

"*Theek hai,*" he said noticing her resolve, "I'll find out more about this boy from Nizar tonight after prayers." Nizar Shaheen was Daddy's good friend. They knew each other from Friday prayers at the mosque as well as many evenings playing cards at the CCI. Nizar attended religious services at both the mosque and the JK. He was also Rehana's father and the perfect person to tell him the truth about Amir.

CHAPTER 24

Saturday, August 20

"THUMP! THUMP! THUMP!"

The two gentlemen had begun a pleasant discussion after Friday prayers at the mosque. Unfortunately for Rahim, Nizar had to cut the discussion short as he wanted to attend prayers at the JK and see his daughter, Rehana. They had agreed to meet at noon for an early lunch at the CCI the next day.

Just before leaving for the Club, Rahim covertly dragged the telephone onto the veranda. Quietly shutting the French doors, he tip toed to the chair at the far side and winced when the plastic seat cover squeaked as he sat. He quickly phoned Jabbar to inform him that Nazeera had been presented with another proposal. He didn't add that it was an odd proposal. Jabbar didn't need to know that.

Rahim wanted to hold onto his daughter, even if it meant going into debt for the rest of his life. Habib's father was surprised Nazeera had received another offer so soon after their visit. He was at a loss for words, but conceded they would present a counter-offer that afternoon.

Jaya had told her to follow her head. The heart would comply eventually. Nazeera's head was spinning weighing the pros and cons of each suitor. The big wild card was the dowry demand. This was a big negative for Habib. If Amir had a similar one, then, the scales could tip in Habib's favor. She had to know what Amir's family wanted, no demanded. She had to know all the facts so her head could make the decision. She had to know. She had to know now!

Nazeera began frantically looking for the telephone. She needed to call Amir and ask him. She needed to know the answer. She couldn't make a decision without knowing the answer. She couldn't think of anything else. She had to find out now.

She saw the long extension cord leading to her parent's bedroom. Frantic for the telephone, Nazeera pounded on the door, "Ammi! I need the phone." She listened as her mother shuffled to the door and opened it.

"*Beta*," she said with a bit of concern in her voice, "What's the matter? I have never seen you like this." Nazeera grabbed the telephone and abruptly turned away from her mother. She had to know now!! Her mother caught her arm and said, "*Beta*, calm down."

Nazeera burst into tears. "Ammi," she said between sobs, "I don't know what to do." Stepping into her mother's arms. "I'm confused. Who should I marry?"

She allowed her mother to lead her to her parent's bed. As they sat down, still holding her hand, her mother said in a soothing voice a mixture of English and Hindi, "Nazeera, you are a dazzling, independent woman. Your father and I are very proud of you. We know you will make the decision that is best for you. We will support it no matter who you chose."

"But, Daddy doesn't want me moving to America," the young girl blubbered to her mother. It was as if Nazeera had been transformed into an eight year old again, "Neither one of the guys will make Daddy happy."

Her mother hugged her again, sighing, "Marriage of a daughter is not always a happy occasion. A lot of parents chose their daughter's spouse. We are allowing you to choose your husband, partially because we were not allowed to choose our own spouses." She began stroking Nazeera's hair, adding softly, "We want more for you than we had, *Beta*. Don't worry about your father or me. We will be fine."

Stifling her tears, Nazeera transformed back into an independent twenty-year old woman. She sniffled and looked up at her mother, "Thank you Ammi, you're right. You and Daddy have given me the opportunity to make the decision that will change my life. The decision is mine. Whichever path I chose, I must live with my decision."

"That's right. So think about it carefully. Your Daddy will be back from the Club soon. We can chat more about this when he returns."

Nazeera wiped her tears again and blew her nose in the tissue her mother offered her. She sat up straight, wetting her lips, "Can I use the telephone? I want to make a call."

"Sure," Ammi said handing her the telephone again.

Nazeera hugged her mother again, then dragged the telephone and its long extension cord into her bedroom. Her mother was being very supportive and she was thankful for that. She didn't even mention astrologers or fortune tellers once. Maybe her mother was changing.

She picked up the telephone and was about to dial Amir's telephone number when she paused realizing, she didn't have it. She had thrown that scrap of paper in the garbage. *Darn!* She laughed and shook her head at the predicament.

Rather than bother her mother again, she jumped onto her bed and reached into her bedside drawer, digging out her Interior Decorating notebook. Flipping to a blank page she drew a straight line, well almost straight line, down the center. Then she wrote in large capital letters, "Habib" and "Amir" on the first line, on either side of the median. Using Jaya's advice, she would consider each man logically - using her head. The heart would come later, right?

She would think about this logically. Starting with Habib, she began filling in the positive and negative aspects. The list came fairly easily: Handsome, wealthy, two half-brothers, from Hyderabad, moving to Bombay, can do charity work or run boutique, will have cook, servant, driver, strong father, prayers five times a day, wear *burkha* on occasion, large dowry demand, Daddy will be in debt, close to home, wandering eye, multiple wives?

The list for Amir was a bit more difficult: Handsome, lives in America, one or two brothers, two or three sisters, strong mother, makes eye contact, respects me, thinks I have spirit, waltzes wonderfully, bad

Hindi, likes travel, few friends, far from home, Daddy will miss me, work, wedding in a week, one and only wife, dowry??

Amir called Rehana every half an hour since he woke up that morning. "Did she respond yet? Did she accept my proposal?" Rehana had responded that no one had called and sleepily suggested he phone Nazeera directly if he was so desperate for an answer.

He was beginning to get worried. Sure, he wanted to know her answer, but he also wanted to start the wedding planning. He only had a week and Indian weddings usually took days to perform all the ceremonies. He would need to ask for more time, that was certain. And what if Nazeera said, "no"? He would have to start the search again or settle for Dilshad. Bandra would be happy with that.

Amir paced back and forth in his mother's living room. He couldn't concentrate on anything. He had to know what she was thinking. Yesterday was bad enough, but he knew she would have to tell her parents and they had even called to confirm that it was a proposal. So much for his personal touch. Was he not clear?

He needed to know her answer. He marched to the telephone and grabbed the receiver. But, before he finished dialing, he quickly replaced the receiver. Wow, this was harder than he thought. He paced up and down the hallway a few more times, trying to work up some courage. Picking up the receiver again, he dialed her number. It began to ring. He was about to give up when a male voice said, "Hall-low."

"Um, this is Amir," he mumbled. Clearing his throat, he asked a bit more confidently, "Is Nazeera home?"

Since both the ladies had insisted on eating lunch in their bedrooms, Akbar had to carry the lunch to them on the wooden tray. Having served Ma'am Sah'b first, it was now Baby Sah'b's turn. Lightly knocking, Nazeera allowed Akbar to enter her bed chamber. The aroma of the food seemed to drift directly to her nostrils as he stepped into the room.

"Hmm, it smells divine. Is that Pomfret?" Nazeera asked her mouth already salivating.

"*Ji, huh, Baby Sah'b. Pomfret* and *Aaloo Gobi.*" Akbar said as he laid the tray at the foot of her bed. Practicing his English, he added, "Very good. Nice tasty."

Nazeera nodded, and leaned forward eyeing her lunch. Just as she picked up a piece of *naan*, the telephone sitting on her bedside table began to ring. Usually Akbar answered the telephone, so she ignored the ringing and took a bite of the potato and cauliflower dish. She would eat the pan-fried fish in a moment.

As expected, Akbar walked to the telephone and stopped the ringing by lifting the receiver. "Hall-low," he said to the caller. He listened for a moment and then turned to her. "Amir-*Ji* calling."

"Oh!" she said with a pleasant surprise, "I want to talk to him!" She wiped her hands on the linen napkin and crawled to the other side of the bed. Following a calming exhale, she took the handset from Akbar, "Amir?"

Amir must not have expected her to answer so quickly because he hesitated and then responded, "Yes, Nazeera. It's Amir."

"We need to talk," she went straight to the point. *What dowry does he or his family demand? Is he lying about his American life?* "But not on the telephone, can you come to the flat?" Without hesitation this time, he agreed.

Quickly devouring her lunch, she anxiously awaited his arrival. Would he or his family have a large dowry demand like Habib? She doubted it. He seemed different from all the others. He was less polished than Habib, but in some ways more real. Her life with him would be full of adventure and travel. Moving to America sounded exciting!

After what seemed like forever, he finally arrived on foot. She had moved to the veranda to better spy on the street activity. When she saw him walking down the sidewalk, she burst open her mother's bedroom door and updated her on the plans. Her mother was a bit scandalized - they were unmarried and unescorted - and simply said as Nazeera ran out of the flat, "*Baap-re*!! Don't let anyone see you!"

She joined Amir at the entrance to the building. He seemed startled to see her exit the lift. Giggling, she led him to her aquamarine

Vespa. Tying the loose ends of her *dupatta* together, she lifted her right leg over the seat and straddled the scooter. "Come sit," she chuckled as she put the key in the ignition.

Amir hovered a second, then lifted his leg over the seat to sit down behind her. Nazeera had driven many girlfriends around town during her college days and was used to having someone sitting behind her. Jaya knew she had to hold on as soon as she was seated; Amir was not so wise. When Nazeera took off with a jerk, he grabbed her waist to avoid falling off the Vespa. She immediately noticed his hands felt warm and comforting, so she did not push them aside. Thankfully, he left them there on her waist the entire ride.

Quickly looking both ways, she skillfully entered Dinshaw Vachha Road headed toward Marine Drive. The pathway near Marine Drive was nearby and a popular place to chat. She needed to know what he was thinking. As they approached the intersection, Nazeera noticed the sidewalk and the concrete sitting ledge were full of people and worse yet, noise. That would not be the nice quiet place she wanted for this important conversation, "This will not do."

Racking her brain for other places to go, she suddenly remembered a place her father had mentioned over dinner last week. She rotated the scooter around with Amir's hands holding her a bit tighter and headed away from Marine Drive. Accelerating, she followed the road past the CCI, past her flat to Jamshadji Tata Road. This was a extremely busy road even in mid-day. To hold on, Amir put both of his arms around Nazeera as she maneuvered the scooter through the cars, motorcycles, carts, bicycles and pedestrians.

This was fun! She enjoyed having his hands and now arms around her waist. *He's holding me really tight,* she thought to herself. This was the first time she had a man on her scooter. Actually, it was the first time a man held her around the waist other than when they were dancing. *It feels nice.*

She weaved in and out of traffic and thought she overheard Amir yelp a few times as they closely approached other vehicles. They passed the Ritz Hotel where he supposedly proposed, passed Sumrat where she lunched with Khushboo and continued through the roundabout. All this was familiar to her. She loved it here. She loved her life here. But, she knew life was going to change. Whether she liked it or not, it was already changing. Her friends were all married or soon would be married. Jaya had moved all the way to Delhi. Khushboo's family was discussing suitors for her. She knew she had to make some hard choices soon or she would end up a burden to her parents. She didn't want that.

She raced her engine a bit faster in response to this thought process. No time to think about this now. His answer to her questions would decide their fate. Her fate. They passed the Gandhi monument and she noticed a few tourists staring at it and taking photos. Onto Madame Cama Road. She deftly maneuvered through the traffic and turned onto the first street headed south, which was Foreshore Road. They passed a tall building and Amir pointed at it, mumbling something she could not hear.

A block later they passed the MVM Banquet Hall and then Badhwan Park, the start of Cuffe Parade. This was newly reclaimed land and was still being developed. She had wanted to see it because the Bombay City Improvement Trust had been working on this for awhile. The growing population of the city had urged the Trust to make the island of Bombay a bit bigger by filling in holes or in this case, just making the island longer. Her father had been involved in part of it and she was naturally curious.

Nazeera thought that since this area is still under development, it would be quieter than Marine Drive. She was right. Most of the reclamation work had ceased for the weekend, so constructions sites were quiet, except for a few stray animals.

Seeing an acceptable spot near one of the sites, she drove the scooter to the side. They had a moment of peace. Finally she could ask him about the dowry. She hoped he would say the right answer.

Amir dismounted as quickly as he could and stretched his back, "Whew! Nazeera you're a crazy driver." He laughed, "But, boy, that was fun!"

Nazeera smiled. Good, she had not scared him off with her scooter or "crazy driving" as he called it. His sense of adventure was another quality she would have to add to the list. He liked to travel and she had always wanted to see The Great Wall of China. Glancing around, she found a long wooden plank balancing on two piles of rubble. It looked like a makeshift bench from the construction site.

She tested it, and sat down. Patting the space next to her, she glanced at her suitor, "Amir, come sit."

He was looking around at the construction site, his eyebrows gathered tightly on his forehead as if he was straining to see something. He turned his head toward her, smiled and stepped over a few rock pieces to join her on the make-shift bench. She braced herself in case his weight caused the bench to fall. It didn't.

"Amir," she started and then stopped. She had never been alone like this with a man. There had always been others; her brother, her parents or at least a girlfriend or two. She should be afraid. She should be nervous. She was neither. She felt safe. He made her feel safe. "Amir, I understand you proposed marriage to me."

He nodded. "Yeah, I wanted to propose to you in person like they do in America. But, I messed it up. I forgot to bring the ring, I didn't get down on one knee and I don't think I told you that you're beautiful." He took her hand in his, "You are beautiful, Nazeera."

Nazeera's heart started thumping. Thump. Thump. Thump. His hands were warm and the warmth radiated from him directly into her veins. Her breathing began to quicken and become heavy. Amir started tracing an imaginary line on the back of her hand with his forefinger. The tiny hairs on her arm stood on end as if she had just been electrified. She was feeling things she had never felt before. He continued for a minute and then flipped her hand. Using the same forefinger, he started tracing the lines on her palm. The sensation slightly tickled and she impulsively pulled her hand away. She had to hold it together!

"Amir," she said slightly panting, "I have something serious we must discuss." She looked down at her hands now regretting pulling them away from him. Exhaling, she asked, "If that was a proposal, then I need to clarify a few things."

He shrugged his shoulders, "Okay, shoot."

She wasn't used to such casual responses. What does "shoot" mean? Must be a cowboy phrase or something. He talked so weird. She cleared her throat and worked up her courage again, this time asking a question she had already asked him, "Um, do you have a girlfriend or wife in America?"

"Nope," he quickly responded, "No wife and no girlfriend. Next question."

He sure answered that quickly, Nazeera thought. *Is he lying? He seems to be telling the truth.* She continued, "*Aacha*, you also said I would...."

"Actually," Amir interrupted, "Since we are being totally honest here, I want to tell you the whole truth." *Oh, here it comes. He's going to tell me he does have a girlfriend. That he's going to marry me, and then break up with her. This is going to be just like Mallika's marriage. He did lie to me!*

"Um, I did have an American girlfriend." Amir continued, looking down at his clenched hands, "Her name was Diane. She was wonderful and very independent. But, things did not work out between us and we broke up a few months ago."

"Do you.... Do you still...like her?"

"Of course," Amir said with a laugh, "We're still friends. But, what I realized when I was dating her is that I really admire self-confident women. Women that are independent and with spirit. You have that Nazeera. I admire that in you."

She blushed. *He admired me? Really? No one has ever said they admired me.* She had been told she was pretty or even beautiful, but someone that actually liked her independence and admired her for that! That was a first!

Her head began to swoon and she forgot her next question. Amir took her hand again and tapped it a few times, "Are you all right?"

"Yes, yes, just thinking..." she covered. "*Aacha*, you said I would have to work, right?"

Amir leaned back on the make-shift bench, nearly falling off. "Yes, I'm still early in my career and so you working would help us pay the bills. Also, my American host family, the Nomla's, are wonderful. They helped me settle into life there. They will help you too. Mrs. Nomla said that working would be a great way for you to make friends and help you adjust to life there."

"Hmm..." she said aloud, but her mind was thinking through his words. *Maybe working wouldn't be such a bad thing. He isn't saying I have to work so he could stay home. It's for a better life for both of us, and to help me adjust to life there. I could still run a boutique! Yes, it was possible! Adventure and a boutique!*

But, now for the real question. The question that would determine her answer to his proposal, "What is your family expecting in a dowry?"

Amir didn't hesitate, "Whatever your parents want to give you is fine. We... I'm not asking for anything."

Nazeera was a bit shocked at his answer. It wasn't rare for a man to ask for no dowry, but Indian men usually asked for something. Their family insisted on it. But, Amir was a modern man and independent of his family. And he admired her independence. No one had ever said they admired her for anything other than her beauty.

Not wanting to show her excitement at his response, she said sarcastically, "Good, because you'd get a goat and two chickens."

She laughed and then he joined her. They both shared a laugh and exchanged smiles. She placed her hand on top of his. Sometime during their conversation he had grabbed her hand again. Their hands were warm and comforting. Safe. She wanted to remember this moment for the rest of her life.

They sat for awhile conversing about his life in America and how her life would be there. It began to grow dark and they sadly decided it was time for them to head back home. "Ammi must be very worried." Nazeera had said as her excuse. She didn't want the afternoon to end, but she knew it was best for them to return home now.

The drive back to the Yashodham flat was less rushed. In fact, Nazeera purposely drove slower to enjoy his hands on her waist a little longer. She didn't care if others saw them. In fact, she even considered taking the longer route home, but she decided against it. She wanted to tell her parents her decision. Amir was the man she wanted to marry.

The couple had been gone almost two hours. She paused long enough at the Ivanhoe flat to drop Amir at the walkway. He kissed her hand as they said good-bye and it gave her goose bumps and the huge smile she wore during the drive home. She drove quickly to the flat. She was anxious to tell her parents the news.

When she rushed into the flat, she noticed it was quiet. Looking around, she quickly summarized Ammi was still in the bedroom. Where is Daddy? Is he still at the CCI with Rehana's father? What were they discussing? Then again, it didn't matter what they discussed, she was marrying Amir.

CHAPTER 25

"THAT IS A GOOD CHANGE"

Still floating on a cloud from her recent excursion with Amir, Nazeera drifted into her bedroom, and plopped onto the bed causing the notebook she had been scribbling in just a few hours earlier to flop onto the floor. She let it lay where it landed. She didn't need it anymore. She had already decided which of the two men she was going to marry.

Picking up her book, *Rebecca*, she piled her bed pillows into a mound and leaned against them. Anxiously, she opened the book to where she had bookmarked. As she read the last page, she smiled to herself satisfied. She knew her ending would be happier than theirs had been. She knew a lot more about Amir than Lady DeWinter knew about Maxim. And, they wouldn't have a scary Mrs. Danvers haunting her dreams.

The front door slammed and Nazeera heard her father's voice as he joked with Akbar. *Ah, Daddy must be finally back from the CCI. He sounds more relaxed than when he left. That's a good sign. The chat with Mr. Shaheen must have gone well. Hopefully he told him what he needed to hear - Amir was from a good family and didn't have a girlfriend.*

This was a perfect time to tell them of her decision! Jumping up from the bed, she straightened out her *kameez* and strode confidently into the living room. She entered the room, ready to tell the world her news, but no one was there.

She turned to retreat back into her bedroom as her mother charged out of the other bedroom, "*Juldi, juldi*, the Abdullah's will be here soon. Get changed!"

"*Kya*? What? Why are the Abdullah's coming again?"

"They are coming with a revised marriage proposal. Now *juldi, juldi*. Hurry up and change into something decent."

What was going on? Why were they coming here with a revised marriage proposal? Had her father called them or had they called here? No matter, her mind was made up. She complied with her mother's wishes and changed into the chocolate brown sari her mother had purchased recently. She knew it made her look dazzling. She intended to reject this revised proposal. She wanted Habib to suffer for insisting on such a large dowry.

Promptly at 5 o'clock, Habib and Jabbar arrived. Since they were expected, Akbar answered the doorbell, and allowed them to enter the flat. They were warmly greeted by the hosts and asked to sit down in the living room, near the photo of Nehru enjoying afternoon tea with them. Nazeera came out of her bedroom, her head held high. She was not interested in this proposal, and anxious for this meeting to be over.

Forcing a smile, Nazeera sat down on the sofa next to her mother. Habib smiled a broad smile as she entered the room, quickly sitting in the chair directly across from her. Stealing a glance at him, she noticed his smile was warm and friendly. Refusing to return his smile, she turned her head toward her father instead.

"As you know," her father said to Habib's father, "We were concerned with your first marriage proposal... as we considered the dowry request... too large. Also, just two days ago, Nazeera received another marriage proposal. So, since we have not formally rejected your proposal, we wanted to give you an opportunity to..."

Nazeera was only half-listening to what her father said. She was watching the man in front of her. *He is definitely good looking. Bollywood movie star good looking. His hair is perfectly coifed. Are those henna highlights in his hair? No, maybe just streams of sunlight. His blue fitted shirt accents his biceps. Those khaki pants look freshly pressed and his black leather shoes recently polished.*

Habib noticed her intently staring at him, so he smiled again. Nazeera's heart began to flutter, even though she didn't want it to. *Was it warm in here?*

Carrying the wooden tray, Shanti approached the group offering soft drinks. Habib looked at the tray and then directly at Shanti's chest, pausing a moment longer than a gentleman should. Looking to her face, he asked, "Do you have any Banta? The ones with the codd-neck bottles?"

The codd-neck was unique because the bottle was filled upside down with the rubber gasket and marble enclosed in the neck of the bottle. When the drink is opened and poured, the enclosed marble helped make the drink more fizzy.

Keeping her eyes averted, Shanti shook her head, "*Ji, nahih.*" Without making eye contact with Habib, she turned her face toward the master of the house. Everyone's eyes turned to see how her father would react. Rahim straightened his back, nodding slightly. Shanti finished offering drinks and scurried away.

Jabbar sipped his lemonade. Turning to Daddy, "As you can see, my son really likes your daughter. I'm sure we can work something out."

Taking a sip of Coca-Cola, Daddy responded, "What are you proposing?"

The two fathers bantered back and forth for several minutes in front of the ladies, very different from the last time they were here. The Abdullah's seemed less aristocratic, a bit more friendly. Even though she was sitting inches from the conversation, Nazeera's mind was miles away. She didn't care what they said. She didn't care about the revised proposal. She was going to marry Amir. Habib was too late.

The suitor sat back in his chair, his hands behind his head and his feet propped up on the coffee table. *Oh, how cocky! He must think I'm in love with him and the only thing standing in his way is the dowry demand. How presumptuous!* Unexpectedly, he glimpsed in her direction. Noticing she was watching him, he gave her a wry smile and blew her a kiss. *How arrogant!* Nazeera did not return the smile nor the kiss.

"...Nazeera? Nazeera?" her father repeated. Nazeera snapped back to the conversation at hand and shook her head. Her father added, "What are your thoughts?"

She had no idea what the question was, but she didn't want to say that in front of the two guests. "Can we chat in private?" she quietly said to her father. The three of them walked into her parent's bedroom. "So, what do you think?" her father asked as Ammi shut the door.

"Sorry, what was the question?" Nazeera asked still in a slight daze.

Daddy rolled his eyes. "Habib is still very interested in you. They now understand the dowry, er.. wedding gift request was too much, so they have modified it. They still want the furnished flat, but it does not have to be in Malabar Hills. It can be anywhere in South Bombay."

"That is a good change. A very good change." Ammi added, "What do you think, *Beta*? We could meet for lunch at the CCI."

It was a good change. Much more manageable and affordable for her parents. She could stay in Bombay and run a boutique. All her childhood dreams would come true. But, there was only one problem with that plan - she would be married to *this* guy - this egotistical, wandering-eye, full of himself guy! Nazeera looked into her father's desperate eyes, "I'd like to stay in Bombay near you and Ammi. But, I no longer want to marry Habib."

"But...." Daddy started to protest, but Ammi put up her hand to stop him. "*Nahih*, No. This is her decision." She flipped her hand dismissively toward the living room, "She doesn't want to marry this boy." She took her daughter's hand in hers, "You prefer Amir, no?"

Her mother understood. With relief in her voice, "Yes, Ammi, I do."

"But...." her father repeated. He paused, then added, "He's an Ismaili."

Still holding her daughter's hand, Ammi gave it a squeeze. For the first time in a very long time, Ammi turned to her husband, looked up into his worried eyes, and said boldly, "She wants to marry Amir. *Bas*, enough. We will arrange it."

Daddy seemed surprised by how confident his wife was being. She usually just went along with things, but today, she was standing up for her daughter. "*Theek hai*, I will speak with them. But, before I give my consent to a marriage with that Amir, I must speak with him."

"Fine," Ammi said squeezing her daughter's hand again, "No to Habib, and Maybe to Amir." She waved her hand at her husband, "Go tell them."

Daddy hesitated as he watched Ammi open the bedroom door. He seemed suddenly older, his eyes drooping. Drudging to the door, he paused as Ammi touched his shoulder. With a heavy sigh, he lifted his chin and stepped into the living room. The ladies giggled and spied on the conversation from the crack in the mostly closed door.

All Nazeera could hear was a murmur of deep voices. Suddenly, Habib exclaimed, "I don't believe it! I want to hear the words from Nazeera directly!"

Without hesitation, Nazeera opened the door and strode into the living room, followed closely by her mother. She sat down in her previous spot opposite Habib, and leaned back folding her arms over her chest.

Shanti chose that moment to return to the group. She carried the wooden tray with the newly acquired Banta bottle, a tall glass and a small bowl of cut limes. Nazeera paused as she watched her suitor gawk at her servant. Shanti poured the soda and offered him a piece of lime. Taking the glass with his right hand, Habib reached forward to retrieve a piece of lime with his other hand, nearly brushing her chest in the process. He squeezed just a touch of lime into his drink.

Nazeera patiently waited for him to take a sip and look in her direction. "My answer is still no, Habib."

He put the glass on the coffee table and threw his hands into the air, "I can't believe you refused me again! You'll have a hard time finding someone as great as me. Especially with that brother of yours!"

Nazeera wanted to unleash some fury with a reply but held her tongue. It was not the right time. *Stay calm. Breathe. Breathe.* Forcing a smile, she simply said, "Good-bye, Habib."

The angry suitor clumsily stood up, nearly knocking over the precious photo of Nehru and her family. His face was ablaze. Pointing at her, he bellowed, "I'll find someone even more impressive than you. That'll show you!" Jabbar tugged on his son's arm indicating it was time for them to leave. "You'll be sorry you didn't marry me, Nazeera!"

Daddy showed them to the door and thankfully the pair left without further incident. The whole group, including the two servants, sighed heavily when the door closed.

"After that, I really don't regret my decision." Nazeera whispered only loud enough for her parents to hear. Relieved, she leaned back on the sofa, closing her eyes. *Why did he say that about my brother? Would Hamid cause an issue with Amir, too?*

CHAPTER 26

Sunday, August 21

"I WANT YOU TO MAKE ME TWO PROMISES"

Soaring from his scooter ride with Nazeera the previous day, Amir was expecting them to call any minute to accept his proposal. So, when the telephone ran, he sprang to his feet and rushed to it. "Yallo!" Amir said with high hopes.

"Hello, darling," Bandra answered, "I have something important to discuss with you. Are you free?"

Amir was not in the mood to entertain his older sister. She was not fond of his choice of bride and had made that abundantly clear. "If you're trying to talk me out of marrying Nazeera, forget it."

"But I have information about Nazeera's family you may find interesting."

"Fine," Amir relented, "Come over, but make it quick." He replaced the telephone receiver and a moment later the telephone rang again. Thinking it was his annoying sister again, he shouted, "Bandra, just come over!"

A deep voice responded, "Excuse me. This is Rahim, Nazeera's father. I was hoping to speak with Amir Virani. May I speak with him?"

Amir winched, so much for winning over the in-laws, "Sorry, Uncle, I thought you were my nosy sister, Bandra."

"*Aacha*," Rahim replied, his voice monotone, "I would like to chat with you young man. There are a few matters we need to discuss. When can you meet?"

"Uncle, my sister is coming over to visit me just now. I could meet you right after that. Say, 1pm at The Sea Lounge?" He suggested Nazeera's favorite hang out place hoping his choice of location would impress his potential future father-in-law.

"*Theek hai*. That would be fine." He seemed adequately impressed. Amir crossed his fingers, hoping the meeting with her father would go well. *It needs to go well. What are the matters he wants to discuss?*

They exchanged good-byes and Amir almost skipped into the living room to update his mother. She was resting on the divan, a blanket thrown unevenly over her legs. As he approached, she fluttered her eyes open.

"How's Farid?" Amir asked.

"Better," Mummy said sitting up on the pillows, "He was in a lot of pain last night. Rehana and I took shifts all night. I think he passed three or four of them. Hopefully they are done. He is resting now."

Amir quickly told his mother Bandra was coming over and he was meeting Rahim at The Sea Lounge in a couple hours.

Smiling weakly, she said, "I will give an update to Farid and Rehana when I see them." She rubbed her son's arm in a motherly way and added, "Do you want me or Farid to come with you to The Sea Lounge?"

Amir did want the support as Rahim intimidated him, but he knew his mother and certainly his brother were in no shape to assist him today. "No, I can handle it." He said with as confident a smile as he could muster.

If Mummy believed him or not, she nodded agreement. With a groan, she stood and went into her bedroom to freshen up. Within thirty minutes she was headed back to Farid's flat. A few minutes after she left, Bandra arrived.

Greeting him more warmly than usual, she sat down at the dining room table. Amir cautiously sat down in a chair perpendicular to her.

"So, what information do you have that I need to know?" They both nodded when Ramu offered them tea.

Bandra started out by saying she thought Dilshad was still a great choice. She was lovely and they made such a nice couple. After Amir politely refused her prodding a few times, she changed the topic to Nazeera. "I had my guy investigate Nazeera and her family," Bandra proudly said. "And he found something. Something very interesting."

Amir was not in the mood to hear gossip, "You had her investigated? Why?"

Bandra refused to be rattled, "Well, because she's not Ismaili. We don't know much about her. Only what the Ambassador told us - which is not much."

"I know enough," Amir admitted. "I don't need to know more."

"Well," Bandra continued, ignoring Amir's pleas, "there was a scandal with her brother, Hamid. It seems he…"

Amir put his hand up to stop her, "I don't want to hear it, Bandra. There is nothing you can tell me that will change my mind. I love Nazeera and I'm marrying *her*. Whatever her family has or has not done will not affect us in America."

"But, her brother." Bandra protested.

"I know what happened to her brother," Amir lied. "It doesn't matter."

His sister sat dumbfounded for a moment and then added, "*Theek hai*. But, did you know she was seen yesterday driving her flashy scooter all around town with some guy on the back? He was holding her waist pretty tight! What a flirt!"

Amir just laughed at his sister's sources. "Yeah, I know that. I was the guy." He was going to explain what they discussed, but concluded he didn't need to explain himself to her. "Good-bye, Bandra."

Her eyes widened and she quickly added, "…And did you know her father has been asking a lot of questions of Nizar Shaheen?"

"Rehana's father?" Amir asked, "Why would he be asking him questions?"

Bandra paused. Slowly a cynical smile crept onto her face. She raised her eyebrows and replied, "He's been asking questions about you and the family."

"That's a good sign," Amir responded with a smirk. "That means

Nazeera has told her parents and they are considering the proposal." Amir smiled from ear to ear. "Her father just called. He wants to meet me to discuss a few things."

"Her father wants to meet you? That's a bad sign," Bandra said in an ominous voice. "Did he say what he wanted to discuss?" *Is she trying to scare me?*

Amir reflected for a moment, "No... he didn't. He just said there were a few matters for us to discuss."

"Hmm..." Bandra said in a tone of impending doom, "A very bad sign." With that, she gathered up her things and left. Amir was relieved to see her go. *But, what if she's right? What if this is a bad sign. Well, no use worrying about it. I'll find out soon enough.*

Amir arrived a few minutes before their scheduled time. He had never been to The Sea Lounge before and didn't want to be late for this important meeting. He took a few deep breaths and exhaled slowly from his mouth to calm himself down as he walked up the red car- peted Grand Staircase to the second floor restaurant. As he reached the top of the staircase, he turned right to enter The Sea Lounge. If he had turned left, he would have walked toward the renowned Crystal Ballroom at the other end of the hallway.

The Taj Hotel was the place just a week earlier he had been anxious to enter. Now, here he was walking up the Grand Staircase and about to have lunch at The Sea Lounge. How different his life was now.

The Sea Lounge had an open floor plan and many small tables and several booths along the window overlooking the Bombay Harbour. Since he had never been to the restaurant before, he requested one of the two-person booths near the window. As he followed the mai- tre d' to the booth, he glanced around the room and noticed it was filled with businessmen, tourists and an occasional couple. Everyone seemed huddled together in secret discussions.

Sitting down in the booth, he took the side facing the front door so he could see Rahim arrive. He checked to make sure the table was set properly and then nervously played with his white cloth napkin. After a moment, he glanced at the front door again and then gingerly around the room. The walls were painted pastel blue and the molding along the archways and the ceiling were white. It was a lovely contrast made even more attractive by the exquisite accents of gold leaf and crystal. The wood floors were covered in places by a brown and blue zig-zag pattern rug. The brown of the rug matched the color of the chair arms perfectly. Someone had spent a lot of time decorating this room. Impressive. No wonder Nazeera liked this place.

Still no Rahim. Was this a test of his patience? He glanced at his watch, it was only three minutes after one. He isn't too late. Since he had scanned the interior, Amir shrugged his shoulders and gazed outside. He was amazed at the view of the Arabian Sea and all the people walking on the sidewalks. Small tug boats were puffing their way through the water near the Gateway of India probably giving rides to and from Elephanta Island. He had taken a similar boat to the Island when he was a child. Seeing the tug boat reminded him that he had meant to visit the Island again during this visit. *Maybe Nazeera would like to go, too?*

He watched a tourist family near the Gateway. They looked European or maybe American with their western clothes and camera. The parents were attempting to take photos of the Gateway while the children were running around in circles with their arms stretched out like airplanes. He imagined them making airplane noises and laughed to himself. The mother was yelling something and the kids stopped the airplanes and came to stand near her while the father snapped a photo. They looked like a happy family, one that he hoped to have someday.

"Hello, Amir?" a strange voice said from beside him. He had been concentrating on the scene outside and had forgotten to watch for his lunch partner. Awkwardly standing up, Amir offered Nazeera's father an outstretched hand. Rahim was a formidable man. He was a few inches taller than Amir with a broader chest. His well trimmed moustache was tweaked up a bit on the corners giving him a serious look. Rahim's handshake was firm and for the first time today, Amir was nervous. "Yes, sir, please sit down."

They sat in silence as each scanned their menu. *This place is expensive! I guess one pays a premium for the view. But, this is Nazeera's favorite spot.* Amir decided to try the cold coffee she raves about. It must be something special.

Rahim ordered a cup of hot Darjeeling tea and *pani puri*. Since his hopefully future father-in-law ordered a light lunch, Amir scanned the menu again and added *sev batata puri*. He preferred the *pani puri*, but he thought it might be odd if they both ordered the same thing. The potato and onion dish was also tasty. They both smiled with their orders and leaned back in their respective booth seats. So far, so good.

"Amir, I understand you have proposed to my daughter," Rahim started, fiddling with the utensils in front of him. "You should have come to me first."

"Uncle, I know I didn't follow protocol, but I was trying to be romantic. It obviously didn't work. In fact, it created more confusion."

"*Ji, huh*," Rahim sighed a deep sigh, "*Theek hai*." They sat silently for a few minutes. A waiter wearing a white buttoned up shirt and matching white trousers brought the ordered drinks and retreated.

Adding two cubes of sugar to his hot tea, Rahim started, "Amir, you seem like a nice boy, but..." He stopped abruptly. Clearing his throat, he glanced around the room as if stalling. He added a touch of milk to the cup and began to stir his tea, "I want to tell you a story."

"Yes, Uncle?" Amir was not sure what kind of story he would tell. Maybe this was a bad sign as Bandra had predicted.

"As you know, we lived in Poona until recently," Rahim stared out of the window and began his tale, "We are friends with the Hussain family. Very good friends. Mahmod was a general in the army and we worked together on occasion. Anyways, we became friends." Rahim took a sip of his tea, added another cube of sugar and continued to stir, "So, when his daughter Mallika was ready for marriage, we were, of course, happy for them. They arranged her marriage with a family they knew from the mosque. Mallika was to marry their son, Khurram."

Rahim paused. They both watched tourists board one of the boats in the Harbour. "A few years earlier, the boy had gone to Ameer-ic-ka to attend University. He graduated with a good degree and had come home to marry."

Amir thought to himself, *Where is this story going?*

The story-teller paused again, sipping his tea. Placing the cup back onto the saucer, Rahim turned his eyes to Amir, "He and his family demanded a large dowry. Very large. And Mahmod had no choice but to pay it, hoping it would buy Mallika a good life in Ameer-ic-ka. The wedding was a grand affair and the couple seemed to be compatible. A few days after the wedding, the boy returned to Ameer-ic-ka promising to send for his bride as soon as the immigration papers were settled."

"Yes, but..." Amir started.

Rahim ignored his interruption and continued, "They waited for six months. Seven months. Eight months. They heard nothing from the boy. Nothing. No telephone calls, no letters, *kuch nahih*, nothing. So, Mahmod hired a private investigator to find him. It took a few weeks, but the investigator found him. He was living in Ameer-ic-ka, with an Ameer-ic-kan woman. When the investigator confronted him, he said that *she* was his wife!" Rahim's voice escalated and he was visibly upset, "He had married the Ameer-ic-kan woman *before* he married Mallika. Can you believe it?! He took the dowry money and ran away! *Kutta*! Dog!"

Rahim's hands were shaking. He took a few calming breaths, and returned his gaze to Amir, "Mallika took it hard. Very hard. She was disgraced. She talked to Nazeera about running away or doing something worse."

This story must be leading to a discussion about my life in America. Nazeera had asked me similar questions without the backstory. "Uncle, I'm sorry to hear your friends had a bad experience with an American guy. But, let me assure you, I have no wife in America. You can call my friends or my boss. You can talk to my family."

The white clothed waiter returned carrying two plates. Rahim remained steadfast as his order was placed in front of him. Amir nodded and the waiter retreated again. They both took a few bites of their lunch, letting the moment grow awkward. Amir could hear Rahim chewing the crunchy *puri* mixture. Suddenly, Rahim revealed, "I had a long chat with my friend Nizar. Rehana's father."

"Yeah," Amir said swallowing a bite, "I met him once. He seems like a great man."

"I have known Nizar for many years. He attends both the mosque and the JK to develop business contacts. He is knowledgeable about both religions."

Amir was not sure where this was going, so he just nodded and took another bite of his *puri* mixture. He regretted getting something with fresh onions. He hoped his breath didn't smell too bad.

"Nizar said he is very fond of your brother. Farid has been very good to his daughter, and his grandchildren, and they're happy. He said that he only met you briefly when you arrived in Bombay, but from that meeting, you seemed similar to Farid." Rahim took a sip of his tea and then added, "He also said that your mother was very progressive and open to Western ideas."

"Very open," Amir quickly responded. "She insists all of her children be educated, even the girls. In fact, I have a sister who is studying to be a doctor."

"I know," Rahim answered a bit annoyed at being interrupted, "What are your intentions with regard to religion?"

Amir had not even thought about this. They were both Muslims, what was the issue? "Uncle, I'm not sure I follow."

"My daughter is a Sunni," Rahim said proudly. Then with a hint of disdain, he added with a flip of his wrist, "and you're an Ismaili."

"Yes, we are Ismaili. My family has long roots in the Ismaili community. My father has helped many people and even started the First Ismaili Bank to help the poor open businesses."

"Let me just ask my question," Rahim said impatiently. "Are you going to require my daughter to convert to being an Ismaili?"

Amir shook his head, "No. We are both Muslims and that's good enough for me."

"*Aacha....*" Rahim drifted. He took another sip of tea and pulled out a folded paper from his right trouser pocket. He glanced down at it and seemed to be mentally checking things off. It must be a list of topics he wanted to discuss. "*Theek hai,* Amir. I want you to make me two promises."

"Sure, Uncle, if they are within my power to make, I will make them."

"*Nahih*!" Rahim replied, his right fist pounding the table. "I will consent to this marriage *only* if you make both promises."

This sounded serious. "Okay, I understand," Amir admitted, "I want to marry your daughter. I will make and keep both promises."

"*Theek hai*. First, you must promise to put aside enough money for a return airplane ticket for Nazeera. If she ever wants to come home, for any reason, I want her to be able to do that."

"No problem," Amir responded without hesitation. "And the second promise?"

"I do not want my daughter to end up like Mallika. Waiting for immigration papers to join her husband. You will take her to Ameer-ic-ka with you now."

That was his intention all along. The only issue he could imagine is a slow passport and immigration office. "It is my intention to take her with me. I want her with me. However, getting a passport and the immigration visa may be a challenge. I may need your help, Uncle, to get this done. But I promise, I will not leave India without Nazeera."

Rahim swallowed the last of his tea. "*Theek hai*, very good." He held out his hand and Amir took it. They shook hands like gentlemen. The wedding was on.

CHAPTER 27

"EXQUISITE THREADING!"

Moments after the two men shook hands, they left the restaurant. Amir paid the bill and shook his head as he descended the Grand Staircase at the high cost of a cup of tea, a cold coffee and two starters. At least the cold coffee had been tasty. In fact, it was the best he had ever had.

He didn't remember walking home, he floated on a cloud. Rahim had given his consent to the wedding. Nazeera was going to be his wife!

Upon arrival at the Ivanhoe building, Amir headed straight to the lift to climb to the fourth floor. Thankfully, the lift was waiting on the ground floor, so he was able to reach their flat in just minutes.

Still floating on a cloud, Amir whistled as he walked down the hallway toward his brother's flat. *I can't wait to update Farid and Rehana. They can use some good news after these past two weeks! But, I won't stay long*, he told himself, *Farid needs rest.*

Knock. Knock. Knock. As he waited for Babu to open the door, Amir heard a murmur of voices. No one came. Knocking again, he double checked he was at the correct door. Yes, of course, he was. He had been there over a dozen times now. Why were there so many voices coming from inside? Why wasn't anyone opening the door?

Did something happen to Farid? A bit panicked, he rang the doorbell twice.

When Babu finally opened the door, he hurried into the flat half-expecting to see paramedics and Farid sprawled on the floor. Instead, he saw family. Lots of family. Farid was sitting on the sofa with a blanket over his legs and a glass of water in his hand. Rehana was at his side with their children, Rabia and Rafiq, playing on the floor near them. Mummy was in her favorite spot on the high back chair scolding the children for making so much noise.

Wandering between the living room and dining room were his three sisters. Bandra was carrying a blanket from the bedroom, probably for Farid or Mummy. Nadia was holding Tarik's hand and leading him back to where his cousins were playing, and Nilofer was pacing the room throwing out various home remedies for them to try.

The group turned their attention from Farid to Amir as he entered the living room. Bandra or Mummy must have told them he was meeting Rahim as the first question out of Nadia's mouth was, "How did the meeting go?"

Nilofer ushered her brother to the loveseat. Everyone fixated their eyes on him as they anxiously awaited his answer. Hearing nothing, Nilofer asked, "So, what did her father say?"

Clearing his throat, Amir walked them through the lunch meeting, the story and the promises. He said he intended to keep both promises. To keep the second one, he would definitely need more time to get Nazeera a passport and travel visa. More than the six days he had left.

Giggling, Nilofer clapped her hands and suggested they call the Khan family right away to welcome them. Rehana stood up, patted Farid on the shoulder and declared, "We need to do more than that. First, we need to organize the formal engagement party. Given our time frame, it should be done as soon as possible."

"Yes, let's do it tomorrow," suggested Amir. He was anxious to get the wedding preparations done. He only had six days of vacation time left, and he figured he would needed at least a week to get the immigration papers. *How much more leave can I even get? Hopefully my boss will be understanding.*

"What do we need to do?" Nadia asked, rubbing her pregnant belly.

"Well, let me get my list," replied Rehana now excitedly. She rushed to the hallway table, opened the top drawer and pulled out the pad of paper with her bride-finding notes. She flipped to a page with a few written lines, and said, "It is customary for the groom's family to give the bride her engagement sari and jewelry. So, if we have the engagement party tomorrow, we need to select her sari today."

"We don't know much about her," Nilofer replied. "What does she like?"

"Let's find out," Rehana said very matter-of-factly. She picked up the telephone receiver and called the Khan flat.

Crossing the dining room to answer the ringing telephone, Akbar greeted the called with his typical, "Hall-low." Listening to the caller's words, he nodded twice. Turning toward Nazeera he announced, "Baby Sah'b. Rehana-*ji* calling."

Nazeera was pacing between the dining room and the living room - back and forth, back and forth, back and forth. She froze when the telephone rang and watched Akbar's expression as he listened to the caller's words. *Is it Daddy? Why hasn't he returned from his lunch with Amir? What are they talking about for so long!*

She heard Akbar's words announcing who the caller was. *Rehana? What does she want? To say good-bye to me since Daddy has said no?* Nazeera was too nervous to chat on the telephone to anyone. Resuming her pacing she pleaded, "Ammi, can you please take the call. I...I just can't talk to anyone right now."

Laughing at her daughter's plight, Ammi put her hand stitching down on the side table and took the telephone receiver from Akbar. She smiled at her daughter as she began chatting with the caller, responding and bobbling her head several times. Nazeera heard only bits of the conversation between her pacing, "*Aacha*", "Very nice boy," "*Aacha*", "Tomorrow", "*Huh*", "*Theek hai*", "Good-bye".

Replacing the receiver, Ammi glanced at her pacing daughter and pulled the telephone and its long extension cord into her bedroom.

Who is she calling now? Why doesn't she tell me what Rehena said? What is going on?!

Nazeera shrugged her shoulders and stomped onto the veranda. Maybe she could catch a breeze while she waited for her mother. It had been another hot steamy day. Beads of sweat were trickling down the back of her purple and white *salwar kameez*. She slumped in her usual chair and leaned back against the cushions. *Oh, it's still hot out here. Maybe Akbar can bring me something to drink?*

Before she could call out to Akbar, her mother stepped onto the veranda giggling like a young girl. "*Beta*, that was Rehana on the phone. Your daddy has given his consent to a marriage to Amir." Nazeera was in shock. Daddy had agreed!

Her mother continued speaking rapidly in Hindi, "There is a lot to do. As you know, typical weddings take several months to pre-pare." Nazeera nodded. There was a lot to do to make the wedding successful - locations to secure, guests to invite, saris and jewelry to purchase, sari blouses to make, flowers to order and ceremonies to organize. "We only have six days since Amir is scheduled to leave on Saturday." *That will need to change. I'll insist on that. Amir must understand they need more time! This is my wedding! Our wedding!*

Nazeera's heart began to beat rapidly and she began to swoon. This was all happening so fast.

Her mother continued, very excited, "Amir knows we need more time. Rehana said he is already planning to ask his boss for additional leave. But first things first, you need to be formally engaged." Ammi sat down on the chair next to her daughter. "Amir's family is coming over tomorrow to present the engagement and wedding saris."

Smiling from ear to ear, she added, "They are purchasing the wedding sari, and I thought you might like to shop for the engage-ment sari this afternoon." Her mother was obviously excited to go shopping, "I just phoned Nusrat Aunty. We are meeting her and your cousins at Kala Niketan on Charni Road in one hour."

Nazeera was still in a daze. She simply nodded. Daddy had agreed!

The *salwar kameez* she was wearing was sticky and wet from perspi-ration. Before she changed her clothes, Nazeera dusted herself heavily with baby powder to absorb some of the sweat and odor. Combing her armoire for another *salwar kameez*, she chose a simple pastel blue and white outfit, hoping the colors would not be distracting when she held the sari fabrics against it.

Nazeera knew exactly what type of fabric she wanted for the engagement sari. Something from her birthplace, Surat, and now a common addition to more expensive saris throughout India – *zari*. This fabric consisted of threads of fine gold or silver woven into sari fabric to add a touch of elegance. She had worn sari fabric with a small amount of *zari* in the borders on prior occasions, but for her engagement sari, she wanted the *zari* to be woven throughout.

Charni Road was a twenty minute car ride from the flat. Their regular driver did not work on Sundays, so the pair caught a taxi from outside the CCI. They arrived only a few minutes before Nusrat Aunty, Pinky and Dolly. Exchanging strong hugs and double kisses, they entered the store.

The bride described what type of sari fabric she wanted. With this goal in mind, the older ladies asked the shopkeeper about the shop's selection of *zari* saris. Nazeera reviewed them, disappointed with their selection.

At the fourth store, their enthusiasm was waning and they gladly accepted the offered glasses of lemonade as refreshments. Ammi and Nusrat Aunty sat on wooden stools and sipped their drinks as the three cousins approached the counter.

Pinky placed her palm on the glass countertop, strumming her fingers, "Do you have any sari fabric with *zari* threading running throughout?"

The shopkeeper approached the trio and listened to Pinky's request. She turned and pulled out fabric similar to what they had seen in the previous three stores. Dolly threw up her hands, "Don't you have anything nicer? This is for a wedding."

An older man walked behind the shopkeeper, reaching for a sari Nazeera had rejected earlier. He started to fold it, as he overhead Dolly's frustrated question. He looked up from the sari and simply said, "*Ache* minute."

He placed the half-folded sari onto the glass countertop and turned around to face the mirror wall behind the shopkeeper. Using a key from the key ring clipped to his trouser belt loop, he placed it into a small lock and turned it to the left. Pushing the small door of the mirror wall to the right, he exposed a mystery cupboard with two shelves full of saris.

Pulling three from the bottom shelf, he laid them in front of the eager girls. Each sari was still wrapped in plastic. He asked if they would like to see any of them more closely.

Nazeera stepped toward the saris and felt relief flow through her body. Finally! This is exactly what she was hoping to find! She looked at them closely, pointing to the third one as one she wanted to see closer. The older man pulled the sari from the protective wrap and with a few quick flips of the wrist, spread the fabric over the half folded one on the counter.

"Wow, this one is beautiful!" Dolly said with some relief.

"What do you think about this one, Ra-Ra?" Pinky asked, looking eager to touch it.

Leaning forward, Nazeera looked closely at the sari. "The threading and fabric quality are good, but do you have something with paisleys and flowers?"

"Ache minute." He turned back to the magic cupboard and pulled a plastic bag from the top shelf. He carefully pulled the fabric out from the bag and with a flip of his wrists, he spread the silver colored sari with gold *zari* threading onto a empty section of countertop. The gold threading was done in rows of small flowers with an edging of larger flowers and gold tassels. There was also a row of small paisley detailing between the small and large flowers.

Nazeera was bewitched, and her eyes began to tear. "This is it!" she said as she wiped a tear of happiness from her right eye, "Ammi, this is it."

Her mother put down her mostly finished glass of lemonade and came to stand next to her daughter. Both of them touched the fabric, being careful to only touch the edge. Now that Nazeera held it, she noticed how delicate it was. And how perfect. *Oh, but the price. I hope it's not too much. It would be silly for them to spend a lot of money on a sari I'm only going to wear for a few hours.*

"Khubsoorat! Beautiful!" Dolly gasped.

"Exquisite threading!" Nusrat Aunty admired, joining the group.

"Really pretty design, Ra-Ra!" Pinky awed.

186

After their moments of admiration, her mother asked the price of the lovely sari and responded with a simple, *"Aacha."*

Does that mean it's too expensive? I really want this sari. With high hopes, she picked up the fabric and draped it around her shoulders. It was perfect.

CHAPTER 28

Monday, August 22

"I WILL CHERISH THIS FOREVER"

Nazeera woke up an hour earlier than she normally did. She was so excited for today's events, she just couldn't sleep. Prone on her back, she laid in bed for several minutes watching the ceiling fan spin around and around. *They'll be here later today to present me with my engagement sari. My engagement sari!*

Jumping from her bed, she enthusiastically opened the armoire doors. Shanti had placed her folded saris on the shelves on the left and her folded *salwar kameez* outfits on the right. Too anxious to make a decision, her head went left, then right, then left, then she just reached into one of the shelves on the right and pulled out an outfit. It didn't matter what she wore right now, she would put on her more formal outfit later. She turned her light off and tiptoed into the dining room hoping not to wake her parents. They needed their sleep. This would be a hard day for both of them. But, especially her father.

Crossing the threshold of her bedroom she noticed the light was already on in the dining room. Someone was already up. Probably Akbar making preparations for lunch or Shanti cleaning the flat.

"Good morning, *Beta*," Ammi said in a soft voice sounding slightly tired, "I see you couldn't sleep either."

"No, Ammi," Nazeera replied as she came down from her

tiptoes and allowed her feet to touch the cool morning floor, "I'm too anxious."

"So are we," her father announced returning from the kitchen with a hot cup of tea, "We both tossed and turned all night. We just came out here to have some tea. We thought we would have to wake Akbar to make it, but he was already awake too. We are all anxious. This is happening so fast."

Nazeera put her hand on her father's shoulders, this wedding was bittersweet. She loved her parents dearly and had enjoyed her childhood. But, with this marriage, they would not be a big part of her adult life. She would be in America and they would be here. Maybe once Daddy retires, they could move there. But, why would they? Aziz and Hamid are here. "Oh!" she suddenly said out loud, "We must tell Aziz and Hamid. They should be here!"

Her parents exchanged glances, "Yes, we were thinking that too. We thought it best to wait a little while to call them. Aziz could come after work tonight. Hamid may not be able to make it. He'd have to come from Delhi."

"Do you really think Hamid will come?" Nazeera asked sitting in the chair next to her father and curling her legs up to her body. The air was cool this time of the morning. She hadn't been up this early in a long time. Maybe years. She considered going back to her bedroom for a blanket, but Akbar arrived with a cup of hot tea for her.

"Good morning, Baby Sah'b," he said gently. She smiled at him and wished him good morning as well. They had been exchanging good morning greetings for over a decade. *Oh, my,* she suddenly thought, *I'm going to miss him too. And Shanti. She knew exactly how to match fabrics and how I like to wear my saris. Who will help me get dressed in America? Who will make my tea? Wait, who would help me do anything?! Wow, this is going to be harder than I thought!* Tears began to form in her eyes and her usual strong resolve shattered into little pieces. She began to cry.

"Oh, *Beta*," Ammi said as she moved closer to her daughter and put her arms gently around her, "Come, come. You'll come back to visit. I especially want to see my grandchildren."

"But... but...." was all Nazeera could say in response.

"We love you too, *Beta*. We will miss you dearly," Daddy said with a slight crackle in his voice. "But, this Amir seems to be a good man and you will have a good life in Ameer-ic-ka."

Nazeera continued to sob and she wiped away a few tears with her *dupatta*. "And," Ammi added with a upbeat tone, "And, his family seems very nice." Nazeera slowed her tears and wiped her eyes again. This was the beginning of the next chapter of her life. Her next adventure, right?

The trio continued to sit at the dining room table as Akbar made them his special cheese and *kothmir* omelets. They ate them happily and enjoyed the breakfast together as a family. The eggs were fluffy and the cilantro gave the dish an earthy flavor. Her father had another two cups of tea and then declared he was ready to phone his sons.

He telephoned Aziz first. Her brother was still at home and very happy with her choice of husband. He said he would meet them at the party tonight. He wrote down the time and the address. That was easy.

Hamid was another story. He lived in Delhi and since they had called Aziz first, they believed he was now at work. Daddy called his work number and had to leave a message with his secretary. She had said he was going to be at clients all day.

After the telephone calls, Ammi took the opportunity to remind Nazeera how to act. They sat on Nazeera's bed and she practiced her demure head pose – head slightly tilted forward and eyes cast down.

Ammi repeated, "*Aacha*, a proper Indian bride should not be too anxious to marry her husband." Sufficiently impressed with her daughter's demure pose, Ammi changed the instruction to respect, "*Theek hai*, let me see you show proper respect to the groom's mother."

Nazeera took her mother's hand and pressed her forehead against it and then kissed it. She practiced this repeatedly until Ammi declared with a head bobble, "*Bas*. Enough."

The tedious process of getting ready for the arrival of the guests was made a bit more fun by the sun shining outside the window. Shanti opened up the blinds in both bedrooms to allow the friendly sun to stream into the rooms. The air had cooled slightly with last night's rain and the fresh air smelled of hope. A yellow songbird came and landed on the windowsill in Nazeera's bedroom. The songbird chirped and then broke into song to entertain them as Shanti helped Nazeera step into her petticoat.

Nazeera knew she would be in a lot of photos today, so she took extra time with her makeup. She put black eye liner on her upper eyelid and then on the inside of her lower eyelid. Then, she added black mascara to make her eyes really stand out. She added a touch of moisturizer to her face and finished her preparations with a touch of *Princess Pink* lipstick. Shanti brushed and brushed her long flowing hair and then twisted it into a loose bun.

After placing multiple bobby pins in her hair to hold it place, Shanti showed her mistress the sari she suggested she wear for the ceremony. It was an aqua marine color which she said would contrast nicely with the silver-gold engagement sari Nazeera had described to her.

Approving the sari selection, Nazeera placed her arms through a silver sari blouse and buttoned the tiny buttons to ensure a snug fit. She stepped into the petticoat and then nodded to Shanti to help her expertly pleat the sari fabric. Lastly, Nazeera screwed the ear backs on her favorite earrings – gold dangling ones she got from her *Nanima* – and she placed a simple gold chain around her neck.

There was a knock on the bedroom door and she heard her father's voice call to his daughter. "*Ache* minute. One minute." Nazeera said surprised anyone was knocking on her door. "I'm almost ready." Shanti finished closing the clasp on the necklace and Nazeera slowly moved toward the door, rustling as she walked. She paused to allow Shanti to open the door and then she proceeded across the threshold. "Daddy, were you looking for me?"

Daddy nodded, "Yes, *Beta*, your mother and I have something for you." Nazeera smiled. Presents!! She cautiously followed him into their bedroom, spotting her mother standing next to the bed. Nazeera smiled when she noticed her mother was holding a red box. She hoped it was jewelry, red boxes were the unofficial box color of jewelry stores.

As Nazeera approached her mother, she examined what she was wearing. She looked stunning in her royal blue raw silk sari with large golden tassels along the border. She wore five gold bangles on her right wrist and one thick one on her left. Her gold earrings had a ruby and gold wreath shaped center and two beaded strands hanging down. As usual, her face was powdered heavily, giving her the fair complexion she was craving, but making her cherry red lips contrast even more sharply.

Ammi waited until her daughter approached, then opened the box and withdrew a gold choker necklace. It was made up of dozens of one inch wide and two inch long gold rectangles strung along a black cord. Hanging from the bottom edge of each gold plate were two small gold balls that jingled when they were shaken. Nazeera knew this necklace was one of her mother's favorites. She had seen her mother wear it to many weddings and other special occasions.

"Nazeera," Ammi said holding back the tears, "We want you to have this necklace. It was given to me by my parents as part of my wedding dowry. Now, I know Amir is not asking for a dowry, but we still want you to have this as a wedding gift from us."

Tears welled up in Nazeera's eyes and she fluttered them repeatedly to keep the tears from smearing her eyeliner. Leaning forward, she gave her mother, and then father, as big a hug as she could without ruining make up or saris. "I know how much you love this necklace, Ammi. I will cherish this forever."

She handed the precious necklace to her father. He struggled with the clasp and cursed a couple times. *Why is he struggling? He's put this on Ammi many times*. Frustrated, he called for Shanti and she came running. The servant gasped at the gift and also welled up a bit as she swapped the simple gold chain around Nazeera's neck for the choker necklace her parents had just given her. Even Shanti knew it was special.

They all wiped their eyes carefully, and headed into the living room. The doorbell rang and Akbar opened the door to Ammi's brother and family. They lived in central Bombay and had taken a taxi to the Yashodham flat to be in attendance for the engagement ceremonies. They planned to stay all day to help as needed, but really, they just wanted to be there. This was an important day for the family and since Nazeera held a special place in their hearts, they wanted to be part of it.

Nazeera was surprised to see Jhoma Uncle, as he worked during the day. *He must have taken the day off of work*. He exclaimed joy as he walked into the flat, wrapping his loving arms around her in a huge bear hug. She allowed him to hug her, hoping he would let go soon. After he released her, he and her male cousin, Khazin, strolled onto the veranda jesting the flat was too stuffy at this time of day. Daddy kissed her on the forehead and quickly joined the men on the veranda. He closed the French doors after himself, but the ladies could still hear the guys laughing about something. At least they were out of the way.

Nusrat Aunty looked stunning in her silver sari with cerulean blue leaves and matching sari blouse. She wore her favorite gold square watch on her left wrist. She had received it from Jhoma Uncle on their tenth wedding anniversary, and she wore it proudly on special occasions, such as this. The watch had a unique gold face with no numbers as the hours were designated by small slivers of gold that had been very delicately placed onto the watch face. The face shimmered slightly as it caught the streams of daylight. The gold of the watch clashed with her silver sari, but she didn't care.

Her daughter, Pinky preferred blue colors and she had selected a baby-blue *salwar kameez* with a dark navy *dupatta* and little tassels on the end. She wore dove-gray *chappals* with a large navy blue daisy hot-glued near the big toe. She liked to spice-up outfits by adding her special touches wherever she could. Dolly preferred the other end of the spectrum and wanted to wear something that would contrast with her mother and sister. She originally had on a pale pink outfit, but at the last minute changed into a hot pink *salwar kameez*. She thought it was more fitting for the celebration of Nazeera's engagement. She was jealous of her cousin leaving India to begin a life of adventure. She wanted desperately to leave the hum drum life in Bombay. Maybe she too could find a husband and move to America? Or England? Or Australia?

Dolly whispered into her cousin's ear, "You look like a Bollywood actress! Amir is a lucky man." The girls giggled, grabbed hands and plunked onto the settee.

Leaning forward, Pinky added, "I can't wait to meet him, Ra-Ra!" The girls continued to giggle. This was going to be a fun day!

Akbar came around and offered the guests glasses of lemonade and mango *lassi*. He had been told several times that morning, by both Daddy and Ammi, to make sure the guests did not get dehydrated with the sweltering August heat. Neither one of them wanted fainting guests!

Taking a sip of lemonade, Nazeera noticed Akbar looked weary today, but still forced a toothy smile whenever he spoke. *It looks as if he hadn't slept well last night either. What's bothering him? Maybe today will be bittersweet for him, too.*

Buzz. Buzz. The doorbell rang and the giggling immediately stopped. *Here we go,* Nazeera thought to herself. *Stay strong, be respectful.*

The cousins vacated the settee and the five ladies formed an ad hoc greeting line in the main hallway. Akbar opened the door and the stream of Virani ladies began. Amir's mother strode in first, and was introduced by Ammi to the other ladies. Nazeera took note of the various saris each one was wearing. Each of them was dressed very well for this important occasion.

Her soon-to-be mother-in-law wore a Persian pink chiffon sari with a rose and silver flower filigree on the border and matching winding vine pattern throughout the fabric. The cultured pearl necklace and earrings she wore complimented the shimmer of the border. Instead of a traditional watch, she wore a silver bracelet watch with a diamond in the twelve position. It jangled as she moved her wrist and the diamond sparkled when sunlight hit it just right. Today, she wore her hair slightly brushed back and her gray and white horn-rimmed glasses. She looked every bit the mother of the groom. Very elegant but yet motherly.

Nadia and Nilofer were both in yellow saris. Nadia in a metallic silk marigold version that seemed to have been wound too tight around her pregnant belly and Nilofer in a sunflower chiffon that seemed to make her smile even more bright. Bandra wore a chocolate brown sari with a *zari* butterfly design. She did not seem happy to be here and kept her hands folded in front of her.

Rehana also wore a pink chiffon sari but unlike Shakila's, hers had little white flowers sprinkled throughout the fabric. She wore three strands of silver necklaces, and contrasted the pink sari with deep red lipstick. Her six year old daughter, Rabia, wore a matching pink dress with little white flowers and a cotton candy pink headband. The two of them crossed the threshold together holding hands and they looked very cute in their semi-matching outfits.

The ladies one-by-one gave the bride a big hug and two cheek kisses. Each of them commented on her outfit or her hair or how pretty she looked. She must have really looked stunning because she overheard grouchy Bandra admit, under her breath to Nilofer, that the bride did look nice.

They mingled for a little while, sipping lemonade or Akbar's fresh mango *lassis*. He also brought some Bombay snack mix and nuts for them to nibble. Nilofer and Nadia wandered onto the veranda and met the gentlemen hiding there. They chatted for a bit, but when Ammi clapped her hands, the entire group congregated in the living room. The three gentlemen hovered in the background, with Jhoma Uncle taking photos.

There was much discussion about who should sit where and the group finally relented to Shakila's insistence that the bride should be placed in the middle of the group. At her father's suggestion, Akbar had pushed the sofa, small loveseat and all the chairs against the settee.

Nazeera would have preferred to be by herself on a chair rather than next to all the sweaty Aunties, but she forced a smiled and sat down in the middle of the seating arrangement. Shakila quickly sat down on her left with Ammi on her right. The three of them filled the settee. Rehana sat next to Shakila at one end of the sofa with Nadia, Nilofer and then Bandra to her left. Rabia sat at her mother's feet and stared at Nazeera. Nusrat Aunty sat next to Ammi on the loveseat with Pinky next to her and Dolly sitting on the arm.

Shakila motioned to Bandra. With a glare, she stood up, crossed in front of the other Virani women and stood in front of Nazeera. As the eldest sister, it was her honor, or in this case her duty, to be the first one to officially welcome the bride. As instructed by her mother, Nazeera kept her head down but she did glance up once to see Bandra was still not smiling. She quickly averted her eyes as Bandra placed the red wedding veil over her head and retreated to her place on the far end of the sofa.

Nearly tripping over her daughter, Rehana stood up and stepped in front of the bride. With slight instructions to Rabia, the two of them placed a garland of fragrant white jasmine and red roses over Nazeera's head. She wished the recipient good health and then returned to her spot on the sofa. Rabia returned to her place, but remained standing and stared at the bride.

Next, Nilofer smiled a broad smile and approached the bride. She slowly placed the engagement sari over Nazeera's right shoulder and draped the glittering fabric across her torso to maximize the amount of fabric showing in front. Nazeera simply smiled to herself. *This is really happening!*

Before Nilofer fully returned to her seat, Nadia eagerly stood up to present the jewelry. She opened the red box to reveal two gold bracelets, a gold necklace and a set of earrings. She slowly waved it in front of Nazeera and then the group, so everyone could see. Nazeera snuck a peek at the jeweler's name on the box. It was TBZ. *Isn't that the jewelry store William's mummy went? Did they buy this today? Is this the jewelry set Aunty had taken all the way to America when she tried to marry Amir to an American woman? Well, it doesn't matter. It's mine now.*

Finally, Shakila stood up using Rehana's arm as a crutch, and turned toward the bride. Nazeera immediately took her hand and did *addabars* to show respect to the elder, just as her mother had shown her hours earlier. She did it perfectly and Ammi smiled proudly. Shakila smiled and placed her left hand on top of Nazeera's head and patted it. After a moment, she mumbled something that no one was able to hear, not even Nazeera, and sat back down.

To make sure the bride and groom, and their families, only say sweet things to each other, Indian tradition dictates each wedding ceremony includes *sherbet*, the group sharing something sweet. As the jewelry presentation had concluded, Ammi called to Akbar. He and Shanti hurriedly scampered into the living room carrying trays of *pista kulfi*. As instructed, they had used all the crystal bowls the Khan's had, even a few sterling silver ones, to provide each person a serving.

The group carefully ate the *kulfi* as no one wanted to spill on their precious outfits, and then the Virani ladies stood up and began saying good-bye. As Rehana hugged Nazeera, she whispered she had something special planned for the engagement ceremony tonight.

Rabia stood by her mother and silently stared at the bride. After a half-hour of hugs and kisses, the ladies finally left the flat.

When Akbar shut the door after the final Virani exited, Pinky and Dolly pounced on Nazeera admiring the fabric of the engagement sari. Nusrat Aunty and Ammi each picked up an earring and pretended to weigh it in their hands. Nazeera slowly removed the veil and garland from over her head. She glanced around the room trying to savor every moment. Once she had mentally memorized the moment, she removed the two bracelets from the box and slipped them over each wrist. They fit perfectly.

The next few hours were filled with stories of the courtship. Pinky and Dolly wanted to know the details, all the details.

"When did you meet Amir?"

"What was your first impression of him?"

"What does he look like?"

"Why did you say yes to his proposal?"

"What happened to Habib?"

Nazeera giggled through most of the answers. She was excited to be the center of attention; but also, the events didn't seem real until she shared them with her pseudo-sisters. The three of them had been close since they were young children. Although they had not lived nearby since before they were teenagers, they called and wrote each other often. Surprisingly, even though Nazeera and her parents had moved back to Bombay six months ago, she had not seen her cousins more than a handful of times. Life had been busy for all of them this summer. But, yesterday, when Ammi had called Nusrat Aunty to update her on Nazeera's engagement, they dropped everything to help her shop for an engagement sari and attend today's events. Family.

The hours between the engagement sari drop-off and the engagement party flew by. Ammi, Nusrat Aunty and Jhoma Uncle sat on the veranda, sipping lemonade and discussing life. Daddy and Khazin occupied themselves with sampling plates of hot food Akbar had expertly prepared. The family grew closer and when Ammi mentioned it was time for them to change into the evenings clothes, everyone was excited and anxious.

Pinky and Dolly briskly followed the bride into her bedroom, giggling the whole way. Pinky combed Nazeera's flowing hair with long brush strokes until it was soft and straight. Then with her left hand she gathered and twisted it into a soft bun. As she strategically placed a dozen or so black bobby pins into Nazeera's hair, Dolly dabbed copper eye-shadow above her black eyeliner. She then continued with face powder to make her skin more fair and finished by caressing her lips with Nazeera's favorite lipstick.

Shanti stepped into the bedroom and watched the last few minutes of her mistress's preparations. Now that the cousins were done, she lifted the sari fabric from the bed and commented on it being so light, so delicate, so precious.

The cousins stepped aside and watched as Shanti helped Nazeera upgrade from her beautiful day sari to the dazzling engagement sari. First, the blouse and petticoat undergarment. Second, the six yards of silver and gold *zari* fabric. Shanti pleated and then tucked the fabric into the petticoat and then around and around Nazeera's waist she went. The remaining sari *pallu* was delicately placed on her mistress's shoulder.

Now it was time for the jewelry! Nazeera nervously opened the TBZ jewelry box she had received hours earlier from Amir's family. Each of the helpers selected a piece of gold. Pinky carefully lifted the long gold necklace over the hair bun and placed it on Nazeera's collar bone. She closed the clasp tightly and stepped aside. Dolly slowly slipped a gold bracelet onto each wrist. Lastly, Shanti fed the long earrings posts into the ear holes and tediously screwed them into place. The bride stepped back to look at herself in the mirror. *Something is missing. What is it? Rings. No, she will receive the engagement ring tonight. No need to wear any other rings. Maybe a nose ring? No, that will be for the wedding.* Then it dawned on her. She wanted to wear the choker necklace her parents had given her that morning. She had removed it when Pinky had been brushing her hair.

Picking up the choker necklace, she handed it to Shanti. The servant placed it on her collarbone and closed the clasp on the back of the necklace. With relief, Nazeera noticed the two necklaces complimented each other. The choker and the engagement necklaces were the exact color of the gold *zari* thread. They looked perfect. She looked perfect.

As Nazeera made her entrance in the living room, her parents stood up to admire her. "*Khubsoorat*! Beautiful!" was all Daddy could manage to say. She noticed a tear in his eye. *Is he crying?*

Ammi had changed into an indigo blue sari with three matching blue stone bangles. She wore matching earrings that were so long they touched the top of her shoulders. Her hair was slicked back to highlight the dangling earrings. Daddy looked very handsome in his dark blue Nehru jacket suit, though he tugged at his neck collar occasionally. *Is it too tight?*

The phone rang and Akbar informed the group the car was waiting downstairs. Daddy acknowledged his announcement and told him to tell the driver they would be down in a few minutes. Ammi took her daughter's hand and squeezed it. *Here we go!*

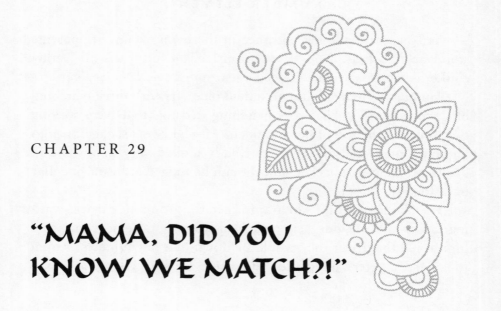

CHAPTER 29

"MAMA, DID YOU KNOW WE MATCH?!"

An hour before noon, Rehana hummed as she rolled her daughter's hair with hot rollers. She was in a great mood. Amir had chosen the girl she had found. Sure, she was a last minute addition, number eleven on the list of ten girls; but, nonetheless, he had chosen Nazeera.

"Owwie, Mama, that hurts!" Rabia shrieked as Rehana twisted her hair around a hot curler.

"Hush, *bacchi*. Baby. Sit still. You want your hair to look pretty, no?" Rehana soothed and continued rolling.

"*Ji, huh*," Rabia replied pouting her lower lip and crossing her arms in front of her. Rehana noticed her daughter was very fidgety. *Of course she is, she's excited to be going to the engagement sari presentation. We both are.*

"The dress is ready," Jasminda said with a huge smile as she entered the bathroom. Giggling, Rabia immediately jumped from the chair and skipped to her *aaya*. Jasminda looked to Rehana for permission to help the young girl put on her dress.

Rehana unplugged the case with the remaining hot rollers and waved her hands, "That's fine. Just watch the hair."

Changing quickly, Rabia twirled around to fluff up the ruffles and enjoy a frilly dress as only six year old girls can do. Suddenly, she stopped. Silently walking to her mother, she looked up with a wide grin, "Mama, did you know we match?!"

"Yes, *bacchi*, I do." Rehana patted her daughter's shoulder and began to take out the hot rollers. Several of them had already started to come loose from the earlier twirling. Her hair had a bit of bounce, but not much. With a sigh, she brushed Rabia's hair and placed a headband in it.

"*Bas.* Now go with Jasminda. I need to finish getting ready," Rehana said with a head nod to the *aaya*. The other Virani ladies were due at their flat in half an hour. They would travel together via taxi and hopefully arrive at the Khan flat by noon.

Jasminda joined the pair and called for the child. The nanny spoke very good English as she was raised in Goa, an English speaking province south of Bombay. She had been hired to help Rehana with the children - dressing, feeding and playing with Rabia and Rafiq daily.

But today, she had been asked to do more. After Rehana and Rabia leave for the Yashodham flat, she was to watch Rafiq and help Babu prepare the elaborate meal for the engagement party. Then, tonight she was to take the children to Nadia's flat, so they could eat and play with their cousin Tarik, and not be under foot when the flat was full of people.

As Rehana screwed the backs on her earrings, Rabia sat on the edge of the bed, and let her legs swing boldly back and forth hitting the frame with a thud. She was jabbering to her mother that she was anxious for the aunties to arrive so she could meet Am-cha's bride. At an early age, Rabia had shortened Amir *Chacha* to Am-cha, *Chacha* meaning father's brother. She loved her original nickname and Amir didn't seem to mind. She knew he had met lots of women and she was excited to meet the one he selected. "What's her name?"

Ignoring her daughter's babble, Rehana hastily stepped out of the bedroom. She quickly noticed she had two ducklings following her, Rabia and Jasminda. *So much for the aaya taking care of my child.*

Rehana allowed them to follow her. First, she confirmed the breakfast dishes had been cleared. Check. Then she confirmed the living room was set up for guests. Check. Then she strode to the kitchen to check on Babu's dinner preparations. Noticing something on the floor, she stopped abruptly. Bam! Jasminda kept walking and fell on top of Rabia. The two ducklings giggled. Rehana did not find this funny. Well, maybe a little. She shot them a stern glance and the two ducklings tried to muffle their silly laughs.

As usual, everyone was late to arrive at their flat and after waiting an extra thirty minutes for Bandra, Shakila declared they should leave as it was already half-past noon. Rehana thought for a moment, *maybe Bandra is so disappointed with Amir's choice she won't even come to this event!*

As the ladies were stepping into the taxis, Bandra finally arrived. Her sister-in-law simply hopped from her taxi to the second taxi containing Nilofer and Nadia and they were off to the Yashodham flat. *Whew, she did come after all.*

❋ ❋ ❋ ❋ ❋

Rather than serving the traditional *barfi* or *kulfi* for the *sherbet* ceremony after the engagement, Shakila insisted they adopt the Western custom of a cake. She had justified her reasoning with a simple statement, "My son is from Ameer-ic-ka."

Knowing the Bombay bakeries that make such Western cakes require at least a week notice, Rehana volunteered to make the cake. She had made several cakes for her children's birthdays, and believed she could make something suitable. She hoped it would look as good as the bakeries. *This is for Amir and Nazeera, after all.*

Baking the two large sheet cakes had been the easy part. Rehana made them in the morning before breakfast. Farid had complained as to the hour she awoke, but she was determined to make the cakes while the rest of the house was quiet.

When Rehana returned home from the Khan flat, she quickly changed into a comfortable *salwar kameez,* checked on Rabia and Rafiq with Jasminda, and headed excitedly into the kitchen. Farid had left while they were gone to have lunch with the groom. *It's fun making cakes when there are no other distractions!*

Humming, she retrieved the cooled cakes from the back counter in the kitchen. She found a serving platter large enough and carefully placed the platter on top of one of the cakes. Flipping it quickly, she nodded to herself at the perfection of the flip, and placed the cake platter on the counter. Under the watchful eyes of Babu, she spread a layer of raspberry jam onto the base layer and then carefully lowered the second layer on top.

Drawing a deep breath, she slowly carved two interconnecting hearts following her hand-drawn pattern, trimming here and cutting there. She placed the discarded cake onto a plate and allowed both of her kids, Jasminda and even Babu to taste. They eagerly gobbled the cake which Rehana took as a symbol the cake was tasty. When she was finally satisfied with her carving, she covered the whole cake with her homemade almond butter-cream frosting and pressed slivered almonds onto the sides to cover up any frosting imperfections and give it a more elegant look.

Pulling out her cake decorating book, Rehana piped a few green vines and added red roses at the end of each vine, creating a bouquet of sorts. She stood back to look at her masterpiece. *Pretty good, but it needs something more. Personalization!* With exhausted and shaky hands, she piped each of their names onto the cake, a cupid's arrow and added the two plastic swans she found on the bottom of her decorating box. *Finally done!* Rehana was relieved when both Shakila and Amir told her the cake looked incredible. *Whew!*

Decorating the cake had taken several exhausting hours. Rehana lay face down on her bed, she was not used to standing for so long. After what seemed only a moment, Farid entered carrying a bottle of cola. "Here, drink this. The rest of the family will be here soon."

With a heavy sigh, Rehana sat up and drank the bottle of caffeine hoping it would perk her up quickly. With a half smile, she announced to Farid, "I'm sleeping late tomorrow."

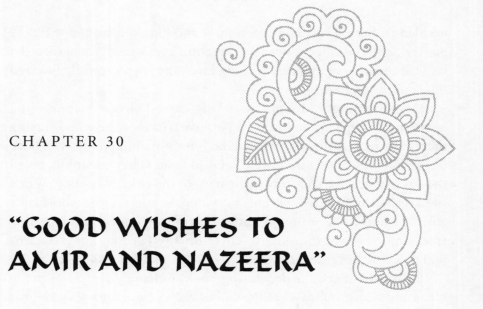

CHAPTER 30

"GOOD WISHES TO AMIR AND NAZEERA"

Amir retreated from the kitchen, very satisfied with the engagement cake Rehana had made for him and his bride. His mother was busy chatting with Babu about the evening meal, so this was his chance to grab the high back chair. He wanted to sit in that silly chair!

Passing through the hallway, he caught a glimpse of himself in the mirror. Out of nervousness, he turned and approached the mirror for the fourth time that evening. He smiled to himself. He looked handsome in his freshly pressed blue suit - the same one that he had worn the night he met Nazeera. Incredibly, that was only ten days ago. He was wearing the narrow blue and burgundy tie and matching handkerchief that he had been given by his American friends the Nomla's, as a Christmas present. He brought it to India specifically for this occasion. He patted his oiled hair trying to tame it. It stayed in place for only a second and then bounced up a bit. *Darn cowlick.* The doorbell rang. He took a few breaths and counted to ten. *Okay, this is it.*

The now familiar foot stomping could be heard throughout the flat moving from the kitchen to the front door. Farid shouted from the bedroom to Babu to open the door. Noticing both of the hosts were still getting ready, Nadia jumped up from the loveseat and wobbled to the hallway. She greeted each of the guests and escorted the trio into the living room. Bandra and Nilofer were sitting on the sofa sipping tea. Now that the guests had arrived, they each stood up and welcomed them to the flat. Amir noticed Bandra wore a cynical smile. *Does she think I may still change my mind?*

The dining room chairs, as well as a few borrowed chairs from the neighbor across the hall, were set up against the wall to provide ample seating. With a heavy sigh, Rahim sat on the dining room chair nearest the wooden bookshelf. Amir wondered, w*hy did he sit way over there? Better view?* Nazeera entered the room demurely and stood at the edge of the furniture formation not sure where to sit. Rehana had changed into a blue sari and silver jewelry and now rushed into the living room to insist Nazeera sit next to Amir on the loveseat. The hostess shooed her sister-in-laws off the sofa to make room for the two mothers. Although Mummy would have preferred her usual spot on the high back chair, she sat next to Lailaa and leaned back on a nearby pillow.

After watching the rest of them be seated, Amir nervously stepped into the living room. All eyes turned to him and he began to welcome the guests one-by-one with the firm handshake he had learned from attending several American business meetings. He knew everyone at the party and sincerely appreciated them being there. Luckily he completed his rounds near the loveseat, so he simply took his designated place next to his fiancé. The gold thread in the sari made her eyes even more dazzling. *Wow! She's my bride. She said yes!! She's my Miss Right!*

Nazeera's brother, Aziz, arrived just a few minutes after Kassim and Nadir. He came armed with a camera, and immediately began circling the flat taking photos. Flash! He took photos of the engaged couple, the mothers, his father, the host and hostess, the aunties and uncles, the cake and even the dinner table. A few other guests got the same idea and so suddenly there were three or four cameras taking photos. Flash! Flash! They were capturing the whole evening on film, which was great because Amir wanted to remember this evening for a long time.

Glancing at his chosen bride, Amir noticed her eyes were blinking frantically - her long eyelashes dancing on her cheeks. *Is she wearing gold eye shadow?* A moment later, Aziz's flashing abruptly stopped, and everyone was staring at him. *What did I miss? Am I supposed to say something?*

Mercifully, Mummy stood up and gestured for Rahim to join her and Lailaa on the sofa. Once he was seated on her left, she took each of their hands in hers and lifted them slightly. "Welcome to our home," she struggled in English, "Good wishes to Amir and Nazeera." Turning toward Rahim, as representative of Amir's side of the family, she formally offered the proposal of marriage of Amir to Nazeera. Rahim and Lailaa graciously accepted.

Mummy hobbled to the loveseat, and stood before her son. Fumbling with the folds of her sari, she pulled out a small square red box. With a smile, she reached toward him with her gnarled fingers. As he did so, Amir was reminded how old his mother really was. He was proud he had fulfilled his promise to her while she was still alive.

Before he even took the box, Amir knew what it held. It was the diamond ring his mother had been given by his father on their tenth wedding anniversary. Mummy knew in America, engagement rings were diamonds, so she insisted Amir give her cherished ring to his fiancé. As he took the box, Amir stood up and gave his mother a long hug and tender kiss on the right cheek. She smiled and fought back tears.

Amir sat down lightly on the loveseat, and opened the red velvet box careful not to let Nazeera see the contents. He glanced in her direction noticing her eyes were still downcast. He took the sparkling ring out of the box, shutting it with a snap. The diamond looked brilliant and he was pleased they had followed Nadia's suggestion to get it cleaned. With a soft whisper he asked for Nazeera's left hand. Holding it lightly, he slipped the jewel studded gold ring onto her finger.

The ring must have been a bit too wide for her delicate finger as the diamond crown immediately slipped off to one side. Nazeera pushed it back upright and then nervously placed her right hand over it to conceal that it had slipped again. They would need to get it fitted for her thinner fingers. She looked up with a smile and pretended that nothing was wrong with the ring. The group cheered and took more photos. Flash! Flash! Flash!

With a sigh of relief, Mummy motioned to bring out the cake. Rehana was smiling at the couple and missed her mother-in-law's cue. Farid nudged her elbow and tilted his head toward his mother raising his eyebrows at the same time. She glanced in Mummy's direction and winced. Scurrying into the kitchen, Rehana returned carrying the white ceramic platter with the two-heart shaped cake. There were many ooh's and aah's as they watched her place it in front of the engaged couple. Rehana stepped back smiling from ear to ear as the flash bulbs blinded everyone again.

The cake sat on the coffee table as they waited for Babu to bring a long serrated knife for them to cut it. This gave the couple a much needed moment to regain their eyesight as the blue flashing dot from the flash bulbs continued to haunt them for a few moments.

Babu handed the knife to Amir. It had two long red ribbons tied to the end. It was a small detail that transformed the knife from one to cut *naan* to one worthy of cutting an engagement cake. Amir took the knife from Babu and leaned closer to Nazeera so she could place her right hand next to his. With a quick glance at each other, they sliced the cake just off to the side. The group again cheered and the flash bulbs blinded the couple. Flash! Flash!

Not knowing what to do, Amir handed the knife to his sister-in-law. Rehana knelt down beside him and proceeded to cut the cake into manageable pieces. With Babu's assistance, she placed them onto her ebony china plates with the gold rim. She gave a plate to Amir and resumed cutting the cake.

Savoring the almond flavor in the frosting and the sweet flavor of the filling, Amir enjoyed his first two bites. He was chewing his third bite when he noticed his soon-to-be wife did not have a cake plate. Thoughts rushed through his mind. *Why has Rehena skipped her? Am I supposed to share my piece with her?*

He was about to share his plate with Nazeera, when he got a mischievous idea, and offered her a forkful. She looked at him with a puzzled expression but quickly figured out what he was trying to do. With a sigh, she raised her eyebrows and opened her mouth. He delicately fed her the forkful being careful not to drop any crumbs onto her sari. Licking her lips, he watched her chew the cake. Good.

So far, so good. He offered her another forkful, but she politely refused and asked for her own plate.

They ate their dessert before dinner, but sometimes that's how things go. After indulging in a slice of engagement cake, the group followed Rehana into the dining room. Babu was still in the process of strategically placing the serving dishes around the table. As they waited for him to finish laying the rice and *naan*, she declared the menu was created in honor of the bride and groom.

There was so much food on the dining room table, Nazeera noticed there was no room for a centerpiece. Beautiful china dinner plates and bowls sat on one side of the table, atop the pristine red tablecloth. Small placecards lay next to each dish with handwritten words scribbled on them. Following Amir around the table, she read the name of the dish and the source of the recipe on each card.

The second card she read said the source of the recipe was her mother. Smiling, she looked at the dish. The *paya salen* looked expertly done. *Did Babu make it from Akbar's recipe or did Akbar secretly make it and bring it over?* Smiling at the slow-cooked goat feet curry, she knew Rehana had definitely made an effort to identify her favorite dishes.

Around the table she went, now with a spry step. There was her mother's recipe for lamb *biryani*. The layered meat, potato, onion and rice dish was commonplace at special occasions such as this. *At least at my house. Biryani is a multi-step, multi-hour dish. What an effort they've made!*

Next to the lamb *biryani* was Rehana's shrimp *vindaloo*. She had never had the spicy shrimp dish. She assumed it was spicy as *vindaloo* preparations were usually spicy. The shrimp looked nice and plump, so she spooned a few onto her plate next to the lamb dish. Stepping forward, she absentmindedly took an *aaloo paratha*, dropping it immediately onto her plate on top of the *biryani*. *Ow!* She waved her hand instinctively back and forth trying to dissipate the heat from her fingertips. That potato flatbread was hot!

Blowing on her fingers, she watched Amir. He seemed to take a spoonful of everything. *No wonder he wants to know if I can cook! He has a big appetite!* His plate was already half-full, but he added a *pomfret* fillet. Nazeera had eaten the bony flat fish before, but it wasn't her favorite fish.. She glanced around hoping to see a dish of *Bombil*. There was none.

Returning her gaze to her fiancé, she watched Amir ladle *Dudhi Daal* into a bowl. *Hmm. Does he have rice in the bowl? No. Is he going to drink it like soup? I guess so. I've never seen that before.* Nazeera enjoyed eating *daal*, so she spooned the lentils with squash over steaming *basmati* rice. *Might as well try it, but my way - with rice.*

Nudging her along, Ammi insisted she try some of the *Palak Paneer*. Nazeera whispered she preferred *Matar Paneer* with the peas over the *Palak Paneer* with the spinach. "Just take a spoonful. The cheese and spinach dish is one of Rehana's specialties." Listening to her mother, she reluctantly took a spoonful.

With her plate now full, she retreated to her designated spot on the loveseat. Amir was sipping the *daal* just like soup. She stared incredulously at him for a moment. *He must have eaten it that way as a child. Or is that something he learned in America?*

Everyone seemed to be enjoying the meal, and she smiled when her brother and father returned to the dining room table feast for a second helping. Aziz had a plate full of *paya salen*. He ate some of the goat meat with a piece of *naan*, then proceeded to noisily suck the marrow from inside the bones. She was envious of her brother as she loved to do that too. *It's the best part!*

Her mother was still eating the lamb *biryani*. Nazeera had enjoyed the sample she had tasted, noticing this version was similar to Akbar's. But, it was slightly different, which meant Babu had used her mother's recipe only as a guide. It was a very common dish for special occasions and Rehena probably had her own recipe that Babu had made several times.

Ammi was staring at a spot above Nazeera's head. From the expression on her face, she was probably analyzing Babu's cooking technique of the lamb and potatoes. Akbar usually pan fried them before he layered the meat and potatoes in the casserole dish. Meat - potatoes - rice - onions - repeat. She knew the layers very well. Babu had not used as many fried onions as Akbar, but he had added a bit more saffron to the rice. Slight changes, and still delicious.

The room was buzzing with conversation in between bites of food. Amir was definitely enjoying his *pomfret*. She watched him with interest as he removed the small bones from the fish filet and took a large bite. He chewed smugly and she wondered what spices were included in the curry. Probably *kothmir* since the curry is green. Most likely minced garlic and cumin. *Hmm.... I guess I better ask her how to prepare that dish. I'm sure Amir will want me to make it for him.*

She laughed to herself and glanced at Rehana. The hostess had her eyes closed, dark patches beginning to form under each eye. She was leaning back on the chair, seemingly enjoying a moment of quiet.

Continuing her scan of the room, Nazeera noticed her father was thoroughly enjoying a plate of lamb *biryani*. With a slight tear in her eye, she turned to watch Bandra as she nibbled on the edge of an *aaloo paratha*. She smiled for an instant but then almost instantly the smile was gone. *What's wrong? Why does she have a constant scowl on her face?*

Shrugging her shoulders, Nazeera turned her head toward her mother again. She still looked lovely though the powder on her face was beginning to fade. Her eyes were afire with conversation and her earrings danced on her shoulders with every word she uttered. She was having a great time!

The evening was a success. The business of the engagement was complete. They had shared something sweet, and enjoyed a delicious meal. Babu collected the plates, returning with a platter of finger bowls with quarters of lemon to cleanse their fingers. Once the cleansing was complete, he moved onto an offering of fruit. As a few of them peeled and ate a custard apple, the questions commenced,

"When is the wedding?"

"Amir, you must ask for more time!"

"Where are you having the reception?"

"Are you inviting anyone from Ameer-ic-ka?"

"You should have it at the Willingdon Club"

"No, the Turf Club is better – out on the lawn."

"What about the CCI – don't they have a lawn?"

"My friend had a wedding at the Taj Hotel. It was lovely."

"What about the MVM Banquet Hall?"

"Are you having the wedding in Bombay or Poona?"

Nazeera noticed Amir was not shaken by the barrage of questions. In fact, he just let the group banter. Instead, he took her hand in his and rubbed it slightly. The couple just let the questions fly around the room. They didn't answer any of them. They would worry about the details tomorrow. Tonight was just for them.

CHAPTER 31

Tuesday, August 23

"AT LEAST A MONTH!"

Rehana sat at the dining room table scratching notes onto a sheet of notebook paper. When Amir walked into the room, she looked up briefly, grimaced, and resumed scribbling on her list. Amir placed his hands onto her shoulders, "Rehana, why are you so serious?"

She jumped slightly at his question. Exhaling noisily, "Aaah, Amir." Glancing at her list, she added, "We have a lot to do before Saturday. Have you asked for time yet?"

Amir sat down on the chair facing her. Leaning back so the back of his head touched the top of the seat back, he said, "Not yet. There is what, a twelve hour time difference between here and Milwaukee." He glanced at his watch and added, "So, it's.... oh, too late to call now. I'll call my boss, Greg, tonight and ask for more time. How much time do you think we need?"

"At least a month!" she pleaded without even looking up from her list.

"Don't forget you'll need time for her to get a passport and immigration visa." Farid added as he joined them in the dining room. He was looking much better and the color in his face improved each day. The kidney stones had passed on Saturday night and he had received a clean bill of health from the doctor's office yesterday just before the engagement party. He kissed Rehana on the forehead and sat down next to her. Smirking, he added, "And you want time for a honeymoon."

Amir remembered his promise to Rahim. He had promised to take Nazeera with him. It was no longer just a promise to keep - he *wanted* to take her with him. He couldn't imagine leaving this country without her. In fact, he couldn't imagine his life without her. "Okay, I'll ask for a month and we'll have to make it work." He placed his head in his hands, "That may be difficult, but I'll make the call." He stared at the table and then just closed his eyes. "What else?"

"Well, we can't set a date or book a hall until we know how much time we have. So, let's start with the guest list. I started one here," she flipped the notebook pages forward a few sheets to a page half-filled with names. "These are the people you will need to personally invite." She tore it from the notebook and handed Amir the list. He stared at it.

"What else?" Farid asked. He sipped the cup of tea Babu had placed in front of him. Mummy entered the dining room and sat down next to her younger son. Babu also brought her a cup of tea. She listened intently to the banter.

"*Aacha*, let me see what's next." Rehana glanced at her list and smiled, "We need to coordinate things with Nazeera's side. I'll call Lailaa-*Ji* and find out who's going to be their coordinator."

"Coordinator?" Farid asked with a confused look on his face.

"Sure, there's usually a person from each side of the family that coordinates schedules, ceremonies, things like that," she explained impatiently. "I worked with Lailaa-*Ji* for the engagement party and so I assume she'll be the one to coordinate things for the wedding, but I'll check."

Both the guys just shook their heads. Wedding planning did not sound fun. "Rehana," Amir said with a grin, "I think you have this very well handled. I trust you to make this wedding great. Just let me know what I can do to help – otherwise, I will stay out of your way."

"Thank you, Amir," Rehana blushed, "I'm glad you think so. I like to plan parties and this one will be great." Rehana flipped her wrists in a little dance, "I'm very happy you choose the girl I found for you."

"I know Bandra is not happy with my choice."

"Well, that's her problem," Farid responded with no sympathy for his sister, "She'll get over it sooner or later. Who's going to be your best man?"

"Well, you of course. You are my brother and the two of you have made such an effort these past few weeks."

"*Nahih*. No," Mummy corrected waving her forefinger at the group, "That will not do."

"Why not?" Amir asked skeptically to his mother. He didn't want to defy her, but if he had to, he would.

"*Beta*, weddings are about more than just the bridal couple. They are about bringing two families together. So, you must not think about yourself, only. You must think about our family and our traditions." She patted Amir's hand like a small boy, "You both have already been involved in weddings of the family. You were the best man in your brother's wedding." Turning to her older son, she added, "And Farid, you were the best man in Nilofer's wedding, no?" Looking from son to son, she concluded, "Although he is not my son, Nadia's husband must be the best man in this wedding. It is his turn."

Nadia and Kassim had been married for almost five years. She was the youngest of the Virani siblings and Kassim was an only child. He knew Nadia came to visit Mummy every few days and often brought Tarik to visit with *Nanima*. He would make them both laugh with his pretend play of pirates or endless hours of coloring pictures. Having her husband as part of the wedding ceremony would be one way Amir could give back to Nadia for her care giving. "Okay, Mummy," Amir said as an obedient son, "Kassim can be the best man."

❋ ❋ ❋ ❋ ❋

Similar conversations were occurring at the Khan flat. They didn't know if the wedding would occur in the next few days or if Amir could get more time, the next few weeks. "He needs to get more time," Ammi kept repeating.

Nazeera had started a list of her own that morning. There was a lot to do to prepare the wedding of her dreams. She realized she wouldn't be able to have everything she wanted – all her friends, her favorite wedding ceremonies or even the *mehndi*. No, wait, that was non-negotiable. They had to have the *mehndi* ceremony. The henna paste applied to the hands and feet helped cool a bride, right? She would use the professional ladies Jaya had for her wedding. They made intricate designs and were very fast. She needed to talk to Jaya. She added *mehndi* to the list and wrote "Jaya" next to it to remind herself to chat with her best friend.

The phone rang. Akbar walked quickly across the room to answer it with his familiar, "Hall-low." He nodded, looking in the ladies' direction, "*Ache* minute." He put the receiver down on the table and came to stand in front of Ammi, "Ma'am Sah'b. Rehana-*Ji* calling."

Ammi leaned over and gave her daughter a hug, "*Aacha*, she's probably calling to work on details." She stood up and slowly walked to the telephone. Her foot was bothering her again this morning, but she was not going to let that stop her from planning her daughter's wedding. She picked up the receiver and began to nod in response to the caller's statements. Nazeera only heard one or two word phrases, "*Ji, huh*," "Me", "More time", "More time".

When she finished her conversation, Ammi tilted her head to the right, "Well, Amir is going to ask for more time off of work. He is going to try for a month." What a relief! A month would give them enough time to plan a wedding. Well, not a lavish affair, but a decent one. Nazeera began to bubble with excitement. "Rehana is going to make some phone calls and will call us later today. She wanted to know who was coordinating things on our side. I told her it was me, that is, unless you have someone else in mind."

"Oh, Ammi, of course you'll be my coordinator! You know exactly what to do." Nazeera agreed. With a giggle, she added, "Now I'm excited about this wedding. I was disappointed I wouldn't have a nice wedding with only a few days to prepare. But, with a few weeks, it'll be fine. I must call Jaya, right away!" She darted past her mother and began dialing numbers.

"Is she going to be your witness?" her mother asked, "What do they call that nowadays, your....your maid of honor?" Nazeera replaced the handset and turned to her mother, "Well, I suppose so. She is my best friend. There are others though – Farah, Aaliya, Khushboo, Jessie, and of course, my cousins Pinky and Dolly. I'm not sure who's the right one."

"Who does your heart tell you is the right one?" Ammi responded with her hands covering her heart, "This is YOUR special day. Who do you want standing next to you. Remember, you will leave soon after the wedding, so think about who your witness should be."

Nazeera reflected for a moment, "Ammi, there's only one clear choice. My best friend, Jaya. Nothing is real without her."

"*Theek hai*," her mother responded, "You best call her and ask her then."

She lifted the handset again and dialed the numbers for her best friend. They chatted for almost an hour as Nazeera updated her on the scooter ride, the revised proposal from Habib, the quick shopping trip, the engagement ceremonies and party. Jaya listened with great interest, repeating, "Wonderful! Wonderful!"

After her friend was sufficiently caught up on the events of the past few days, Nazeera paused and asked, "Jaya, would you come to my wedding and be my maid of honor?"

Jaya laughed and said, "Nazeera, I can't be your maid of honor."

Nazeera suddenly grew nervous. *Is she laughing at me? Why did she said no?* She stammered, "Ww...why?"

"Silly girl, I'm married," Jaya said with a chuckle in her voice, "I'm no longer a maid. I would be your matron of honor. And, Nazeera, I would be honored to be yours."

A wave of relief swept over Nazeera. She had her matron of honor. Jaya would be at her side throughout the entire wedding. Everything would be alright now. "Thank you, Jaya."

They chatted for another hour about the guest list, the outfits and all the things that would need to be done for the wedding. As a Hindu, Jaya admitted she wouldn't be any help with the Muslim wedding ceremonies. But, she said she could be a great help with the *mehndi* night and had a few names of people in Bombay she would contact to see if they are available to apply the henna paste.

When they were done talking, Nazeera skipped from her bedroom to the veranda where her mother was sipping a glass of *nariyal pani*. Her mother's foot was elevated on a cushion and she was leaning back in the chair resting. Nazeera sat down hard on the chair next to her mother and quickly updated her on the conversation she had just had with Jaya. When she was done, she exclaimed, "Oh, Ammi! This wedding will be great!"

Her mother took her hand and smiled weakly, "*Beta*, I also believe this wedding will be great. However, there is something we have not yet discussed."

Nazeera's smiled changed to a frown, "What, Ammi? What's wrong?"

"Nothing is wrong, *Beta*. But, there are certain things that must be done for a wedding. Certain people should be invited in person."

The bride shrugged her shoulders, "Are you talking about Hamid and Amina *khalaji*?"

"Exactly. Your older brother and my younger sister are ones we must invite in person," Ammi seemed impressed Nazeera knew who she was referring, "Have you given any thought as to how we will do that?"

Nazeera looked at her feet. She had hoped to avoid this family politic nonsense. "Ammi, maybe this would be best handled by you and Daddy."

Her mother gave a short laugh and then seemed to ponder her words for a moment. "*Beta*, maybe you're right. Maybe your father and I should handle this. I will discuss it with him when he returns home tonight."

CHAPTER 32

Wednesday, August 24

"MONDAY, SEPTEMBER FIFTH"

Amir called his boss at exactly 9 o'clock - 9 pm in Bombay and 9 am in Milwaukee. He knew Greg, his boss, got to work about 7 am and then proceeded to have two cups of strong black coffee with a little non-dairy creamer and two sugar packets. He calculated that by about 9 am, Greg would be in a more receptive, maybe even a generous, mood. He was right!

The phone call went better than expected. Greg was understanding of Amir's need for additional time and granted him a one month leave of absence. Unfortunately, the leave would be unpaid and taking it would mean he would not be eligible for the end of the year bonus. The extra month was costing him dearly, but it was a small sacrifice for a decent wedding and to make Nazeera happy. He thanked his boss profusely and even invited him to the wedding. Greg initially laughed at the idea, but then with a more serious tone said he might come.

As soon as Amir awoke Wednesday morning, he called Rehana to share the news. He heard her jump for joy on the other end of the phone line. She insisted they all change quickly and head over to the Khan flat to set the date!

Akbar allowed them to enter the flat, but they walked into an empty living room. Lailaa, Nazeera and a white bearded man were sitting on the veranda. Amir strained his neck to see them. It looked like they were intensely discussing something. When Nazeera saw them arrive, she leapt from the veranda to join them in the living room, closing the French doors behind her. She wore a pink *dupatta* draped over her head.

"Hello," she said a little out of breath, "We weren't expecting you."

"I hope we're not disturbing you," Rehana started, peering over Nazeera's shoulder, "We just wanted to share our good news with you and we didn't want to wait." Nazeera quickly turned her head to the veranda and saw her mother put her hands over her face and shake her head. "Um, sure," she said turning back to her guests, "What news?"

Farid asked if they could sit down. Shaking her head, Nazeera was clearly flustered. *Something must be wrong*, Amir immediately thought.

"Oh, sorry, yes, please, sit," Nazeera said motioning toward the seating area. She called for Akbar and Shanti to bring some drinks. "Sorry, we, um, I mean, I am, um, I'm a bit distracted at the moment."

"I hope everything is okay," Amir said. Nazeera turned to him, her lower lip was quivering. "What's the matter?"

Nazeera bit her lower lip, "Never mind. You said you have news?"

"Very good news," Rehana started.

Amir interrupted her. He wanted to be the one to tell her! "We have an extra month."

"What?" Nazeera responded.

"We have a month to plan the wedding, get the paperwork done and even have a honeymoon." Amir clarified with a gigantic smile. "Isn't that great?!"

Nazeera smiled at him, "Yes, that's great." Her voice did not convey the same amount of enthusiasm. *Did she hear what I said?*

Amir took her left hand and asked in a soft voice, "Naz, what's the matter?"

Naz? He liked that nickname for her. It was short and to the point and it seemed no one else called her that, so it was something unique to him. *What's bothering her? Who is the guest on the veranda?*

Suddenly, the veranda doors opened. Lailaa and the white bearded man stepped across the threshold and approached them. *"As-salaam-alaykum.* May peace be upon you," the white bearded man with a round white pill hat said to Rehana. His eyes were solemn and his voice deep. His beard was a bit scraggly but rounded on the bottom just under his chin. He wore simple white *kurta pyjamas* and carried a cloth bound Quran in his right hand. He tucked the Quran under his arm, put his hands together in front of his chest, and nodded to her in greeting. He repeated this statement, hand gesture and nod greeting to Farid and Amir.

He offered a common welcome greeting from one Muslim person to another Muslim person. In response, they gave the correct response, *"Wa-alaykum-salaam,"* which translates to "And may peace be upon you, too." Amir hesitated before he gave his response because he was out of practice speaking in Arabic. Also, Ismailis exchange different greetings as they had done with Jamila.

The white bearded man sat down on the empty chair next to Farid and started chanting something in Arabic, or was it Urdu? The guests glanced at each other and Lailaa took a few deep breaths before she sat on the loveseat next to Nazeera. The room had a solemn feeling. *This man must not bear good news.*

When he stopped his chanting, he said in broken English, "I come house to read fate." He paused for effect, "Much confusion, much stress. Wedding now no good, make later. Need groom date and time." He turned to Amir, "You groom?"

Amir nodded. *Was this guy really going to dictate when they get married?* "Um, Nazeera, what's going on?"

Nazeera was about to explain but Lailaa put her hand on her daughter's thigh to stop her, and said, "Amir, I have called this *jyotishi* to read the fate of you and Nazeera. He has said a wedding this week is not good." She started to cry, "The marriage would be doomed."

Rehana took a Coca-Cola from the variety of soft drinks offered by Shanti. Holding the glass, she said, "Aunty, we come bearing good news." She waited for Lailaa and Nazeera to turn their heads toward her and then she added, "Amir was able to get another month of leave. We have four more weeks. The wedding does not have to be this week."

Lailaa's tears of sorrow quickly turned to tears of joy, "Really?! We can have the wedding a few weeks from now?!" She turned to Nazeera and grabbed both of her hands a bit harder than Nazeera liked as Amir noticed she winced. "There is a chance for you to have happiness with this man after all." She turned toward the astrologer and asked with high hopes, "What dates are good for their wedding?"

The white bearded man was in deep contemplation and had not heard the conversation that occurred in English. Lailaa repeated the question in Urdu and waited for his reply. He replied in broken English, "Need date and time of groom."

It took a moment for Amir to realize what the man was asking for. When he did, he reached into his wallet and retrieved a small scrap of paper with some numbers on it. Mummy had written his birth date and time when he had first arrived, just in case the bride's family wanted to consult a *jyotishi*, which was a very common practice. Amir handed the piece of paper to the old man.

"*Aacha*," replied the astrologer as he looked at the numbers on the paper. He returned to the veranda, pulled out various charts and books, and started calculating. He looked up every once in awhile but then put his head down again. He started shaking his head, and Lailaa's face cringed. She and Nazeera raced to the veranda, clearly worried.

While the ladies were on the veranda, Rehana asked him and Farid if they should have consulted an astrologer before the formal engagement. Vedic Astrology has a deep history in India of determining the compatibility of two people. It is a compatibility match based on the lunar constellations and assigns points for factors that influence marriage. The more points obtained, the better chance of a successful and happy married life. The maximum possible point total is thirty-six.

The two men shrugged their shoulders and Rehana stormed off to the veranda, probably to find out what the *jyotishi* was saying. Amir wanted to know too, so he followed her with Farid only steps behind him. Lailaa was crying again. The white bearded man was speaking in Urdu, so Nazeera attempted to translate for Amir. "He...he is saying our match is not good. We scored only fourteen points." She then whispered in his ear for clarification, "Fourteen is below the eighteen they believe to be the minimum needed for a satisfactory marriage."

"That doesn't matter," Amir said not convinced this astrology business meant anything. "We don't need this man to tell us we're compatible."

"But, Amir," Nazeera pleaded, "My mother believes this mystic. After what happened to Hamid.... She won't consent to our marriage if he says we're not compatible." Tears welled in her eyes, "If only you were born at a different time."

Amir shook his head in disbelief. *What is this about Hamid? And the time I was born made this match a no-go?* He tried to ask the astrologer what date and time he had for him but the white bearded man could not understand his American English. Lailaa stepped in to translate, thinking it was a good idea to verify all the information. Mummy's handwriting must have been confusing as the astrologer had entered "10:14" rather than "20:14" into his charts. With the correct time in hand, he turned from the group and began to recalculate. This time, he came back with a huge smile, showing his red stained teeth. Too much chewing on *paan* can cause that. *Paan* is a beetle leaf often chewed after dinner to refresh one's mouth. It was India's version of mint, but if chewed too often, it could leave an ugly stain on the teeth. Amir thought it looked like a tomato had exploded in his mouth.

The *jyotishi* bobbled his head. He then proceeded to explain in Urdu the time change for Amir made all the difference. The compatibility score was now twenty-five and the marriage has an excellent chance of success. Amir rolled his eyes. He couldn't believe that Lailaa and Nazeera were deciding their fate based on the time he was born and that ten hours made all the difference. He sat back in his chair and just let the rest of the group continue listening to the rant of the bearded man. He couldn't understand most of it anyway.

After a few minutes, Nazeera came over to him and sat on the arm of the chair. Whispering into his ear, she explained, "Ammi believes in these predictions, I don't. She consulted a *jyotishi* after her second miscarriage. He told her the time and day to try for a child and she followed it exactly. She had three children that way – two boys and then me. Exactly what she had planned for. So, even though it seems like mystery science to us, she believes it's true." Nazeera turned to look at her mother whose face was full of smiles and light. "She's happy we're compatible and that our future looks good. He is now suggesting wedding dates."

The group glanced over at the couple every once in awhile and Rehana even laughed once. The whole group was more jovial and relieved now that the match had been approved by the stars. The astrologer suggested a few dates and Nazeera heard "the fifth" as an option. She jumped up from the arm of the chair and said, "Yes! The fifth. My birthday is on the fifth, so it's my lucky number. I want my wedding to be on the fifth! Ammi, please!!"

Lailaa laughed and for the first time all day, she seemed to relax. "*Beta,* there are other dates to consider. But, if you want the fifth, you can have the fifth."

Rehana opened her purse, and pulled out a calendar. "That's a Monday. A bit of an odd day for a wedding."

"Monday, *theek hai*," the astrologer bobbled his head again.

"Well, that's settled then," Lailaa declared. "The wedding will be on Monday, September fifth."

Amir and Farid looked at each other and just shrugged their shoulders. I guess the wedding date is set. Monday, the fifth. That would be Labor Day in America, and most people would have the day off from work. Maybe a few of them would come to the wedding! Maybe his boss, Greg, or his friend, Kabir. Maybe even his college roommate, Sam.

Rehana was exhausted. It was evident when she fell asleep on the five-minute taxi ride back to the Ivanhoe flat. As they stepped into the entryway, Amir excused himself and hurried into his mother's flat. Nilofer was sitting with Mummy in the living room. They both abruptly stopped talking as he walked into the flat. They eagerly listened to his story of the astrologer time mix-up and the setting of the wedding date.

Nilofer shook her head in amazement. She couldn't believe this was happening so fast. "How can I help?" she offered.

Amir shrugged his shoulders. *How can she help? I have no idea what's next on Rehana's list.*

"Do you have a hall?" Nilofer asked.

"No, we don't." Amir replied, "That must be what's next on the list."

"*Theek hai*, I'll take care of it."

Nilofer phoned the fourth floor flat and checked with Farid. Rehana was resting but glancing at her list, he noticed she had written down five possible locations. Nilofer jotted them down.

She first called the Turf Club where she and Nadir had married two decades earlier. They had a wonderful wedding with hundreds of their family, friends and acquaintances from the JK. Her father had also insisted on inviting many of his business contacts since he was so well networked in the community. All told, there were about five hundred people in attendance, an average-sized wedding. The guest count may not have been grand, but the location was the best in town. Well, at least that's what they thought.

Hoping to secure The Turf Club for her little brother, Nilofer name dropped their father's name a few times in her conversation. The reservations manager simply said he was sorry, but they did not have any openings for Monday, September fifth.

With a frown, she hung up the receiver and scratched The Turf Club off the list. *Theek hai*, onto the next one, The Cricket Club of India. They always had room and the location was perfect, right across the street from the Yashodham flat building where Nazeera lived. The meeting room was not ideal, but they couldn't be too picky since the wedding was just two weeks away. Nilofer held her breath as the telephone rang several times. She was about to give up when someone answered it. Explaining in her most pleasant voice, she said she was a Club member interested in booking the meeting room for a wedding. She could hear the man on the other end flipping pages, probably in the reservation book. He mumbled something, then announced the Club was not accepting reservations for that night. So sorry. She laughed in disbelief. Amir wondered, *why is this so hard?*

Crossing, The CCI off the list, they noticed the Taj Mahal Hotel was next on the list. Amir was thrilled she was calling the Taj Hotel as the Crystal Room was on the same floor as Nazeera's favorite hang out, The Sea Lounge. Nilofer tried to keep his expectations low as it was a very prestigious location and they usually required reservations months in advance.

She dialed the numbers, and waited patiently for someone to answer the phone. The lady that answered was very polite and talked in a sing-song voice as if she was bobbling her head as she spoke. Well, that's what Amir imagined as he listened on the other phone extension. Nilofer explained who she was and what she wanted.

The lady simply said, "*Ache* minute." Both Nilofer and Amir held their breath and crossed their fingers for good luck.

"Ma'dam," the sing-song voice said when she came back on the line, "I have good news. Ver-rry good news." Amir swore the lady did a head bobble and flipped her wrist when she rolled her "r". She added, "The Crrist-tal Rroom is avaaail-able, only."

Big exhale! Amir started to breathe again. Nilofer clarified, "So, the Crystal Room is available on Monday, September fifth." She said it very slowly to enunciate the date.

"*Ji, huh*, the date is available. That's good, no?" responded the voice with a head bobble, "You want reservation, no?"

"Yes!! Yes!!" Nilofer said a bit louder than she needed to. Exhaling again, she added a bit more calmly, "*Ji, huh*. Please reserve it. The name is Virani."

"Ver-rry good. Ver-rry, ver-rry good." The lady said. "I'll mar-rr-rk it down, only. Rrrra-jesh will be your on-site coordinator. Call him to make arrrrr-angements. *Theek hai*?"

"*Shukriya-ji*! Thank you!" Nilofer concluded. "Yes, we will call him to coordinate. Thank you again."

They hung up the telephone receivers and exchanged hugs. Nilofer had found a hall! Amir thanked her profusely and watched as she scampered into the bedroom to update Mummy.

Amir wiped the beads of sweat from his brow and called Farid and then Lailaa. His brother was overjoyed and his soon to be mother-in-law seemed pleased. Grinning, he thought to himself, *the wedding will be perfect*.

CHAPTER 33

Friday, August 26

"ARE YOU SURE I SHOULDN'T COME WITH YOU?"

A few days had passed since the location was secured, but Nazeera still had mixed feeling about it. She thought it was very thoughtful of Amir to have requested the Crystal Room, since it was a beautiful location. *But didn't he realize how difficult it will be for me and my family to go back to that room? It will conjure up all the bad memories of Hamid's wedding fiasco! But, then again, this is my wedding. Things will be different.*

Hamid had met Johara during a bridal viewing organized by their mothers. They had been immediately attracted to each other and dated with chaperones for over seven months. Johara was lovely, respectful and submissive - all the traits her parents were looking for in a daughter-in-law. Nazeera and the bride had become friends, though Nazeera was much more independent.

On the day of the wedding, Johara confided in Nazeera that she was bothered by the *jyotishi's* calculation of only eighteen points of compatibility. She had to decide if her love for Hamid was strong enough to overcome a marriage doomed to mediocrity by the stars. The astrologer had been hired by Ammi to predict their fate, just as he had done for her and Amir.

The wedding ceremony requires three verbal consents from the bride, to make sure she had not been forced into the marriage. Over the years, it has become tradition for the bride to hesitantly say 'huh' or 'yes' the first two times she is asked, as an Indian bride is not supposed to be anxious to marry. When asked the third and final time, she is to give a louder and more distinct 'huh'.

As Johara sat in the center of the Crystal Room, under the red wedding veil and flower garland, Nazeera could see she was uneasy as she mumbled, 'huh' the first two times. When the *Qazi* asked her the third time, Johara hesitated. The *Qazi* repeated the question, and to everyone else's surprise, the bride responded, 'no'.

Hamid was obviously upset when he heard she had said 'no'. First, he verbally lashed out at their mother for hiring the *jyotishi*, then he physically lashed out at any nearby furniture in the ballroom. Storming out of the Crystal Room, he jumped down the Grand Staircase and hurried out of the Taj Hotel. Shoving the driver aside, he drove off in the wedding car dragging flower garlands behind him.

Not used to driving with flower garlands all over the windshield, he soon crashed the car into a concrete barrier. Daddy had to use his police connections to save Hamid from a night in jail. A few days later, he moved to Delhi to live with a college friend.

If her eldest brother came to her wedding, it would be his first time back to Bombay since the almost wedding a year ago. Nazeera thought she should call him and invite him. Then she could convince him to come to her wedding in spite of the location. But, he was her brother and he deserved a personal invitation. Her parents were leaving for Delhi tonight to invite both Hamid and Amina *khalaji* personally. Nazeera wanted to go along, but the three of them decided it was best she stay in Bombay to continue with the wedding preparations. There were only eight days before the wedding and each day was precious.

While her parents were packing for the weekend trip, Nazeera lay on her bed, mentally going through the list of things she needed to do while they were gone. First, she needed to write her girlfriends and invite each of them to the wedding. Maybe one or two of them would be able to make it to the wedding on such short notice. *Do I have their addresses? Hmm, maybe I should just call them?*

"*Beta*," Ammi said entering Nazeera's bedroom, interrupting her thoughts, "Do you know where the brown suitcase is?" Her mother sat down next to her on the bed. She was wearing a pastel blue *salwar kameez* with the *dupatta* hanging loosely around her neck. She rarely wore these two piece outfits, reserving them almost exclusively for when she travelled.

Nazeera sat up straight in her bed. *Ammi doesn't look nervous to see her sister again.*

"I think it's on top of my armoire." They both turned their heads toward her armoire and looked up. There it was. The suitcase blended very well with the armoire, so it was the perfect hiding spot for it. Her mother stood up and reached for the suitcase. It was too high for her even when she tried again on her tip-toes. Nazeera smiled out of the corner of her mouth. Her mother always forgot how short she really was. The armoire was at least another foot taller than her tallest reach. She called for Akbar and he came immediately carrying a stool. He easily reached and obtained the suitcase. Placing the piece of luggage on the ground, he stepped back smiling his toothy smile.

"*Shukriya*, Akbar," Ammi said glancing at the suitcase, "Please bring it to my bedroom. I have a lot of packing to do." She kissed Nazeera on the forehead and then exited quickly from the room. Akbar nodded to her and followed her mother carrying the suitcase.

Nazeera gave them both a little laugh, then reached into the top drawer of her bedside cabinet. She pulled out her notebook and address book and sprawled onto her bed facing toward the window. She kicked her feet into the air and let them sway back and forth like windshield wipers on a car. Glancing at the list of names next to her, she selected "Vidya" first. Vidya had been her friend since she was thirteen years old and they had lived only a few houses from each other in Ahmednagar. They walked together to and from school every day for a year. She had worn her hair in one long braid that reached just above her tailbone. *I wonder what she looks like now.*

A giggle came over her that bubbled into full laughter. *I wonder if she ever married Anil!* He was a handsome boy and all the school-girl's were in love with him from afar. Most of them just giggled as he walked by, but Vidya was different. She was determined to make him notice her. She talked about him on their daily walks and the two of them planned for months how she would say "hello."

On the second to last day of the school term, Vidya told Nazeera "today is the day"! For a bit of confidence, she wore a lavender ribbon in her long hair as lavender was her favorite color. When they arrived at school, Vidya walked straight up to Anil and said "hello." He smiled and replied the same. They talked for a few precious minutes before the bell rang and they scurried to class. The next morning's walk was filled with Anil, Anil, Anil. As they walked into the school yard, he approached her and they walked into the building together.

Nazeera left Ahmednagar the following day, as her father was transferred to a government post in Poona. For a couple years, the two school friends wrote letters, and she learned Vidya and Anil had begun to court with parental permission. Nazeera had been very surprised as her friend had been promised to another young man when she turned eighteen. That would have been two years ago. *Who did Vidya marry?* Nazeera ended her letter by inviting Vidya's husband, "whomever it may be". She laughed as she signed her name. *This will be interesting.*

Striking her pencil through Vidya's name, Nazeera moved her pencil to the next name - Pushpa. *Oh my, I haven't thought about her for several years.* She started the letter and then stopped. *Maybe I shouldn't invite her after all.* They had a very odd past. They both liked the same boy, no, man!

After Ahmednagar, the Khan family moved to Poona. Since her father was in the government service, he arranged for her to continue horseback riding lessons with the army cadets. She had loved horses since she was ten and had started riding lessons. The instructors in the small town of Ahmednagar were elementary, so Nazeera was excited to be taught more advanced riding techniques by the army cadets. There were only four of them in the class, Nazeera, Pushpa and sisters Atia and Anjum. The sisters were constantly trying to outdo each other in class, so Nazeera and Pushpa became friends by default.

That was, until Bijli came to town to demonstrate jumping as part of a horse show. He was a tall handsome army cadet from nearby

Bombay. Bijli was his last name, his full name was... what was his full name? Oh, well, it's not important. He was an excellent rider and both she and Pushpa developed a crush.

Every other month, there were horse riding competitions in Poona or Bombay. Surprisingly, Bijli seemed to be at each of them. After one of the more tedious competitions, he came up to the two of them and congratulated them both on winning a trophy. Nazeera thanked him for his kind words, and Pushpa simply smiled at him. She was too dumbfounded to even speak to him. But, after that meeting, she would not stop talking about him. Pushpa was more obsessed with Bijli than Vidya had been with Anil.

The last time Nazeera saw Pushpa was about six months after Bijli had first congratulated them. He was demonstrating a compli-cated hurdle jump when he fell off his horse. Pushpa yelled at the top of her lungs, "Bijli!!! Oh, Bijli!".

The sisters glared at her in amazement and Nazeera just laughed quietly to herself. Pushpa had embarrassed herself in front of the whole arena but she didn't seem to care. Thankfully, Bijli responded in a gentlemanly manner and simply nodded to the concerned audi-ence he was fine.

After the demonstration, much to Pushpa's frustration, he walked past the obsessed teen and directly toward Nazeera, congratulating her on her recent trophy win. Pushpa was determined to be noticed, so she pushed Nazeera out of the way and stood in front of her. He ignored the impetuous girl, and instead turned his head to continue his conversation with Nazeera. Pushpa fumed and did an about face, her long braid smacking him in the chest as she retreated. She didn't return to the riding lessons for the rest of the term.

Nazeera chewed the end of her pencil and decided not to invite Pushpa after all. They were inviting Bijli and she didn't want to create any tension. Bijli had become a friend to the family during their time in Poona. His station was moved from Bombay to Poona during her college days, so they grew closer often discussing horses. She heard he had been recently promoted to second lieutenant and had a prom-ising army career. But, he could be nothing more than a friend. She decided a long time ago she didn't want to marry an army cadet and move every three years like her father or even William. She wanted a more stable life. Bijli understood this and that made it easier for them to be just friends. She crossed Pushpa's name off the list. No, it wasn't worth the headache.

The next name on the list was Khushboo. Well, that would be an easy one. Even though her own engagement was a bit complicated, she was sure Khushboo would come from Thane for the wedding. She composed the letter quickly and crossed Khushboo's name off the list.

With a tired sigh, she allowed her fingers to glide down to the fourth name on the list, Jaya. She was not going to simply write her best friend, she would call her personally and invite her. Maybe she could still join her parents on their train trip to Delhi! Then she could invite Jaya personally. But, then she would have to deal with Hamid and *Khalaji*.

Jumping from her bed, Nazeera skipped toward the living room. Her parents were there finalizing the instructions to Akbar and Shanti. Both of the servants were nodding obediently to her father's orders. As she skipped into the room, the whole group turned their heads toward her. Ammi said softly, "*Beta*, we thought you were sleeping. We didn't want to wake you."

"I was writing letters, inviting a few friends to the wedding," Nazeera said with an angelic smile. "Are you two ready to go?" *I should really be going with them. Both Ammi and Daddy will have a hard time dealing with Hamid. If I went with them, I could visit Jaya!* "Are you sure I shouldn't come with you?"

This time Daddy spoke up. He had been placing some papers into his satchel, "No, Nazeera, you need to finish your letters and go shopping with Nusrat Aunty and your cousins for wedding items. Your mother and I can handle the conversations with your brother and *Khalaji*." Her father looked warmly at her and she knew he was trying to be brave for her and her mother. This was going to be a hard trip for both of them and she really should be going with them. But she had to admit, there was a lot to do in their absence.

"I wish we had more than just a few days to prepare for this wedding."

"I know, *Beta*, I know."

Nazeera felt moisture form in the corner of her eyes. *Why am I crying now? Is it tears of joy or sadness?*

Maybe she was feeling overwhelmed with all the wedding preparations. But, Ammi and Rehana were handling most of it. No, it was probably the realization she would be leaving her parents soon to go to a far away land. She knew she was leaving for America, but she didn't realize she would miss them this much. Especially her father. She would miss him most of all. She would miss their chats about Art and horses, and their special moments sipping *faloodas* on the veranda. Would he give her a painting? Of course he would. Nazeera drew a deep breath, resolved to ask him for a painting when they returned. He would surely give her whichever painting or sketch she desired. But, which one did she want?

Blinking her eyes repeatedly to hold back the tears, she gave each of them a long hug and good-bye kisses. Noticing a tear in her father's eye, Nazeera watched him slip the satchel over his shoulder and glance at his watch. Cursing the driver for being late, he picked up the two suitcases, and noisily walked toward the front door.

Just as Akbar opened the door for Daddy, the doorbell rang. Relieved, he handed the suitcases to the driver. Turning toward Ammi, he placed his right hand on the small of her back, and announced with a shaky voice, *"Chalo,* let's go."

Her mother gave her a brave smile and simply said, *"Khuda Hafeez.* May God go with you."

"Khuda Hafeez, Ammi."

Nazeera watched her parents exit the flat and enter the lift. Suddenly, she didn't want them to go. *No, this is too soon. This isn't really happening.* She leapt to the veranda and leaned forward on the railing, waiting for them to appear. After a moment, she could see them approaching the car. Wiping tears from her eyes, she watched as the driver opened the passenger doors and then put their suitcases into the trunk. Ammi and then Daddy slipped into the backseat of the Ambassador car. Waving her arms frantically, Nazeera called repeatedly to them. They must have been too far to hear as they didn't wave back. She did see her mother glance up once but she didn't acknowledge Nazeera which meant she had not seen her. Her eyes followed the car down the street and she even stepped onto one the squeaky chairs to be able to watch the car for a few more seconds. When it was finally out of sight, she turned around and slumped into the chair. Using her *dupatta* as a towel, she wiped the tears from her eyes. They were gone.

Akbar approached her holding a wooden tray and a *falooda*. She didn't notice him for several seconds. When she looked up and saw him standing there she thought she noticed a tear in the corner of his eye too. *Oh, I'm going to miss Akbar too. I'm going to miss everyone!*

But, leaving home was part of growing up, right? Akbar had left his home and came to work for them. He had a family to support. She vowed to herself to help Akbar even though she was going all the way to America. If she was going to work, then she was going to help her family. She would send money back to her parents and she would help Akbar too. He had done so much for her over the years, especially with the cooking. *He's like family too.*

Nazeera smiled at him, taking the cool drink. He knew it would help her feel better. She thanked him. Akbar replied with a simple head nod, turned and left her alone on the veranda.

Wiping more tears, she chastised herself. *C'mon, Nazeera, pull yourself together. I need to call Jaya and talk to her! No, that could wait for a bit. I need a distraction. Maybe I should call Pinky and Dolly and go see a movie. A romantic Bollywood film would be a perfect distraction. Wait. I bet they don't have Bollywood movies in Milwaukee. Oh, my! I better go see one now, I may not see another one for a long time.*

Placing the untouched *falooda* on the table, Nazeera sprinted toward the telephone. She dialed the numbers she knew from memory, and waited impatiently for someone to answer the line.

"Hello," a familiar voice said with a slight surprise.

"Hello Aunty, this is Nazeera." She was slightly out of breath from her crying and sprint. She took a few breaths and asked, "Are either Pinky or Dolly at home?"

"*Ache* minute."

While she waited, a thought occurred to her. It was odd that Nusrat Aunty was answering the telephone directly. *What happened to their servant? Why didn't he answer the telephone just as Akbar always did for us?* She shook her head to eliminate the thought from her memory. *Maybe she was just sitting right next to the phone.*

That's why she sounded so surprised when I called. Yes, that must be it. She began to tap her foot in impatience. *What's taking so long?*

"Sorry, *Beta*, they have gone out." Aunty said when she came back on the line, "But, we will see you tomorrow, no?"

"*Ji huh,* Aunty," Nazeera replied trying not to allow the disappointment she felt come through in her voice, "Tomorrow."

They hung up the phone and Nazeera was suddenly exhausted. She went back to the veranda, picked up the *falooda* and took a long sip allowing the cool liquid to squelch her thirst. Leaning back in a nearby chair she closed her eyes.

She must have fallen asleep because the doorbell startled her awake. Nazeera sat up quickly, then glanced around to identify where she was. Suddenly the activities of the last hour came rushing back to her and she felt sad again. She was alone. Just like she will be when she moves to America. Alone in a strange country with a man she has only known for a few weeks. Maybe this isn't a good idea. Maybe she should just stay here and marry Habib. At least then she would be near her friends and family.

"Baby Sah'b," Akbar announced stepping onto the veranda, "Mr. Abdullah to see you."

Mr. Abdullah. Who is that? Must be someone from Daddy's office. I'll just tell him Daddy has gone to Delhi on personal business. He can leave whatever paperwork he wants.

Nazeera took another sip of the drink sitting next to her. It was now warm and the glass had several beads of sweat running down it. She wiped her moist hand on her *dupatta* hoping this Mr. Abdullah wouldn't notice. Taking a cleansing breath, she stepped over the verandah threshold into the living room.

The visitor was standing at the front door, awaiting permission to enter the flat. As Nazeera entered the living room, her eyes grew wide. She recognized this man. Mr. Abdullah was not someone from Daddy's office. It's Habib. *Why is he back?*

He stood very tall and looked, oh so very handsome. His crisp white shirt fit his body perfectly. Obviously tailored. Habib wore a red and yellow silk tie with a paisley design. His dark gray jacket and slacks complimented his freshly polished black shoes. He looked like the Western businessmen she saw on billboards, but, he was a more attractive version. He is more formally dressed than when he was here with his father and brother last week. *Is he here on business?*

Heart thumping faster than she expected, Nazeera asked, "Habib, what are you doing here?"

Habib ran his fingers through his hair. His perfectly coifed hair was now standing up a bit. It gave him a bad boy look and made her heart start beating faster. *Why am I reacting this way?*

Blinking his eyes a few times, he asked meekly, "Can I come in?"

She nodded and Akbar stepped to one-side, allowing Habib to enter the Khan home. He hesitated and then quickly removed his shoes, as a sign of respect. She motioned with an extended hand for him to take a seat in the living room. He silently walked into the main sitting area and took a seat on the sofa. Nazeera nervously sat in the chair opposite him. *Why is he here? And alone? Highly unusual and improper. Was he waiting for Ammi and Daddy to leave? Is he here to threaten me? Thank goodness Akbar is here to protect me if Habib attacks.*

"Nazeera," Habib said breaking the silence, "I apologize for visiting you in your home like this. Are your parents at home?" *So he didn't know they were gone. But, still, why is he here? I've told him no twice already!*

"No, Habib, they've gone out for the evening." She didn't want to tell him they would be gone for a few days. He didn't need to know everything. "What are you doing here?"

He ran his fingers through his hair again making Nazeera's heart beat a little faster. He must be nervous or maybe his head itches. "Um…." *Here is the confident Habib. Not so confident anymore.* She laughed to herself and just let him stew with his thoughts. He started biting one of his nails. Realizing what he was doing, he quickly put his hand under his thigh. Exhaling, he said, "Um… Nazeera."

Clearly Habib was here to say something, but it wasn't coming out. She was starting to lose patience and was about to tell him to get out. As she leaned forward in her chair to get up, Shanti came into the room carrying the sterling silver tray. She nervously approached the couple and put the tray down on the coffee table. She poured two cups of tea and added the sugar and cream to his tea as he had instructed her last week and offered it to him. He quickly glanced at her, mindlessly taking the cup and saucer from her, "*Shukriya*".

Nazeera was impressed he was not gawking at Shanti as he had done his last two visits. In fact, he barely acknowledged her presence only inches from him! Shanti was also shocked and wore an astonished look as she prepared Nazeera's tea and then retreated. Something was different. Something had changed. Habib was not as cocky or confident as he was last time.

The cup and saucer shook in his hand. He noticed a bit of tea spill onto the saucer and hurriedly put them down on the coffee table. He looked down at his feet and then suddenly looked up, "Nazeera, I'm a fool."

That was an understatement. To think she had considered marrying him. That was, until he came to her father demanding a king's ransom for a dowry, er, wedding gift. There was no way she would let her father go into debt, and postpone his retirement, just to get her married. That happened all too often in India and she would not allow that to happen to her father.

Her brief moment of desire turned quickly to anger. "Yes, you are a fool, Habib. What nerve do you have showing up here after what you said and …. and did last week." *How can I forgive him for what he said about my brother? And the way he gawked at Shanti. His eyes had lingered a bit too long on her. Maybe he's planning to marry us both. Muslim men can do that. But isn't that only during times of war?*

Habib rushed across the room, grabbing her hand in his and almost spilling the tea she still held in her hands. He bowed and placed his forehead onto their joined hands. His hands were warm. "Oh, Nazeera, we should never have demanded such a large dowry. I didn't mean the things I said about your brother or you. My father thought it would make me look more successful to live in a nice place and that you would be impressed by it all. But, honestly, I don't care about the flat or the money. I just want to marry you."

What? Did he just say what I think he said? He wants to marry me? He doesn't care about the flat or the money? Where is this coming from? "So, what are you saying, Habib?"

Habib looked up and stared directly into her eyes causing her heart to flutter. She was mad at herself for feeling this way. She had never had a man hold her hand like this before, not like this anyways. And, except for that ride with Amir a week ago, she had never been alone with a man before. Suddenly she felt a wave of heat rise in her bosom and upward into her cheeks. She stood up releasing her hands from his grip and causing him to lean backwards.

"I want you to marry me. Forget the dowry. Just marry me."

Nazeera turned away from him and awkwardly placed her tea cup on the coffee table nearly missing the edge of the table. *Why is he tempting me like this?* And her parents were away for a few days personally inviting her brother and aunty to her wedding to Amir!!

Out of the corner of her eye, Nazeera noticed Akbar and Shanti cautiously peering their heads out of the kitchen so they could hear the conversation in the living room. She frowned, and waved a hand at them to indicate they should scoot back into the kitchen.

She looked down at Habib. He looked like a lost puppy sitting there on the floor. "What made you change your mind like this?"

Habib gulped hard, and began staring at her toes. She allowed him to take her hand again. "Well, after you said "no" again last week, I was devastated. I was sure you were going to agree to the revised proposal. We thought the only issue was the cost of the flat and so modifying it to a cheaper one would make it acceptable."

He looked up at her eyes and added, "The whole trip back to Hyderabad, I kept thinking about you. I couldn't get you out of my mind. Your body, your face, your long beautiful hair." He paused for effect, "I think I love you, Nazeera."

She blinked a couple of times and shook her head in disbelief. *Is he really saying these things? This is what I wanted to hear last week. Before Amir's proposal. Before I got engaged.* "Well, it's too late now, Habib. I'm going to marry Amir."

"*Ji, nahih*! No!" he replied defiantly. "No, I won't accept that. I want you to know that I'm offering you marriage. No dowry, as I know you won't stand for it. You can stay in Bombay near your family and friends." He kissed her hand twice softly and then turned his puppy dog eyes toward her, "I can give you a good life, Nazeera. Please marry me instead."

Her heart was racing now. *Marry him instead?! Stay in Bombay near my friends and family! This would be perfect! Well, almost perfect.* She withdrew her hand, looked down at him sitting at her feet and sighed. "Habib, I'm engaged to Amir." She paused, her head was spinning, "I'm not sure what else to say."

Habib jumped up, and gave her a gentle hug. His warm body felt nice against hers. She could feel how strong his arms were, and how muscular his body was. He lifted her hand again and kissed it with his moist lips. The kiss was tender yet it reached all the way to her toes. *Why hadn't he shown a bit of this tenderness earlier!* She slowly withdrew her hand and stepped back. Trying to hide the wobbling of her voice she said softly, "Good night, Habib."

As if on cue, Akbar entered the room and escorted him to the door. He picked up his shoes, and turned to her, "Think about what I said, my darling." "Oh, my!" she said to Akbar as he shut the front door. "Can you believe this?" Akbar didn't reply. She knew he couldn't comment on her suitor choice, it was not his place.

At least she had a choice. He had not been given a choice. Akbar and his wife had a marriage arranged by their families. He was sixteen and she was fourteen and they first met on their wedding day. She remembered him saying his wife had been immature at first and they fought often. But each time they made up, their love grew stronger. They had seven children and he often said he loved her very much. She had become the stabilizing force in his life. Although he worked in Bombay for the Khans, he wrote to her often and they talked on the telephone the first Sunday of each month. He always looked forward to his long weekends when he could go home to see her and their children. Nazeera hoped she would feel the same way about her husband, whichever one she choose.

"I need to call Jaya!" Nazeera exclaimed, dragging the telephone and its long extension cord into her bedroom. She closed the door with her foot and plopped onto her belly nearly knocking the notebook off the bed. Her pillows flew in the air before settling back down askew. She dialed Jaya, and tapped her fingers impatiently on the telephone while the phone rang.

When she heard her friend's voice on the other line, Nazeera exploded. Jaya laughed and calmly replied, "Slow down, slow down. Tell me everything from the beginning. What is this about Habib?"

CHAPTER 34

Sunday, August 28

"MAKE SURE YOU GET YOUR OWN BUTTONS"

The days seemed to fly by for some and linger endlessly for others. Rehana was frantically addressing wedding invitations, decorating the flat, and preparing pre-wedding ceremonies. Mummy again insisted on a wedding cake "like the Ameer-ic-kans have". She wanted her son to have an Ameer-ic-kan wedding in India. Amir had laughed at the thought, and simply went along with it.

Lookmanji's did not make cakes, wedding or otherwise, and all the pastry shops she usually patronized did not make multi-tiered American wedding cakes. Rehana thought seriously about making it herself, but Farid talked her out of it. She was busy enough with everything else. She didn't need *another* stressor. He volunteered to make the telephone calls to find a bakery that would make the cake. Rehana smiled at him gratefully, writing Farid's name next to the item on the list.

Amir felt guilty Rehana was doing so much work and now even Farid had an important task. Sheepishly, he walked into wedding prep central and asked what he could do. She glanced at him with a slightly annoyed look on her face. "Well, I assume you've done the normal things grooms do." She paused for effect, "Wedding outfit?"

He was shocked. Of course! He needed to get his own clothes and he better get them quick! He only had one week left before the wedding. Embarrassed at having to ask the question, "Um, Rehana, what is the telephone number to a good tailor?"

Rehana looked up from her long to-do list, and smiled weakly. She looked exhausted and he again noticed faint black patches under each eye. Before she could answer, Farid put a hand on his shoulder. "I'll help him, dear."

The groom turned to his older brother, "Thanks." Amir glanced back to Rehana. She had already returned to her list. *Probably best to leave her be.*

The two brothers exited the room quietly, and rode the lift silently down to the garden flat. Their mother was more than happy to see them and she waved them into the living room with grand gestures. She wore a cream colored sari with a hot pink sari blouse. It should have been an ugly contrast, but it actually made her seem more youthful and spry. She gave them both huge welcoming hugs, and then proceeded to pinch Farid and then Amir's cheeks, just as she did when they were young children. *Why is she acting so playful? Is she buttering them up for something? A conspiracy?*

"*Betas,*" Mummy started, "I have a surprise for you." Her surprises usually involved food, so both of them automatically looked toward the kitchen to see what Ramu was going to bring out for them. He did not appear. Amir glanced back at his mother and noticed that she was giddy like a schoolgirl, "My brother is coming to the wedding!" She meant her half-brother Aly. Her own mother had died just after her birth and she was raised by her maternal aunt until her father remarried when she was five. As Mummy told it, her step-mother treated her like Cinderella, but that union had produced a son, Aly.

When she was sixteen years old, her step-mother arranged for her to marry Karim. Her wedding day was the last time she saw her father and step-mother, and the first time she saw her husband. When she looked up from her hands and into his eyes, it was love at first sight for both of them. They were happily married for over three decades and had produced five children, before he suddenly died of a heart attack. Since Ismaili tradition does not allow women to visit gravesites, she has Farid lay a fresh red rose on her beloved's tombstone each year on their wedding anniversary.

Mummy's only regret with marriage was leaving Aly. He was the only joy in the gray household she was raised. His wife died in child-birth, and he has not ventured from his home in Pakistan since then.

"That's good news," Amir replied, "It'll be nice to see Aly *mamu* again. It's been a long time." It always seemed odd to call your uncle a *mamu* but that's what he had been taught to call his mother's brother. "When does he arrive?"

Mummy, still giddy, clapped her hands like a child about to open birthday presents, "He arrives on Friday. He will call when he has finalized his travel plans." Farid and Amir couldn't help but laugh. They hadn't seen their mother this happy since before their father died. The three of them laughed together, the first time in years. Amir was thankful Aly *mamu* was making such an effort to come to the wedding. His visit would be a nice distraction for his mother.

When they stopped laughing and talking about Aly *mamu*, Farid asked for the address of a tailor shop. Smiling, Mummy hastily wrote it down on a scrap of paper and handed it to her eldest child. Before he took it, she pulled it back and said to Amir, "Make sure you get your own buttons. Nirmil, is a good tailor, but his buttons are terrible. Just terrible." She handed Farid the piece of paper and then waved her hands dismissing them both, "Go to Fashion Street or Chor Bazaar. They have good buttons."

Their mother waved her hands dismissively again, then turned and scampered into her bedroom giggling. The brothers looked at each other. *Their mother was crazy.* "We should call Kassim to join us," Farid suggested as Amir rolled his eyes, "I know, I know, but he is the best man after all."

They made it to Fashion Street via a pleasant walk on M G Road. The slight breeze from the Arabian Sea was a welcome relief from the roasting heat of the day. The sky was a soothing blue and the clouds were white cotton puffs dotting the otherwise clear sky. It was just past noon and the sun beat down on them like a relentless master, but the breeze made the walk tolerable, and Amir admitted it was a good day to be outside, even if that meant shopping.

Fashion Street was really just rows and rows of vendor stalls selling various clothes, shoes and even belts. Farid was familiar with the maze, and led the way dodging pedestrians and tourists. The three of them weaved through several stalls until Kassim lagged behind and then finally stopped at a book seller's stall.

The best man picked up a thin book, and flipped a few pages. Farid impatiently crossed his arms in front of him as Kassim replaced the thin book and picked up another one. He flipped a few pages and then began to read aloud to his captive audience. Amir recognized the words as Hindi, but he couldn't understand enough to appreciate the poem, so he just nodded for the sake of good manners. Kassim must have taken Amir's nodding as permission, so he continued. When he finished the poem, he placed the book on top of a pile of books, picked up another one and started reading again. This time, Amir couldn't understand any of the words Kassim said. *What language is that? Marathi? Guajarati? Why does he insist on reading these poems to me? Are they love poems? Is he showing off because he can read more than a few languages?*

Amir knew something like this would happen with his sister's dreamy husband. "*Chalo,*" he said to hurry his best man, "Farid's waiting". They both glanced into the depth of the labyrinth. Farid was now two stalls away probably acutely aware of Kassim's tendency to read poetry aloud in different languages. He was pretending to look at some carved wooden boxes.

They continued through the web, with Kassim stopping only one more time to admire the mirror work on some beaded belts. The brothers had continued walking and their brother-in-law came running to catch up with them. They continued left, then right, then left. Kassim seemed to be tempted to veer off again when Farid abruptly stopped at a stall under the shade of a low banyan tree.

The stall was really a square space with a few tables lining the outer rim and one long table along the center. The outer tables were stacked high with bolts of fabric. One table had cotton, several tables were covered with silk and one table was a jumble of miscellaneous fabrics. The center tables were filled with countless jars of buttons, cuff links, and spools of thread. Hanging from the back wall of the stall were wedding outfits in various stages of completion. An old wooden counter stood under the outfits. As they entered the stall, Amir smiled to himself. *This guy will have the perfect buttons.*

Farid remembered the stall and the man from the time of his wedding. That was nearly a decade ago, but the stall and the guy were still there. Amir thought it would have been nice to find the buttons at a modern shopping center, but there was something comforting in knowing this man has dedicated his whole life and made his living from selling buttons and fabric. *He must be good. He doesn't look like he is starving.*

"*Namaste*, Manish," Farid said with a slight bow, palms pressed together. He waited for the old man to turn to them and acknowledge his greeting. He added, "We're looking for buttons for a wedding *sherwani.*"

"Wedding *sherwani?*" the old man eyed each of the gentlemen, "Which one of you is the groom?" The *sherwani* is typical wedding attire for a groom in North Indian weddings. It is traditionally an off-white colored long coat falling just below the knees, buttoned up in front with a Nehru collar. It can be a simple outfit or it can be made more lavish with gold *zari* thread or even added colors - typically red, the wedding color. Amir wanted to keep his outfit simple and had explained this to Farid.

Amir blushed and raised his hand slightly, "I am."

The shopkeeper limped slowly toward the groom. His left leg was slightly shorter than his right leg, but he didn't use a cane. Growing used to the limitations his leg gave him, he just dealt with it. After a few strides, he reached Amir's side and glared at him. Turning him around, he said in broken English, "Humph, Ameer-ic-kan. *Theek hai.*"

For an old man with a limp, he was pretty spry. He disappeared behind the wooden counter and came back with two trays full of gold buttons. "Nice buttons. Come see. Come see." Amir gazed at the trays. The old man was correct, they were attractive buttons. Round, square, triangle. Too many choices. Manish picked up the one closest to him. "What do you think?"

"Farid, what shape are the buttons on *sherwanis?*"

"Any shape, but most grooms prefer round." Manish answered self-declaring himself the expert on wedding buttons. He pointed to two rows of round buttons, "Come see. Come see."

Kassim's eyes grew wide in excitement. He picked up a round button and held it against Amir's buttoned shirt.

"Wait! Wait!" the button-*walla* exclaimed as he rushed to Amir's side and placed a piece of *sherwani* fabric over his shirt to provide the illusion he was wearing a wedding outfit. Kassim picked up each button and one by one held it against Amir's chest. Farid stood back slightly and the old man held a mirror so the groom and his best man could also see. The trio waved their heads from side to side deciding which ones looked best. After what seemed like an hour, they narrowed the selection down to three. "Amir, chose one of these."

Smiling at the remaining choices laying on the purple velvet tray, Amir bent down to closely examine the buttons. One of them had a little horse on it, one had a plus sign and the third had a small raised circle. He set the one with the plus sign aside, too mathematical for a wedding. He then picked up the remaining two and glanced from one to the other. He really liked the one with the horse because it reminded him of Nazeera's riding passion, but that one might not be the best for a wedding. He held up the one with a simple dot in the center, "This one."

"Good choice. A very good choice." Manish kept repeating as he found the jar of gold buttons with a dot in the center. They purchased twenty buttons, more than enough buttons for the *sherwani*. Kassim insisted on paying for the buttons as part of his best man duties, and Farid and Amir watched in agony as he counted the *rupees* one by one. Manish finally handed the precious gold spheres to Kassim and thanked them for coming, pressing his hands together and bobbling his head. The three gentlemen held up their hands and bid farewell.

The shopping experience had been exhausting for Farid who was still recovering from the kidney stones episode. He suggested they purchase the wedding turban another day. Amir saw his brother was tiring but also knew they wouldn't have a chance like this again. Before they left Manish's stall, Amir clumsily asked for his recommendations on nearby stalls that sold wedding turbans. The old man smiled and they all noticed his teeth and gums were tinted red from years of eating *paan*. His mouth looked like the astrologer's mouth from Nazeera's flat.

The button-*walla* pointed his long gnarled finger toward the way they had come, recommending a stall halfway back in the maze toward the poetry book stall. The trio thanked him again and began to weave their way back through the labyrinth. After only thirty seconds at the turban shop, Kassim decided he was more interested in poetry books and excused himself. Farid seemed immediately relieved as he proceeded to sit down in a nearby chair. He slumped over and exhaled deeply. Amir put his hand on his brother's shoulder and looked quickly at the turban-*wallas* selection of wedding turbans. There weren't too many to chose from which made it easier for him to select the gold one with a nice red ostrich feather plume reaching upward from the front center. He would look like a *maharaja*! Very regal. And the plume gave the impression he was a few inches taller than he actually was. *Maybe I'll be taller than Rahim on my wedding day?!*

Turning to show Farid, he noticed his brother was looking slightly better, but best to get him home. Amir slipped off the turban and paid the turban-*walla* without bothering to barter. He picked up the box with the precious hat and plume and tapped Farid on the shoulder, "*Chalo*".

Kassim was reading a poem aloud to the book-*walla*. *What language is that? Maybe Bengali?* The vendor appeared to be listening intently and inspired by the words, but Amir could tell he was just trying to please his customer. When the two men approached their brother-in-law, he read louder and with more flourish, waving his hands for dramatic effect. As he finished the poem, he put the book down and waited for applause. Only the shopkeeper clapped. Disappointed his brothers-in-law were not in awe, he turned and left the stall without another word.

CHAPTER 35

Monday, August 29

"DOES HE REALLY LOVE ME?"

The wedding was exactly one week away. Nazeera lay on her bed staring at the ceiling. The sound of car horns honked through her open window. It was still early in the morning, but the air was already heavy making the room very stuffy. The whine of the ceiling fan echoed in the room, providing only whiffs of air movement. Not enough to offer any real relief. Akbar was in the kitchen banging pots and pans around making something for lunch. Shanti had come and gone and at least she was made ready for the day.

However, Nazeera wasn't sure she wanted to handle today. She wanted to just stay in this room and be a kid again. She wasn't ready for the real world. The world of marriage and America. *And Amir wants me to work. Where? What am I qualified to do? What good is that silly English degree? I'll probably end up pulling chicken feathers or cleaning houses. No, I will not do servant work. Maybe I could still run a boutique! Maybe I could sell glamorous clothes like they wear in the Hollywood movies.* Nazeera smiled.

She sat up, propped two pillows behind her and hugged her knees. She would miss this room. Even though she had only lived here for a few months, it now symbolized home. Her father would be sad, no devastated, when she left. Her mother would be sad too, but she wouldn't miss her as much. She enjoyed their shopping trips, but Ammi had always favored the boys and the shopping trips only made their parents fight more. Maybe her leaving home would provide some relief. A married daughter and two sons in great careers. What more could parents desire, right? Then her father could retire, and they could start the next phase of their life.

The phone call last night had been very quick. She had been sitting on the veranda with her feet propped on a chair as the hours of shopping with her aunty and cousins had created blisters on her feet. They had found all the wedding clothes, gifts, and a few outfits for her to take to America. It had taken them two days and twelve stores, maybe more but Nazeera stopped counting after twelve, to find everything they needed. She was grateful they had the driver and car at stand-by. "I don't think I can walk another step." Nusrat Aunty said when they settled into the car late Sunday afternoon. They were all exhausted.

The sun had been setting and the sky was a dazzling red. Nazeera remembered thinking the sun's rays looked like golden rods streaking against a claret carpet. She must have fallen asleep because Akbar woke her when he came out to the veranda with the telephone. She blinked a few times to make sure she was not dreaming. When she realized she was not, she sat up very straight. "*Aacha* Akbar, *kaun hai*? Who is it?"

He declared it was her mother, handed her the telephone, and retreated back to the kitchen. She shrugged her shoulders and put the receiver to her mouth and ear, "Hello, Ammi."

The phone connection was poor and the occasional crackling was distracting. Ammi said she was calling from one of the many stops the train was making on the trip back from Delhi to Bombay. In between crackles, she updated Nazeera by saying both Amina *khalaji* and her cousin Naveed would be coming to the *mehndi* and wedding. Murad *mamuji* may not be able to come, it depends on his work schedule. Nazeera was a bit disappointed her uncle would not move heaven and earth to attend her wedding, but then again neither of them had come for Hamid's wedding, er, non-wedding last year. She would be content with her *khalaji* and cousin attending.

Things had always been tense between her parents and Murad *mamuji*. If she remembered the story right, her father was supposed to have married Amina *khalaji* and Murad *mamuji* was supposed to marry her mother. But two weeks before the wedding, Murad, who was wealthy and very much into politics and appearances, insisted he wanted to marry the prettier sister and chose Amina over Lailaa. Their parents relented, because they wanted an influential son-in-law, and simply swapped suitors - Amina married Murad and Lailaa married Rahim. The room usually got tense when all four of them were present, so Murad *mamuji* not coming to the wedding might actually be a blessing.

Her parents were due back any minute, and Nazeera was sure her father would rush off to work right away. He usually had several meetings on Mondays and he had already missed all the morning ones due to this impromptu trip. She was relieved they had been able to connect with Hamid at the train station before they left and personally invite him to the wedding. He was initially reluctant to attend the wedding at the Crystal Room, insisting he couldn't show his face in Bombay again. But Daddy persisted and Hamid finally agreed because it was Nazeera's wedding, and he didn't want to miss saying good-bye. He said he would co-ordinate timing with *Khalaji* and Naveed so they would all take the same train. That way their father would only have to send the car and driver once. That was, unless *Khalaji* brought a lot of suitcases!

Nazeera laid back on her pillows letting her legs go straight in front of her. She closed her eyes and let her mind wander. It's all happening so fast. Khalaji is coming to the wedding. So is Hamid! Jaya said she would be here on Friday. Friday, Friday, how was she going to tell her parents about Habib's heartfelt proposal last Friday? *Why am I even considering it? Wasn't he the heathen that insisted on a large dowry that would have put Daddy into debt and delayed his retirement? But, now he says he loves me and just wants to marry me. Without a dowry! Does he really love me? Is there another reason?*

And what about Amir? The man I'm planning to marry in a few days! He said he cares for me and he never insisted on a dowry. But he lives in America! Marrying him would mean leaving this world behind and starting anew. Maybe that is my destiny now. Ammi and Daddy could come visit. But, Daddy didn't like to fly.

She needed to chose one of them. She had already chosen Amir, but Habib made an interesting and compelling counter-offer. She could run a boutique and stay in Bombay, just as she had always wanted. She could keep her friends, attend the same parties and visit home often. It was her dream come true! Was it now an old dream? She would, of course, need Shanti to help her dress each day. And Habib had looked at her a bit too intensely on his first two visits. Maybe Shanti was the real reason Habib was so anxious to marry her.

She threw a pillow at the bedroom door, and yelled, "Aaargh!" *Does Habib really love me? Do I love him?*

Nazeera's mind was racing. She began a mental list of reasons why Habib might want to marry her other than love. *Daddy's government connections might be a big asset to his import-export business. That would be convenient, yes very convenient. Plus, a Muslim man was allowed by Islamic law to marry more than one woman. Do they still allow that in India? If they did, then Shanti, though a Hindu, could be Habib's second wife. And Shanti would probably jump at the chance to improve her position in life. But that would mean I would have to share my husband with her. That just didn't seem right.*

She started pacing the floor stopping at the window. She watched the pigeon she startled take flight, and fly from her window sill toward the opposite building. Hanging in one of the windows near the pigeon's head was a large photo of the Taj Mahal. Hmm, maybe this would be like the days of Shah Jahan. He had three wives including the famous Mumtaz Mahal. He loved her the most even though she was not his first wife. They were married for nineteen years before she died giving birth to their fourteenth child. His other wives were nothing compared to her. So, yes, she could be like Mumtaz Mahal and win her husband's love by captivating his heart and bearing him numerous children. Maybe Habib would even create a Taj Mahal of sorts for her. The thought of a white marble monument in her honor made her laugh. *Yeah, right.*

The front door slammed. Ah, Ammi and Daddy were home. Nazeera almost skipped to the living room to greet her parents. "I'm so glad you're home!"

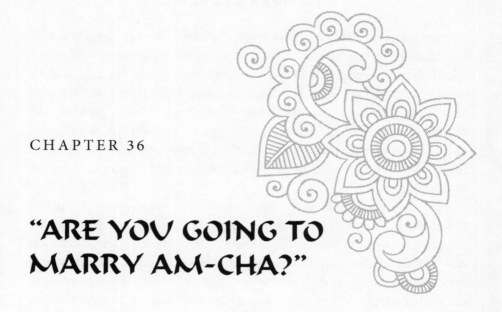

CHAPTER 36

"ARE YOU GOING TO MARRY AM-CHA?"

It had been three days since Rehana had chatted with Ammi regarding wedding preparations, and they had agreed to meet for afternoon tea at the Ivanhoe flat. Ammi had taken a nap almost immediately upon arriving home, so Nazeera had not had a chance to tell her about her Friday night visitor. Daddy had also changed his clothes quickly, and left for the office claiming he was late for a meeting. He probably was. He had a lot of meetings.

The ladies got dressed for afternoon tea with the soon-to-be in-laws. They knew Rehana would be there but weren't sure who else she had invited. Ammi hoped Shakila was there. Nazeera did not. Amir's mother intimidated her.

The driver stopped the car at the closed gate in front of the building, and Nazeera pushed it to enter the small courtyard. This was the second time they were visiting the building where Amir was staying, but the first time she really looked around. It was an interesting Art Deco style building with long straight lines and curved verandas. Nazeera vaguely recalled Amir pointing and saying something about the building as they drove by on her Vespa. Was he telling her where he was staying?

They followed the same path they had taken a week ago and

pushed the button to call the lift. The arrow above the lift doors indicated it was already on the fourth floor. While they waited for it to descend, Ammi straightened Nazeera's scarlet red sari pleats. Bothered by her mother's needless primping, she gently pushed her mother's hands away. Turning to look at her, she noticed Ammi was wearing a dove-gray sari with large deep blue flowers. As usual, she wore a lot of face powder and bright red lipstick. It didn't do much to bring out her natural beauty, but she thought it did and I guess, that's what matters.

The lift car arrived and they stepped into it, pushing the button for the fourth floor. As the lift began to ascend, Nazeera considered telling her mother about Habib's visit and his revised wedding proposal. He had said he loved her and wanted to marry her without any dowry! She turned toward her mother and hesitated when she noticed her mother seemed content. In fact, she was humming slightly, something she rarely did. She was happy. No need to change that now. She could tell her mother later. It could wait.

The lift doors opened, and they walked down the carpeted hallway toward their destination. The door was already ajar, so Nazeera knocked hesitantly and peered her head into the flat calling cautiously, "Hello?!"

Rehana noticed them right away and came rushing from across the hallway to them, "Welcome, welcome." She was wearing a forest green sari with silver *zari* threaded in a leaf pattern. She looked like a shiny palm tree. She smiled and ushered them through the dining room and into the living room.

Arriving moments earlier, Amir and Shakila were just being seated. Shakila sat in the high-back chair, while Amir sat on the loveseat and indicated to Nazeera to sit next to him. It seemed like an eternity since she had seen him and even longer since that afternoon when he had declared he loved her. *Did he still love me? Has that changed? Do I love him? Enough to marry him?*

As Nazeera sat down, Amir took her hand in his. Unexpectedly, her heart started to pound against her chest. She glimpsed at her fiancé and saw his face had turned red and his hand was suddenly warmer. *Maybe he's nervous too. Maybe he truly does love me. Amir is kind and caring, and would never cheat on me. I'm sure of that.*

Sure, he has his faults, but they're minor ones. Ones I can live with and overlook for the sake of a happy life.

Babu came into the living room carrying a sterling silver tray with the typical afternoon tea components. He silently placed the tray on the coffee table, and began pouring cups of tea. The bowls of flowers and Bombay mix she remembered from the engagement party had been replaced with platters of colorful pastries and sandwiches.

The banter surrounded them, and Nazeera ignored the murmur. They were talking about some detail she did not care about. After a few moments, Amir tapped her hand and mumbled something to her. It was a little hard to understand him with his American accent. Not knowing what he had said, she just nodded her head and smiled, hoping the question was about the tea. It must not have been about the drinks as Amir repeated what he was saying a bit slower. She turned from him and looked to her mother for guidance. Everyone was staring at her.

"Sorry, what was the question?" Nazeera asked feeling suddenly hot.

"We were wondering how you felt about exchanging the saris gifts at the time of the *mehndi*." Rehana explained to the bride, "Since the gift of saris to the ladies of the groom's family is a tradition from your side of the family, why don't we do that before the *mehndi* since all the women will be present at your parent's flat."

That made sense, she smiled and said, "*Ji, huh.*"

Satisfied with her answer, Nazeera leaned back on the loveseat cushions. Suddenly she felt something move from beside her left hand. She jumped back and leaned on Amir for protection. Two big brown eyes glared back at her. She held her position and Amir put his arms around his fiancé wrapping her in security. Suddenly a whole body appeared stealthily. It was Rabia, Rehana's daughter. She had been there at the engagement gift event and had stared at Nazeera then. She was staring at her again now, and suddenly asked, "Are you going to marry Am-cha?"

Did she mean Amir? "Yes, I am," Nazeera said more confidently than she felt at that moment.

The little girl smiled and tilted her head to the right than left. She asked the bride her name and Rabia replied, "You're pretty,

Niiizzzeearaa *Chachi*. I mean, Nazzeer Chi. No, I mean, um, Nazer-chi, Naz-chi. Bye Naz-chi!" she scampered over to her mother's side, kissed her on the cheek, and then disappeared into her bedroom. *Naz-chi? Did the little girl just create a nickname for me? Is Nazeera Chachi really that hard to say?*

Farid laughed. "She likes you, Nazeera or she wouldn't have given you a nickname already. She's been following Rehana around trying to help with the wedding planning. She's loving all of this."

The group sipped their tea and continued discussing the wedding. The invitations had all been sent or personally delivered. Amir sent a few to America and already followed up with telephone calls. He said most were not able to attend as they did not have passports, but his friend Kabir Mehta was planning to come with his American wife Carmen. Also, his boss, Greg, would come if he could get a travel visa. He was planning to drive all the way to the Indian Consulate in Chicago sometime this week to try and get one.

Ammi updated her portion of the guest list by saying her sister and nephew were coming from Delhi and her eldest son Hamid would also be attending. Shakila proudly responded that her brother was coming all the way from Pakistan. Amir simply shook his head, this wasn't a competition.

Scratching lines on her list, Rehana changed the subject, "*Aacha*, onto the timing of the display."

"What display?" Nazeera asked not sure if she missed part of the conversation.

"The display of the wedding gifts." Rehana replied very matter-of-factly. "The traditional display of the gifts from the groom's side to the bride, the bride's side to the groom and the bride's parents to the bride."

"There will be no display of gifts," Nazeera said defiantly removing her hand from Amir's grip and taking a sip of her tea. It was too hot and it burned the tip of her tongue. "No one needs to see what gifts we receive. It's none of their business." The tradition of showing the gifts was meant to be a show of wealth and to a certain degree generosity. Gold and jewelry were common gifts as they were something that could be worn or converted to cash at a later date if the couple needed it. Clothes and food were also common gifts though they were given only after the gold and jewelry gifts.

"My dear," Shakila said speaking boldly, "It is tradition. For Farid and Rehana's wedding, we had a grand display of the gifts. Rehana's father gave them all the furniture for the flat. For Nilofer and Nadir's wedding we had a grand display that took up three tables, and for Nadia and Kassim's we had a similar one. It is what is done."

Nazeera had always thought the tradition was ridiculous, and she wanted no part of it. "That may be tradition in your family, but it is not tradition in mine." She turned to her mother for support. Ammi avoided her gaze by taking a sip of tea. "Also, my father is in the government service. Showing any amount of wealth could raise some eyebrows. I don't want my father suspected of bribery, just because you insist on showing the wedding gifts."

It seemed as if smoke was coming out of Shakila's ears as she glared at Nazeera, then Amir. Returning her penetrating gaze to Nazeera she fumed, "Young lady, this is how it is done."

Also smoldering, Nazeera added, "Not at my wedding, it's not." As soon as she said the words, she regretted them. She was basically yelling at her soon to be mother-in-law, the woman she was supposed to revere above her own mother when she married her son.

Much to Nazeera's disappointment, it was not Amir who suggested the compromise, it was his brother Farid. "How about a small display of gifts. That would keep with tradition without being too showy."

Both women glared at him, but Shakila reluctantly nodded, "*Theek hai*". Rehana quickly changed the subject before Nazeera could protest. She and Shakila exchanged one final heated stare before they both turned their focus to the conversation. Nazeera purposely avoided Shakila's glances for the rest of the afternoon.

Amir's mother was obviously used to getting her own way. Well, that was not going to happen with her. It was probably just as well they would be living in America. Couldn't his mother see how showing all that gold and jewelry would look to Daddy's superiors? They wouldn't understand he and Ammi had been saving for these gifts since she was born. In fact, a few of the gifts were her mother's own jewelry. One such item is the tiger claw necklace made from a tiger Daddy had shot in the jungles of India, when the tiger hunt was a sport and at times a necessity.

Not only did Shakila's stubbornness upset Nazeera; but also, Amir's silence. *Why isn't he saying anything? Will he stand by my side in a fight or cower in a corner? Maybe he's not the right one for me after all. I'm much too independent and determined to be married to a wimpy guy!*

The conversation swayed from topic to topic, and then suddenly stopped. Ammi started giving hugs and kisses as good-bye salutations. Nazeera did the same, approaching Amir's mother politely, "Good-bye Aunty."

"Nazeera," Shakila whispered with a curt tone, "Just remember you are number eleven."

Is she insulting me? "Excuse me, Aunty. What did you just say?"

With a slight head bobble and a dismissive wave of the hand, "Just remember, you were number eleven on the list."

She is insulting me. Nazeera was tempted to say something sarcastic in response, but this woman was going to be her mother-in-law. She had to show her respect. She bit her tongue and quickly scurried after her mother who was standing near the lift.

The lift ride down to the car was fairly quiet. Ammi simply said, "We raised you to be independent, but maybe you are too independent." Nazeera began to protest but her mother raised her right hand to stop her.

CHAPTER 37

"HOW COULD HE REFUSE A PARTY IN HIS HONOR?"

Only a half hour after the intense afternoon tea, Bandra phoned to invite them to dinner. She said she felt terrible she has been in a bad mood the last few days, and she wanted to make it up to them. Farid and Rehana were pleased with the invitation as they both needed a distraction from all the wedding planning. Mummy always enjoyed eating dinner with one of her children, so she also accepted the impromptu invitation. Amir was more suspicious of his sister. Was this another ploy? He hesitantly accepted the invitation only after she said the dinner party was going to be in his honor. How could he refuse a party in his honor?

Bandra and Salim lived in a hard to find location off of Colaba Causeway. They had lived in the same building for the past couple decades and the city sort of grew up around their building. As they walked up the steps from the sidewalk to the foyer, Amir noticed his mother was smiling a very smug smile. *What has she done? Did she tell Bandra about the outburst from Nazeera? Do they think Dilshad now had a chance? Well, she's sadly mistaken.* The heated discussion between his fiancé and his mother convinced him that Nazeera was exactly the woman for him. She was independent, confident and principled. She cared more about her father's reputation than she did about offending her soon-to-be in-laws. That was the spirit he admired and now loved.

The lift was an old-fashioned Otis brand elevator. It moved slower than molasses, and when it finally arrived after an almost ten minute wait, they noticed it was extremely small. The lift car was a five foot by five foot square with mirrored walls. It made the room seem more crowded and for the first time in a long time, Amir felt claustrophobic. *Why did they have to live on the top floor?*

They squeezed into the box, and Farid hit the button for Bandra's floor by reaching past Rehana who was sandwiched between him and the wall. Mummy seemed to be sweating from the excessive heat in the car as well as the stifling heat in the foyer. The sun had set already, but the humidity in the air lingered.

They finally arrived at the correct floor after what seemed like another ten minutes of agonizing ascent. Pouring out of the lift car, Mummy wiped her neck and chest with a tissue she pulled from her small purse. They walked down the tiled hallway to the door. Farid hit the doorbell, stepped back and sighed. It was too hot for this much activity.

A moment later the door opened, and Bandra welcomed the small group to her home. She and Salim had a large flat with a magnificent view of the Arabian Sea. They had the veranda doors propped open and a refreshing breeze ebbed and flowed through the living room making the flat at least thirty degrees cooler than the hallway.

The newly arrived guests settled themselves onto the living room chairs, and Salim signaled their servant, Sabu, to bring a round of drinks. He returned carrying a wooden tray filled with chilled glasses of Coca-Cola and water. As Amir took a glass of water, he noticed an elephant inlay on the bottom of the tray. He thanked Sabu for the water, to which the servant simply grumbled, moving onto the next guest.

The water was very refreshing. Amir took another long swallow and began to glance around the room. Bandra's flat was furnished with expensive but comfortable furniture. They had a large tan Persian rug in the center of the living room with the typical sofa, loveseat and two chairs configuration. The furniture was dark brown almost black with tan and white throw pillows. One of the chairs had a footstool that looked well used. A blue cut glass bowl of cashews sat in the center of the coffee table. There were already a few handfuls missing from it.

The ceiling fan was humming nicely and the whole flat had a serene atmosphere. Carrying his glass, Amir stepped onto the veranda to watch the waves wash up on the shore. The gentle breeze coming off the sea tasted salty on his lips. *This is nice. I can see why they've lived here for so many years.* He took a sip from his glass and simply sighed.

A woman stepped silently onto the veranda, and came to stand next to Amir touching his arm with hers. She did not say anything and they simply stood together in silence. He glanced out of the corner of his eye and confirmed it was Dilshad. She was wearing a lavender sari with some sort of swirls. Her hair hung loosely around her shoulders and she wore long dangly earrings. He wasn't surprised to see her. He suspected she was the real reason Bandra invited them to dinner. Her earrings jingled as she tilted her head toward Amir, "What a lovely evening."

"Yes, a very lovely evening," he responded without breaking his gaze of the waves lapping on shore. After several moments, he turned to look at Dilshad moving away from her slightly, "It's been a long time since I've stood on this veranda. Do you visit here often?"

They made small talk about her friendship with Bandra. Dilshad relayed the story of how a misadventure with an immigrant couple at JK had brought them together. It was obvious she adored Bandra and Amir was certain the feelings were reciprocated.

During a tale of a shopping adventure, Dilshad tilted her head back and laughed a somewhat exaggerated laugh. As she did so, she placed her right hand on Amir's bicep. He laughed along with her, more out of awkwardness than her silly story. *Did she place her hand there on purpose? Is she flirting with me?*

"Maybe we should head back inside," Amir suggested once he composed himself.

Dilshad slowly stopped laughing, rubbing her hand on his arm. With raised eyebrows, she gave him a wry smile, "Fine."

Placing his hand on the small of her back, he escorted Dilshad back to the living room. The rest of the group were scattered throughout the room. Bandra and Salim were socializing with Mummy, while Farid and Rehana were chatting with Bandra's daughter, Daania.

Immediately spying Amir and Dilshad return from the veranda, Bandra shot them an inquisitive look. Amir ignored his sister, instead using the better lighting to take a better look at the woman standing next to him. She was indeed wearing a lavender sari with large magenta swirls. She wore a sleeveless sari blouse allowing her arms and midriff to show. Amir could not help it, but his mouth dropped.

The group filed into the living room and his mother played along with the plan by seating Dilshad in the love seat and Amir on the sofa, at right angles to each other. Amir was now convinced the plan was for the two of them to converse and for him to admire her beauty and forget Nazeera. Farid, Salim and Daania found dining room chairs and sat down to a quick conversation about the latest cricket match, making Daania completely bored. Bandra sat next to her preferred bride, while Rehana sat next to her brother-in-law, munching handfuls of cashews.

"You're looking lovely this evening," Amir admitted to Dilshad. She smiled knowingly at him, and blinked her eyes audaciously. *She is appealing,* Amir told himself. *If I wasn't so in love with Nazeera, this woman might've had a chance.* He knew both his sister and mother preferred Dilshad over Nazeera. She was after all the same religion as him, her family was known to his family, and she was stunning. All very good reasons he should have selected her.

But, if she is this perfect, why wasn't she placed higher up on the list? If I had met her first or even second, especially before the doctor who wanted to wait or the nawabzadi whose father yelled at me, things might've been different. Why had they waited so long to introduce her? There must be a reason. She must have a flaw, somewhere.

"So, I hear you went shopping on Fashion Street yesterday," Dilshad said blinking her eyes again at Amir. "Did you find what you were looking for?"

Amir leaned forward so they could talk more privately. His hands were inches away from hers. He was tempted to take her hands in his to rile his sister. Instead, he told her about their quest to find the perfect gold buttons. She appeared to listen intently, and be fascinated by every word he uttered.

More sets of eyes were watching them then Amir realized. When Bandra announced dinner was ready, he saw everyone turn from them to peer into the dining room. *What are they all expecting to see?* Dilshad and Amir started the buffet line at Bandra's request, with the rest of the family lining up behind them.

The food display was not as appealing as Rehana's presentations, but each dish did look delicious. As Amir circled the buffet, he remembered Bandra was a fabulous cook. She had always made the best tasting *shammi kebabs*. Salivating at the thought of them, he searched the table discreetly looking for the minced lamb meat skewers. *There they are!* They looked perfect, with bits of *kothmir* sticking out of the meat. Licking his lips, Amir eagerly took two *kebabs*. Deciding to indulge in this rare treat, he took two more.

While they enjoyed the food, Daania shared she had saved a drowning girl at the CCI swimming pool yesterday, Dilshad shocked the group saying she was almost crushed by a school bulletin board, and Bandra bored the group with her adventure finding new *chappals* on Colaba.

During Bandra's never-ending story, Dilshad threw up her hands in mock laughter. As they came down, her left hand accidentally, or purposefully, landed on Amir's thigh. She left it there for several seconds, caressing it gently, before whisking it away. Her hand was warm, but Amir felt nothing. No increase in his heart beat, no flush of his face, no sweat beads on his upper lip. No thrill. He was now convinced more than ever he was not attracted to her in a romantic way.

The lingering flavor of the cloves from the *shammi kebabs* sat on Amir's tongue. They were delicious lamb skewers when he ate them, but now he needed something sweet to neutralize the taste. After a short moment, his wish was granted. Soon after the hand incident, Sabu gathered the empty dinner plates and retreated to the kitchen. He returned with the elephant inlaid tray filled with several small bowls of *kheer*. Everyone must have enjoyed the creamy rice pudding as the room was instantly quiet. *Maybe everyone needed the sweet-ness of the kheer to counteract the spices from dinner.*

Amir used this opportunity to glance around the room, and he caught his sister making hand movements to Dilshad obviously trying to convey a message. Leaning forward slightly to watch his sister, Amir dropped his spoon. He rolled his eyes, and leaned forward to get it, "Sorry". Dilshad also leaned down at the same time, and they knocked heads. "Sorry," he repeated. She smiled, holding her lips only inches from his. She started to lean forward, and he quickly retreated holding the spoon.

Grumbling, Sabu collected the empty dessert dishes while Bandra distracted the rest of the group by offering them a cup of Darjeeling tea. Amir was concerned Dilshad was getting the wrong impression from him. She was almost throwing herself at him. She touched his arm, caressed his upper thigh, knocked his head, and longed for a kiss. But, still he felt nothing but friendship for her.

He forced himself to be civil during the tea service, and jumped up when Farid announced it was time to go. Dilshad smiled sweetly at Amir, blinking her eyelashes again, as she rose from the loveseat. She gave him a tender hug and kissed both of his cheeks lingering a bit longer on the second kiss. *Why is she lingering? Is she thinking I'm going to kiss her?*

Turning from Dilshad, Amir stepped toward his older sister to give her a departing hug. He could tell she was miffed, as she barely returned it. Brushing past him, Bandra hugged and kissed her friend saying a little louder than she should have, "He's a fool".

The four of them left the flat three hours after they arrived. The taxi ride back to the Ivanhoe building was slowed by the usual Bombay traffic. There seemed to be traffic at all hours in this city!

"Dilshad looked stunning, didn't she?" Mummy asked.

"Yeah, she did," Amir had to admit. Mummy turned toward him with eyebrows raised. Rehana also turned to him with her forehead creased probably hoping she wouldn't have to start the wedding preparations all over again with a different bride. "She's very nice. I can see why Bandra is friends with her."

"But what do you think about her as a bride?"

"A bride for whom? For me?" Amir teased pointing to his chest,

"Mummy, I already have a bride." Rehana sighed deeply in relief. "I'm marrying Nazeera next Monday. Meeting Dilshad tonight did not change that. In fact, it reinforced that I made the right choice. Both women are beautiful, but Nazeera is independent and smart. I enjoy Dilshad's company and she tells great stories, but I only have feelings of friendship for her."

Mummy sat back in her seat, and remained quiet the rest of the ride home. Amir thought she was plotting another plan. She probably was; she was used to getting her own way. Farid nodded off in the front seat and began to snore very loudly. After several moments of silence except for Farid's snoring, Mummy whacked him on the shoulder startling him awake. She was obviously frustrated.

CHAPTER 38

Tuesday, August 30

"I'M GOING FOR A WALK"

After the encounter at afternoon tea yesterday, Nazeera was convinced the wedding would be cancelled. She was sure Amir's mom would call it off, refusing to let her son marry such a non-demure, bold, independent woman. Well, if Amir was out of the picture, maybe Habib could be back in. It was time to tell Ammi about Habib's proposal. *Marrying him wouldn't be so bad. Would it?*

Her mother had gone into her bedroom immediately upon their return from the Ivanhoe building. She was visibly upset, taking dinner in her room, and even refusing telephone calls. Nazeera had knocked and knocked on her mother's bedroom door to no avail. She wanted to talk to her mother; no, she needed to talk to her. These mood swings were hard on everyone in the family. Even her father had slept on the settee in the living room because Ammi wouldn't allow him to enter the bedroom.

She wanted to apologize for the outburst yesterday. Nazeera was protecting her father, didn't they all see that? She didn't mean to be disrespectful to Shakila, but she needed to convey her point of view. Why was it so hard for them to understand it was hard for her father to be a Muslim in a majority Hindu government? Showing wealth might bring suspicion where none was warranted.

"I'm going for a walk," Nazeera said aloud to anyone listening. Throwing up her hands, she stormed out of the flat. Impatiently pushing the lift call button five or six times, she decided she couldn't wait for the stupid lift. She turned, and jumped down the stairs two at a time.

The sun shone on her face as she exited the Yashodham building, and she had to lift her arm in front of her eyes to shield them from the blinding sun. Standing in the front courtyard she was undecided - walk to Marine Drive or drive her scooter to The Sea Lounge. Pacing, she concluded she needed to walk not ride. Starting up Dinshaw Vachha Road, she walked past the CCI and Hotel Marine Plaza. At the busy street corner, she turned left onto NSC Bose Road and walked toward the Oberoi Hotel. Looking around quickly, she crossed the road jogging in front of a black Fiat to avoid being hit. A man with a cart full of *paan* stood on the corner. His teeth were red with the indulgence of his wares. She headed straight for the wall ignoring the *paan-walla's* calls to buy his items. Glancing around and noticing no one was watching, she removed her *chappals*.

Climbing up, Nazeera stood on top of the flat and wide cement wall. On her left was the Arabian Sea and a sea wall that looked like a multitude of used wine corks poking out of the water. On her right was a red brick pedestrian walkway with dozens of people, dogs and an occasional bicycle. She could jump. That would be it. She wouldn't need to decide between Amir or Habib. She wouldn't have to apologize for being herself. She wouldn't have to worry anymore.

But, her life was not that bad. She had two men interested in her. Granted both of them had issues. Amir had a mother who thought she knew better than anyone else, and Habib had a father who dominated his household. But, both of them would be living away from their parent's home. In fact, Amir would be living on another continent from his mother!

Sitting down, she let her feet dangle over the cement wall. She leaned back on her hands and let the sunshine pour onto her face. Instinctively, she closed her eyes, wishing she had brought sunglasses. Sigh. *What do I do now?* The sound of the waves crashing onto the sea wall was relaxing. An occasional crying seagull flew overhead.

The car horns and vendors calls blended together into a weird Bombay white noise. She blocked them all out. She had to think.

When Nazeera returned from her walk, she was surprised to see her mother sitting on the sofa in the living room. Her legs were curled up under her, and she was scratching names off a list. *Had Rehana cancelled the wedding? Has Ammi been calling all these people to tell them I blew it?* Nazeera's heart was racing, and the room began to spin.

Ammi looked up from the list, "Aaah, *Beta,* you're back." She patted the seat next to her and moved her feet to the floor. Nazeera reluctantly went and sat down next to her mother, still feeling light-headed. "Let's review the guest list to see who we need to call."

"To cancel the wedding?" Nazeera asked, feeling dizzy, "I...I," She couldn't even finish the sentence. She was amazed her mother was sitting here so calmly calling people to cancel her wedding!

"*Baap-re,* what nonsense." Ammi replied turning to face her daughter, "The wedding is not cancelled."

"It's not?" The room stopped spinning.

"*Nahih.* You are who you are. If Amir wants to marry you, even if you are independent and speak your mind, then *theek hai.*"

"So, Rehana didn't call to cancel the wedding? Amir's mother hasn't stopped the wedding."

"*Nahih, Beta.*"

A weight was lifted. Suddenly the world wasn't crashing down around her. She smiled to her mother, simply saying, "*Aacha.* Fine." She was more relieved than she wanted to admit. But, now she was back to the original dilemma of Amir or Habib. "Ammi, I have something I need to tell you."

Her mother looked a bit annoyed, but put her pen down and looked at her daughter, "Yes, *Beta. Yea kya hai?* What is it?"

Bursting with tears, Nazeera apologized for the outburst at Rehana's flat. Her mother accepted the apology, replying, "There are times when one has to be humble to the in-laws and elders. When I was your age, I was forced to mar...." she abruptly stopped and pretended to review the names on the guest list.

Nazeera took this opportunity to add, "There's one more thing."

Her father fumbled with the keys in the lock. Stepping into the flat, he announced he had come home early to help with the wedding preparations, if he could. Nazeera's face lit up, and she rushed to give him a hug. Patting her head like a child, he hugged her back holding her close.

"We're just going over the guest list," Ammi updated him.

"Daddy, I'm so glad you're home. I can tell you both together."

Her father sat down in the chair near the sofa and leaned back. Shanti brought a tall cool glass of water on the small circular tray used for serving solo drinks. Daddy thanked her, drank about half of the water, then responded to his daughter, "Tell us what?"

Nazeera returned to her spot on the sofa, "Um, Habib came to visit me last Friday." She described the whole scene with his declaration of love and his revised proposal. Ammi was in shock. "How dare he come when we are not home!" Daddy was more concerned as to the reason for his change of heart. They speculated as to why. Nazeera was tempted to say she thought it was because of his interest in Shanti, but she wasn't sure, so she kept quiet.

"How do you feel about him, *Beta*?" Her mother asked, placing her own hand on her daughter's knee.

"I don't know," Nazeera said, her face in her hands. She described her conundrum between staying in Bombay with Habib and leaving for America with Amir. Listing the pros and cons, they concluded Habib had more pros but also more cons.

"Which one do you care about more?" Ammi asked simply. Nazeera noticed she didn't use the word, "love". It was hard to fall in love with someone you hardly knew. Caring, turns to affection. Affection to love. "Which one do you think will make you happy?"

Nazeera started to cry. Marrying Habib would allow her to stay in Bombay. She could open the boutique she always dreamed of, and continue meeting her friends. A life of familiar experiences. Marrying Amir would take her away from this life to start a new one on a different continent. They would only have each other. None of her family or friends. It would be a life of new experiences.

"Sleep on it," her father suggested trying to be patient.

Stumbling into her bedroom, Nazeera plopped onto the bed. Her parents were making this very easy for her. She could pick either guy.

It was all up to her. No pressure from them to make a diplomatic match. No arranged marriage where she was forced to marry a guy she had never met. No pressure to even marry. It was her choice. She could say "yes" to either of them. In fact, she already had.

She leaned back on her pillows, staring at the spot on the ceiling she had been staring at all too often lately. *They asked me which one would make me happy. But, which one is that? The guy that will let me stay in Bombay but I question his fidelity or the man that will take me away but would remain faithful? Neither option is ideal, that's for sure. But, which one will make me more happy?* She turned onto her stomach and placed a pillow over her head. Aargh!!

It would be simpler if they just told her what to do. Then she could blame them if things didn't work out. If she made the choice, she could only blame herself. This must be what growing up is all about. Making your own decisions and then living with the consequences. She only had a few days before the wedding. Was she marrying the right man?

CHAPTER 39

Thursday, September 1

"AACHA"

Nazeera noticed her mother was humming more often. She must be happy preparing this celebration, having tea and cakes with family friends inviting them personally to her daughter's nuptials. Since the wedding was proceeding as planned, she assumed Ammi was thinking Amir was the groom. *He's a good guy. Handsome, smart and caring. Why am I now doubting my choice? Why am I even considering Habib? Is it because he has movie star looks and a lot of money? Am I that shallow?*

Her mother was babbling about the events of the day, "Mohan will be arriving today. You remember him, no? He was our tailor in Poona. He has agreed to come to Bombay to make the sari blouses, adjust our wedding outfits, and help in any way he can. The cotton mattresses for the guests will be delivered this afternoon. Is ten enough? Well, there were the sofas and the settee too. And Aziz's flat isn't too far. People could stay there, no?"

The doorbell rang followed by a loud knocking on the door. Akbar hurried out of the kitchen and peeked through the spy-hole. Turning to Ammi, he whispered, "It's Mr. Abdullah."

Frowning, Ammi nodded to indicate it was all right to open the door. Nazeera scurried into her bedroom to peer from a crack in the doorway. She wasn't sure what her answer to him was yet.

Habib smirked as he crossed the threshold, and entered the

living room. "As-salaam-alaykum, Aunty" he said with a slight bow. Removing his shoes, he stepped boldly forward.

"Salaam, Habib," Ammi responded, gesturing to an empty chair. She moved the invitation list out of sight of her impromptu visitor, and sighed, "Nazeera told me you revised your proposal."

"Yes, Aunty," Habib started, "I realized after our last meeting that I truly love her and want her as my wife." Nazeera blushed at his remarks. She couldn't believe he was saying these things to her mother. She inched the door open a bit further. She dared not open it much more for fear of someone seeing her.

"*Aacha*, so you..." Ammi started, but then stopped as Shanti entered the room holding the wooden tray full of soft drinks. Her mother selected a Coca-Cola and Nazeera watched as Shanti walked to Habib and held the tray at his eye level.

To her surprise, Habib selected the drink nearest to him and said, "*Shukriya*." He did not look up. He did not offer her an extra wry smile. He was a gentlemen. Maybe he's changed! Nazeera's heart raced and she was suddenly warm. She waved her hands in front of her face to try and cool herself down.

"*Ji, huh*," Habib took a sip of lemonade, and continued, "Yes, she's lovely and I want her to be my wife."

Ammi watched him for a moment, then simply repeated, "*Aacha*." Why wasn't she talking more? What was she waiting for?

"Um... yes, and since your husband has excellent government connections, he can help my company with its customs issues. My father and I figure the connections alone are worth the cost of the dowry. So, we dropped the dowry request."

"*Aacha*." The truth was coming out. Her mother took a long sip of her Coke. Why did she keep repeating the same word? Is she waiting for Habib to dig himself a hole.

"It was actually my father's idea. He's a smart man. A very smart man." Habib was talking very fast. Ammi began tapping her foot but let him continue. "He thought since our Bombay branch is still in the early stages, well, connections are very valuable. No custom delays. No fines. We could grow our import business very quickly."

Ammi just nodded. Nazeera couldn't believe what she was

hearing. Exploiting Daddy's government connections just to grow his business. That's just another form of extortion. No way!

Continuing, Habib must have thought her mother was not convinced, "And Nazeera will be a great hostess to all the VIPs we will need to entertain. She can supervise the kitchen, and charm them with her beauty. She will wear only the latest fashions and since I'll be travelling a lot, it'll be nice for Nazeera to have Shanti to keep her company."

"Shanti?" Ammi sat forward in her chair, her eyebrows bunching together. Nazeera winched. She saw Shanti and Akbar both step out of the kitchen. Habib could not see them as his back was to them.

"Yes, of course. I can see Nazeera needs her to be a great hostess, so of course, she must take Shanti with her. She will have a nice life with us. I will double her salary, of course, and help you find a replacement."

"Shanti is not going with you. She is staying here." Nazeera noticed Shanti's face change from a frown to a smile. She didn't want to leave here, especially to go with him.

"But, Nazeera..."

"*Nahih*, No," Ammi yelled, her face was red and her leg was visibly shaking. Tell tale signs she was upset. *This guy doesn't really love me! He doesn't really care about me or my dreams. He only cares about what this marriage can do for him - either wealth from a flat or Daddy's connections. It's time to get rid of him for the third and final time!*

Stepping defiantly from the bedroom, Nazeera strode into the living room. Reaching him in seconds, she blurted, "Habib, I've heard everything you've said. I have considered your proposal, but my answer remains the same. I'm going to marry Amir. He treats me and my family with respect, and he truly loves me. Neither of which I believe you do. Please leave now."

Habib was shocked. He stood up and looked softly into her eyes, "Nazeera, darling," he started, trying to grab her hand. "Come now, you know I love you. I told you as much last Friday."

"*Juldi chalo*. Hurry up and leave!" Ammi said very loudly and with a quick flick of her wrist. "Akbar!"

Akbar rushed into the room, but it was Nazeera who gave the

orders this time, "Help Mr. Abdullah leave." Grabbing his elbow, Habib was escorted to the door. As he picked up his shoes, he turned back toward Nazeera with his puppy dog eyes to try and melt her heart again. This time it didn't work.

To avoid hearing further pleas, the ladies stepped onto the veranda and closed the double doors behind them. Leaning back in their chairs, they sighed at the same time. "*Bahut shukriya*, Ammi. Thank you very much."

"*Kyon*? Why?"

"Because you stood up for me and supported me." Tears welled up in Nazeera's eyes. She wasn't sure why she was crying, but her mother's unwavering support of her made her sentimental. Something she normally was not. "I love you."

Her mother placed her left hand on Nazeera's arm. "I love you too, *Beta*." After a moment she added, "I figured out the boy was trouble after that second meeting, but you needed to figure it out for yourself."

They exchanged smiles and leaned back again in their respective chairs. Nazeera closed her eyes and felt a sense of triumph. The touching moment between mother and daughter was interrupted by Akbar stepping onto the veranda, "Excuse me, Ma'am Sah'b. You have guests in the living room."

Both ladies sat up with a jolt. *What? Is it Habib again? Did he bring his father for reinforcements? Oh, the nerve of this man. How many times do I need to say no to him?* Feeling her face turn red and her pulse quicken, Nazeera threw open the French doors with a flourish ready for battle.

"How dare you...." she started, yelling at Habib. But, it was not Habib standing in her living room. It was another man. She felt her mother step around her to greet the guests. Nazeera was stuck in one spot dumbfounded, her heart racing. She needed to calm herself down. Way down.

"Rehana," Ammi said with a sigh of relief. She moved forward past her daughter to embrace her guest and gave her the usual welcome kisses on her cheeks. She turned to the man standing next to her, "Amir". She embraced and kissed him too, more warmly than she had ever before, "So good to see you." She nodded approval to

Akbar who had let them into the living room as though they were family already. He quickly collected the glasses from the previous visitor and retreated into the kitchen.

Nazeera was planted in her spot. *Has Amir noticed I can't move? What's taken him so long to come to me? It's been three days! Are they here to call off the wedding? So, I will go from two proposals to none in one day? Is he going to marry another girl next Monday?* Tears welled up in her eyes. What an emotionally draining day. Her throat was parched, she felt it tightening.

"Nazeera," Amir said as he approached her. Rehana and Ammi were sitting on the sofa conspiring about something. "Nazeera," he repeated with a gentle tone. She snapped back to reality and blinked a few times. She noticed he was not smiling. This was serious. He had never looked that concerned before. He was probably trying to think of the right words to say to get out of marrying her.

With her hands on her hips she mustered up some confidence and declared, "So, are you here to cancel the wedding?"

Amir frowned and shook his head, "Why would you think that?" She remained defiantly planted in one spot, but now she was confused. Approaching her, he gently took her right hand, led her over the threshold, back onto the veranda. He placed her in the chair she was sitting in only a few minutes earlier, and dragged the chair her mother had occupied toward her chair.

Picking up her hand again, he smiled a genuine smile, "Naz, I know we haven't known each other long, but I think I know you well enough and you know me. Why would you think we were here to call off the wedding?" He paused and searched his mind tilting his head slightly, "Do you think it's because of the disagreement you had with my mother?"

Nazeera could only nod. She was trying hard to hold back the tears. Amir continued, "Silly girl. I'm not mad at you. In fact, I'm proud of you for standing up for what you believe in, and for worrying about your father's reputation." Nazeera couldn't help but let a tear roll down her cheek. Her eyelashes were moist with tears. Tenderly, he wiped the tear from her cheek, "I admire you and I told my mother that after you left. C'mon," he said with his American accent, "I think your confidence and wit are perfect and will be great in America." He raised her hand to his lips and gently kissed it. "I can't wait to make you my bride."

The roller coaster of emotions was too much for her and she burst into tears. She felt Amir's arms envelope her and draw her close. She allowed him to hold her and she noticed he smelled of gardenias and hair oil. His arms were warm and comforting and she felt safe. Almost as safe as she felt in her father's arms.

After a few minutes she forced herself to stop crying. She wiped the tears from her cheeks and tried to blot the moist eye liner with the sides of her forefinger. With a deep breath, she sat up straight and exhaled. Inhale. Exhale. The tears disappeared and her breathing returned to normal. Amir stood up, offering his hand. She took it, and rose to stand by his side. He smiled at her and said reassuringly, "Everything will be okay."

He led her over the threshold, back to the stark light of the living room. The two ladies were sipping sodas and chattering wildly. Amir placed her in the chair next to Rehana and stood beside it leaning on the back of it. Nazeera looked down at her hands and noticed black smudges from her eye liner. She pulled a tissue from the tissue box and dabbed her eyes to salvage what she could.

The wedding couple sat silently, listening to the two coordinators continue coordinating. Shanti came out with the wooden tray of refreshments and a bowl full of Bombay mix snacks. She noticed Akbar had included fresh mango *lassis* for Amir and Rehana. He had never offered *lassis* to Habib. *Interesting.* She took a tall glass of *lassi* and gulped it quickly since she was dehydrated. The liquid was refreshing and just what she needed. She felt a bit better.

Most of the arrangements had been made. Between the two coordinators, the wedding had been pulled together in less than two weeks. The *mehndi* ladies were coming from Andeheri, a suburb north of the airport. They were the best in town and had agreed to come on Saturday. Since this was not December, high wedding season, some of the best artists in town were available on short notice.

The next topic to be discussed was the jewelry. Nazeera had hoped to simply avoid this conversation as this was the one that got her all riled up days ago. Alim, the Virani family jeweler, was going to come by Rehana's flat later that day to show her the bridal jewelry he had available. The ones the family purchased will be presented to Nazeera before the *nikkah*, the wedding ceremony. These were gifts from the groom's family and part of the gifts Shakila wanted displayed. Did they want to be there to see the sets? Did Nazeera have a preference for gems or colors?

Ammi indicated she didn't need to be there when Shakila met with Alim. Nazeera was exhausted and not in the mood for making any decisions. She didn't really care what her mother-in-law gave her, as she knew it would be in good taste.

Wanting to lay down, she stood up and began to leave the living room. Her mother shot her a stern look.

Covering her faux pas with a smile, Nazeera shifted her weight and sat back in the chair. She turned to Rehana and thanked her for all she had done for the wedding and added she was fine with whatever jewelry is selected.

Tinkle. Nazeera looked around for the source of the sound. Tinkle. It was Rehana's chandelier earrings. The sound reminded her of the earrings she had received from Amina *khalaji* for her fifteenth birthday. They were long strands of brilliant blue sapphire gems that tinkled as she walked. She loved them and wore them often. Her mother warned her sapphires were bad luck. Actually, they were either very good luck or very bad luck and best to be avoided. Ignoring another of her mother's silly superstitions, she wore the earrings during an important horse riding tournament. She was guiding her horse Tej expertly around the track and was in position to win first place. The earrings must be giving her very good luck. Silly superstition!

There was one round of five jumps left to complete. Easy. She had led Tej through similar courses before without problem and today she had the good luck earrings! Nazeera felt very confident she could beat Pushpa to win first prize.

Her ride started without incident. But, as she neared the last hurdle, she heard the tinkle from her earrings and as if that triggered an omen, she shifted her weight slightly on the black horse causing him to jump prematurely. His forelegs cleared the hurdle but his back legs hit the wooden bar causing it to fall off. The crowd who had been cheering wildly fell silent as they knew what that meant to her final score. She lost the tournament by only a few points to Pushpa, who went directly to Bijli to gloat. She blamed the earrings and swore she would never wear sapphire jewelry again. Her mother was right.

"No sapphires!" Nazeera blurted. Her mother nodded knowing the superstition. Rehana simply shrugged and wrote the note down.

"Great. We have only one more topic to discuss." Rehana held her breath for a moment and then added, "Our Imam will not perform the *nikkah* because you aren't Ismaili."

"What does that mean?" Amir asked speaking loudly, and a bit heated. "That's crazy. We're both Muslim."

"Well, we will need a neutral Muslim *Qazi*." Rehana turned to Ammi, "Does Rahim know any priests at your mosque? Or should I chat with my father?"

"I'm sure he does. I'm sure between Rahim and your father, they will find one that will perform the ceremonies."

With that settled, they said their good-byes. Amir held his fiancé in a warm embrace. With his American accent he repeated, "Everything will be okay."

Nazeera believed him. She was going to marry him Monday!

CHAPTER 40

Friday, September 2

"IN FACT, SHE SEEMED VERY HAPPY"

The train was to arrive at Victoria Terminus (VT) at half past six. Aziz and Nazeera were slated as the train greeters, but just after lunch, Aziz phoned the flat relaying the bad news that his supervisor had asked him to stay late at work. Fortunately, Daddy was able to come home early, and took his son's place as greeter. Ammi wanted to join the pair and welcome her younger sister, but knew she had to stay at the flat and supervise the dinner preparations.

They arrived at the train station a few minutes early. Father and daughter aimlessly wandered toward the entry of the building, passing green bushes and flowering plants. Nazeera was too excited to patiently stand and wait, so she began to pace up and down the sidewalk, stopping at a brass plaque mounted on the wall. It read, "The Victoria Terminus was named to honor Queen and Empress Victoria of England. It opened on the date of her Golden Jubilee in 1887. The style of the Terminus has influences from both Victorian Italianate Gothic Revival and traditional Indian Mughal architectures."

Each time the exit doors opened, Nazeera quickly looked to see if the person exiting was someone she knew. Here comes an older gentlemen. No, she didn't know him. Now, here comes a young mother and son. No, she didn't know them. Oh, here comes a young man and an older lady. She looks vaguely familiar, but the guy doesn't. Who is he? Is that *Khalaji*? She walked a bit slower than the young man, but they were both headed directly to her father. She saw Daddy notice them, stand up straight, pat down his hair and straighten his shirt. Was he nervous?

Amina *khalaji* was wearing a purple and blue *salwar kameez* and a light weight white sweater like some Indian woman do when they're slightly cold. Her hair was placed into one long braid for the trip and she wore comfortable-looking brown *chappals*. Even after travelling for several hours, she still looked fabulous. "Hello, Rahim," *Khalaji* said placing her hand on his forearm. "So nice to see you again so soon." She leaned forward and gave him a kiss on the cheek. Nazeera saw her father's face flush a bright cherry red, as she joined the little group and gave welcome hugs to her aunty and her cousin Naveed.

Thankfully, Daddy had arranged a second car for their trip to the flat. The two drivers approached them, and began to carry the suitcases to the car. As expected, *Khalaji* had several suitcases. Her father stayed with the first wave of guests, as Nazeera returned to the glass doors awaiting the next wave.

Suddenly, Nazeera heard a scream. It was a scream of joy, and she looked frantically around to find the source. Rushing toward her was Jaya! Screaming in return, Nazeera hurried to her best friend.

"Nazeera!" Jaya exclaimed as they exchanged hugs. They giggled together for a moment, then she turned to the man standing next to her. He seemed oddly familiar. "You remember Sanjay?" Suddenly she remembered him. Of course, Jaya's husband. He looked so different without all the wedding garb.

She led them to the first car, and the driver loaded the suitcases into the back while they climbed into the car. Sanjay sat in the front seat next to the driver, while Nazeera and Jaya sat in the back seat to catch up on the events of the trip. He tried to say a few words, but then remained silent, probably finding it difficult to talk to the friends.

Once everything was loaded to her father's satisfaction, he ordered the drivers to head back to their flat. The trip to VT had taken only ten minutes, but the return trip took four times that. Not only did they have to deal with the never-ending Bombay traffic, but unexpectedly the traffic came to a halt. They could hear shouting voices through the crack in their windows. As they inched past the commotion, Nazeera noticed a motorcycle driver gesturing wildly to a man with an oxen cart. A taxi driver was also yelling something. As they slowly approached the accident, Jaya exclaimed the cart had tipped over and there was fruit scattered all over the road. Nazeera peered over Jaya's shoulder to see the man on the motorcycle give a handful of *rupees* to the man driving the oxen cart and drive off. The man in the taxicab just threw up his hands and returned to his vehicle.

By the time they arrived at the flat, the group was famished. Thankfully, the food was ready and with a head nod from Ammi, the food was brought out to the dining room table. One by one the travelers refreshed in the bathrooms, and returned to the dining room wearing smiles at the smell of the feast Ammi and Akbar had prepared.

"Aaah, this smells wonderful," *Khalaji* said waving her hand to her nose. She was not a good cook, and relied completely on their hired cook for their meals. Amina had always been astonished her sister could make anything tasty from a piece of meat and a few spices.

The seven of them squeezed around the table meant for six with her parents on opposite sides of the table. Akbar placed all the food on metal trivets so it could be served family-style. The steaming dishes were passed clockwise except for the *naan* which Sanjay accidentally passed counter-clockwise.

"This is delicious," Naveed said with his mouth full of chicken *biryani*. Then a moment later he added pointing to the dark green crystal shaped vegetable spiced with mustard seeds, "Is that your *bhendi*?"

"Of course. It's my specialty," Ammi gleamed, passing the okra dish to her nephew. He was eating like he had not eaten food in days. "You're a wonderful cook, Lailaa *khalaji*," he kept repeating.

"Is *Mamuji* coming to the wedding?" Nazeera said changing the subject from her mother's okra dish. Amina *khalaji* looked down at her plate. Naveed finished swallowing his bite of okra, and said, "Papa's still in Delhi. He had some government business to finish up. He'll come down on Sunday evening."

"*Theek hai,*" Ammi said in a matter-of-fact tone. Nazeera knew her mother was not fond of Murad after the way he had rejected her before the wedding. She probably would have preferred he didn't come at all; but, he was married to her sister, and weddings are a time for family to come together. Even if you don't like them.

Nazeera glanced around the table. Everyone was enjoying themselves. The food was excellent as usual, the conversation was still civil, and she had Jaya by her side. *What a perfect evening!*

Her best friend seemed happy. In fact, she seemed very happy. She wore a huge smile and was engaged in the conversation. Sanjay leaned forward and whispered something in Jaya's ear. *Are they discussing her? The food?* Nazeera grimaced when she saw that both Sanjay and Jaya had only taken the okra and *Matar Paneer* dishes. No chicken. No lamb. Are they vegetarians? A lot of Hindus are vegetarians. Maybe Jaya had become a vegetarian when she married Sanjay. They will need to serve more vegetable dishes. She'll let her mother know.

Suddenly, Daddy bellowed, "*Are-re!* Yikes! Did I forget my son?!"

Khalaji nodded knowingly, "Hamid called our home just before Naveed and I left for the train station. He said he got detained, and would come down on Sunday."

Daddy was noticeably relieved, "*Aacha,* Sunday."

The rest of the dinner proceeded uneventfully as the group gobbled the various curries. After Shanti cleared the table, Akbar returned with a sterling silver platter filled with bowls of *gajjar halwa.* The combination of grated carrots, condensed milk, and plump sultanas was a sweet end to the delightful dinner.

With full stomachs, the group dispersed. *Khalaji* followed Ammi into her parent's bedroom where the sisters would be sharing a bed. Nazeera led Jaya to her bedroom where they would do the same. Daddy, Sanjay and Naveed began to stake out spots in the living room where they would sleep on one of the rented cotton mattresses. Naveed looked out the window, and suggested they sleep on the veranda instead since it was such a warm night. Sanjay agreed, and as the two men walked to the veranda, he relayed a story of how he had often slept under the stars on his grandparent's farm.

Sitting in the corner of the veranda, diligently working was Mohan, the tailor. He had eaten his dinner with Akbar and Shanti before the other guests had returned from VT. He was now hand-sewing a sari blouse for Ammi, using a candle for light. He too had planned to sleep on the veranda, so the boys laid their mattresses next to his.

Nazeera would have seen her future husband if her guests had arrived at the Bombay Airport rather than the train station. Amir and Farid arrived at the airport at half past six. They decided to wait outside baggage claim for the arrival of their uncle from Karachi. Mummy wasn't sure if Aly *mamu* would be coming alone or bringing a companion. The brothers hoped he was coming alone since they only had one car.

The heat of the day was starting to dissipate, and the slight breeze whistling though the airport pick-up area created a very pleasant evening. There must have been a lull between planes, as there was no one else waiting outside baggage claim. They sat down against a cement pillar and watched a few passengers walk by them.

Amir wondered if this area would be more crowded in the mornings. He would be returning here on Sunday to pick up his friend Kabir, and his wife Carmen. At least one of his friend's from America was coming to the wedding. His boss, Greg, had phoned this morning at 2 am, he had forgotten about the time difference, saying he was not able to get a tourist visa and would miss the wedding. Amir had said he was sorry, but he was actually relieved. He could now concentrate on the wedding, not entertaining his boss.

A crowd of people came through the sliding glass doors. The brothers shot up and began searching the heads for a familiar one. It had been a decade since the brothers had seen their mother's brother. Did he look different? What if he grew a beard or shaved his head? One by one the people walked by them. They all headed for cars parked in the parking lot or toward the taxi queue. No Aly *mamu*.

Another wave of people stormed through the sliding glass doors, and they searched the crowd again. This time there was a head that looked vaguely familiar. "Aly *mamu*?!" Farid yelled. The head turned and started walking toward Farid. Weaving through the crowd, Amir joined them. He didn't look much different than he remembered. A bit older and rounder, but otherwise, the same. He wore a pastel blue *kurta pyjama* and a little white pill box hat. He was carrying a duffel bag and a mirrored cloth bag filled with magazines. He was unshaven and looked worn-out. The trip must have been hard on him.

"Come, come," Farid insisted as he took the two bags and began walking to the waiting car. The old man stopped and placed his hands together, nodding to each of them, "*Ya Ali Madad.*" He smiled and waited for their reply. The brothers exchanged glances, and gave the correct reply.

Aly *mamu* approached Amir. He paused only a moment before pinching his cheeks, saying something in Urdu that made him laugh. Amir just smiled. He had no idea what his uncle had said. He followed them to the car trying hard to understand what they were discussing. He had a hard enough time with Hindi, but Urdu was impossible. The two languages were similar but certain words and pronunciations were different. Farid understood most of it and replied the best he could in Hindi and broken Urdu.

They walked and talked as they exited the pick-up area. When they reached the car, the driver eagerly took the bags, while Amir hastily grabbed the front seat. The dutiful host, Farid, held the back seat door for their uncle. The old man pinched Farid's cheeks, then slid into the car.

The ride was uneventful as Amir looked out of the window and ignored the chattering in the back seat. It sounded like a Bollywood movie but without the subtitles. He had forgotten more Hindi than he realized. Hopefully he won't ever be alone with Aly *mamu*.

After an hour of listening to the two of them chatter, they reached their destination, passing through the intersection with the motorcycle, oxen cart and taxicab well after it had cleared. As they entered the flat, Mummy came running from the high-back chair in the living room to the hallway, nearly knocking her half-brother to the floor with her hug. She giggled like she was five years old and tugged on his arm dragging the tired old man into the living room. Amir placed his bags on the small table Babu had set up in Rafiq's room. The little boy was going to share Rabia's room while Aly *mamu* stayed in Bombay. Rafiq was pleased with the move as he got to play a lot more with his big sister.

When he returned to the living room, Amir discovered only Mummy and Aly *mamu* were there. Farid and Rehana must have retreated to their bedroom or went to check on the kids. He hovered for a moment beside the loveseat, listening to them prattle in mixed Hindi and Urdu. He had no idea what they were saying. *Time to leave.*

Hoping no one would noticed him slinking out, he tiptoed out of the flat and down the hall to the lift. He hit the call button and stepped into the lift pulling the scissor doors shut one at a time. He rode the lift down to the main floor enjoying the silence more than he had expected.

CHAPTER 41

Saturday, September 3

"A, M, I, R"

The activity started a few minutes after 11 o'clock in the morning. Nazeera was sitting at the dining room table enjoying a steaming cup of Darjeeling tea and a lukewarm bowl of cream of wheat. She and Jaya had stayed up late talking about her life in Delhi, the upcoming wedding ceremonies, and possible *mehndi* designs.

As close friends sometimes do, they even playfully debated the usage of the word '*mehndi*'. Nazeera insisted it could be used interchangeably with the raw product of henna powder. Jaya maintained the powder was called henna, and once it was applied to the hands it was called *mehndi*. After several minutes of discussion, they concluded they would ask the experts.

The Andeheri ladies arrived an hour earlier than expected. They looked surprised, and yet relieved, to have reached their destination after only an hour-long taxi drive. As they entered the flat, they apologized for arriving early, but not wanting to be late starting the bride, they had given themselves extra time to get to the flat. The spider web of Bombay roads were akin to a maze. Usually the twelve mile journey from their home in Andeheri, north of the airport, took over an hour, sometimes two or even three!

After removing their *chappals*, one by one each newcomer greeted the members of the household with a sincere, "*Namaste*". The sisters introduced themselves as Shakun and Jyoti. Since Nazeera was still eating breakfast, Ammi offered her guests something to eat. The sisters gladly accepted, and the threesome headed to the kitchen.

The ladies caught Shanti off-guard, as she was moving fresh lemons from a canvas bag to a wooden tray. She watched them approach Akbar, and help themselves to a cup of tea and a bowl of cream of wheat. When they had nearly finished eating their impromptu breakfast, Shanti excitedly approached them and asked in Hindi, "How can a mixture of henna leaves and lemons leave a stain on the hand?"

Nazeera heard the question from the dining room and, eager to know the answer herself, leaned into the kitchen trying not to disturb the flow of the conversation. Smiling at Shanti, Shakun replied, "It's a secret recipe."

"But, how do you actually make it?" Shanti asked again anxiously, not satisfied with the abrupt response.

Shakun squatted, and removed a few items from her multi-compartment plastic carrier filled with tools of their trade. She laid a few pinches of henna powder in her right palm and began wiggling her left forefinger through it, "First, you must remove any twigs and lumps from the ground henna leaf powder. See, here's a twig. Then you must sift it until it is very fine. Very fine." Shanti leaned forward to watch Shakun remove the twig and a small stone from the powder. "Second, you add a hot liquid. Most people add hot tea to the mixture but Jyoti and I have found a mixture of hot tea and hot coffee produces much better results." Shanti nodded her head enthusiastically at learning their secret. Shakun put the powder back into the plastic bag and returned it to her plastic carrier.

Picking up a fresh lemon as a prop, Jyoti added, "Then, you add *limbu* and mustard oil to the powder, and stir the mixture carefully. You want the paste to be thick like mud." Shanti nodded her head as she listened.

"But, you must be careful!" Jyoti continued, "Too much lemon juice and the paste won't harden. Too much mustard oil and the paste won't pipe well." Shanti grimaced as if this warning was too much for her to handle.

"When the mixture is well mixed and the right consistency," Shakun added picking up a thin plastic cone of henna paste, "I let it cool for an hour or two, checking it occasionally to make sure it's still moist." Nazeera leaned over to look at the paste they had made, and would be placing on her hands and feet soon, "Once the mixture has the right consistency, I put it on my henna shelf and let it sit."

"For how long?" Jaya asked joining the group in the kitchen.

"One day is good, but two days are better," Jyoti responded in English with a head bobble. "Two days, very good." She handed the cone of henna paste to Shanti who looked at it from all directions before giving it back to the artist. She thanked the *mehndi* experts for their description. Nazeera stepped forward and asked what was the difference between henna and *mehndi*?

Jyoti laughed. "Well, henna comes from an Arabic word and *mehndi* comes from a Sanskrit word. The term *mehndi* is mostly used in India. Some people use the terms interchangeably, but I prefer to refer to the flower paste as henna, and the henna painting process as *mehndi*."

"*Aacha*," Nazeera said smirking at Jaya. They were both right.

Followed closely by Shanti, Shakun marched out of the kitchen ready to commence decorating the bride. Applying the *mehndi* to the bride is a multi-hour event, and the beginning of the pampering of the bride. Nazeera was very excited, she was finally the bride! As soon as she sat in the chair, her adrenaline started pumping through her veins. She was wide awake now!

Jaya had advised Nazeera to wear something out of fashion or at least well worn. The henna paste was supposed to stain the skin, but it was strong enough to also stain fabric or hair. Nazeera wore an old pastel pink *salwar kameez* with a large daisy pattern. It was the outfit she wore when she wanted to be comfortable.

At Ammi's suggestion, Shanti had placed old bed linens on the armed chair, to keep it from getting stained by the henna paste. Nazeera, giggling with excitement, happily sat in the chair. Jyoti, the younger but more experienced sister, asked the bride if she needed to use the bathroom before they started. Nazeera shook her head, but on second thought, admitted she had better use it since she would be sitting for hours. After she returned, she sank back into the chair. The sisters sat on stools on either side of Nazeera's throne placing their plastic carriers by their sides. Trying to calm Nazeera down, Shakun gently stroked the bride's palms with her own forefinger, explaining she had been applying *mehndi* for almost two decades.

When Nazeera was sufficiently relaxed, Shakun asked her if she had any decorative preferences. "Yes, I do." Jaya was standing nearby and handed Shakun the piece of notebook paper with the list of ideas she and Nazeera had created late last night. In line with general Islamic doctrine, they did not list any animals or people. Instead, the list included: paisleys, Mogul flowers, vines, leaves, spirals, water drops and waves. Nazeera wanted her finished hands to look like delicate laced gloves.

Ammi approached her daughter and leaned over Shakun's shoulder to whisper in her ear. Her whisper was loud enough for even Nazeera to hear, "Please add Amir's name to your design. But, hide the letters well. I want my new son-in-law to have trouble finding the letters on their wedding night." She then smiled knowingly at Jaya. Nazeera blushed.

Each lady gently picked up a bride's hand and laid it flat. From the small cut at the tip of the spherical shaped cones a green-brown mixture flowed onto Nazeera's hands. The mixture felt cool on her skin as each of them began their design. Jyoti worked on the bride's right hand and started with a large paisley in the center of the palm much to Nazeera's delight. She piped a daisy flower inside the paisley, then sat back for a second. Leaning forward, she added a line around the first paisley and wiggled the cone back and forth to make waves between the two paisleys. To finish the initial design, she piped a few dozen L-shaped tassels on the outside. Sensing Nazeera was pleased, she continued working her way outwards to the fingertips adding an exaggerated daisy flower, more waves, geometric designs and occasional paisleys.

Shakun had the bride's left hand where the groom's name or initials were usually hidden. She made two paisleys in the center close enough that they formed a lop-sided heart. She added a five pointed flower in the center and leaves flowing up and down the palm. Swirls, leaves and flowers surrounded the paisley pair.

Then as if just remembering she needed to add the groom's name, she looked up to find Jaya hovering over her like the mother of a newborn. Exchanging whispers, Nazeera heard Jaya enunciate, "A, M, I, R".

Ammi leaned forward as Shakun completed the 'R'. Scanning her daughter's palm, she declared "*Bahut aacha*. Very good. He will have a hard time finding the letters!"

Each artist continued her designs up to the elbow, using various geometric designs to connect the patterns. Shakun added a heart here and there. She said it was her own little touch to keep the bride in a loving mood.

Nazeera was getting tired of holding her hands and arms in the same position. It had been over an hour and she wanted to move. Being a bride was hard work! Jyoti must have sensed her uneasiness as she began to talk. Until then, both the artists had been silent, diligently working on their masterpieces. "Do you know how long *mehndi* has been decorating brides?"

"Since the 1300's when Shah Jahan built the Taj Mahal." Nazeera replied in a loving but playful mood relieved for the distraction. She loved the story of Shah Jahan and the Taj Mahal, a symbol of love and eternity.

"*Ji, nahih*. Before that."

"It was written in the Vedas, Hindu texts, a couple thousand years ago." Jaya added. Then speaking as a new bride herself, "Doesn't the *mehndi* symbolizes good luck?"

"*Ji, huh*, it symbolizes good luck, good health, and good ...." Jyoti hesitated and said in a soft whisper, "sexuality." The four ladies laughed nervously. Nazeera looked around to see if Ammi or *Khalaji* were listening. They weren't.

Shakun added, "The deeper the color of the stain on the hand, the more good fortune in the marriage. This has been the tradition in India for over five thousand years." No wonder this is an important wedding ritual for Indian brides. It's been a tradition since before Alexander the Great.

The ladies continued their artistry in silence. Needing further distraction, Nazeera allowed her eyes to wander about the room. Jaya was standing nearby, inspecting the work done by the sisters, *Khalaji* was chatting with Mohan on the veranda, and Ammi was supervising Akbar and Shanti as they prepared the dining room table for the lunch buffet. *I wonder what Daddy and the boys are doing?*

Her father, Naveed, Sanjay and Aziz were at the CCI. They were not welcome at the *mehndi* ceremony and had decided to spend the day swimming, eating and playing cards at the Club. The plan was devised soon after Akbar and Ammi began preparing the food for lunch. At first, they were quiet since everyone was still sleeping. But after a few people awoke, probably due to their banging and clanging, they carried on with the normal sounds of cooking. Soon, the whole flat smelled of fried *pakoras*, and Naveed snuck a few before being shooed out of the kitchen by Ammi. Poor boy didn't get much home cooking.

The ladies reviewed the masterpieces each had created, then flipped over Nazeera's arms to do the backside. This took much less time as the patterns were larger and less intricate. They were more than halfway complete when the aromas of the fresh, hot food overwhelmed the room. Ammi declared the food was ready, and the artists agreed to take a break.

The lunch buffet was laid on a green tablecloth purchased for the occasion. Green being the color of the henna plant leaves and thus the color of the day. Nazeera indicated with raised eyebrows and a head nod, she would like some food. Being a dutiful matron-of-honor, Jaya filled a plate with food she thought would be easy for her to feed the bride.

Carefully picking up a *pakora*, Jaya placed it just in front of Nazeera's mouth. The bride leaned forward and took a bite. It was delicious. Yum! She was hungrier than she originally thought. She eagerly took another bite, and then a third to finish the little fried potato ball. She eagerly ate the second one, then Jaya moved onto the main course. She watched as her best friend mixed the chicken *tikka* and rice together. Anticipating the baked chicken with red cream sauce, Nazeera leaned forward and opened her mouth. Jaya scooped the mixture with her fingers and awkwardly fed her friend. Patiently eating, Nazeera finished all the food on the plate, especially enjoying the potato and cauliflower dish as it was the least messy. Not entirely full, but exhausted from the effort, she told Jaya she had had enough. Jaya nodded and scampered to the dining room to fill a plate for herself.

Ammi must have remembered Daddy had left the camera for her, because she began to take photos. Wandering around the room, she snapped photos of everyone and everything - the two *mehndi* artists, Jaya feeding Nazeera, *Khalaji* sitting on the veranda, Mohan and the sari blouse he was working on, Akbar and the food on the table, and Shanti near the flower garlands decorations. Once Jaya was done feeding Nazeera, she had her take a photo of mother and daughter.

After the sisters finished washing their hands of the curry and rice, the *mehndi* application to Nazeera resumed. Checking the progress of the arms, they nodded to themselves satisfactorily. Nazeera had not moved much and the designs were still intact. They finished the patterns they had started on the backside of the arms, replaced the cotton balls near her elbows to allow Nazeera to rest her arms, and began discussing the patterns for her feet. Similar to the hands and arms, the ladies started with a center design and worked their way outward. But, unlike the hands, they didn't decorate the bottom of the foot, only the top and half-way up the shin. That was sufficient, as it was all one could see under a sari.

When the application was complete, Nazeera sat back trying not to move. Each movement caused some of the drying *mehndi* to flake off thereby stopping the color transformation of her skin. She watched as the ladies all stepped onto the veranda to enjoy a glass of Akbar's *faloodas*.

Aaah, this is nice, Nazeera thought. She leaned her head back slightly and held her hands palm out as if she was floating at the CCI swimming pool. Suddenly, she was hit by a splash! Sitting up quickly, she screamed, "*Are-re!*"

Jaya jumped back in surprise by her friend's reaction. "It's just *limbu*," she replied very matter-of-factly, stepping forward to continue her duty. *Oh, yes, the lemon juice.*

Laughing at herself, Nazeera leaned back in the chair. The lemon juice helped prevent the henna paste from cracking and flaking, allowing it to work its magic and create a deeper red color on her skin. And as they said, the deeper the color the better the marriage. Her marriage to Amir. One to last a lifetime. Nazeera closed her eyes to help her relax and just let her mind wander. *Just relax. Breathe. Just a few more hours. Thank goodness I used the bathroom before they started. Inhale. Exhale. Amir. Marriage. America. Adventure. Is it really like the Hollywood movies? Big cars and big houses?*

Nazeera could hear someone in the dining room removing the lunch dishes and replacing them with some other dishes. Probably for the afternoon tea with the Viranis. Thank goodness they wanted to keep this visit short, as they needed to return for Amir's *pithi*, well wishes ceremony. Wedding ceremonies can span several days, so her mother and Rehana had decided each side would host their own ceremonies, as they were slightly different traditions.

After the *faloodas*, the group had a little time before the first wave of guests arrived. Ammi and *Khalaji* stayed on the veranda supervising Mohan, while Jaya sat by Nazeera's side often dabbing *limbu* on her skin with a cotton ball. Nazeera tried very hard to remain still, but it was hard not to bounce around the flat like she always did. The two of them sat in silence, since they had exhausted their conversation from their multi-hour catch up session the previous night. Jaya picked up a fashion magazine and started flipping through the pages, showing Nazeera a photo every once in awhile. Jyoti and Shakun were in the kitchen showing Shanti how to grind the henna flowers and leaves with a mortar and pestle.

After less than an hour of calm, the doorbell rang. Everyone became instantly erect, as Akbar strode across the living room and opened the door for the expected guests. Shakila strode in first leading the parade. They greeted Ammi, *Khalaji* and Jaya warmly, gave a nod to the *mehndi* artists, then fawned over Nazeera's *mehndi* application.

"*Khubsoorat*, beautiful," Nilofer admired.

"Lots of paisleys," Rehana added.

"Let me see if I can find Amir's name," Nadia pondered.

After the bride's hands and feet were sufficiently admired, the Virani women sat in pretty much the same places they had sat a few days earlier for the engagement ceremony. On the Khan side, *Khalaji* stepped away from the seated group and sat next to Jaya and Nazeera, allowing her sister to be the center of attention for this ceremony. Ammi had changed into a rose pink silk sari with small pastel blue dots. Nazeera noticed both mothers were wearing pink as Ammi sat down next to Shakila who wore an onion pink sari with tiny coral flowers.

After they enjoyed their afternoon tea with the small cakes Akbar had reluctantly store-bought for this special occasion, Ammi stood up and retreated into her bedroom. She returned with an armful of the sari gifts Nazeera and Nusrat Aunty had purchased last weekend. Her family tradition was for the bride's family to give the groom's family a sari to wear at the wedding. The giving of the saris was a way to encourage the ladies in the groom's family to welcome the new bride.

She laid the saris on the spot where she had been sitting on the settee. Looking directly at Shakila and letting her eyes wander amongst the group she said in Hindi, "We hope you are as happy as we are with this wedding. We think Amir is a very nice man and will be good to Nazeera. It is a tradition in my family to give a sari to each member of the groom's family. It is then traditionally worn to the wedding, but you can decide if you want to wear it or not." Ammi glanced at Jaya who came running.

Looking between the saris to be given and the saris the ladies were wearing, Ammi picked up a baby-pink raw silk sari with cerulean flowers along the border and matching glass beads. She handed it to Jaya to deliver to the named person. "Shakila, this sari is our gift to you." Jaya handed the sari to the mother of the groom and returned to Ammi for the next one. Nazeera noticed Shakila visually inspecting the handiwork of the sari fabric.

Bandra was wearing a ginger brown sari with sky blue flowers scattered here and there, so Ammi picked up a peacock blue sari with silver geometric block printing, "Bandra, this is our gift to you." The sari gifting continued for each of the remaining ladies with Nilofer receiving a gossamer gray sari with a paisley design, Nadia receiving a burgundy sari with silver elephant block printing, and Rehana receiving a chocolate brown sari with blue and silver flower stamps.

After Ammi's gifts were distributed, Rehana picked up a bag sitting on her lap. She reached in and carefully pulled out a delicate ocean blue raw silk sari with silver and black geometric block printing. She gently handed it to Rabia who scampered to Ammi, the blue frills on her dress bobbing up and down as she walked. When the little girl reached her destination, she unceremoniously dropped the precious sari onto Ammi's lap, and scurried back to her mother's side. Placing a hand on her daughter's shoulder, Rehana winced and said, "Lailaa, to honor your family's tradition, we are presenting you with a sari. This is our gift to you." Ammi was tickled by the thoughtfulness of the gesture, and giggled as she admired the sari she had just received.

The ladies admired their saris and the exquisite block printing. It was a unique technique where a wooden block is dipped into paint, then carefully stamped onto the fabric. It was harder to do on silk and the ones they had been given were very well done. Expertly done.

As the ladies admired the saris, Rabia wandered over to see the bride. Nazeera glanced down, when she felt a warm presence at her feet, to see two big brown eyes staring back at her. Sitting with her legs crossed legged in a non-lady like fashion, the little girl smiled at her. *How precious!*

Nazeera wanted to grab Rabia and give her a hug, but she knew that gesture would mess up all the *mehndi* on her hands. So, she resisted the urge and remained still, simply smiling back to the owner of the big brown eyes. The girl turned her head, and began focusing on the intricate *mehndi* designs on Nazeera's feet and ankles. Her head moved about as if she was trying to take it all in. At second glance, she seemed to be tracing one of the vines with her finger in the air. She looked totally content.

Flash! Flash! Jaya took a group photo of the ladies with and then without their new saris draped over them. Each of them had another cup of tea and then Akbar came to check if more water was needed in the tea pot. A male presence in the room reminded Rehana of the *pithi* ceremony for Amir. She abruptly jumped up, announcing they had to leave. Regretfully they said good-bye and began the long process of hugs and kisses. Nazeera was smiling, saying good-byes to everyone though she continued to sit very still on her throne. The ladies rushed out the door and one of them hit the button to call the lift.

After the ladies left, *Khalaji* and Jaya slumped down onto the sofa, while Ammi made a phone call. Nazeera began to chat with them and noticed the big, brown eyes were still staring at her feet. Pointing and whispering loudly, she said "Um, someone is still here."

With a friendly smile, Jaya led Rabia to the front door. She opened it to find Rehana approaching it. The two of them exchanged knowing smiles, and Rabia changed hands lagging behind her mother as they approached the lift.

"I think you have an admirer," Jaya laughed as she returned to her position on the sofa next to *Khalaji*.

Nazeera shrugged her shoulders, "I guess I do". The three of them laughed for a moment, then each of them one by one leaned back onto pillows. They had only a few minutes before the next wave of guests, family and friends, came for the *mehndi* celebration. Nazeera heard a voice from behind her. Ammi was still on the telephone. *Who is she talking to?*

CHAPTER 42

"GOOD LUCK"

Pacing the flat, Amir wondered when the ladies would return from the Khan flat. They had left for afternoon tea several hours ago, and should've returned by now. Farid was frantically doing his best to keep the family content with tea and snacks.

"I bet you fall off!" Yasmeen jested to her cousin. Daania was standing on one foot on a little red table. The table was sitting on an old bed sheet laid out in the middle of living room, the furniture pushed against the walls.

"Don't mess up the flowers!" yelled Zarin from his seat on the sofa. He and Tarik were playing with a few of the younger boy's matchbox cars. "They'll be back any minute."

Amir glanced at the kids. Hopefully they're back before the kids ruin all the items set up for his *pithi* ceremony. *Where are their aayas?*

The little red table stood above a Hindu swastika made of red rose petals, orange marigold petals and uncooked white rice. The swastika, one of India's oldest known symbols, represents good luck and auspiciousness. The Ismailis, who have adopted a few Hindu rituals, adopted the use of this symbol in their wedding celebrations.

It consists of four arms of equal length, bent at right angles in a clockwise direction. Amir tilted his head a quarter turn to view the Nazi swastika. How unfortunate, the symbol of good fortune, had been so tainted by Adolf Hitler and his Nazi empire.

"You better get off!" Rafiq scolded, "Mama said 'No touch'." The girls giggled at their little cousin, but complied, much to Rafiq's satisfaction.

Babu was returning to the living room carrying another tray of sweets when the ladies noisily walked into the flat. "Aaah, they're finally back," Farid sighed in relief. "We were wondering what happened to you. I had Babu serve tea and some snacks."

Smiling her approval, Rehana simply said, "We were having a good time. Nazeera looks enchanting." Amir smiled at her comment and watched as his sister-in-law scampered into the bedroom to put her new sari onto the bed. He nervously scanned his outfit once again hoping he was appropriately dressed. Farid had warned him to wear an old shirt and trousers. Since he didn't have anything old, he had borrowed them from his brother. The trousers already had an oil stain, probably from a fried *pakora*, but Amir didn't mind. At least he wouldn't ruin one of his suits. He thought it was odd Farid had said he didn't want the clothes back. They seemed like nice enough clothes. Was he going to get that dirty?

Mummy grabbed two pieces of the *khaju kathri*, then snapped her fingers for Yasmeen to get out of the high back chair that had been pushed in front of the veranda entrance. She sat down in the chair and readied herself for her son's ceremony. She chewed the sweets slowly savoring each bite. Aly *mamu* leaned forward and grabbed two of the sweets, returning to his place on the loveseat. He chewed them slowly commenting something to his sister in Urdu.

The room was full of familiar faces. The women were starting to form a line and Rehana was gesturing for Amir to step onto the little red table. His heart was thumping in his chest. *Why am I nervous? This is the pithi. Just a simple well wishes ceremony done by the womenfolk. Rehana said they would put some turmeric paste on my cheeks and throw flowers over my head. How hard is that?*

Rehana checked on the tray she had prepared earlier. It included all the necessary items - a yellow paste made of chickpea flour, turmeric powder, mustard oil and rose water, flower petals of red roses, orange marigolds and white jasmines and colored uncooked rice. She gestured to her husband to light the oil in the small clay pot or *diya* sitting in the center of the swastika. He fumbled a bit as it was under the table, but he was able to light it on the third try with the matches singeing his fingers slightly. He grinned as he retreated with a final warning to his brother, "Good luck."

Wondering why the *diya* had to be lit at all, Amir hoped his butt wasn't going to get too hot. The symbolism of 'warming up his loins' or 'lighting his fire' seemed ancient but it seemed to make the ladies happy. He wanted children and if this *diya* would help with that, then so be it. He could put up with it for one evening.

Leaning forward on her tiptoes, Rehana placed a red rose and white jasmine flower garland around Amir's neck. He felt silly, but it was part of the ceremony so he wore it in silence. Nadia stepped to his left side and placed a red *dupatta* with a thin gold tassel border over her head and then over his. She said to the group that Kassim had graciously picked up this *dupatta* from the JK earlier that day specifically for this ceremony. Amir watched as Kassim blushed and waved his hand to the group.

Tarik came up and stood next to Amir. "Hello Amir Chacha," he said with a smile. The three year old saw his mother holding the red fabric over his uncle's head, so he went to Amir's right side and lifted the fabric over his head and held the little bit of cloth between him and Amir Chacha. *How precious even little Tarik wants to help. I need all the help I can get.*

When all was ready, Rehana gestured for Mummy to go first. Swallowing the last bite of *khaju kathri*, she grunted as she stood up from the comfortable high-back chair. Zarin took this opportunity to jump into the now vacant chair. As she approached Amir, she placed her hand on his shoulder in a reassuring way.

Stepping in front of Amir, while Rehana held the tray, Mummy followed each prompt as to what to do next. First, she dipped her fingers into the yellow paste and rubbed a little on each of her son's cheeks for 'well wishes', then she picked up a few flower petals and rice and threw them over his head three times to 'get rid of evil spirits and thoughts'. Finally, she placed her hands on the side of his head and then placed her knuckles on either side of her own head and cracked them to 'remove pain'. For fun, she teased, "How many children will you have?" She cracked her knuckles on her temples again and they cracked one-two-three times, "Three children!"

Mummy returned to the high-back chair, shooed Zarin from it, and watched as the rest of the ladies lined up haphazardly to have a turn. The well wishes were given, the evil spirits gone and the pain removed. The number of children varied from zero to five. When the aunties were done, Tarik sat down on the ground in a big slump letting his end of the *dupatta* fall onto Amir's shoulder.

The nieces then wanted a turn. When Rabia threw the rose petals over her uncle's head she whispered just loud enough for Amir to hear, "You better make Nazchi happy."

Amir smiled at her comment and whispered back, "I'll try."

Rabia retreated with a huge smile, as if she just helped to make their marriage a success. As she sat down cross legged on the floor at her mother's feet, the blue ruffles of her dress flew upwards.

Sensing the ceremony was over, Amir nervously glanced around the room to see if anyone else wanted a turn. No one did. *Good, I can stand up and stretch my legs. And get my butt off this hot table!*

"Not yet," Nadia jested grabbing a small clay pot from the side table. She placed it on the floor at his feet, and still holding the red *dupatta* over his head, suggested he step off the stool and break the pot with one step. *What did this symbolize? Well, whatever it did, it's part of the ceremony.*

Amir stood up and stretched. Now to destroy the pot. He stepped forward and with one footfall smashed the pot into several pieces. Cheers rose up from the ladies. Tarik asked innocently to anyone in the group, "Why did he do that?"

No one else heard Tarik's question, and rather than answer the little boy, Amir planned to run away before he got smeared again. He took only one step away from the clay pot shards when Nadia warned, "Hold on".

Carefully Nadia removed the special red *dupatta*, and placed it on the side table. Mysteriously, she turned to the other women and yelled, "Now!" Grabbing her brother's arm, she added, "We want to wish you lots of luck." Before Amir knew what was happening, she pulled the shirt cuff upwards until the fabric ripped. She continued pulling and ripping until his entire shirt sleeve had come off. "Yeah!"

What has she done? She ripped off my sleeve?! Yikes!

Suddenly, Nilofer grabbed his other arm and proceeded to do the same with the other sleeve. Amir was feeling accosted, covering his face with his hands to protect himself. Bandra spread her feet out wide to steady herself. Grabbing the bottom of his shirtback, she ripped it in two. There were two slices of shirt hanging from his back. "Stop it." Amir tried to say. No use. The three sisters continued to rip and tear the shirt to shreds until he was totally shirtless.

Farid and Kassim laughed boastfully. They remembered having the same thing done to them. "Why didn't you warn me?" Amir laughed to Farid as he came to sit down next to him on one of the dining room chairs.

"It's one of those things you need to experience for yourself. That's why I gave you the old shirt. I've been saving it for you." Farid laughed again, "If you had made it to Nadia and Kassim's wedding, you would have known this was coming." Amir just laughed. Touché.

As Babu brought out the dinner dishes, Amir followed his brother into the bedroom to get a fresh shirt. He first tried to wash his face to get as much of the dried turmeric paste off of his cheeks as he could. He wasn't totally successful so there was a slight yellow hue on his cheeks where the paste had been. He slipped into his own trousers and put on a fresh shirt provided by his brother. *Okay, the worst part is over. Time to eat.*

CHAPTER 43

"I'M SO GLAD YOU CAME"

The doorbell rang. "Here we go," Ammi sighed as she gave the nod to Akbar to open the door and let the next phase of the evening begin. He had just cleared the area of the cups and plates from the afternoon tea. Good timing.

Each of them were dressed in different shades of green *salwar kameez*. The cousins giggled as they approached the bride, gawking at her decorated hands and arms.

"Oh my, Ra-Ra, how intricate!" Pinky said with a jealous tone. "Can I squeeze *limbu* on them?"

Nazeera knew both of her cousins would be anxious to help, and Jaya needed a break. "Sure, you can do the left side," Nazeera said to Pinky, "and you can do the right," she said as she turned to Dolly. The cousins did their duty and then scampered to find the *mehndi* artists.

Jyoti was already busy decorating Nusrat Aunty's hands. "Lots of paisleys, I just love paisleys." she kept repeating.

Pinky sat next to her mother on the settee, "I would like both my hands to have one pattern. One large pattern."

Bobbling her head, Shakun said, "I have a wonderful two hand pattern." Pinky nodded enthusiastically and held her hands open face together. She watched as the artist made a flower on one hand and continued the outline onto the other hand. Filling in the empty spaces with leaves, flowers and geometric shapes took the expert only minutes.

When Nusrat Aunty and Pinky's hands were done, they watched as Shakun made a three leaf pattern in Dolly's palm, adding climbing vines to each of her ten fingers.

The trio carefully walked to the veranda holding their hands in front of them as if they were surgeons about to go into heart surgery. *Khalaji* was sitting next to the door. She had already washed her hands of the dried henna paste and was now sipping lemonade.

"Come, come," a voice called. Nazeera directed her attention away from the veranda, and looked about the room trying to find the source of the voice. "Come, Nazeera," the voice called from the bedroom.

Using only her elbows for leverage, she awkwardly stood up from her throne. Waddling like a penguin on her heels, she waddled to the bedroom, passing both Akbar and Shanti who looked like they were suppressing laughs. Jaya and Ammi were on either side of the bathroom sink with the lukewarm water already filling the basin. As Nazeera approached, Jaya turned the faucet off and began waving her hands with anticipation. Ammi skillfully helped her daughter plunge her painted hands into the water. Rubbing the dried paste from her hands, it began to flake. As the henna paste was being removed, Nazeera saw the color of her skin was a deep burgundy. Nazeera was satisfied. *The deeper the color, the better the marriage.*

The superb color was very evident when all of the dried paste was removed. Nazeera smiled from ear to ear as she examined her hands back and forth, and up and down. She looked like a bride. A very colorful natural lace gloved bride. "This is perfect," she said as she showed her mother and Jaya.

After removing the dried paste from her arms, and feet, Nazeera changed into a pale blue *salwar kameez* with big paisleys because the one that she had been wearing did indeed have a small stain from the henna paste and the cuffs were wet.

She added a touch of *Princess Pink* lipstick to her lips, and black mascara to her eyelashes. To make her eyes even more sparkling, she added fresh black kohl eyeliner and dabs of copper eye shadow. Perfect. She looked like a princess. A bridal princess. Then just like a princess entering a room, she floated into the living room to show off her *mehndi*. The friends who had arrived while she was in the bathroom rushed up see her, nearly knocking her over.

Vidya, who was wearing a royal blue sari with a *mehndi* green stamped border bobbled her head approvingly. Nazeera hugged the friend she had not seen in almost a decade. "Did you marry Anil?" were the first words out of her mouth. Vidya pointed to a guy hovering aimlessly near the French doors. She said she had recently given birth to their second child. The girls grabbed hands and giggled.

After a moment, Nazeera was surprised to see her friend Shilpa sitting on the sofa with Jyoti decorating her left hand. She rushed to her friend, peppering her with questions about her life for the last several years. Shilpa answered meekly, saying she still lived at home with her parents, and had not yet married even though she was in her mid-twenties. This was her first trip to Bombay in five years, and she was thankful Uncle had met her at the train station. Nazeera looked around. She didn't know her father was meeting people. *What else don't I know? Who else is coming?*

"Where's Khushboo?" Nazeera asked seeking out her mother. "She said she was coming. Where is she?" What about the other friends she'd invited? Where was Jessie, another friend from high school or Vim, her last roommate from college? She hadn't known either of them long, but she had kept in touch with them, and hoped each would come to the wedding celebrations so she could see them before she left India. *I'm leaving in a week! I may never see any of them again!*

Suddenly, Nazeera was overwhelmed again with the thought she would never see her friends, her cousins or her beloved Aunty again. She wouldn't see Jaya or her parents without a special trip home. No more lunches at the CCI or cold coffee at The Sea Lounge. No more mango *lassi* on the veranda. The room started to spin. Goose bumps formed up and down her arms. She was cold and the *mehndi* on her hands and feet started to tingle. Her heart was racing wildly. Nazeera grew quiet as she slumped onto the sofa.

Her mother came and sat next to her. Placing a tender hand on her shoulder, Ammi said, "*Beta*, your friends are all trying to come. It is just harder for some. Your father went back to VT to get Khushboo and Vim. Jessie is not able to make it. She has a family commitment, but she sends you best wishes."

Nazeera could feel her heart beat slowing to a more normal rhythm. Her mother knew how to calm her down. The hand on her shoulder was just what she needed, and Ammi had said exactly what she needed to hear. Turning to Shilpa, Nazeera gave her a hug, "I'm so glad you came." The unexpected hug surprised Jyoti who made an odd leaf pattern on Shilpa's forefinger. The two of them looked at each other and winced. Jyoti tried to fix it, but ended up adding similar odd-shaped leaves to the other fingers so they would all match.

As Jyoti started on Shilpa's second hand, the bride bounced onto the veranda where her cousins and Aunties were sitting. She wanted to spend as much time with them as she could before she left. She glanced at their hands and admired Pinky's two handed pattern. After Nazeera gave her stamp of approval on the patterns her cousins got up and went to the bathroom to wash off their dried paste. They had an important mission yet to do.

Farah and Aaliya were sitting quietly in a corner of the living room, watching the other ladies flutter around the room, as the *mehndi* on their hands dried. Nazeera listened as they did their usual routine of watching, commenting and giggling. Everyone seemed to be having a good time.

The smell of freshly made *samosas* wafted from the dining room, as Akbar laid a large platter of the warm pastries in the center of the table. The light pastry dough enveloped the spiced potatoes, peas and onions mixture. The quick deep fry made the pastries crispy but still flaky. Ammi insisted Akbar make them half the size he usually did so they could be eaten with one hand. An important detail when one hand may be painted with *mehndi*. The *samosas* were pounced upon by the hungry guests. Some took the savory mint green *kothmir* chutney, while others opted for the sweet dark brown tamarind chutney. Anil, Vidya's husband, must have been famished as he took five *samosas* and both chutneys!

Slowly chewing each mouthful, Nazeera savored the flavors of Akbar's creation. It was his own recipe and one he made often. She made a mental note to ask him for the recipe. Maybe he would send her some in America! No, that would be silly. She took another bite and let her eyes wander around the room. The marigold flowers garlands Shanti had hung around the veranda railing were a brilliant orange. A flowery curtain was also outlining the French doors of the veranda as well as the front door making each guest duck or sneak through them as they entered or exited. There were vases on every table filled to capacity with fresh flowers. She inhaled deeply to fill her lungs with the intoxicating fragrance. The cousins approached Nazeera, each wearing her *dupatta* over her head, looking as if they were about to leave the party. "Where are you going? You can't leave yet."

Dolly laughed, "As soon as your father returns with the car, we're going to the Ivanhoe flat to deliver some *mehndi* to your groom."

"Don't you need something sweet to offer him?" *Khalaji* reminded them of a critical part of the ceremony. The group looked around with slight panic. Spotting an unopened box of Indian sweets on the sideboard, Dolly grabbed it. "We can stop and get another box on the way home."

With a flourish of breeze and a whiff of freshly cut marigolds, the front door opened, and Daddy, Sanjay, Naveed, Aziz, Khushboo and Vim entered. Nazeera was shocked all six of them fit in the car. No wonder Khushboo and Vim look a bit rattled. She rushed to her friends, giving each of them large welcoming hugs. Naveed and Aziz were still holding their suitcases, so the ladies were able to hug her back. "I'm so glad you made it!!"

Pinky and Dolly left quietly with a full cone of the *mehndi*, a wrapped box of Royal Sweets *barfi*, and directions for the driver. They were the delegates from Nazeera's side to "share" the *mehndi* used on the bride with the groom. This was meant to be a bonding moment for the bridal couple, but it was basically a fun event for the cousins.

Khushboo followed Nazeera to the settee where they chatted about her train journey. After a moment Shakun drew near, asking the new guest what design she wanted on her hands. "Something simple and only on my left hand. I want to be able to eat some dinner." Shakun suggested a few different designs and Khushboo settled on a pattern with a vine with three flowers placed at three, six and nine o'clock with more vines coming out of the center design and creeping to the fingers. This was a design more often done on the back of the hand, but it was exactly what Khushboo wanted. Something simple and yet still classic.

Being a bit more daring, Vim wanted a flourishing pattern on her hands. Jyoti suggested a wild geometric pattern to which Vim enthusiastically agreed.

CHAPTER 44

Monday, September 5

"LET'S START GETTING YOU READY!"

The sun shone high in the sky before anyone stirred in the Yashodham flat. The servants were the only ones awake. Akbar had made a steeping pot of Darjeeling tea, but no one came for it. Shanti went early to the vegetable-*walla* to get the freshest fruit, but no one came for it.

While they waited for the group to stir, the servants each picked a corner of the kitchen. Akbar continued the letter he had started to his wife about all the wedding festivities. He thought she would enjoy knowing what Baby Sah'b was wearing, and how the *mehndi* looked on her hands and feet. Shanti flipped through the pages of Nazeera's latest fashion magazine, studying different hair styles and sari draping.

Mid morning, Daddy awoke and stretched. Sleeping on a cotton mattress on the floor was not the most comfortable. He called Akbar and told him to bring him a cup of tea and a kothmir omelet. He must have decided it was time for everyone to get up because he spoke louder than normal. One by one the houseguests began to stir, helped by the mouthwatering smells coming from the kitchen.

One by one the ladies used the bathrooms, taking showers and freshening up. Jaya placed plastic bags over Nazeera's hands and feet to help keep the *mehndi* designs intact. It made it extremely hard for her to wash, but beauty was more important today. The ladies changed into their day clothes and then filed out into the living room. Six hours until the wedding.

The guys were sitting on the veranda by the time the ladies appeared in the dining room. Akbar was kept busy serving them breakfast and accommodating the various things the women wanted to eat. Khushboo, Shilpa and Vim slept on cotton mattresses in Nazeera's bedroom. The five girls had giggled into the night talking about today and Amir.

Khalaji walked into the living room wearing a coral sari with royal blue triangles. She was radiant and strode about the room like a Bollywood movie star. Nazeera noticed her father watch her walk about the room. His eyes always seemed to follow her. *Is he still in love with her?* Maybe that's why Ammi had kept him and *Khalaji* apart for all these years. She watched as *Khalaji* batted her eyelashes at Daddy, then sat down next to her mother. *Is she teasing him?*

Nazeera watched her father for a moment. He rubbed his face with his hand, turned his head, and paid attention to the conversation on the veranda. Aziz looked like he was pushing imaginary furniture with his hands and moving Sanjay and Naveed as if they were sofas and chairs. They must be strategizing how to set up for the *nikkah*, wedding ceremony.

Mamuji was standing off to the side with his arms akimbo. He and Hamid had arrived last night just in time for dinner. Ammi had borrowed a table from their neighbor, Lalu Aunty, and adding it to their table, had formed one long table covered with several different table linens. Akbar had spent most of the day preparing the meal with Ammi supervising and helping when she could between entertaining guests. They served four non-vegetarian dishes and four vegetarian dishes. She offered both *gajjar halwa* and *gulab jamuns* for dessert.

Just after dinner, *Mamuji* had pulled Nazeera aside. He insisted they talk in her bedroom and for an instant she had been nervous. She swallowed the big knot she had in her throat, and followed him into her bedroom. He couldn't do anything with all these people in the next room. Could he?

She sat down on the bed and he sat next to her. "Nazeera. Your *khalaji* and I only have Naveed," *Mamuji* started, "We never had a daughter. I always wanted a daughter...well, I wanted to get you something special for your wedding." He paused and looked up at the ceiling, as if the words he wanted to say were hovering just above his head. He handed her a red box with gold trim. She opened it and stared at them. "I had them specially make these earrings. They were supposed to have been ready on Thursday, but they weren't ready until late Friday. So I had to take the Sunday train."

The bride looked at her *mamu* with shock. The earrings were 22k gold chandelier earrings. She had seen a similar pair on one of the models in her fashion magazine. She shook them slightly to hear them tinkle. "You... you had them make these earrings for me?"

Shrugging his shoulders, he replied, "*Ji, huh,* you are very special Nazeera. Like I said, I always wanted a daughter...I mean...after what happened with your mother...I thought...I...."

"*Mamuji*, I know what you mean," they shared a smile. "But, I don't know if I can accept them. They're so expensive."

"Please, Nazeera. It is a wedding gift, and something for you to remember me...us...me and Amina...when you are in Ameer-ic-ka."

"Does *Khalaji* know about this?"

"No," he replied looking at his hands.

"Oh, *Mamuji*," Nazeera said, overwhelmed by his generosity. He was always giving expensive jewelry to *Khalaji*, and now, he was giving her something special. "*Bahut Shukriya*! Thank you very much!" she exclaimed, wrapping her arms around his head, her moist cheeks tickled by his sideburns. She surprised herself by giving him an impromptu kiss on the cheek, and rushed out of the bedroom to show her parents.

Both of her parents were surprised by the generous gift. Nazeera noticed her father seemed agitated. Was it because the gift was from *Mamuji*?

"Nazeera, Florence is here. Let's start getting you ready!" Ammi said with a bit of excitement in her voice. Her mother's voice returned her to the present moment. *Oh, yes, the wedding nikkah. Florence. Hair. Whew. Lots to do. Lots to do.* She looked down at her half eaten kothmir omelet, shrugged her shoulders and threw up her hands. *Oh well.* She quickly finished the last sip of her lukewarm tea, and hurried into the bedroom where most of the women were already waiting.

Florence was their hair dresser. She had a rule to only made home visits if it was a special occasion and she really liked the person. Thankfully, Nazeera met both of those criteria. Florence was ecstatic to be the one to do the bride's hair. What an honor, she repeated several times. She was a petite Chinese lady in her mid-40's who had immigrated with her husband and two young girls to Bombay about a decade ago. Her husband managed a Chinese restaurant next to the hair salon. Ammi and Nazeera often got an order of Kung Pao Chicken after they got their hair done.

"What we do today?" Florence started as she ran her fingers deftly through Nazeera's long flowing black locks. "Tight bun good. Perfect for *nikkah* and reception. Last all day. You pin head covering in place. No worry about hair." She expertly raised the long hair into a bun. Nazeera smiled coyly and looked to the panel of onlookers. Ammi smiled and cooed. Jaya suggested a bit of tightening on the left side, then nodded approvingly.

Florence brought her eldest daughter, Maggie, to be her assistant. She had been warming up the hot rollers in the corner, and setting up the line of hair brushes and roller pins on the bed. Nazeera sat on one of the dining room chairs someone had dragged into the bedroom.

Brush, brush, brush. When Florence had straightened and softened the hair, she nodded to her daughter who began the routine of handing her hot rollers and roller pins. The hair was brushed into a small band, then slowly rolled up until it was near the top of Nazeera's head. Florence worked quickly brushing, rolling and pinning the bride's entire head in just a few minutes.

While Nazeera sat with hot oval shaped plastic tubes on her skull, Florence and Maggie moved to the chair adjacent the bride. Ammi was excited when it was her turn. She had short hair, so Maggie handed her mother smaller rollers. Brush, roll and pin. Repeat.

One by one, the bridal party and guests were primped. After Nazeera's rollers were cool and removed from her hair, Florence combed and bobby pinned it into a gorgeous bun laying just below the crown of her head. When the crowd was sufficiently impressed,

Maggie sprayed the bride's hair with what Nazeera thought was about a half a can of hairspray. No strand of hair would dare move now!

After Florence and Maggie cleared the room of the numerous brushes, rollers and umpteen roller pins, Jaya pulled out the gold and silver silk engagement sari from the armoire. "Why are you wearing this one?" *Khalaji* asked, "You should be wearing red. Brides wear red."

"*Khalaji*, I know red is the wedding color, but I love this sari." Nazeera's face lit up as she described the fabric, "The gold and silver *zari* threading makes this sari shimmer and I think it's too pretty to wear just once. I have another sari for the wedding reception and I didn't think it was necessary to purchase another lavish sari for the one hour *nikkah*."

Shaking her head disapprovingly, *Khalaji* raised her eyebrows and clucked, "Tsk, tsk, tsk. That's not how it's done."

Putting up her hand, Ammi simply said, "*Bas*, this is Nazeera's decision. If she wants to wear this sari, even though it is not wedding red, so be it." With that, *Khalaji's* challenge was squelched.

Shanti began pulling out the items Mohan had made over the past few days. His talents as a tailor were evident in the perfectly fitted sari blouses and petticoats for the bride and a few of the guests. The undergarments Nazeera had worn two weeks ago at the engagement party were from her gray sari. The ones Shanti held in her hands were made specifically for this sari.

The long process of getting the bride ready commenced. The petticoat, the sari blouse, the eye liner, the eye shadow, the makeup, the lipstick, the sari, the pinning and pinning to keep everything in place. Finally, the jewelry.

The wedding necklace her parents purchased for her was very delicate. The gold neckline lay on her collarbone with strings of gold almond shaped pieces dangling flat against her chest. Each almond had a green painted circle and a red semi-precious stone. The earrings were gold strings of identical almond shapes, jingling with every step Nazeera took. The matching nose-ring was clipped onto her nose and strung along her cheek and pinned into the side of her bun. Nazeera disliked wearing nose-rings, but today, she wore it proudly.

Finally, the red wedding *dupatta* or veil. Since she was not wearing a red sari, Nazeera conceded to a red veil. She believed it accomplished the same basic thing. The *dupatta* she wore today had sentimental value as her mother wore it during her prayers.

The doorbell rang and the ladies heard a rush of voices enter the flat. "Amir must be here!" Khushboo exclaimed. She had not yet seen this mysterious bridegroom, and was anxious to see him. She opened the closed bedroom door slightly, and peered out to sneak a peek. Returning to the ladies who were finishing their own dressing, declared, it's not him. Vidya entered the room holding a small piece of paper.

"Hello darling," she said giving Nazeera an air kiss. "You look just divine!" Vidya and Anil had just arrived from his parent's home in Juhu, a nearby suburb. She handed the paper to Ammi, and found an empty spot on the bed next to Vim.

"Is Amir here?" Khushboo questioned with an impatient look on her face.

"Not yet, but the *Qazi* is here. He and his two witnesses shared the lift with me and Anil."

Ammi quickly read the note, winked at her daughter and left the room. Nazeera was immediately suspicious. "I wonder what that's about." Nazeera asked Jaya who was finishing the clasp on her own necklace.

As the matron-of-honor, Jaya wanted to wear a sari to complement the bride. Nazeera had told her she planned to wear the gold and silver *zari* sari, so Jaya decided to wear a gold sari with large paisleys stitched along the border. She wore her gold wedding necklace with mother-of-pearl spokes from a central collar and matching earrings.

"Maybe Amir's changed his mind," Shilpa jested. "My own wedding was called off because the groom had second thoughts."

"*Bas*. He loves her. He'll be here," Jaya said as much for the other ladies as for Nazeera. She had yet to meet the mysterious Amir, but based on what Nazeera had said, he did care for her and she believed he loved her.

The doorbell rang again. Suddenly, there was commotion and a loud rush of voices. A lot of people must have just entered the flat. Khushboo played spy again and opened the door slightly to see who it was. She gave the group a play by play, "It's Amir and his family. His mother is here. His sisters are here. A few children are here. One of them is looking around.... Oh, I see Aziz and Hamid. They just came into the living room from the veranda....."

"Do you see Ammi?" Nazeera said a bit nervously. *Why am I nervous? Amir is here, no reason to be nervous.*

"Let me look....." Khushboo the spy said scanning the living room, "Yes, I see her. She's chatting with the *Qazi* and your father. They're pointing to different parts of the flat. I think they're planning how to conduct the ceremony." Khushboo shut the door and came back to the group. "Why didn't you get married in a mosque?"

"Well," Nazeera started. Khushboo is Hindu and didn't know all the customs of Muslim weddings. Actually, half the ladies in the room are Hindus. Hmmm... she hadn't noticed that before, but that was not uncommon in India where the majority of the population is Hindu. "In Muslim weddings, there is a marriage contract signed by the bridegroom and the person giving the bride in marriage. In my case, my father. They sign the document and then the *nikkah* or wedding ceremony actually begins."

"So, your father is giving you in marriage? Is that what that means?"

"Yes, basically. But I must still consent to the marriage. It's a formality here since I have already agreed to marry Amir and want to marry him, but in arranged marriages, it could be important."

"Interesting," Vidya said, "Mine was a little different. The main part of my consent was the *Saptapadi,* where we take the seven steps around the Holy Fire as a couple. Anil held my right hand in his right hand, which was really awkward by the way. I led him around the fire six times, and he led the last one. When we finished the last circuit, we were married."

"Seems short." Jaya said, "My wedding involved vows and then we walked around the Holy Fire."

"We had some vows too. But they were really short."

The group laughed and then collectively their eyes moved toward the door as it suddenly opened. In came Ammi, followed by Rehana who gushed over the bride as she entered. Rehana explained the various steps of how the next hour would go, "The bridegroom ceremony was going to start soon, then Amir and the gentlemen would move into your parent's bedroom. Once they are out of sight, you and the other ladies can come into the living room. Once your ceremony is over, Amir will return for the bridal couple blessing."

"And the mirror ceremony," Nazeera said reminding Rehana she wanted the old-fashioned ceremony. It was not a ceremony often done at non-arranged marriage weddings, but Nazeera thought it was very romantic. Since they had not seen each other for a few days, she thought it was still a fitting ceremony.

"Yes," Rehana nodded, "And the mirror ceremony." There was a knock on the door. Khushboo, who had been standing guard, asked the visitor, "*Kaun hai?* Who is it?"

The knocker said he was Farid, and the bridegroom ceremony was about to start. We were to wait here until we heard another knock. "*Theek hai,*" Rehana replied.

The *nikkah* was beginning. Nazeera's heart started to beat faster. *Today is my wedding day. The day we've been planning for several weeks. No, the day I've been planning for years. I've finally found a man I want to marry and he loves me. The true me. So, why am I nervous? Why am I feeling faint? Maybe I should eat something? Too late, I don't want to mess up my makeup or the dupatta. Breathe... breathe...breathe....*

CHAPTER 45

"HUH, HUH, HUH"

The *Qazi* sat cross-legged on the prayer rug, eyes closed, chanting words in Arabic. The red and blue Oriental rug normally under the furniture in the living room was moved to the center of the room with Rahim's burgundy prayer rug in the direct center. It was only large enough for the *Qazi* and Amir to sit upon. The all-blue clad priest was chanting words Amir didn't understand. They sounded like verses from the Quran, so he simply bent his head in reverence and listened. Every once in awhile, he glanced around the room out of the corner of his eye to notice Rahim, his soon to be brothers-in-law, Kassim and the two mosque witnesses also had their heads bent down. *Good.*

Trying to be discreet, Amir glanced at his watch. Starting only fifteen minutes late, not bad. Most Indian events started late, up to two hours late, and he had nicknamed this tardiness as "Indian Standard Time."

Sitting in the center of the room, he was pleased he wore his gray suit. He had Ramu freshly launder and press it for today. He wore a white dress shirt, but the ironing-*walla* had added too much starch and the collar chafed his neck. He didn't want to adjust it as it would draw undue attention. He just moved his neck a little, trying to ignore it.

The henna stained beard of the *Qazi* bobbled up and down as he raised and lowered his voice. His words filled the room and elevated the ritual to a religious event. The white pillbox hat he wore sat slightly askew on his head, showing wisps of white hair. Amir was tempted to push the hat onto the top of his head, but thought better of it. When the *Qazi* had finished chanting, he closed his eyes, and said a few more verses from the Quran. Opening his eyes, he looked directly at Amir.

"Is marriage contract done?" he asked in broken English as he knew Amir was not well versed in Hindi. Rahim and Nizar, Rehana's father, had met with the *Qazi* at the mosque on Friday night. The *Qazi* agreed to marry the two Muslims even though one was a Shia and one a Sunni. He believed as long as they were both Muslims, they were not breaking any Islamic law; otherwise, the couple and the marriage would be doomed. The marriage contract was a formality but still an essential part of the *nikkah*.

"*Ji, nahih.* No," Rahim answered, "It needs to be signed."

"*Aacha.* And *mahr*? Marriage gift to bride?" the *Qazi* asked directly to the groom. "What you decide?"

Amir looked at Rahim. They had not discussed this. The *mahr* is the amount paid to the bride so she would have some cash or property of her own. It was often a token amount as it was meant to be the start of a woman's financial independence from her parents. One thought was it gave her some security in case the husband did not treat her well and she wanted to move out; another is this is the amount of money she could live on if her husband died.

Recalling the conversation he and Rahim had at The Sea Lounge, Amir had agreed earlier to provide enough money for an airline ticket for Nazeera to return home for any reason. That was like the *mahr*, same basic concept, right? He calculated the cost of the airline ticket, converted it to Indian *rupees* and then doubled it. It should be plenty for her to return. He blurted out the amount hoping it was enough.

Rahim looked at him in shock. Amir hoped his look meant the amount was adequate. The *Qazi* scribbled the amount on the document. He passed the contract to the witnesses to review and they both nodded their approval. Then it was passed to Amir who signed as bridegroom, Rahim who signed as the one giving Nazeera into marriage, and Kassim as his personal witness. As Kassim signed, Amir's breath stopped for a moment. *It's really happening! I'm moments away from being legally and religiously bound to Nazeera.*

Hobbling onto the rug, Mummy awkwardly sat down in the chair next to Rahim. Amir flushed, and whispered to his mother. "What are you doing here?"

She must have thought all the others had the same thought, as she said aloud and proudly, "Amir's father died a few years ago. Since I am his only living parent, I insist on being here."

"But...." the *Qazi* began to protest as this was traditionally a men-only ceremony. Deducing Mummy was determined to be included in her son's *nikkah*, he relented, "*Theek hai.*"

Taking the signed contract from Kassim, the Muslim priest verified it was signed, and handed it to the witness closest to him for safe keeping. Silently, he nodded his head to indicate the ceremony was about to begin. Obediently, the men donned their hats in reverence to Allah. The *Qazi* adjusted his pill box hat, straightening it on top of his head. Rahim and the two mosque witnesses placed white furry pillbox hats on their heads, signifying their high rank within the mosque. Not having a hat, Mummy flipped the sari *pallu* to cover her hair and most of her forehead. Amir carefully placed a black furry hat on his head. It was a sentimental hat, as Rahim had worn it when he married Lailaa three decades earlier.

The *Qazi* glanced around the room to ensure everyone had their heads covered. He motioned to the two brothers who promptly stood up. Aziz approached first, placing the flower wedding garland over Amir's head to rest on his shoulders and chest, immediately making him the groom. Next, Hamid as the eldest brother, came and stood next to Amir. As an added blessing, he held the Quran over Amir's head for the entire ceremony. The two men had met only fifteen minutes before the ceremony and now he had one of the important roles of Amir's marriage to his sister.

"*Bismillahir Rahmanir Rahim*. In the Name of Allah, the Most Beneficent, the most Merciful," the *Qazi* chanted. He continued chanting in Arabic further declarations of faith, and then three verses from the Quran. He finished with a Prophetic saying on marriage.

Turning to Amir, he asked solemnly in English, "Amir Jooma

Virani, son of Karim Farid Virani, do you take Nazeera Zamani Khan, daughter of Rahim Hamid Khan as your wedded wife?"

"*Ji, huh*, I do." Amir said more confidently than he felt. He wanted to say 'I do' just as they did in the American movies. *Whew! The hard part is over.* The *Qazi* concluded with more words in Arabic, closed the Quran and did a head bobble. The bridegroom's part of the ceremony was done. Now it was Nazeera's turn.

There were some words, then chanting, then more words, then silence. Khushboo had spied on the groom's ceremony for awhile but with all the Arabic chanting, she grew tired of standing, and retreated from the doorway to the bed. Hindu weddings were usually done in Sanskrit, which was even more difficult to understand. With no play-by-play, the ladies just waited for the bride's turn.

Unfortunately, the room was getting very warm. Their combined body heat, the residual heat from the rollers and the sweltering heat of the mid-day sun was stifling. The ceiling fan was already spinning at high speed, but it was not providing any relief. Ad hoc hand fans were made from torn notebook pages or magazines laying in the corner. Even the open window and occasional breeze proved inadequate. The ladies were baking and the makeup and hairdos were beginning to melt.

Relief finally came when there was a knock on the door. A grateful breeze gushed into the room as the door opened. One by one they filed out of the hot bedroom and into the cool living room. The veranda doors were propped open and a wonderful breeze from the Arabian Sea immediately enveloped the group. The gentlemen had moved into her parent's bedroom and the prayer rug where Amir had sat minutes earlier was now vacant. A pillow was placed on the rug and Nazeera was helped by Jaya and her mother down to the pillow. It was hard to maneuver with the sari and red veil pinned in place!

As soon as Nazeera entered the room she heard the room swell with admiration. The guests probably couldn't see the beads of sweat on her forehead and under her armpits. She was thankful for the heavy veil covering her face and shoulders helping her act demure.

Maybe this is why Indian brides always kept their heads down. They're sweating!!

Scanning the room with her peripheral vision, Nazeera noticed a lot of legs in saris and trousers sitting or standing along the walls. *There's Pinky and Dolly, oh, and there's Mamuji. And there are Akbar and Shanti serving drinks. Good, that should keep the guests cool on this hot day.* She knew her father and brothers were in the bedroom with Amir. Where were the kids? She had expected Rabia and her big brown eyes to be sitting at her side by now. In fact, there were no kids. Their *aayas* must have taken them to the park or to the Club for *kulfi.* Good planning.

The *Qazi* gestured to the now vacant seats near the center of the room and indicated that Ammi and Jaya should sit in them. Shakila was wearing a pastel pink sari with pink flowers sparkling with silver embellishments. She was already seated just to the right of the *Qazi.* *I wonder if she was part of Amir's ceremony, too?*

Her mother sat where her father had sat minutes earlier, with Jaya and *Khalaji* to her left. The rest of the ladies found spots in the empty chairs or along the wall. When everyone had found a spot to sit, the *Qazi* nodded to one of the ladies sitting along the wall. Rehana stood up and walked toward the center of the room. She placed a wrist garland on each of Nazeera's wrists just below where her dozen bangles were hanging on her arms. She then stepped aside, to allow Nilofer to place a large flower garland over the bride's head. Nazeera found out later that Bandra had volunteered to decorate the bridal suite at the hotel in Juhu, so she was not in attendance at the *nikkah.*

With the wedding garland in place, the *Qazi* lowered his head and started chanting in Arabic. The room quieted down again and the *Qazi's* chanting was the only sound in the flat.

"*Bismillahir, Rahmanir Rahim.*" He began just as he did with Amir's part of the ceremony. Blessings from Allah were an important start to any event, especially a marriage. He read the same verses from the Quran and then re-read the Prophet's statement on marriage.

Unlike the bridegroom's part of the ceremony, the bride had to agree to the marriage verbally. Amir's affirmation was not needed as he had signed the marriage contract. Nazeera had not signed anything yet. She would sign the contract after she verbally agreed - then the marriage would be legally binding. The *Qazi* was going to ask her three times if she was willing to marry Amir. She had to say '*huh*' or 'yes' each time. If she said 'no' at any time, the wedding was stopped. This is the step where Johara had said 'no', so her wedding to Hamid had been stopped.

The *Qazi* turned to Nazeera and said, "Nazeera Zamani Khan, daughter of Rahim Hamid Khan, do you take Amir Jooma Virani, son of Karim Farid Virani as your wedded husband?"

Still with her head down and eyes cast downward, Nazeera said softly so only the *Qazi* and Jaya who was seated right next to her could hear, "*Huh*". She had said it softly as her mother had instructed her to do. *Brides were not supposed to be too anxious to marry.*

The *Qazi* repeated his question again, and Nazeera repeated a slightly louder, "*Huh*". With the last question she straightened up and said loudly, loud enough for several people to hear, "*Huh*". Nazeera looked up briefly to see her mother beaming with pride, as she did her demure bit and the '*Huh, Huh* and *Huh*' perfectly.

The witness holding the marriage contract then approached the bride and had Nazeera sign the document agreeing to the marriage. She noticed the *mahr* had been written in. *How had they decided on such an odd number?* Jaya took the paper and with a shaky hand signed as the second personal witness. *Why is her hand shaking?*

Ammi asked Shanti to bring her daughter a glass of cool water. She complied, but afraid to approach the bride, she gave the glass to Jaya instead. The matron-of-honor helped the bride take a few sips, being very careful not to drip any water onto the sari or the veil.

"Take a sip yourself," Nazeera suggested. Jaya reluctantly complied by taking a quick sip. She took a second sip and then sighed. She must've been dehydrated too.

When Nazeera was ready, *Mamuji* knocked on her parent's bedroom door, and Amir was led into the room. He still wore the wedding garland but his head was now uncovered. Nazeera kept her eyes downcast with the veil covering her face and profile. She had to strain, but she vaguely saw Amir sit in the *Qazi*'s vacated spot. Someone shifted part of her veil to cover his head as well. Now they were sharing her red wedding veil.

The room grew quiet as Jaya placed a mirror on the rug between them. When instructed, Amir leaned forward to peer into the mirror. At the same time, Nazeera leaned forward and tilted her sari *pallu*. She saw his facial reflection change from slight confusion to utter delight. She blinked her long eyelashes at him and smirked. Flash! Aziz snapped a photo of the couple. Flash! A few other cameras also tried to capture the moment. Flash!

Slowly, the wedding veil was removed. As Nazeera pushed back the sari *pallu*, she allowed it to fall on her shoulders exposing her full head. Her hair bun was still in place though a few strands were beginning to escape. She looked up from her clenched hands and straight into Amir's eyes. He was staring at her in wonderment. *What is he thinking? Hopefully he thinks I look pretty. He's staring at me intensely. That's good, right?*

Kassim brought a box with the Western style wedding rings. Amir selected her ring and gently placed it onto her right ring finger. Nazeera picked up his and with hands shaking, placed the ring on his right ring finger. Now, everyone in America would know they are married.

Next they had to share something sweet. Approaching the couple with a tray of *barfi*, Akbar wiped a tear from his eye. He placed the tray on the mirror and quickly retreated. Nazeera picked up a piece of coconut *barfi* and fed it to her husband. Amir then picked up a piece of pistachio *barfi* and fed his wife. They had shared something sweet to help ensure they would always be sweet to each other. A round of applause filled the room.

Kissing her hand just above the newly placed wedding ring, Amir said he would see her later. He and his side of the family were returning to the Ivanhoe flat. It had been arranged he would return in a couple hours to take her to the reception hall. Reluctantly, Nazeera nodded jingling as she did.

CHAPTER 46

"DID YOU LIKE THE BAND?"

There are multiple ways a groom can collect his bride from her father's house to escort her to the wedding reception. Kassim suggested Amir hire a white horse and gallop up to the main door of her building and call out to Nazeera. This is what he had done when he had collected Nadia. Amir seriously thought about it for a minute, because Nazeera would love to see him on a horse, but then dismissed the idea as he would probably fall off it.

Farid and Nadir had hired bands to play at their bride's homes. The band members had banged on their drums or tooted their horns loudly to notify the bride and all the neighbors her groom was coming to collect her. Farid said his band had played for almost an hour before he arrived. Rehana admitted her father's hearing was impaired for two days afterwards.

Salim had rented an elephant and her *mahout*. He rode in a specially made carrier like a *maharaja*. Bandra loved the idea of being carried around the streets of Bombay like a queen, but practically, she had had a hard time climbing on and off the elephant's back with her wedding sari. He advised Amir not to do this one.

Amir spent the nights after the engagement party laying in bed imagining how he wanted to collect his bride. He wanted something memorable. Nazeera deserved that. After all, she was leaving her whole life here to join him in America. She deserved a good bridal collection.

After much thought and a couple changes of plans, he finally decided to keep it simple. That was his style and one he hoped she would appreciate. He hired a band but not a very obnoxious one. He asked them to start playing softly at the Yashodham flat about thirty minutes before he was scheduled to arrive, then build to a big but not obnoxious crescendo a few minutes before he arrived.

Kassim and Salim oversaw the decoration of Salim's black Ambassador sedan with dozens of long strings of tuberose flowers, red roses and orange marigolds. Amir had changed into his wedding *sherwani* and as he buttoned the gold buttons he had specially purchased for this outfit, he smiled at himself. He looked rather dashing. Farid helped him place the wedding garland around his neck, then the turban with the obnoxious plume. The turban put the outfit over the top and they both laughed. *At least it would hide his silly cowlick!* Now he looked like a Mughal emperor about to hold court. The final touch were the *mojri* or curly toed golden slippers.

Dressed in a Western suit, Kassim came to collect the groom. He and Mummy would follow the bridal car to the reception. He helped Amir maneuver through the doorways with the tall turban on his head and into the car. The driver wore an all-white western looking suit with a white sailor hat and black brim. He had been hired for the whole day to drive the bridal couple to and from the reception. Now, he held the door open with his white gloved hand, and Amir stepped carefully into the decorated car. He hoped he would be able to get out of the car without losing his turban or the feather.

The normally five minute drive to the Yashodham flat was made much longer as the driver inched down the road. He claimed he was having a hard time seeing through the multitude of flower garlands on the windshield. About a quarter mile away, Amir began to hear the drums beating and the horns blowing. *Wow, that's loud. Hopefully Nazeera is not going deaf!*

When the band spotted the decorated car, they started playing even louder. They had now been playing for nearly an hour, and Amir was sure his bride and her family had been sufficiently informed of his arrival.

Knowing he couldn't exit the car without help, Amir waited in the car for Kassim to approach him, "Please get Nazeera. I think she's had enough." Kassim laughed and hurried into the building to tell them the groom was finally downstairs.

A few minutes later, Nazeera stepped out of the building wearing a snow white sari and a beaded white headband in her black hair. The top of her head was covered by her sari *pallu* and she walked with her eyes downcast. The sari had been a gift from Mummy for the wedding as she insisted brides wear white in America. Nazeera wanted to wear red for the reception, but she went along with her mother-in-law's request to please her.

Hamid was walking just behind her holding the Quran over her head. Her parents followed with Lailaa wiping tears from her eyes, and Rahim not looking as confident as he usually did.

Scurrying past the family, Jaya helped Nazeera into the car. She sat down in her seat and leaned back. The pair sat next to each other for a moment before Amir finally spoke, "Did you like the band?"

Wiping away a tear, she replied, "Yes, it was nice. A bit loud though." The two of them laughed. Maybe that was part of the purpose of the band - to give the couple something to laugh about on the way to the reception. Amir glanced behind him and noticed they were leading a convoy of cars. Hopefully the driver doesn't take an hour to get to the reception.

CHAPTER 47

"MISTER AND MISSES AMIR VIRANI"

They arrived at the Taj Hotel, forty-five minutes after their reception was supposed to start. *Indian Standard Time*, Amir thought to himself. The flower garlands on the windshield were a hazard. The two of them waited in the car for the driver to open the door. Nazeera said she would need help getting out of the car and Amir admitted he would too. They laughed again and just waited for help. Soon, Kassim came to help Amir out of the car and then he in turn helped Nazeera out of the car, stepping on the hem of her sari and almost toppling her over.

They followed the group through the front lobby, letting the various family members hold back the crowds to let them pass like movie stars. Waiting for them in the lobby was Rajesh, the hotel wedding liaison. He welcomed them to the Taj Mahal Palace Hotel and escorted them one flight up the Grand Staircase. He paused just outside the unopened double doors leading to the Crystal Room waiting for the trailing family members to ascend the staircase.

At Mummy's request, Rehana had coordinated with Rajesh to have a white wedding bouquet for Nazeera to carry as she entered the reception room. Although an unusual request, Rajesh had arranged with the hotel florist for a white wedding bouquet composed of white roses and calla lilies to be placed on a special table just outside the doors. He now picked up the bouquet, and as though it was something he did every day, handed it to Nazeera who reluctantly took it. Amir winked at his bride. He knew she didn't want to carry the bouquet, but did so to appease his mother again.

Rajesh stepped toward the door, threw them open with a flourish and crossed the threshold holding his hand back with his palm open to indicate the bride and groom should wait there.

"Excuse me!! Excuse me!!" he started with a booming voice and waited for the murmur in the room to quiet down a bit, "Please stand and welcome Mister and Misses Amir Virani". He then turned and nodded to Amir and Nazeera to proceed into the grand room.

The friends and family were standing, and began to clap as the bride and groom entered the reception hall. Amir felt Nazeera's hand slip into the crook of his arm, and he placed his hand over it. They stepped across the threshold together into the reception room. The flashes of the photographers nearly blinded them but they continued walking forward. Flash! Flash! Amir could see the platform on the left side of the room, so when he reached the middle of the room, he turned left and led his wife to the platform.

When they reached their destination, he saw she was still not smiling. "Jaya, could you hold the flowers?" Amir asked, thinking she must really hate the bouquet.

"*Ji, nahih*. No." Nazeera admitted, "I just want to sit. My shoes are too tight." Jaya and Amir both looked down at her shoes and noticed her feet were already swollen and red.

The platform they sat on was two steps up. Just enough height to set them apart from the rest of the guests, but not so high that they felt out-of-touch. There were two throne type chairs in the middle of the platform. Each was a white wooden chair with royal blue velvet cushions. On either side of the thrones, were cushioned benches with royal blue velvet fabric. Amir and Nazeera took their places, with Nazeera on Amir's left facing the audience. They were now ready to hold court.

For the first picture, Jaya sat next to her friend and Kassim sat next to his brother-in-law. The photographers, using the tripod he had set up, snapped the first seated photos as Kassim was talking.

Flash! They took a few more photos and then the group changed. Flash! Flash!

Nazeera's family was next. Lailaa and Hamid sat next to Amir with Rahim and Aziz next to Nazeera. Aziz gave his sister a hug and whispered loud enough for the group to hear, "I think you made the right choice." Nazeera elbowed him in the ribs and the two of them laughed.

"Hold still," the photographer said. Flash! Flash!

"I should have brought my camera too," Aziz said in between smile poses. "But, I'm sure we'll see these photos all over Ammi and Daddy's flat now." Flash!

"So, when are you getting married?" Nazeera said through her teeth. Flash!

"Hopefully soon. I think I'm ready to start looking." The photographer stopped and started waving his hand for them to move off the stage. "You'll have to come back for the wedding."

"Of course I will!" She leaned toward her brother and gave him a warm hug, "Thank you for helping me these last few weeks. You should visit home more often."

"*Aacha*, I'll try and eat dinner over there a couple times a month. I actually miss Akbar's *samosas*!"

As the group got up to leave, Amir turned to Lailaa and whispered in slow Hindi, "*Shukriya-ji*." She looked startled by his Hindi words. He added in English, "Thank you for believing in us and for supporting Nazeera's decision. I will take good care of her."

She smiled at him and patted his shoulder. She kissed his cheek, "*Aacha, Beta, aacha*." He watched her cross the stage and noticed Nazeera was now chatting with Hamid.

Trying to eavesdrop without being obvious, he could only hear Hamid's response, "I'm fine. Don't worry." *What is that about? Oh well, it didn't matter, he said he's fine.*

Next it was his family's turn. After the photographs, Mummy gave her son a hug and kisses on each cheek. She then stepped to Nazeera. Placing her right hand on the bride's shoulder, she whispered so only the three of them could hear, "Remember, you were number eleven."

Nazeera paused for a moment, turned to Amir for confidence, and replied, "And who did your son marry?"

"You."

"*Ji, huh,* so now I'm number one."

Mummy smirked, and turned to Amir, "I hope you are happy now."

Smiling, Amir answered, "I am Mummy." He watched his mother descend the platform. He placed his hand over his bride's hand. *She'll be fine in America.*

One by one the family groups came onto the stage for their photo with the bridal couple. Rehana and Farid followed Mummy with Rabia insisting on standing next to Nazeera. She toyed with the bridal bouquet, and Amir thought for a moment Nazeera was going to give the whole bouquet to the little girl. As they exited the stage, Rabia called back loudly, "Bye Nazchi".

Since they weren't sure of how many people could attend their quick wedding, Rehana and Lailaa decided to serve a simple buffet dinner. Rajesh had arranged for white-clad servers to carry sterling silver trays with appetizers and mingle throughout the room making sure every guest was offered something to eat at least three times. As for drinks, well, Amir wanted to serve wine as they did in American weddings, but given this is India and a Muslim wedding, no alcohol could be consumed. To make it special, Rehana worked with Rajesh and the hotel made a special punch using mango and lemonade. It was very tasty and the kids consumed it readily.

When all the formal family photos had been taken, the bridal pair relaxed for a moment and watched the crowd. Amir was surprised at the number of people at the wedding, especially for a Monday night. He estimated there were about two hundred-fifty people at the wedding. Rehana was keeping the exact count, but he didn't really care what the exact number was.

The respite was short-lived as a few friends began to form a line at the bottom of the stairs. Some of them said they had made the extra effort to see Amir as they had not seen him in years, and some had said they had come to see Nazeera since she was leaving India in a week. Thank goodness they had hired a good photographer so they would have photos of all of these people.

A few groups came and went, then Kabir and Carmen climbed the two steps to the stage. The two of them chatted for several minutes, and for the first time in days, Amir understood every word his friend spoke. No mixed Hindi-English conversation! They left the stage with Carmen promising to take Nazeera shopping at an American department store followed by dinner with their husbands.

A few more groups came and went. A tall lone gentlemen strode onto the stage. He obviously knew Nazeera as he glanced in her direction as he offered his hand to Amir. He introduced himself as Captain G.H. Bijli from Poona. He said he knew Nazeera from her horseback riding days. When Amir let go of the Captain's hand and he moved toward his wife, he noticed Nazeera's face change from boredom to extreme joy. She reached for him, drawing him close to her in a big hug. He hugged her back, and gave her a soft kiss on each cheek. Amir shifted his weight slightly to overhear him mention he was still riding horses and his wife was not able to come. They chatted for another few minutes about each other's lives and then he descended the stage. Nazeera was beaming.

Suddenly, the music changed from soft background music to loud dance music. Amir saw Kassim standing next to the drummer egging him on. Dozens of people were dancing on the pseudo dance floor waving their hands in the air. He turned to his bride and noticed she looked like she wanted to join them, but was too exhausted. It had been an exhausting day. He motioned to Rehana. She scurried to his side, and he asked, "When are we going to do our wedding dance?"

"We can do it whenever you're ready." They both looked at his watch and agreed they would do it in fifteen minutes. Another Western custom they were trying to incorporate into this wedding - the first dance. Ten minutes later, Rajesh arrived carrying a tall slender vase with a single red rose. Rehana had told him when they were discussing the bridal bouquet, the groom wanted to wear a red rose boutonniere for the first dance just like groom's wore in America. Rajesh had kept the red rose safe in the corner, and now he pulled the rose from its vase, cut it near the base of the flower, and removed any remaining thorns. Rehana arrived just in time to help Amir remove the flower garland and instruct Rajesh where to pin the boutonniere.

The band began playing a slow song. Amir stood up and gallantly offered his hand to Nazeera, who seemed oblivious to what they had been doing. He asked her if she wanted to dance. She smiled up at him, took his hand, and placed the bouquet on the seat cushion next to her chair. They walked, still holding hands, across the room to the dance floor, the crowd parting as needed. He took her hand in his and they started dancing.

"Did you ever think when we first danced a month ago, we would end up married?" Amir asked her as their bodies swayed to an Indian ballad.

"Honestly, no," Nazeera replied, "I thought you couldn't dance."

"And now?" he asked thinking he was doing the fox trot rather well tonight.

"You definitely can dance the slow dances. I think we'll skip the fast dances tonight." They continued their first dance together as husband and wife, posing for the photographer and a few family photos. Flash! Flash! When the song ended, Nazeera asked if they could return to the stage so she could sit down. Amir figured her feet must be hurting again so he led her back to her throne.

A few more friends came up to the stage to chat with them. Rehana stepped onto the stage, waiting patiently for the friends to leave. When they descended the steps to leave the platform, Rehana followed by Kassim approached them. "It's time to do the wedding ceremonies." Amir and Nazeera exchanged nervous glances.

"First, Amir, please come with us." Rehana said waving her hand. Amir looked to Nazeera for support. She just raised her eyebrows, and offered, "Good luck".

Rehana removed the red rose Rajesh had pinned to his *sherwani* and instructed Amir to stand still. Unsure what was next, he spread his legs to brace himself for whatever they had planned. Hopefully not another round of the turmeric paste or tearing his clothes off. He noticed Kassim was standing nearby, so at least he had a male companion in this ceremony. Following Rehana's instructions, Kassim and Nadir placed a full-body flower garland over Amir's head. The garland was made up of long strings of white tuberoses and red roses. It looked like a miniature version of the garlands decorating the car. Farid then stepped forward and he and Salim placed a heavy gold shimmer over the garland to cover his head. "The gold garland was borrowed from the JK for extra blessings."

Amir stood very still. He could barely breathe from the multitude of flowers covering his face or move from the weight of the gold. The photographer must have been taking several photos as he could see flashes of light. Flash! Flash! Salim, who was still standing near Amir's left began to laugh and couldn't stop. *Great, I must look ridiculous.*

Whomever wanted to bless him, formed a line and one by one, they followed Rehana's instructions. First, for fertility, they held the unopened coconut with both hands and circled it in front of Amir's face, or where they thought his face was. Then, for bountiful blessings, they picked up a handful of red rose petals and white rice and threw them over his already flower covered body. Lastly, they gave him something sweet so only sweet words would be uttered from his lips. Rehana had purchased a whole box of mixed *barfi* from Lookmanji's just for this ceremony. It was all gone by the end with Amir feeling a bit of a stomach ache.

Jaya was the first to perform the blessing of the groom ritual. When she had finished feeding her best friend's husband, she whispered, "Good wishes, Amir." Mummy and Aly *mamu* were next to follow Rehana's instructions. After the ritual, Aly *mamu* took his hand and said a blessing to him in Urdu. Amir didn't understand what was said, so he simply nodded. Nazeera must have understood the words as she replied, *"Shukriya, Mamuji.* Thank you, Uncle."

Nadia and Nilofer followed with their kids. While the adults performed the ritual, Amir watched the kids played with the strings of flowers. Tarik toyed with one string like a kitten would toy with a ball of string. Zarin and Yasmeen were a bit more gentle with the flowers, but they still were amazed by the amount of flowers on each strand. When one of the flowers fell off the garland due to Zarin's touching, Yasmeen quickly picked it up and placed it in her hair.

Bandra was the last female family member to perform the ceremony. She reluctantly followed the various steps. When she was done, she leaned forward so only he could hear and said, "I wish you well." For the first time, in a long time, she smiled.

When the ceremony was over, Rehana instructed Kassim and Salim to help Amir out of his flower and gold canopy and asked Nazeera to come with her. Nazeera gave Jaya a nervous look as she handed her the bridal bouquet and stood up to follow her sister-in-law down the stairs. Amir was relieved to be able to breathe normally again and watched as the two ladies crossed the room to sit at a table set up on the dance floor near where he and Nazeera had danced a half hour earlier.

He watched as his mother hobbled across the room followed by Farid carrying a glass bowl full of coins. Amir instantly recognized the set up. *Oh, they're going to do the coin ceremony. Great!* His mother sat across from his wife and reached forward to take her hand. Farid put the large glass bowl in the center of the table and then stepped back.

Rehana stood up and spoke loudly to the collective guests, "Our family welcomes Nazeera and her family into ours. As a gesture of generosity, we will do what we call the coin ceremony." She turned to the glass bowl, "This bowl is filled with silver coins. Nazeera will scoop as many coins into her hands as she can hold."

Sitting on his throne, Amir noticed Nazeera looked worried and was frantically looking around the crowd for someone. Maybe she was looking for her mother or Jaya. He reached over to Jaya, and suggested she go and stand next to her friend. She nodded repeatedly at the suggestion, placed the flowers down on the stool and hurried to Nazeera's side. She placed her hand on Nazeera's shoulder for reassurance, then stepped to the side and stood next to Lailaa who had also moved closer to the table.

Following Rehana's instructions, Nazeera stood up and reached into the bowl. It had a wide mouth but steep sides which made it difficult for her to hold onto the coins. Mummy noticed this flaw, so she asked her new daughter-in-law to remove her hands from the bowl and hold them in front of her. Nazeera complied and watched in amazement as Mummy proceeded to scoop the coins out of the bowl and cascaded them into her open palms like a waterfall.

Giggling in spite of herself, Nazeera listened to the clinking sound of the coins landing on her skin. When her hands and forearms could hold no more, she sat down sloppily on the chair trying not to lose any of the coins. Amir glanced at the glass bowl and noticed it was nearly empty. His mother lifted the bowl pouring the remaining few coins onto Nazeera's already overflowing outstretched arms.

After the photographer captured the grateful bride, Rehana and

Farid began removing the coins from her arms and placed them back into the glass bowl. When the bowl was filled again, Mummy pushed it toward Nazeera to indicate she should take the whole thing. Nazeera looked toward her mother who nodded approvingly. Turning back and looking Mummy in the eyes, Nazeera said, "*Shukriya-ji*". She tried to lift the bowl but it was too awkward with the sari and garlands and all the bridal finery. Kassim came to her rescue and lifted it, and followed her back to the stage. He placed the heavy bowl on the little table Rehana had used for Amir's ceremony.

The crowd began to mingle again and the bridal couple had a moment to themselves. After a little while, people started coming up to them to say their well wishes and good-byes. Rajesh stood by the bottom of the stairs and simply said, "It's ready." Amir looked at Nazeera, but she didn't know what was next. *Now what? What ceremony would they be doing now?*

Rajesh gestured for them to follow him. Amir took Nazeera's hand and helped her down the stairs. They crossed the room weaving their way between the guests. On the other side of the room was a long table with the wedding cake on top. Mummy stood next to it, with her arms gesturing toward the cake, "Just like in Ameer-ic-ka!" She then waved her hands in front of the cake and added, "Surprise!"

The cake was just like the cakes he had seen in the movies. Three white frosted tiers with a larger base layer, a smaller middle layer and a smaller still top layer. The top tier had a circle of white roses and the start of roses cascading down one side and around the middle tier and continuing to the bottom tier. He knew Farid had been on the phone several times with the bakery to order this Western style cake, but he didn't know it would be this perfect.

Rajesh handed him a serrated knife with one red and one white ribbon tied to it. He gestured for the two of them to hold the knife together to cut the first piece. Nazeera approached Amir and their hands touched as they held the knife. With a single thrust, the knife slid through the cake easily. As they removed the knife from the cake, a bit of frosting clung to the edge. Nazeera swiped it with her forefinger, and slipped it into her mouth, "Yum!"

Amir handed the knife back to Rajesh. He didn't want to be responsible for cutting this cake! While they remained in front of the cake, Rajesh cut them each a piece and placed them on two plates. Jaya took the plates and followed the bride and groom back to their thrones. Amir attacked the generous pieces of white cake. He was more hungry than he thought. He glanced at Nazeera and she had done the same. Neither of them had eaten since they had arrived.

Slices of cake were served to all the remaining guests. Everyone was surprised by the cake and how delicious it tasted. Even Rahim admitted the "Ameer-ic-kan wedding cake" was a nice touch.

"Last ceremony," Rehana said with as cheery a voice as she could muster as she approached the exhausted pair. She picked up the red and the red and blue *dupattas* sitting on the side table and stepped up to stand next to them. Turning to the photographer, she said, "Please take a lot of photos."

Rehana handed the red *dupatta* to Amir to place around his shoulders while she and Jaya helped Nazeera wrap the red and blue one around her shoulders. Amir looked at Nazeera, and shrugged his shoulders, "I guess this is the knot ceremony." She looked confused.

Once the *dupattas* were in place, Rehana called her daughter to the stage.

"Rabia, as the youngest niece, would you like to tie the knot?" The young girl had been staring at Nazeera, "*Ji, huh*, Mama, I do. I do." Rabia rushed onto the stage and began fumbling with the *dupatta* fabric attempting to tie a knot. She tried a few times but each time it came loose. After the third failed attempt, Rehana helped her daughter make the knot, and Rabia stepped back proudly.

Turning to the remaining guests, Rehana announced, "This is the last ceremony. The wedding knot ceremony. If any guests want to participate in the ceremony and give their blessing to the couple, please step forward." A few people came eagerly forward, and noticing there was a line forming, many more of the guests got in line. Amir thought just about all the remaining guests were in line! *This ceremony will take the rest of the night!!*

Since this was a couple blessing ceremony, the steps were slightly different from the ceremony performed on Amir over an hour earlier. First, the well-wisher circled the couple with an unopened coconut, then threw various flower petals and rice over their heads three times and then finally fed them something sweet.

Rather than feed them *barfi* after they just had wedding cake, Rehana asked Rajesh to prepare small cupfuls of sugar water. As before, Rehana prompted each guest through the three steps, and when it was time to give them something sweet, she handed them a small cup. Rajesh was on stand-by to make sure there were enough cups filled with the sweet water. After a dozen or so guests, the routine became the cup was given first to Amir who took a sip and then he handed it to Nazeera who finished it and gave the empty cup to Rajesh. This routine continued for nearly an hour with many of the guests leaving soon after they gave their blessings to the couple.

One of the first groups in the line were from Nazeera's side - Nusrat Aunty, Jhoma Uncle, and her cousins. Nusrat Aunty gave them both a big hug though it messed up Jhoma Uncle's circling of the fertility coconut. She had simply said, "Be happy, Ra-Ra." Jhoma Uncle performed the ceremony perfectly and then shook their hands adding, "Be good to each other." The cousins were surprisingly serious and Pinky and Dolly kissed Amir and then Nazeera on the cheeks. Their brother Khazin just nodded to the couple before stepping off the stage.

Farah and Aaliya were next, and they followed Rehana's instructions in their own way alternating steps. "We'll miss you," Farah said. "Parties won't be the same without you," Aaliya added. Nazeera had taken their hands in hers and said they must keep in touch through letters. Each of them promised they would. Farah added maybe Nazeera can find her an Ameer-ic-kan husband!

About halfway through the line, were William and his mother. They explained they had received the personal wedding invitation from Ammi, and he had asked for special leave to be able to attend the wedding. They had arrived during the coin ceremony due to the traffic from Poona. As William threw flowers on them, he apologized to Nazeera for not being able to meet her a couple weeks ago for afternoon tea. At this last comment, Amir looked at the man standing next to him a bit more closely. He looked very sharp in his uniform. If he is from Poona, maybe he's another Captain friend from the horseback riding days.

As the mother gave Amir the sugar drink, William leaned over and whispered something in Nazeera's ear. Amir couldn't hear what he said but she immediately leaned forward, tugging on the knot, to give him a big hug. Wiping a tear, she asked him to keep in touch. William kissed the wet spot softly, "Good-bye, Nazee."

Pounding onto the platform, the Ambassador took Amir's hand. Shaking it several times, he repeated, "Congratulations, *yaar*, congratulations. I'm glad it all worked out." He stepped toward Nazeera and kissed her sloppily on both cheeks, "Best wishes, *yaar*."

When the last guest had performed the ritual, Amir looked with sugar-glazed eyes to Rehana to untie them. "Sorry, I can't do it." She gestured to the oldest two nieces who had been impatiently standing nearby waiting for the ceremony to end. They both hurried onto the stage with Daania pushing past Yasmeen.

"How much will you pay us to untie it?" Daania demanded with her hands defiantly on her hips.

"What?" Amir looked at them both incredulously. Were these girls blackmailing him? He didn't remember this part of the ceremony. This must be something new, or maybe it was just Daania. He looked to Nazeera for help and she shrugged her shoulders. She had no idea how this part of the ceremony was supposed to go. This was his family's ceremony.

"How much?" she repeated. Sensing Amir wasn't going to give her anything, she suggested, "Two hundred *rupees*." Amir countered with "twenty *rupees*" and Daania quickly agreed. He had no money on him, so Kassim paid the girls on his behalf. With the *rupees* in their hands, the knot was untied and the couple was free to mingle with the remaining guests.

Most of the remaining guests were family members gathering up children. Amir concluded it was time for them to make their exit. Stepping off the stage, he led Nazeera to Rehana and his brother. "We are going to take off now and head to the hotel. Thank you for everything, and for walking everyone through all the ceremonies."

Rehana blushed and was speechless for the first time all night. Farid shook his brother's hand and said, "Have a good night."

They began heading toward the main doors when both of them noticed Nazeera's parents sitting off to the side. "I'd like to talk to them," Nazeera said with a bit of urgency. With Amir at her side, Nazeera took each of her parent's hands and looked from one to the other, "Ammi, Daddy, are you all right?"

Rahim stood up and gave his daughter a hug. "Yes, *Beta*, we are fine. We were just discussing how wonderful this wedding was. What a nice family you have married into."

"Yes, they seem nice enough," Nazeera conceded. "Some of those Ismaili ceremonies have Hindu roots, but they're his family's ceremonies, so I guess they're special to him." Amir just nodded.

"Don't be concerned about the source of the ceremony," Lailaa started, "What is important, is all of these people came to give you their blessings and well wishes for a long and happy marriage." Nazeera started to well up, her bottom lip quivered. "Don't cry, *Beta*. Always know your father and I love you. And, we'll see you tomorrow night at dinner, no?"

After clearing his throat, Rahim added, "I've got a copy of the marriage certificate and tomorrow I'll start the paperwork for your passport and immigration visa." Stepping toward Amir, he added, "I chatted with Nizar earlier. He has a connection at the immigration office. He's going to make some phone calls to try and hurry up the process."

"Thank you, sir," Amir responded. "That will definitely help."

"*Shukriya-ji*, Daddy," Nazeera smiled at her father. With a sigh, she added, "How's Hamid really doing?"

"*Theek hai*. Hamid told me, he and Murad came here yesterday before they came to the flat. One of the bellboys let them walk around the room. He said the room looks and feels so different from last year, it didn't trigger any memories of his wedding fiasco."

"So he's all right?"

"*Ji, huh*, he'll be fine, *Beta*." Rahim said squeezing his daughter's hand. He added, "On another note, I've decided to give you that painting you like so much - the woman with the sitar. You can consider it an early birthday present."

"Oh, Daddy! I love that painting! *Shukriya-ji!*" Tears began to run down her cheeks and she hugged them both, lingering a bit longer than any of them had expected. "See you tomorrow at dinner." She forced a smile and breathed in deeply. She exchanged her parent's hands for Amir's. He thanked them both for their love and support, then led his bride out of the Crystal Room.

CHAPTER 48

"CAN I OFFER YOU ONE?"

The driver must have taken a wrong turn somewhere. He seems to be turning left and right almost constantly. *Aren't we going to a hotel in Juhu? It's just on the other side of Chowpatty Beach. Where is he actually taking us?*

Nervously, Nazeera glanced out the window. It was hard to see anything because it was dark outside. A flash of light appeared on the far horizon. That's Chowpatty Beach! Great, they weren't lost, but still a long way to go. Giving into her aching feet, Nazeera slipped off her silver *chappals* and wiggled her toes, making sure to hide them under the petticoat of her sari. The tight *chappals* had left a dent on her feet, and she was tempted to lean down and rub them. But she didn't want Amir to see her ugly feet yet. They did look prettier with all the *mehndi* on them, but once the decoration wore off, it would be back to her ugly feet.

She glanced nervously in his direction. Amir had already removed his turban and was loosening the top button on his *sherwani*. "Naz, why don't you take off your *chappals* since they've been bothering you all night." Nazeera just smiled and agreed to his suggestion. She still kept her feet hidden under the petticoat.

"I don't know why my mother and Bandra chose this hotel. It's so far away from the reception hall," Amir said with a yawn. He yawned again, and for a brief second Nazeera thought he might fall asleep on the ride to the hotel. Great, that's all she needed on her wedding night. A husband that fell asleep before they....

After another half an hour, they finally reached their destination. Before the car stopped in the hotel driveway, Nazeera could hear cheers. "Hurrah!" "Yeah!"

Looking around, she saw several members of Amir's family standing on the hotel steps. *There's Rehana and Farid. Oh, and there's Nilofer and Nadir and their kids Zarin and Yasmeen!*

Quickly slipping her *chappals* back onto her swollen feet, she waited for the driver to open the car door. Amir slid out of the car first, then held out his hand for his wife. She took it and leaned on it as she hobbled her way up the blue carpet lined concrete stairs to the lobby.

The hotel seemed nice enough, not too lavish but not too ordinary. There were marble accents on the thresholds and the lobby was freshly polished. As they strode into the lobby, she felt like a Bollywood actress arriving at her movie premiere. Cameras were flashing, people were cheering, and everyone's eyes were on them. *There's Nadia, Kassim and Salim. Wow, there's Bandra and even Daania. Oh, and my brothers Aziz and Hamid. I'm so glad they're here, too.*

Amir now looked wide awake and jested back and forth with his family and brothers-in-law. Salim handed him the room key for room 5966, and the group followed the two of them like celebrities as they moved across the lobby. They stepped inside the lift car and waited while the driver placed their little suitcases just inside the doors. Amir, still holding Nazeera's hand, reached forward and hit the '5' button for the fifth floor. He gave a final wave good-bye. The group responded with louder cheers and well wishes. Nazeera had been silent this whole time. The doors shut with a thud. They were suddenly alone in the lift.

As the lift doors opened, a little bell chimed to indicate they had arrived. Amir stepped off first, releasing her hand to grab the two little suitcases. Nazeera stepped out of the lift and paused at the plaque on the wall. It indicated room, 5966 would be to their right.

She glanced down the long hallway. Taking a deep breath, she slowly followed her husband. Her feet were very swollen now. Each step was painful. *Can I take off my chappals again!?!*

Struggling to keep up with him, they finally reached the room door. Amir put the suitcases down and began fumbling with the key. It was an old fashioned skeleton key with a curly handle. He seemed to be having problems finding the right position for it in the lock. This way, that way. He tried several different combinations. *Why is this so difficult?*

In a few moments, she was going to enter the room where they would spend their first night together as husband and wife. She looked down the hallway back toward the lift. *Is it too late to run? I could make a getaway if I started now. But, where would I go? No, I need to be brave. Confident. This is what brides all around the world are doing.*

Amir finally opened the door, and pushed it with his hand. He quickly stepped forward, and dropped the two suitcases off to the side. Propping the door open with his left foot, he called, "Naz, come here."

She approached him cautiously, and in one swoop, he swept her up into his arms. Not knowing what else to do, she wrapped her arms around his neck as he carried her effortlessly across the threshold. She giggled in delight. He strode into their room, and let her kick off those silly *chappals* before he laid her gently onto the flower covered bed. She was still giggling as he shut and locked the room door.

The bed had been covered with a red rose and white tuberose flower petal heart. The desk table had a wooden tray filled with various desserts and sweets including some Indian *barfi* and chocolate covered strawberries. A bottle of Perrier sparkling water was chilling in a bucket of ice and there were two wine glasses next to it. "Would you like a glass of Perrier?"

She had always wanted to try the bubbly water, so she agreed. Amir poured two glasses and brought one to her. Nazeera held it delicately by the stem, as she saw someone do at a restaurant, and they both clinked their wine glasses in a sort of 'cheers'. He took a long first sip, gulping a little. She brought the lip of the glass to her mouth and sipped delicately. The cascade of the cool liquid was refreshing and the bubbles tickled her throat. It helped squelch her thirst for the moment. She took a few more sips, then handed him the glass to put down on the bedside table.

Amir crossed the room, and brought the tray of sweets to her side. Scanning the tray, he picked up a now melting chocolate covered strawberry and glanced at her. *Is he going to feed it to me?*

He moved the tray slightly to the middle of the bed, and inched a bit closer to her. Taking a big bite of the strawberry, he said, "Oh, these are good. Can I offer you one?" She smiled and nodded. Her heart was beating loudly. *Can he hear it?*

Leaning closer to her, Amir held the decadent fruit just beyond her lips. Nazeera opened her mouth and took a small bite causing bits of the hardened chocolate to crack and fall into his waiting hands. She glanced into his eyes as she slowly chewed. Her chest heaving at his presence. The water had helped her relax. She felt warm and safe. Their gaze met and she leaned forward and took another bite of the strawberry. She felt him move closer to her. He placed the remaining strawberry back onto the tray and leaned forward to kiss her.

His kiss was soft. Her heart was beating wildly. Thumping against her chest. She leaned into his arms and kissed him back. He engulfed his arms around her and their exchanges grew more passionate. *This is really happening. This is our wedding night! The start of our life together. The start of our great adventure. And he still has to find his name on my palm!*

THE END

Acknowledgements

A very special thank you to my parents, Jhoma and Nusrat Merchant, for sharing their stories with me. I cherish the time sitting together as I listened to you relay your adventures. An added thank you to my mom for providing me with insights into traditions, recipes and names. This book would not have been possible without your trust, inspiration and help!

A big thank you to my wonderful and supportive husband, Bill, who allowed me to fulfill my dream of writing this story. An added thank you for giving me constructive thoughts to refine the story - such as the addition of Amir's family tree. Another big thank you to my fantastic son, Tarik, who encouraged me every step of the way. I fondly recall the many hours we sat at the kitchen table with me working on this book and you writing your own stories. Keep being creative!

Thank you to the many people who listened to my brainstorming and plot refinements. There are too many to name, but a few people deserve special acknowledgement and I thank each of them for their help: Sharifa Merchant, Jenna Lester, and Kim Schroeder. The story would not have been the same without your input!

About the Author

Zia McNeal is a first generation Indian-American. To celebrate her first birthday, she returned to Bombay (now Mumbai) as the first grandchild born in America. Her next projects include another Indian-inspired novel and a juvenile fiction book with her son. She now lives in Minneapolis, Minnesota, with her husband, Bill, and son, Tarik.